Book

STAR

Visit BVLarson.com for more information.

Dust World

(Undying Mercenaries #2)
by
B. V. Larson

UNDYING MERCENARIES
Steel World
Dust World

Copyright © 2014 by the author.

ISBN-13: 978-1497591714
ISBN-10: 1497591716
BISAC: Fiction / Science Fiction / Military

Earth meets the Galactic Empire, a Timeline of Events:

1922 – Radio broadcasting sweeps Earth, becoming the first of many forms of streaming transmissions that reach out into space at the speed of light.

1943 – Imperial Galactic outposts pick up a growing tide of transmissions from Earth. They open a case file and launch a study.

1947 – A rash of UFO sightings is recorded on Earth as the investigation by the Galactics begins.

1969 – NASA lands two men on the Moon, taking humanity's first step into the cosmos. The alarming advance is reported to Galactic Central.

1977 – Voyager 1 is launched on a mission to explore beyond the limits of the Solar System.

1993 – The European Union is formed, becoming the first of many multi-national conglomerations to follow.

1995 – The first exoplanet is discovered circling 51 Pegasi, a main-sequence star. Thousands more discoveries soon follow.

2012 – Voyager 1 becomes the first man-made object to travel outside the Solar System. The violation is carefully noted by Galactic observers.

2025 – Worldwide economic collapse hastens the formation of multiple political blocks and increased nationalism. China, the EU and the North American Collective (NAC) enter a new Cold War era.

2041 – Earth's first and only colony ship, *Hydra*, is launched toward Zeta Herculis. The colonists are primarily political exiles from the NAC.

2052 – Having detected humanity's rise in technological prowess and various violations in conduct, the Galactic Empire is compelled to act. Local Battle Fleet 921 is dispatched to the Solar System and Galactic Rule is established.

2054 – On Earth, cultural shock gives way to acceptance. The former rival political blocks form Sector Governments, underneath a central Hegemony Government, which in turn is ruled by the distant Galactics.

2058 – Earth's first mercenary legion, Victrix, executes two successful missions during their initial year of operation, bringing home much needed Galactic Credits and proving Earth is a viable new member of the Empire.

2076 – Legion Varus is formed to handle clandestine off-world missions.

2081 – An outbreak of rebellious factions in Brazilia Sector is put down. Seven million are killed in the subsequent purge.

2099 – James McGill is born.

2121 – McGill joins Legion Varus. During his first tour, he's instrumental in ending all mercenary contracts with

Cancri-9, a disaster that is later ruled to be unavoidable. Earth subsequently enters an economic downward spiral.

2122 – *Hydra*, Earth's one and only colony mission, finally reports to the home world. The colonization of another star system has been achieved, but it is a violation of Galactic Law. Legion Varus is dispatched to handle the situation…

*"The slain care little if they sleep or rise
again."*
– Aeschylus, 479 BC

-1-

Right from the start, I didn't enjoy my four months of shore leave. The veterans and adjuncts told us that after a year of blood and hard living we were bound to have trouble settling back into our old lives. The Legion psychs gave us a short speech about "disconnection problems" before we were released and sent marching down the gangplanks into Newark spaceport, and they suggested we should contact the legion if we felt we needed help.

I laughed that off, went home to Georgia on the sky-train and then endured the cubical-party my parents threw for me in our hab's rec room. A dozen neighbors and friends had gathered, so I glued a smile on my face. All the while, I wanted nothing more than to get away from everybody.

For the next few weeks, I think I was in shock. Civilian life didn't seem fun to me anymore. The first chance I got, I hunted down Carlos and some of the others from my unit. We got seriously drunk. That felt good, but it only lasted for a few hours.

Staggering home again, I awakened to find my mom making me breakfast. I ate it, threw it up in the bathroom, then ate some more.

"You want to talk about it, James?" she asked.

"No," I said. "I'm fine."

"Getting things off your chest can really help."

5

I looked at her, and she forced a smile. I could see the worry in her face, and it bugged me.

"Telling war stories won't help anything," I said.

She dropped her eyes to stare at the floor, and she hugged me briefly. "You should try to get back into your old routines," she said.

I did as she suggested for the next month or so. I tried to fall back into my old habits, but I felt disconnected from gaming buddies, old girlfriends from school and even my own parents.

It wasn't all me. I could tell that. Oh sure, people I knew smiled at me whenever I came around. They patted my back and fed me sandwiches. A few even bought me drinks.

But when they looked at me, they stared a little too long. There was darkness in their eyes while they did it, too. They could see something in me—something different. There was a distance between me and everyone else, a separation. It took me a while to figure out what it was.

"You aren't sure that I really *am* James McGill," I said to my dad suddenly one Thursday night in June.

"What?" he asked, startled. He'd been lying on his back, watching a streaming ballgame on the ceiling. It was the only flat surface large enough in our tiny apartment for a big screen. He adjusted his recliner, and it pushed him up into a vertical position. He paused the game. "What did you say, son?"

"I can't blame you for not knowing who I am," I said. "Sometimes, I'm not entirely sure myself."

My dad gave me a small, nervous chuckle. "I don't know what you're talking about, James."

"Let me spell it out for you. By my count, I'm on my fourth body. I'm not in the skin I was born with, Dad. Do you get that? I *died* out there in space. I died and was reborn with a fresh body built from alien slime."

Another nervous chuckle from him. Had his eye twitched a little? It hadn't been a wink, I was certain of that.

"Sure," I continued, "I *look* like the old James. I have his familiar laugh. I have the same hair, I like the same brand of beer and I can still kick most people's ass in an online shooter whenever I bother to log in."

6

My dad stared at me for another long second. Then he straightened up. "You're my kid," he said firmly. "You're still my kid. I'm certain about that."

I smiled. "Thanks, Dad. But I'm undeniably *different*. You have to admit that."

"You've grown up, that's all. You've been out to the stars. People always have trouble coming home after being in a war. That's been true throughout history. Maybe you should contact the legion. Maybe the bio people can help."

I snorted. "Yeah," I said. "They'll give me a shot of something. They'll bleed me and order me to piss in cups until I run dry. And if they don't like what they find, you know what they'll do?"

My dad shook his head slowly.

"They'll kill me again, that's what. I'll be recycled, hoping for a better grow."

Dad looked horrified. "I don't understand…"

I stopped him with a raised hand. I had never told my family about what really happened when you died and came back. I'd skipped all that. It wasn't clean, and I suddenly felt bad for burdening my father with all this crap.

"I'm sorry, Dad. I'm going for a walk."

"Wait," he said, jumping up out of his chair and grabbing my arm.

I looked at him.

"There's something else. You've got the wrong idea. You haven't been watching the news, have you?"

I frowned, shaking my head.

My dad sucked in his breath. "People aren't thinking about how you died. They don't think of you as some kind of zombie—you can forget about all that. We don't think like that because we haven't experienced it. What we're wondering is just what your legion did out there, son."

It was my turn to look confused.

My dad pointed to the ceiling. "Notice how we stream games and junk all the time? We don't want to watch the news. No one does. People are scared, James. That's what's wrong with them."

"Scared? Why?"

7

"Because Cancri-9 has dropped our contracts. They canceled them *all*. Germanica, Solstice, Victrix—no one is flying out there to work anymore. The news agencies aren't saying why, but they do often mention that Legion Varus was the last to serve on Steel World."

I felt a sudden squeeze in my guts. This was much worse than being feared as a member of the walking dead. I'd thought things were bad before, but now I was beginning to get the real picture. This wasn't about me—not exactly.

"You're telling me that everyone thinks Legion Varus screwed up? That we somehow pissed off the princes and lost our best interstellar trading client?"

He nodded slowly.

I let out a sigh that left me empty. "They're right, in a way," I said. "But they're also wrong. There was nothing we could have done to keep those contracts from getting canceled, Dad."

"What happened out there?" he asked me, his voice barely above a whisper.

I almost told him the truth then, but I stopped myself. We weren't supposed to talk about it. Legion Varus didn't have as many rules on conduct as most legions did, but secrecy in the area of mercenary contracts was definitely one of them.

"I can't talk about that. But believe me, the dinos on Cancri-9 were going to screw us one way or another. They were never Earth's friends."

Dad nodded slowly. "Okay. I hope knowing the truth makes you feel better."

"Yeah sure," I said, trying to laugh it off. "People think my legion ruined the planet's economy single-handedly. That's a lot better than thinking I'm a freak."

"No, no," he said. "It's not *ruined*. Sure, we're in for some hard times. Some belt-tightening is overdue, that's all."

I reached for the vid controller which rested on the table next to Dad's recliner. I flipped it to the news—to the financial browsing section. I climbed into the chair beside my father's and stretched out on it.

My dad quietly reclined his chair again, and we stared at the ceiling together. I watched vid after vid—they were all the same.

Planet-wide, we were going into a recession. At least, that's what the suits called it, but the more excitable people called it a "crash". The more they talked, the more I became concerned. Companies and governments were announcing shortages, rationing and layoffs everywhere. District governments, Sector governments and even Hegemony had declared budget shortfalls and were listing their proposed cutbacks. All alien tech commodities were off limits for civilian purchase. Every Galactic credit on Earth had to be wrapped up into something they called a "relief fund". I had to wonder who was going to feel "relieved".

My mom showed up then, returning from the store in the middle of a streaming netcast that showed idle legionnaires sitting on park benches in Asia. They looked bored and pissed off.

"Dammit, Pete," she said accusingly. "I thought we weren't going to tell him."

"He figured it out," Dad said. "He was bound to catch on eventually. The whole world is talking about it."

She huffed and carried her purchases into another room and began putting stuff away.

I turned my attention back to the screen. An article scrolling at the bottom of the display caught my eye. Had they just mentioned Legion Varus by name?

I clicked on the link and after a few bonus commercials you couldn't skip, we were treated to a raving politician who blamed my legion by name for destroying interplanetary relations without authorization.

"But we didn't screw up!" I shouted at the screen. "The lizards planned it all out before we even got there. This guy doesn't know what he's talking about."

My mom came back into the room after hearing me shout. She looked worried.

"What happened up there, James?" she asked me.

I almost told her the whole story. We'd been briefed not to, but I almost did it anyway. Legion Varus was "special" in ways

9

no one else understood outside the Hegemony Government. We fought for new contracts in space. We fought for new territories and protected our old ones. The saurian people on Steel World had decided to try to challenge our rights under Galactic Law to monopolize mercenary contracts in the region. We'd stopped them, but in doing so we'd lost Steel World as a client planet. We would have lost much more if they'd beaten us and become a new trading rival on our doorstep. Disaster had been averted, but we were still in for hard times.

I looked from one of my parents to the other. I knew they wanted me to explain it. I knew they wanted to be able to tell their neighbors, friends and even my own relatives that their son wasn't part of some renegade legion of losers.

But I couldn't. The stakes were too high. I'd already made enough mistakes on my first campaign. I wasn't interested in making any new ones at home.

I shook my head and sighed. "I can't. The whole story is Hegemony-level. Top-secret, classified—whatever you want to call it."

They looked disappointed. We all fell into a brooding silence. I couldn't stand it, and about five minutes later I went to our tiny storage chamber. I managed to get the organizer robot to spit out my stored bag, then I headed for the door.

My dad intercepted me.

"Give us some hugs, at least," he said.

"Huh?"

"You're leaving, aren't you? You got the call."

I stared at him for a brief second. He thought I'd been called up by Varus, but really I'd been planning on finding another couch to crash on.

"I've got to go," I said.

There were hugs, and my mom cried. This scene was familiar to me. We'd already done this once, more than a year ago. Back then, I'd been starry-eyed and nervous. Now, I felt emotional but resigned.

"Here," my dad said, pressing a box into my hand. "A replacement. You said you lost your old one."

I looked at the box.

"What's this?"

"Open it. We were saving it for your birthday."

I mustered a smile and opened it. I found a knife inside, a mean-looking thing. It was no pocketknife, it was a combat model. A real one, not a cheap knock-off from another sector.

I tested the edge and smiled. "Thanks, Dad."

"You never told us how you lost the first one," my mom said, wiping away a tear.

I shook my head, marveling at the blade. The metal was dark except for the edge which was so fine it shone white. "No, I didn't," I said. "And you don't want to hear that story."

I'd lost my pocketknife the third time I'd died on Steel World. The first time, I'd been torn apart by lizards, but I'd found it again in the piles of recovered equipment. When I'd been executed later on, my belongings had been returned to me when I was revived—but that third time…well, that had been the charm. I'd been blown to bits and my knife had been blown up with me.

"Thanks guys," I said, and gave them an honest smile. I hugged them both again and left.

I walked out of my parent's building, and I didn't go back. I didn't bother to take the sky-train this time. That was too expensive, and I wasn't in any kind of hurry.

I spent a week heading north on bumping public trams. As long as I was careful, I knew I had enough money to last for months. I decided to have myself a little vacation. I checked out a few towns, walked on a lot of beaches and watched a lot of vids on my tapper.

Something went wrong with my tapper unit on the sixth day, however, and I couldn't get it to access the net anymore. I wasn't sure if it was related to billing or if it was a technical issue. Tappers were organic screens embedded in the flesh of your forearm. The beauty of the system was that you couldn't lose it, and it was supposed to keep you connected to the world at all times. There weren't any batteries to be recharged, either, as it fed off the electrical impulses naturally generated by the human body. Even when a soldier died, his tapper was faithfully reconstructed by the legion revival units because it was organic, just like any other part of the body.

11

After my tapper died, I spent most of my time dozing on beaches with my head on my ruck. This wasn't as peaceful as it sounded as I often dreamed about lizards tearing off human limbs and making excited gurgling noises as they fed.

The summer days were fairly enjoyable for me despite my dreams. I felt like I was experiencing Earth. There weren't any officers yelling at me or worried parents eyeing me oddly. I felt like a ghost gliding through the world, and I kind of liked it that way.

I usually wore my fatigues, but as a precaution I covered my legionnaire's patch. The wolf's head of Varus was on far too many net broadcasts lately—and never with a happy story attached.

My wanderings drew me farther north every day. I knew where I was going: back to the Mustering Hall where this had all started. The legion people would be there. They'd know what the score was. They'd know when we were going to ship out again. It was all supposed to be a secret—but someone always knew what was really going on.

-2-

It was a Monday night when I arrived in Newark. The tram dumped me on a street I didn't know. I'd never liked this city; the best I could say was it wasn't the worst place on the planet. These days, most of Newark looked more like a warzone than some of the warzones I'd walked through. People said there were nice areas, but I'd never seen one. I guess if you're rich enough every town has a nice section—but I didn't know any rich people.

I headed through darkening streets looking for the Mustering Hall. The Hall's doors were automatic, and I knew that the building would be closed to the public after eight, but I thought maybe the doors would let me in because I was a legionnaire. The only other option would be to find a room to rent, which was going to be hard. Without my tapper, I couldn't access my account. I didn't have much cash left on me, and I'd decided it would be best if I let my folks have the rest of the credits left in my account, anyway.

They were going to need all of it if the news reports were right. The crash was looming closer every day, and people were already hardening their hearts and scrambling to move their money someplace safe.

My own account had once contained genuine Galactic credits. They were hard currency, good anywhere in the Empire on any planet. But by decree, the real money had been swept from my account and exchanged for Hegemony credits. Hegemony cash was better than district money, but it was only good on Earth. As my parents might be in trouble, I'd let them keep most of it. All their accounts were in District money which was spiraling lower in value every day. With Hegemony cash to draw on, I was at least fairly sure they wouldn't starve.

I found the big building at around nine p.m. and tried the doors. They flashed up my info, but they didn't open. Instead, the door buzzed and flashed a red hand at me, the universal stop symbol. I wasn't getting in tonight. The door didn't even talk to me or give me a reason. It was one of those older, dumber, not-so-smart-doors.

Turning around and muttering curses, I froze. I wasn't alone.

Three figures stood near. They weren't in my face. They were standing back a ways, keeping out of the circle of concrete covered by the security camera over the door. I could tell by their easy stances they had this down to a routine. They knew where they could be seen and recorded. They'd probably followed me from the drop-off point and knew that the door wouldn't let me in.

I had a few choices now, I realized. I could try to bluff my way through them, or I could call the police on my tapper—but that wasn't working. Besides, the police might not be getting paid anymore. Maybe they wouldn't come down here, and these thugs knew it. Maybe the muggers paid the police more than the Local Gov did, and the cops were never going to come even if they did get my distress call.

My third option was the least appetizing. I could stand close to the door and the camera, shivering here all night, hoping they'd keep away until morning came. I already knew I wasn't taking that option. I wasn't going to huddle here and have them laugh, watching me take a leak against the building when the urge came.

My eyes narrowed and I felt myself getting pissed off. This is something that happens to me now and again, often at the least opportune moments. Call it a character flaw if you like— it was what it was. Normally, I'm an easy-going guy. Ask any of my friends. I can put up with a lot of shit day-to-day.

But tonight I was done taking any more of it, especially from these three losers with their little trap.

14

What had me pissed off the most was wondering how many legionnaires they'd shaken down, robbing them when they came too late to get in the door. Probably, they'd usually gone for hopefuls, not full-fledged legionnaires. Poor kids who'd come down here hoping to join up. Maybe they'd mistaken me for one of them as I'd covered my insignia.

Instead of trying to slip past them or bluff them or hugging the dumbass smart-door like it was my mama, I walked directly toward the nearest of them. He was also the largest, although not as tall as I was.

Their easy stances changed as I approached confidently. The leader stood his ground while the other two walked slowly toward me from the sides.

I ignored the sidekicks. I went straight for the leader.

"You lost, boy?" I asked loudly.

He frowned at me. I could see his lower jaw, although the rest of his face was shrouded in a dark hood. Criminals wore hoodies all the time when they were on the street. It was illegal to cover your face to avoid facial-recognition cameras in most cities, but people still did it all the time.

"I think you're the one who's lost," he answered with a snort of amusement.

"What's your name, kid?"

"Frigging yokel," he laughed. "I'm the taxman. And it's time to pay your taxes."

The self-proclaimed taxman put out his hand with his palm up and made a grabbing gesture.

"You'd best put that begging hand away," I told him, "before you lose it."

His amusement vanished. "What? You crazy? Give me your cash. All of it. Can't you count? We got three men against one fool."

"No," I said, shedding my outer jacket and leaving it draped over my right hand. "There's only one man here. Only one legionnaire talking to three pieces of trash."

My patch stood out. It showed the full stripes of a specialist. Above that was the wolf's head of Varus. I hadn't yet qualified for a particular specialty, which would add symbols to my sleeve, but Centurion Graves had given me the promotion before I left the ship. On our next mission, I was to train en route. I was best qualified as a tech or a weaponeer. I wasn't sure yet which path I would be placed upon—but I was kind of hoping for weaponeer.

"You haven't got no ray-gun," the leader said.

The other two had stopped on either side of me, standing just out of reach with their hands in their pockets. They might have weapons in there, or they might not. Like I said, I was pissed off, so I hardly cared one way or the other.

"You know what happens if this goes the wrong way?" I asked.

"Yeah, you die."

"No," I said. "I can't die. Not like you can. I'm right here next to the Hall. My mental engrams are being recorded at a constant rate, and my body scans were stored over a year ago. If I die, I'll pop right back out in the morning. If you losers die, you'll stay dead. Forever."

"Crazy mother," the leader said. "All right, you can walk. But keep your shit to yourself if we ever meet again."

I chuckled and shook my head. "You ladies don't get it yet. You're the ones that are in trouble, and you're not going to walk. Not today. I can't have you jokers shaking down recruits tomorrow night. This ends now."

"*What?*" demanded the thug on the left. "Why are we even listening to this fool?"

"Shut up, Abhi!" the taxman hissed.

"So, it's the taxman and Abhi, did I get that right?" I asked. "Anyone else want to give me a name or a tapper ID?"

At that point, I thought I had the situation in the bag. They were crumbling. I had the leader cowed and one of his sidekicks was in rebellion. I figured I'd frog-march them all to the nearest cop station before this was over.

But I was wrong. I'd yet to hear a word out of the third guy, who silently stood to my right side.

The quiet man pulled out a weapon at this point in the conversation. It wasn't a gun, not exactly. Gunpowder weapons are strictly-controlled and rare in cities these days. But what he pulled out of his coat was a weapon nonetheless. A riveter, to be exact. A construction man's tool.

16

In my time, most buildings were formed using puff-crete as the primary building material. An alien commodity, it could be shaped into any form and when it set, it was harder and lighter than carbonized steel. But its very strength was a problem because often construction crews needed to connect slabs of puff-crete together. How did one do that with a nearly indestructible material? The answer was a modern-day riveter.

The weapon was small, not much bigger than a power drill. But it operated more like a snap-rifle, accelerating rivets to fantastic velocities and hammering them home at close range. Those rivets could kill just as easily as bullets could—they were possibly even more deadly because they hit with fantastic speed and force.

The third man's move left me no choice but to act. Sure, I'd played the part of a tough guy who didn't fear death—but I was a liar. I feared death quite a bit, possibly more than these three clowns combined. I'd experienced death, and I didn't want to go through it again.

Dying is kind of like getting vaccinations. Every kid starts off curious and clueless when the needles come, but they learn very quickly to fear them. I had experienced the needle one too many times, and I wasn't interested in a repeat performance.

I had my new knife concealed under the jacket I'd shed earlier. Taking it off had served two purposes: it had revealed my rank, but it had also hidden my only weapon.

I hadn't planned on putting the new weapon to use so soon. I hadn't figured it would come out of its sheath until I left Earth—but I'd been wrong.

I took one quick step toward the guy lifting the riveter and reached out with my knife. He got a shot off, unfortunately. I was clipped in the left hip. A burning line that felt like a dog-bite sizzled there. I hoped he'd missed the bone, but I didn't have time to worry about that now. My left leg was still holding me up, but I didn't know if I was on borrowed time or not.

The quiet guy didn't have time for a second shot, as the riveter kicked up and almost flew into his face. The tool had released so much energy it had recoiled and caught him by surprise. He was clearly an amateur with a makeshift weapon rather than an expert who used it in his daily routine.

One lunge, one slash—that was all I had time for. My knife flickered and took his hand off at the wrist.

The other two were reaching for us. They were yelling something but I no longer cared what they were saying. This was on.

The taxman had the presence of mind to grab onto my knife hand with both of his. It didn't save him. I dropped my knife and jerked him forward, using the momentum of his motion against him. He stumbled over his buddy, who was no longer the silent type. He was on his knees and howling by now, the fingers of his remaining hand clamped over his stump, trying to stop the torrent of blood that was splattering everyone's shoes.

The taxman went into a belly flop when I let him go, and I kneed him on his way down. He grunted in pain.

Abhi was behind me then, and I took a fist in the kidney. Three or four more blows landed on my head and shoulders. They hurt, but they didn't put me out. He threw his arms wide and looped them around mine, trying to bear-hug me.

The taxman scrambled for the riveter, and I knew I couldn't let him have it. I couldn't just pick it up because this Abhi guy was on my back, so I kicked it away toward the smart-door.

I broke Abhi's hold, and then I broke his jaw. None of them seemed to be trained in hand-to-hand. Legionnaires usually died a time or two in boot camp—we took our training very seriously.

Abhi ran off into the night holding his face together and sobbing. I looked around and noticed that the one-handed guy had disappeared, too. I couldn't blame either of them.

But the taxman wasn't through yet. He ran toward the smart-door. He was going for the riveter.

"Give it up, man!" I shouted, snatching up my knife. I rushed after him painfully. My hip slowed me down.

He made it to the riveter first, and he lifted it up, grinning. His face was fully exposed, his hood having fallen to his shoulders in the struggle.

"You're dead," he told me.

"You're on camera," I told him.

18

His face faltered. He knew it was true. His hands tightened on the riveter. I knew he could hammer a chunk of metal into my breastbone in an instant. I couldn't even dodge effectively, and there was nowhere to hide.

I watched his face, twisted and deciding—kill me and go to prison, or run and go to prison anyway for the list of other crimes his face was now attached to?

As I wondered which way his mind would twist, the door behind him buzzed and opened.

-3-

The taxman glanced over his shoulder. I couldn't blame him for that. He was caught between me and whoever was stepping into the situation behind him.

I didn't wait around for his surprise to subside. I didn't have time to reach him with a kick or a punch. So, I threw my new knife at him.

Throwing a knife accurately isn't easy even if the weapon used is balanced and built for the purpose. I'd been combat-trained aboard my legion's ship for months, but we hadn't done much in the way of knife-throwing.

My whirling blade sailed past the taxman, missing him by a hair. Instead of its intended target, it thunked into the smart-door behind him.

"McGill! You asshole!"

"Carlos?"

I couldn't believe it. He was standing there, his stocky form silhouetted in the doorway.

I winced when I saw the knife had nearly hit him, but I didn't have time for apologies. I came forward, closing with the taxman. He turned back to me, lifting his riveter, and I knew I was screwed. I couldn't reach him before he could pull the trigger.

Thick arms came out and latched onto the thug's wrist. Carlos had finally made his move. The riveter fired, over and over. The concrete at my feet sparked with tiny yellow explosions.

Carlos and I tackled him a second later, and he went down, but he still had both hands clamped onto that damned riveter. Not wanting either of us to be shot in the foot in the struggle, I ended the fight by slamming the smart-door into the taxman's head repeatedly. Finally, he stopped moving.

We stood over the unconscious thug, breathing hard.

"Making friends again, huh McGill?" Carlos grunted out.

"As always."

By this time, Hegemony MPs had reached the scene. The smart-door must have alerted them. We explained the situation, and they arrested the thug at our feet.

"What's his name?" one of them asked me.

"He said he was the taxman," I explained.

The MP twisted his lips. "Very funny guy. He can tell his next joke in the District auto-courts."

The MPs hauled him up, carrying him between the two of them like a sack of potatoes.

"He's not dead," I said.

"I figured."

"Shouldn't you call an ambulance or something?"

The MP snorted. "They won't come out here. We're going to have to drive him to the District hospital ourselves. It's a jurisdiction thing."

I frowned and shrugged as they hauled him off.

"I don't get you, McGill," Carlos said. "One second you're in a death fight with that loser. The next, you're worried they'll stub his toes."

"He might have a broken neck. They should put him on a stretcher or something. He's not like us, he's a civvie. He won't get a new grow if they screw up his body."

Carlos laughed and shook his head. "He would have killed you if he could have. Get over it."

"People are desperate, Carlos," I said. "I don't know what his story is, but I'm sure it's not a happy one."

"What can we do about it?"

"We can bring home the bacon," I said. "We can go out there and win new accounts, new planets for our legions to serve."

Carlos snorted at me. "Yeah, sure. We're going to save the Earth. You always have big, dumb ideas. I think it's because you're so tall. The air is too thin up there for your brain to work properly."

Lines like that had often brought Carlos and me to physical blows. But I restrained my irritation. It was just his way of talking, and I'd gotten used to it for the most part.

"What are you doing here at the Hall, anyway?" I asked him.

"Mustering back in, same as you."

We'd been told we'd be contacted and brought back to the same Mustering Hall where we'd been recruited after shore leave was over. But it hadn't been long enough for that yet.

"By my accounting, we've got nearly three more weeks of leave," I said.

"What? Didn't you get the call? We're supposed to be here *now*. That's why the adjunct sent me up here when you buzzed the door. The computers alerted him. Why didn't you check in with your tapper?"

"It's not working—and no, I didn't get that call. I came back to see if there was any news about our next contract."

We were walking through the Hall by this time. I was still limping, but it wasn't that bad. I figured if I got the wound sprayed over by a flesh-printer, I'd be right as rain in a day or two.

The Mustering Hall was a loud, echo-filled chamber, nearly as big as a football stadium. As the non-legionnaires had been kicked out, only official people were left still milling around.

"Lucky you," Carlos said. "You would have been reported AWOL if you hadn't shown up by tomorrow night. Anyway, here's the update: our contract *was* canceled. We've got a new one, though. We ship out in less than a week. No one seems to know where we're going or what the mission is."

I nodded. "I hear there are a lot of legion contract cancellations happening."

"Figures," Carlos said. "Everyone's getting a vacation except for us. Same old Varus bullshit. Whatever the new job is, I bet it's going to suck."

I couldn't argue with him on that point.

On the way down to Legion Varus' offices, which were located on the lower floor, we ran into two legionnaires. They were standing on either side of the escalators, loitering.

I could tell right off they were from a different legion than we were. They had shiny black boots, and their legion patch depicted Taurus, the raging bull. The emblem indicated they were both from Germanica, a respectable outfit. I noticed that the symbol was bigger than our wolf's head symbol. In fact, their patches were so wide they were hard to ignore.

Germanica was one of the famous legions. I'd tried to join them when I'd first come to the Mustering Hall last year. They hadn't wanted me, and I'd joined Varus instead.

Carlos and I glanced at these two, then moved to walk between them to the escalators, but they moved to bar our way.

"What do you losers want?" asked the legionnaire on the right. She was a black woman with a pair of the thickest thighs I'd ever seen on a fit person.

The legionnaire on the left gave a bark of laughter at her comment. He had his arms crossed—and they were big arms, I had to give him that. He had reddish curly hair that was cut so tightly it looked like he had a cap on his head. He was a specialist too, same rank as me, but his second patch indicated he was a weaponeer.

"You want to go downstairs where the rats live?" the woman asked. "That's it, isn't it, rat?"

"Yeah?" Carlos said, puffing up his chest a bit. "You clowns from Germanica shouldn't talk big. I hear your last contract was cancelled. And I do mean your *last*."

Their faces, which had been bullying and amused, suddenly displayed rage. Carlos had a special gift when it came to making people want to hit him. I knew Germanica had lost their contracts, everyone had. Their contracts had mostly come from Steel World, but that was all over with now.

"You little shit," the redheaded weaponeer said, stepping forward and poking Carlos with a thick finger. "That's why we're here. We want to talk to you Varus bastards. You're the reason we lost our contracts in the first place."

As legionnaires from different legions, we were technically in the same overall force. But there was a strong sense of rivalry between the different outfits. In the past, troops from various military services hadn't always gotten along. There had always been Army-Navy rivalry, for example. But with legionnaires it was even stronger than that. We were more like armies from different allied countries. We operated independently, and we had complex relationships.

In the case of Legion Varus, however, the relationships weren't complex. Pretty much everyone else despised us.

I put my hands up in a cautioning gesture. I figured we could settle this calmly. After all, I'd just been in one fight, and that was usually my limit on any given evening. But before I could speak words of peace and wisdom, Carlos had his mouth open again.

"Unemployed," he said, then laughed. "*We've* got a contract, and you're standing in the way of one of Earth's few sources of hard currency. I wonder why the aliens picked us over you guys? Maybe because we get the job done instead of whining about how our cush deals went sour. I'm glad you pukes got cancelled. Maybe you'll have to do some real fighting next time out."

The redhead's fist was pulling back before Carlos even finished his little speech. I couldn't recall seeing a guy's face go from white to red quite that quickly before. The situation might have been a record for Carlos, who often generated this sort of response from people.

"Stand down, Specialist!" called a voice.

We looked and saw an officer striding in our direction. She looked small but mean. She had a Hegemony patch on her shoulder, a globe, and under that there were two bars which served as the universal emblem of rank for adjuncts.

I could tell the redhead was uncertain. His arm stayed up and cocked. I could almost see in his mind that he was weighing a night in the brig against the joy of punching Carlos. It was a tough call, and I couldn't blame him for hesitating.

Not helping matters, Carlos was smiling at him and tapping at his chin with his middle finger, begging for the punch.

The female legionnaire from Germanica defused things. She put her hand on the redhead's fist and gently pushed it down.

"These rejects aren't worth it," she said, giving each of us a sneer. "You know, you're right, we did lose our contracts. But we got new ones: bullshit missions because of Varus!"

The two stepped aside and left. The adjunct glared us, watching as we separated. When we'd safely passed down the escalator, she disappeared.

"I was totally going to take down that ginger-headed moron," Carlos said. "He's lucky a couple of girls were there to save his sorry ass."

"Uh-huh," I said.

Carlos looked at me, and his expression turned thoughtful. "What do you think she meant about getting new bullshit contracts?"

"I don't know. Maybe they have to take on crappy jobs like we do. Maybe that's why they're hating us right now."

"They always hate us. But yeah, that makes sense. I bet they're trying to carve out new territory. Ha! That serves them right! Let them do some hard fighting and dying for a change."

"You're a bitter little man, Carlos," I told him.

He glared at me, but then he looked thoughtful again. "Do you think everyone on Earth blames us for what happened? For the lizards dropping contracts with all the legions?"

"Probably. The news-nets are pushing that idea. They never accuse us directly, but they hint around all the time. They talk about how the very last legion to set foot on Cancri-9 was the 'notorious' Legion Varus. Then they go into a brief discussion about what a bunch of losers and misfits we all are."

"But that's just a cover story, right? I mean, Hegemony Gov knows we're the best, right? That's what you said the Tribune told you."

I glanced at him and felt a guilty pang. The truth was the Tribune hadn't told me any such thing. He'd said we took on the jobs that no one else wanted, and that we did essential work. But that pretty much describes morticians and school janitors who sprinkle smart-dust on barf stains, too. Just because you had a hard, necessary job didn't guarantee anyone would respect you for it.

I decided to maintain the fiction, however. Now wasn't the time to bring Carlos down any further.

"Yeah," I said. "That's right. We're the best in the system. They're just jealous."

"Damn straight."

We reached the Varus offices and walked into a wardroom. It wasn't big enough to hold all the soldiers present, so we had to stand in the back, shoulder to shoulder. There must have been a hundred people in the room, which was built to hold half that number.

"Glad you could make it, McGill," Veteran Harris rumbled at me.

I touched my fingers to my cap and flashed him a smile he didn't return.

"Eyes front," he said.

I looked forward and saw another familiar face. It was Primus Turov. She was the leader of my cohort, which was mostly made up of people from North America Sector. She didn't like me, but fortunately she wasn't looking in my direction right now. The only thing I liked about the woman was her posterior, which I found myself staring at right off.

With an effort, I tuned into the briefing. I had the feeling she'd been talking for quite a while.

"Our destination world is still a secret, but our mission is not. We're to grow Earth's territory. We've lost certain critical accounts, and they aren't coming back. Because of that, our entire world is feeling an economic bite."

"More like an economic swallow," whispered Carlos.

Veteran Harris must have been waiting for this moment, as he'd positioned himself nearby. It was like he'd known that one of us would eventually make a comment. His boot slid sideways, crashing into Carlos' shins. It was a move I'd seen him use before, usually on recruits who weren't showing the appropriate level of respect. Carlos made an odd sound that made me wonder if he'd consumed a small animal in a single gulp. The troops around us grinned faintly, without ever taking their eyes off the Primus. I had to admit, I was grinning too.

The Primus' head turned, and she stared at us coldly for a second or two before continuing with her speech and her walk. That woman really knew how to walk. It had to have something to do with her hips and the heels of her officers' boots. Hell, I don't know. I felt like I was being hypnotized by some kind of exotic snake as I listened and stared.

"This campaign will be different," she said. "As you muster back in, you'll all be required to pass a specialized battery of tests."

There were groans. I glanced at Carlos, but he was keeping his lips compressed together tightly, resisting his natural urges. Veteran Harris' arm lashed out twice, slapping recruits who'd dared to voice their dismay.

Discipline in a modern legion was very physical. I'd read a bit about the old Roman legions during my shore leave. The historical records had stipulated a long list of harsh punishments for soldiers in ancient times. One or two had stuck out in my mind. When a Roman citizen signed on for military service and took the oath known as the *sacramentum*, he knew what he was in for. The *sacramentum* stated that he would serve Rome on pain of punishment up to and inclusive of his death. The discipline was much more rigorous in those days, and Earth had revived the old model in response to the Galactic Empire's requirements.

In ancient Rome, an officer had the power to summarily execute anyone under his command. Depending on the nature of the crime and the disposition of the commander, punishments varied. A man might be fined a few silver coins for minor infractions, or he might be publicly flogged until his skin hung from his back in bloody strips. For serious crimes like treasonous behavior, the standard penalty was to be sewn into a leather sack full of snakes and tossed into a nearby lake or river to drown while the serpents presumably went mad and chewed on the disgraced soldier.

Although I'd never heard of anyone being drowned with reptiles, I was pretty sure some commanders had thought it over—especially if they were dealing with a guy like Carlos.

"Yes," said the Primus loudly with her hands on her hips. She'd stopped strutting around and now looked deadly serious. "I'm talking about a few tests: blood, core-samples, the works. You'll have to pass physical stress-tests, too. I don't want any weaklings on this campaign. The stakes are too high."

Core-samples? I didn't even know what the hell that was, and I exchanged worried glances with a few others nearby.

"We're heading to a harsh environment," Turov continued as if that explained everything. "I'm only making sure we're all fit to do our duty. Accordingly, I want everyone to spend the night in the Hall instead of heading out to the spaceport. We don't have the facilities to do the testing on the transports, and *Corvus* won't be in orbit until the very hour we launch. We'll do the tests here, and they will be administered by Hegemony personnel."

Another round of groans and cuffing sounds swept the chamber. This wasn't good news. As harshly as my legion's personnel treated us, they were at least on our side. They'd been in battle with most of us, and some of us had even developed personal relationships with the bio specialists.

That wouldn't be the case with the Hegemony people. They weren't our friends. If the reaction of the two Germanica legionnaires was any indicator, this was going to go badly. Most members of other legions had spit on us before, but now they thought they had a real reason to hate us.

"Any questions?"

I knew I shouldn't, but I did it. I raised my hand.

"For God's sake, McGill…" Harris muttered.

I knew why he wanted me to stay quiet. Primus Turov and I went way back—in a bad way. She'd tried to have me executed—in fact, Harris himself had done the job, killing me with a grin on his face. But I'd managed to weasel out of that with an unauthorized revival. That had never sat well with Turov. The very fact I was still breathing annoyed my superior officer. It hadn't been a good place to start off a relationship, but I hoped she might forget about it eventually.

"Sir?" I asked when she called on me. "Has the legion considered trying to counter all the bad press we're getting? I mean, everyone on the planet hates us now. They think we single-handedly brought financial ruin to Earth."

I don't know what Primus Turov had expected me to ask—maybe something like "where's the bathroom?" but I was pretty sure from her shocked expression that my question had taken her by surprise. She paused for a moment before answering.

"Legion Varus' reputation isn't an issue," she said. "Remember—all of you! We aren't in this for the glory. Fame would only make our job harder. We'll fix public opinion by fixing the problem, not by going on a PR campaign. What we want is to be forgotten about again. We fix things, but we don't do it with fanfare. That's our mission."

The meeting broke up after that. Carlos let out a sigh.

"My life flashed before my eyes when you opened your big yap," he told me. "But she took your question seriously. Must be bothering her, too."

"Yeah, sure," I said. "It has to be bothering all the brass. How'd you like to be in charge of a unit like this for years only to have people talk crap about you online all day long?"

"That's the sad thing about it."

"What do you mean?"

Carlos shook his head. "I mean that even if we *do* fix it, we won't get the credit. People will stop being mad, sure, but they'll probably never know what we did or why."

I thought about it, and I had to admit to myself that he was probably right.

"How about that Turov, huh?" Carlos asked when we'd rolled out insta-mats alongside the train-gliders and stretched out to sleep.

I'd thrown my arm over my eyes—they never turned off the lights down here. I lifted my arm slightly and looked at him with bleary eyes.

"What about her?" I asked him.

"I'm talking about her butt," Carlos said, rubbing his face and yawning. "Don't pretend you didn't notice. How can I want to screw someone and want to kill her at the same time?"

I chuckled. "My father could explain that to you. He says that's what marriage is all about."

-4-

The next day was an entirely new flavor of Hell. These Hegemony bio-types had to be the most heartless bunch I'd ever encountered.

It turned out that a "core sample" was just what it sounded like. They drove little round tubes of steel into our abdomens, tubes that had very sharp ends to them, and left them in our guts while we howled, squirmed and sweated.

The real trick came when they pulled these meat-thermometers out of our bodies. They didn't want to give us infections or cause organ failure—that would be inconvenient and require an expensive regrow. They wanted to take their measure of our guts and heal us back up from the inside.

In order to accomplish this, the tubes were equipped with flesh-spraying tips. Ever so slowly as the tubes were withdrawn, they spit out enough fresh human cells to knit up our punctured bodies. We were left with nickel-sized scars on our bellies and tears running down our faces.

"I want to congratulate you, Specialist Franklin," Carlos said, his voice coming out in hitches. "You've invented the perfect torture device: plenty of pain, but no chance of relief through death."

He got a laugh out of Franklin with that line. She laughed quite heartily. I had to wonder if she really *did* get a charge out of taking core-samples.

Afterward, the circular scars were tender, but we could function. Holding our sides, we moved slowly and painfully to the next chamber, anxious about further tests.

I was surprised by what happened next. Instead of giving us a break, or making us take a sit-down test at least, they put us into sparring chambers. These were sealed, bubble-like affairs. They looked like tents. Carlos and I separated with a nod.

"Good luck, buddy," Carlos said. "The bio told me what's coming up next, and you're going to need some."

"What—?" I began, but he was gone, shunted off down through a line of groaning troops. Everyone had a hand on their side and a grimace on their face.

As I entered my tent a robot grabbed me. It was skinny, a pile of wires and steel tubing. It had fingers—lots of them, and the damned thing seemed to be trying to frisk me.

I've gotten into trouble in the past by abusing robots. In fact, I take a certain degree of pride in my ability to mess with them. But as the legion people never seemed to be happy with my changes to their scripts, I thought I would give the tech who operated this thing a chance.

"Can someone please explain why I should put up with this?" I asked loudly of the plastic, shivering walls.

No one answered me. That was typical of legion tests. They often wanted to see how I would handle a situation. Sometimes they were testing my psychology as well as my physical abilities. On other occasions, they just didn't give a damn what I thought about anything and didn't feel like bothering to tell me what the plan was.

It was hot and humid in the tent. The pressure felt higher, too. There were no ventilation sources I could see, and as far as I could tell, the whole chamber was being filled up with a continuous blowing fan that pumped hot wet air into the dome. It was about thirty feet around and nearly as tall. I could easily stand up and walk around inside—that was, if the robot let go of my shirt.

Instinctively, I resisted the robot. It's just something in me, I guess. I could stand a bio driving what amounted to a metal spike into my guts, but having a robot molest me—that was too much.

31

The machine managed to get my chest-wrap open. We didn't have shirts, not exactly. Legion uniforms were fairly dumb as smart-clothes went. They only knew enough to fit a man's form and hug up against him, adhering to skin and other smart-cloth.

Having the robot rip my shirt open was too much for me. I was already sore, pissed off and hot. I narrowed my eyes at the skinny bundle of metal sticks.

I figured that someone had to be watching—this wasn't my first rodeo—so I decided not to attack the bot directly. Instead, I grabbed its right hand, pushed against its right shoulder, and simultaneously swept my foot behind it, stepping on its power cord. It was a judo move tailored for the target enemy.

The effect was quite gratifying. The robot lost its balance and flipped onto its back. It crashed onto the floor with a jangling sound I quite enjoyed.

"Test failed!" shouted a voice from a hidden speaker.

I looked around but still didn't spot the camera. The tent was hotter than ever, but I was frowning now and becoming stubborn.

"Sir? How did I fail the test, sir?"

"We aren't playing Q and A. Exit the tent, soldier!"

I didn't budge. "Your robot seems to have malfunctioned," I said.

The robot tried to get up, servos whining. I kept my foot on its cord, so it couldn't stand.

"You struck the machine," said the voice. "That's a clear demonstration of malice right there. I'm calling that intolerance under mild stress and discomfort. Test failed."

"I repeat, your robot has malfunctioned," I said, trying to sound reasonable, even cheerful. Sure, I felt like belting the owner of that voice, but I spoke pleasantly and even managed to inject a note of concern into my tone. "I tried to catch it as it fell. Maybe the heat was too much for the machine."

There was silence for about ten seconds. Taking a chance, I stooped over the robot and appeared to be trying to help it. In reality, I groped its chest panel until I found a set of hair thin wires. I gave them a little tug, and the robot stopped struggling.

A moment later, a rustling sound made me turn around. A small, portly woman with blonde hair and twisted lips came in. She put her hands on her hips and glared at me. She was a tech, a type of enlisted specialist that worked with advanced equipment—like robots.

"This automated unit checked out two hours ago," she said in concern. "Why isn't it operating now? What did you do, Specialist?"

"I don't know. Maybe it has a faulty balance gyro. I didn't hit the thing—it just fell down."

She glared at me, then checked out her robot. Her face changed from anger to concern. "It's lost power…"

"Like I said—"

She stood up suddenly and put her finger in my face. "You're one of those clowns from Varus, aren't you?"

I slapped the patch on my shoulder. "I wear the wolf's head with pride, Specialist."

Cursing, she dragged her robot away. I offered to help, but the tech waved me back.

"Just keep away from my equipment. You know what I'm going to do? I'm going to pass you. That's the worst thing I could do…yeah, you're getting an A-plus, asshole!"

I frowned and, not knowing what to make of her threats, I exited the tent immediately. Outside I sucked in gulps of cool air in the open Hall.

I saw a familiar face just coming out of another tent. The girl's name was Kivi. It had been a few months since I'd seen her, and she was a sight for sore eyes. She had that classic short-girl body: short limbs, but with plenty of curves. Her hair was curly and her eyes were quick. She was from the Mideast somewhere originally, and right now she looked hot in more ways than one.

I couldn't help smiling as I ran my eyes over her. She was in a state of undress and struggling to get her smart-clothes to adhere to her body again.

Her eyes flicked over to me, and she caught me watching her. She smiled.

"You made it through the test?" she asked me.

33

"Of course," I said, having no real idea what the test had been about.

She pursed her lips. "I'm kind of surprised. Did the robot undress you completely?"

I blinked, then I caught on. So that's what it had been trying to do. "I let it," I said, "just the way I was supposed to."

"You've changed, then."

She walked toward me and began flicking at my specialist patch. She didn't have one.

"Looks like we might not be in the same unit any longer," she said.

"We'll have to see," I said. I lifted up a hand and touched her elbow. It just felt like a natural thing to do.

Kivi and I had been intimate on a number of occasions. We'd broken up long ago, but several months apart tends to make a man forget about whatever it was that had pissed him off in the first place.

She smiled up at me shyly, but I wasn't fooled. Kivi didn't have a shy bone in her body.

"I passed, according to the tech," I said, "but I don't know why the hell they would give us such a freaky test in the first place."

"I'm not sure. But I'll bet we're heading somewhere hot and wet."

I thought about that, and nodded. "Testing how easily we're irritated by heat and pressure?"

"I guess."

"You feel a little warmed up," I said, looking down at her and smiling again. "How about we go get a cool drink before these Hegemony bastards torture us some more?"

"Good idea," she said, and we headed up a short flight of steps to the ring of booths that surrounded the central testing area. Half the booths were occupied by various legion representatives while the rest seemed to be concession stands selling things.

I bought Kivi a beer and we drank fast. You never knew how long you had before you were caught goofing off in Legion Varus.

As it turned out, I was just lowering my face toward hers to kiss her when my tapper buzzed on my arm.

I could tell hers was going off too. She winced a little. The vibration under your skin never felt right. Most of us had them set so that they only made tones or flashed colors on the skin. But legion rules were clear: we had to have them set to vibrate for emergency incoming orders.

She raised my arm to eye my tapper, which I'd had fixed earlier today. When she let it go, I naturally allowed my hand to come down and rest on her shoulder. She smiled and reached up in response, throwing a hand around my neck.

"Forget about it for a second," she whispered.

Then she kissed me, dragging my face down to meet hers. We had a serious height difference…but we'd always managed to find ways to get around it.

* * *

The next day went by quickly. We were tested some more, and the tests themselves made me feel suspicious about this mission. Most of the metrics being measured centered on our tolerance for irritation, pain, heat and pressure. Could we take it? The answer for most of us was *yes*. The legionnaires in Varus weren't like most of the others I'd run into. We might not be the smartest or the best-equipped, but we could take a beating and keep marching on.

By the third night, we were tired but not defeated. We were herded aboard a sky-train going to the spaceport sometime after midnight. No one complained. No one said much of anything. We were going off-world and, unlike fresh recruits, we knew that meant we'd be in for a rough ride.

Fortunately, the officers didn't play any tricks on my unit on the way up to *Corvus*. We weren't here to go through boot camp. We were veterans: flat-faced, dark-eyed. No one smiled or fooled around much. We all had the feeling that we were going to have entirely new reasons to regret signing up before this mission was over.

Corvus was an amazing sight just as it had been the first time I'd laid eyes on her. Over five kilometers long, the ship was of the dreadnaught class. She had sharp angles, sleek lines and acres of burnished metal hull plates that were so long they boggled the mind. *Corvus* was big enough to carry an entire Earth legion plus a crew of aliens call "Skrull" and all of our equipment. Thousands of troops tramped aboard from dozens of transports which had lifted off from spaceports all around the planet.

After we'd found our assigned quarters, we were summoned to the mess hall for a unit-wide briefing. I was happy about that, as were most of the rest of my comrades. Often, the brass didn't bother telling us what we were facing. This time, they'd felt the need was great enough to clue in the grunts.

"Zeta Herculis," Centurion Graves said, as if that explained everything.

He stood at the front of the mess hall with a laser pointer aimed at the wall-screen. Depicted in blazing color was a system with two stars: one was a big K-class with an orangey hue to it, the second was a smaller white dwarf.

Graves looked around the group, and we stared back blankly.

"My God, people," he said. "Don't they teach you anything in school anymore?"

Carlos perked up. He couldn't help it.

"Yes, sir! They teach us to join the legions and see the stars, sir!"

Veteran Harris stepped closer to Carlos and loomed over him. I could tell he was angry and dying for a hint from Graves that he should lean on Carlos, but Graves didn't give him an excuse.

Carlos' comment seemed to amuse Graves. He chuckled and shook his head.

"Yes, I guess that's all troops come in with. Heads full of happy-talk and lies. But today, we're going to tell you a little secret: we're not alone in space."

I don't think a single one of us knew what the hell he was talking about, but we knew enough to keep quiet and stare. Even Carlos kept his mouth shut.

"That's right, Earth isn't alone. There's another colony out there in space. Right here, in fact."

He smacked the wall-screen which comprised one entire end of the mess hall. The wall didn't even shimmer. It wasn't a projection, but an image generated by photosensitive organic LEDs sprayed onto the wall itself.

A murmur swept over us. A lot of hands raised. We were allowed to do that during a briefing if we had a question.

"Tech Specialist Elkin?" Graves asked, calling on a woman in the front row.

My eyes searched for her. There she was, sweet Natasha. Like Kivi, I'd had a thing going with her back on Steel World, but it had fallen apart after returning home to Earth.

Natasha Elkin was quite different from Kivi in manners and appearance. She was soft-spoken but always knowledgeable and confident. Her cheekbones were high, like a girl in a magazine, but her eyes squinched up and disappeared when she smiled. She was tall, with a fit body and a nice face.

"Sir?" Natasha asked. "Are you talking about the failed exploration mission of 2049?"

"Ah-ha! Yes, exactly. I'd hoped one of you had heard of it. Nice to have someone with a real education in the room."

I was baffled but unsurprised. Natasha had always been something of a brain and a natural teacher's pet. I had it on good authority that she'd once built her own pet out of artificial parts and been expelled from school for the infraction.

"For the unenlightened, I'll explain," Graves said. "Back in 2049, before even I was born, Earth sent a mission to the stars. The Hydra project."

When he said that, a light finally went off in my head. I remembered having read about that mission. People at the time had believed *Hydra* had triggered the interest of the Galactics in Earth. As far as I could recall, the ship left Earth and was never heard from again.

"The Hydra mission was to explore and colonize an exoplanet we'd seen only in telescopes at that time," Graves continued. "All our measurements told us that the world was Earth-like and had large bodies of liquid water. We've since found inhabited worlds even closer, but we didn't know about them at that time."

Natasha raised her hand again. I rolled my eyes. She loved showing off when she knew something the rest of us didn't. Graves called on her.

"Sir? I thought the mission was lost."

"That's what the official story was. But I'm here to brief you on what really happened—at least, as much as we know. You have to understand that our human-built propulsion systems were woefully inadequate when the ship left. To travel the thirty-odd lightyears to the target star system took more than fifty years in local time."

There was as murmur of disbelief around the room.

"That's right," Graves said. "Even given the effects of time-dilation at great speed, we have to assume that people lived and died on that ship before they arrived. Some must have been born en route, and others probably never lived to see the end of the journey. Shortly after they left—right about when the Galactics arrived to graciously invite us into their Empire—we lost contact with the ship. But that was partly by design. The newly formed Hegemony government signaled *Hydra* to go radio-silent. They were worried that if the Galactics found out we'd already launched a colony ship, we'd be destroyed."

I looked around the room. People were frowning, taking it in. This news was big. It was strange to think that Earth had sent out a vessel to the stars without any helpful alien tech. I felt proud just thinking about it. By their faces however, I could tell that to others the thought was disturbing.

"We didn't hear from *Hydra* for about seventy years. A few months ago we finally did get a short message from them, saying the mission had reached their target star, and they'd set up a colony there. Here's the shocking part: they sent that message to us thirty-five years ago. That means they reached the world in question and have been living there ever since. At least, we *think* they're still alive. A lot can happen in thirty-five years."

38

I raised my hand then. I was becoming curious about a key detail that had been left out of the briefing.

"Sir?" I asked. "What are we supposed to do when we get out there? Who do we have a contract with?"

Graves pointed at me. "Good question, McGill. What does all this business about a lost colony have to do with Legion Varus? Well, we *do* have a contract. We've been hired to aid the colonists—if they're still alive, that is."

I frowned. It still wasn't making sense to me. "Aid them? To do what?"

"We're not sure. But we're assuming they need some kind of military support. Maybe they have a civil war on their hands, we aren't clear on that. They don't have modern communication systems at this point, so they can't send messages that travel faster than the speed of light."

The Galactic Empire we all lived within was anything but transparent. Every member world only knew as much as they needed to know about the rest of the star systems out there. Earth only sold mercenary contracts to neighbors within a zone about a hundred lightyears across. That was our territory. Beyond that, the star maps were blank in our computers. We were only given information that had been deemed necessary to perform our trade duties—namely, to provide mercenary troops to neighboring worlds.

"Let me answer your next question before you ask it," Graves said, looking around the room. "Why do we think our colonists might be under attack? Well, it has to do with Galactic chatter. We monitor local messaging as is within our legal rights. We've picked up traffic, messages concerning this star system. It's our belief that the Galactics have discovered our colony."

Natasha had her hand up again. "What if they aren't under threat? What if they plan to produce mercenaries of their own to compete with Earth?"

Graves' face hardened. "In that case, our mission parameters will change. We've been charged with discouraging them from engaging in competitive enterprises."

Discouraging them. I rolled those words around in my mind. I hoped the colonists weren't going up against us.

39

Hegemony was already hurting, and I knew that Varus would have to "discourage them" with violence. I felt bad for the colonists. What a grim situation they must be in. After spending nearly a century cut off from Earth, they finally make contact and what do we do? Send out a force to *discourage* them from trading the one thing that might turn them into a productive member of the Empire. It didn't seem fair.

"But Centurion Graves," I blurted out without raising my hand. "Sorry sir, but don't they have to come up with some kind of trade good? If they don't—they'll be erased."

Graves looked at me flatly. "Would you rather Earth be erased instead?"

I thought that one over. "No, sir."

Graves straightened up, and I knew he was about to dismiss us. I waved my hand at him one more time.

Veteran Harris stepped close. I could feel him behind me. It made the skin on the back of my neck crawl.

Finally, Graves gestured for me to speak.

"One last question, sir," I said. "Who hired us to go out there? I mean, if the colonists are just starting out, they don't have any credits, do they?"

"No," he said. "They didn't do it. Hegemony did. We're working a contract from them. Essentially, Earth is paying for this trip."

"Can we do that?"

Graves chuckled. "Of course. Any member of the Empire can buy their own goods and services. The Vellusians invented puff-crete, remember? I can assure you that they can, and do, use the stuff themselves."

I thought about that, and it made sense. Our legion had to be contracted to take it out of circulation, meaning we couldn't do any other work at this time. They also had to pay expenses, such as to the Skrull for carrying us out here in *Corvus*. It seemed odd and expensive, but perfectly legal, to buy your own services. I wondered if we gave ourselves a discount.

As we filed out of the briefing, I was still frowning in thought. Hegemony was hurting for money, but they'd decided to spend some of their last coins on rooting out a potential rival. Since they were sending out my legion, I didn't think this was going to end well for the colonists. Varus was only brought out to do the dirtiest of jobs, and this one looked like it was going to be the worst yet: fratricide.

They could hang any pretty words on it they wanted to, but that's how it stacked up to me. We'd been hired to kill our own kind. I was sorry to be a part of this mission already. The more I learned about it, the less I liked it.

-5-

"Are you having bad feelings, McGill?" Veteran Harris asked me a few minutes later in our barracks.

I didn't even look at him.

"You *do* understand you're not paid to have feelings of any kind, right?" he asked me, getting in my face. "None of us are. The stakes are too high for any of that crap. All of Earth—everything you love and live for—is in danger."

"I get that, Vet," I said, "but this is bullshit."

"Now don't get like that on me. We don't even know the whole story. You have to trust in your officers and your government. Didn't they teach you that in tech school?"

"I dropped out, remember?"

"That's no excuse. Get your head straight. If I give the order, I need to know you'll pull the trigger—no matter what you're aiming at."

I sighed and grumbled. Harris stalked away to harangue others. Morale was low. We'd been under the impression we were heading out to fight an alien race to expand our territory. Instead, we were apparently going to have to kill our own kind before they could set up shop and compete with us. That just didn't sit well with me—or most of the others.

One notable exception was Carlos. He was positively cheery.

"Why the smile, Carlos?" I asked him after the ten-minute buzzer for lights-out went off. "You have a secret murdering soul in your chest?"

"Sure do," he said. "Same as you. But that's not it. I'm happy because this is going to be an easy run. *Finally*, a mission a guy can sleep through. Just think about it! A few scrawny colonists who've been sitting in a tin-can ship for fifty years. They'll probably be wearing loincloths and giving each other rides in antique rickshaws. They won't have a chance against a polished outfit of pros like us."

I stared at him. "And that makes you happy?"

"Sure does. What? Did you want to fight another horde of crazy lizards?"

"No," I admitted. "But I don't want to be gunning down women and little kids, either."

"We won't have to do that!" Carlos said. "We'll just show up and scare them. Make them think of some other way to make a trade deal with the Galactics."

"What if they don't have anything else worth selling?"

Carlos shrugged. "No idea. But hey, do you think they'll have girls on this colony? I mean...they'd have to be pretty starved for a real man by now, wouldn't you think?"

I took a swing at him. I'd done it before, but usually he'd started it. I think I surprised him because he jerked his head back too late. I caught the tip of his chin with my knuckles, and he stumbled away, cursing.

We thumped each other a few times, then began wrestling. I was winning easily, but Veteran Harris' big boots clumped near, and he pulled us apart like two school kids.

"What's wrong with you clowns?" Harris demanded, glowering at us. Then he let go of me and shook Carlos. "You started it, didn't you?"

"That's an unfair assumption, Vet," Carlos complained. "McGill swung first."

"Doesn't matter," Harris said. "I know it's your fault."

"What? Why?"

"'Cause McGill is an asshole, but you're worse."

A few minutes later we were on our bunks with the lights out. I rubbed at a bruise on my cheek.

"Seriously," Carlos whispered from the bunk above mine. "You think they'll have girls on this rock?"

"Don't worry," I said. "I'll save them for you. You'll get to slaughter *all* the civvies."

"That's not what I meant, dammit," he muttered. "Just forget about it. And I'm sorry if I hurt your feelings. No one seems to know when I'm joking around."

"That's because you joke about things that aren't funny."

Eventually, I drifted off to sleep. I dreamt of screaming colonists with legionnaires running after them, hosing them down with pellets and sizzling beams. I didn't really believe it could happen, but Legion Varus had done some questionable things in the past—and Earth was desperate.

* * *

Centurion Graves summoned me to his office at the end of our first week in space. I'd been expecting his call. It was time for me to begin my training as a specialist. I'd have to learn fast, as by the time we made planetfall and I jumped out of *Corvus*, I'd be expected to function in my new role.

Earth's legions had three flavors of non-coms in the enlisted ranks—four, if you counted the Veterans. As a specialist, you could become a Bio who basically served as a medic in the legions. It was a little more complicated than patching up the wounded, however. You had to learn how to operate the revival machines. I shuddered just thinking about that job. I didn't want to work with those machines. Call me squeamish, but I didn't even like the idea that I'd been birthed by them repeatedly after dying.

Fortunately, I knew the bio people in the legion pretty much hated me and would probably veto the idea. I wasn't worried I'd end up working with them. That brought it down to two possibilities: I could be a Tech or a Weaponeer. Techs were just what they sounded like; they handled the drones, our weapons and our combat suits. Maintaining the hardware was a big job in a space-going military force. I knew I could do that kind of work, and I had the education for it. I rather suspected they would assign me there. But they didn't.

"James McGill," Graves said slowly. He made it sound as if my name left a funny taste in his mouth.

"Sir?"

He stared at me for a second. "You're a lot trouble. Did you know that?"

"Yes sir. My mama tells great stories about my early days."

He chuckled. "I bet she does. I just reread your psych report, you know."

I didn't flinch. After all, they'd let me into this legion. When I'd first joined up, the other legions hadn't wanted me due to a few spikes and curls that showed up on the tests. They'd labeled me a troublemaker, the same as Graves was doing now, and they'd passed—all of them. But Legion Varus had signed me on willingly enough.

"I kind of figured that was all behind me by now," I said.

Graves shook his head. "I'm not talking about the original tests. I'm talking about the ones they did before we shipped out from Earth. You failed, you know, with flying colors. You lost it in the pressure tent."

I glanced at him in surprise.

"Yeah, sure," he said. "You had a cover story for beating on your robot. Did you really think there weren't any cameras recording it all? Worse than that, you failed to follow orders on several additional occasions, doing whatever you damned well pleased."

I snapped my eyes back to the forward wall. "Sorry about that, sir."

"Don't be. We brought you along anyway, didn't we? Really, I wasn't surprised by the results. But you have to try to keep a lid on it this time, okay? Do me that little favor. Follow orders this time out and don't kill people who get in your way—unless they're the enemy. Do I make myself clear?"

"Crystal," I said.

Graves sighed. I could tell he didn't believe me.

"Let me level with you, Specialist. I don't know how this is all going to go down. We have no real idea what we'll be facing. According to our estimates, there shouldn't be more than twenty thousand colonists assuming a reasonable level of attrition and breeding over the last seventy years. On top of that, they'll be wielding pitchforks with any luck."

He paused, looking over a flimsy slip of dynamically updating computer paper. He put it down.

"But I don't buy these predictions. I don't think we're going to get lucky this time out. We're probably going to be facing an organized and well-equipped military force."

I frowned at him. "How is that possible, sir? How could the colonists have advanced equipment? It costs too much—and we know they couldn't have brought it with them."

"Loans from the Empire," Graves said. "We know the imperials know about them. If they are offering them membership, they'll be given some starter cash."

Frowning, I shook my head. "They do that?"

"That's how it works," he said. "It has to. Think about it. How did Earth suddenly become an interstellar power back in the late 2050s? We didn't have two sticks to rub together back then, and if we had, we wouldn't have been able to use them due to some copyright infringement with our neighbors. Every fledgling planet is allowed to borrow Galactic credits to get started. Seed money, essentially. That's how we financed our first tickets on ships like this one. They flew us to distant worlds and were paid with low-interest, government-backed loans that we couldn't refuse to take. We had to be able to buy passage, plus our guns and suits, somehow."

I nodded, thinking about it. The early days weren't often talked about. I knew the history written about in my school textbooks had been cleaned up. There had been many shady deals, civil wars and upheavals they'd seen fit to leave out. Apparently, they'd also left out details like taking loans from the Galactics.

"So, this could be a battle between two human legions?" I asked in concern.

"Something like that, but don't worry. We should have the upper hand. They've been cut off. They started off with discipline when they left Earth, of course, but it was more like a scientific expedition than a military one. I think they must have a tight organization to have reached the stars and survived. Still, I don't see how they can match our experience and expertise if it comes down to a fight. I expect Legion Varus will win this conflict in the end."

I felt uneasy, but managed not to say anything.

Graves stared at me. "I'm going to break one of my own rules, McGill," he said. "I'm going to ask an enlisted man what he's thinking. I never do that."

"I'm thinking that humans should not be killing humans, sir."

"See? That's just the kind of crap I don't want to hear. Didn't we just lay out the basis for an understanding not five minutes earlier? You're not supposed to think about things like that at all. You're no good to me if you're questioning your orders before we even land."

"Sorry sir. You asked."

"So I did," he said, leaning back in his chair. "All right. Let's do this. Let's talk about your promotion and how you'll fit into Legion Varus after today. First off, you should know that I've been transferred—or rather, Primus Turov has been. She's been given command of a heavy cohort. The Tribune felt she didn't have the right feel for training fresh troops. Turov is taking her senior officers with her—including me."

He looked at me as this sank in. Graves was out of my unit? I was surprised, but the more I thought about it, the happier I became.

"Congratulations, sir," I said quickly.

"I guess that's an appropriate response," he said. "I'm finally being moved out of kindergarten. No more light infantry. No more riding herd on fresh recruits in pajamas."

Graves tapped at a set of orders that appeared on the flimsy slip of plastic on his desk. Words shifted on the film, and his identifying icon blossomed into place. He'd signed the computer scroll with his fingerprints.

He'd transferred out! I hadn't dared hope for this. It would be *so* good to have Graves out of my hair. The guy was a capable officer, but he was as cold as a lizard in a snow bank.

I noticed my name was on the electronic slip of plastic. I felt elated to see I had new orders as well.

"I'm taking your squad with me, by the way," Graves said a moment later, dashing my hopes. "I'm putting you into heavy

47

armor, Specialist. I'm making you a Weaponeer, too, so you'll have to bulk up in the gym. What do you think about that?"

I froze for a second but managed to swallow my shock.

"Thank you, sir," I said diplomatically.

"That's what I figured," Graves chuckled. "I can always tell when my troops are sweet on me. Now, get the hell out of here."

I left with sagging spirits.

* * *

The months passed quickly. I learned how to operate heavy armor, which was radically different from the thin smart-cloth suits I'd become accustomed to. Overall, that part of the change was a good one.

My new weapon wasn't as easy to get used to, however. The old hands called it a belcher—a heavy, plasma-firing tube. It was about five feet long and felt like it weighed five tons. I'd handled one of these units before in combat under dire conditions, and I didn't find it much easier to operate one now that I'd been issued a weapon officially.

The plasma-tube was something like an RPG in size but heavier and bulkier. It had manual controls and a power pack you had to lug around on your back. The tube itself was difficult in every way. Just adjusting power levels and cranking the focus from tight to diffuse was a workout.

As per Graves' suggestion, I spent my mornings exercising with weights in the portions of the ship that maintained active gravity-wells. I did this vigorously, as we didn't even know exactly what conditions would be like when we reached the target world. What if the gravity was double that of Earth? I didn't want to be caught dragging my weapon behind me in the dirt with my exoskeleton groaning and sparking, unable to keep up with the rest of the squad.

Training in body armor was another new experience for me. The light infantry really did have the worst of it, I could see that now. The best part was that Veteran Harris showed no new inclinations to kill me during training. It wasn't that he'd gotten over our little rivalry, but rather that he feared damaging my equipment. In order to kill an armored trooper shouldering a belcher, you had to do a lot of damage. That would almost certainly wreck the armor I was carrying around. The fact that all of our equipment was virtually irreplaceable made matters worse for my trainers.

On my first campaign into space, nothing had been more expendable than human flesh. The officers hadn't been overly-concerned with our gear, either. We recycled what we could, but if a smart-suit stopped knitting back up, or a snap-rifle didn't operate properly—we tossed it. Legion Varus, for all our bad reputation, had always been awarded a generous budget of Galactic credits from Hegemony.

Those days were gone. Now that my gear was worth more than my flesh, everyone inspected my equipment whenever I fell down. It was like being ordered around by accountants. I said as much to Veteran Harris, who didn't enjoy listening to my opinions.

"McGill," he said, "you just make damn sure you don't wreck anything when we get down there. You're a specialist now, a big-time weaponeer. Yeah, I'm all impressed. But you remember you're the greenest frigging weaponeer on this deck, and I mean that. So, learn from your betters, boy. They're all around you."

We were standing in a sandy pit with scorched puff-crete walls in every direction. In order to operate a weapon like a plasma cannon aboard a spaceship in flight, you had to make damned sure it didn't puncture the hull. The legion techs had achieved an appropriate level of safety by building up a puff-crete bunker several layers thick all around us. That way, they could just construct a new wall of the material every time we wrecked the nearest one. As a further precaution, they made certain there were always a few more layers outside the bunker to keep us from reaching the actual hull itself.

I took a second to eye the crowd in the bunker with me. It did seem like the heavy weapons squad I'd been assigned to for training was made up of experts. They snapped each component into place with practiced precision. It seemed to me that all the most muscular guys in the cohort were there.

49

Veteran Harris never looked at the rest of the weaponeers. He was watching me. He had his hands on his hips staring at my hands as I worked with my weapon, waiting for me to make the slightest mistake.

"No, no, no!" he shouted a moment later as I pushed a cartridge into the base of the weapon. "You have to slap it in, boy. It won't lock right if you just toy with it!"

I slapped, and apparently I did that wrong too, because he ripped it out of my hands and whacked the cartridge with a big hand. He tossed the weapon back to me. I caught it, but not without staggering.

He glared. "You're hopeless. I'm telling Graves this was a big mistake. He should keep you with the light troops, where at least you know what the hell you're doing."

"Sorry Vet," I said. "I don't know why I didn't get assigned to heavy weapons training during shore leave."

Harris shook his head. "Doesn't work that way. Too expensive."

I thought about it and nodded. We weren't like a national standing army, we were mercenaries. Our treasury was based on active contracts not taxpayer dollars coming from some borrowed government pot. An active duty legionnaire was paid about triple what a man got while sitting on his hands at home. That's why they didn't like to have us muster back in until it was go-time—meaning they had a new contract.

"That's why you didn't put us through boot camp the first time out, right? Cheaper to do it on the flight to the target world, and then throw us into the fight. After dying a few times, we figured out how to be proper soldiers."

Harris shrugged. "That's about the size of it. But you're failing at weaponeer school. You don't know how to handle your suit or your weapon. What's worse, we won't have time to properly train you on artillery systems at all."

I was about to apologize again when another broad-looking fellow stepped up. It was none other than Specialist Sargon. He'd been something of a big-brother to me on my first campaign. By that I mean he'd bullied and abused me but taught me a few critical details almost by accident.

"Harris is right," he said, looking me up and down. "That kit isn't on right. Your exo-systems are working overtime hindering your arm-motions. You can't work against your suit, you have to make it work *for* you."

Harris eyed Sargon. "Specialist," he said. "This training is just a refresher for you. Take over coaching McGill."

Sargon looked at him in surprise. "Did I just step in something?"

"That's right," Harris said. "Carry on."

He left, clumping away in his armor. I thought I heard a rumbling chuckle as he went. Harris was an excellent non-com, but he worked hard to avoid work.

Sargon looked at me and shook his head. He heaved a sigh and reached out with thick, gloved fingers. He grabbed my shoulders first and began yanking on straps and placing my armor into a new configuration.

"That's not feeling right," I complained.

"Pulling the hairs out of your armpits, isn't it?" Sargon asked with a grin.

"Yeah, I think so."

"Good. That's just where you want it. You'll get some callouses up there, but you have to have the epaulettes riding high and tight. They'll spread the weight over your back where you want it."

I nodded, wincing as he screwed around with more settings and straps. I felt like I was wearing a corset.

"You'll get used to it. I recommend you shave around the tight areas and apply a thick coating of powder."

I wasn't used to this kind of thing—tight clothing. I'd been wearing light weight smart-cloth all my life. It always fit perfectly and adjusted itself if it didn't.

"Now," Sargon said. "Fully extend your arms and clap your hands together. Then do it again."

I did as he asked, and the results were painful.

"Why aren't these suits built right in the first place?" I grunted. My skin was already getting raw as I pin-wheeled my arms.

"They are, but the nanites in your smart-armor are lazy, see," Sargon said. "They like to take the easiest path to forming

51

around your body. That isn't what we want. We have to get the shell to sit right for balance and mobility. Comfort comes last. But don't worry, if you keep moving like this, they'll figure it out and start loosening up. Once you have them trained, you can set them to freeze in the new configuration."

After a few minutes of moving around, I did feel my suit ease up. I was surprised. "That's a lot better. But I wish I'd greased up first."

Sargon chuckled. "Every new man in heavy armor thinks that. For Weaponeers, it goes double. We have such a heavy load to carry we can't let the suits get lazy. They have to perform at max efficiency."

Around us, most of the troops ignored me. They threw Sargon a nod as they finished their target practice and left. I looked longingly after them. My bunk would feel good after a shower and a rubdown with whatever I could get out of the squad's bio. I was sure I had a dozen abrasions all over my arms and torso.

"Forget about the other weaponeers. Forget about target practice, too. You aren't ready yet. A man has to be able to shoulder a tube right before he can hope to aim it accurately."

I spent the rest of the day moving around in my new armor. By the time Sargon let me go, I was carrying my weapon at a lumbering trot.

"Thanks Sargon," I told him when we were done. "I needed the one-on-one."

Sargon nodded and slammed his fist into my chest. At first, I was a little alarmed. But it didn't hurt. He was grinning, so I grinned back. The blow had staggered me back a step, but I could barely feel it. I remembered I'd seen heavies interact that way now and then. They liked to kick and punch each other in armor. The sight had always made the light troops feel inadequate.

We split up and a few hours later it was lights-out. I drifted off to sleep, beginning to dream. In my troubled sleep that night, Sargon had a great time pummeling my helmet to the delight of everyone in the unit.

-6-

A few more months slid by. Each day left me exhausted but a little more functional. I'd always known that being a weaponeer would be physically taxing, but overall, it was worse than I'd feared.

Maybe if I'd had a year or two to get into shape, it would have been easier. But I didn't have that kind of time. No one in the legion did. We had a mission to perform, and the arrival date wasn't going to be shuffled back because I wasn't ready to do my job.

Each day, I took time out to visit the forward observatory which was just below the green-zone that served *Corvus* as a park. I often found couples making out in the dim-lit interior. I usually went alone, making a special effort to look at the stars.

Corvus was a warp-bubble ship like most starships in the Empire. We didn't completely understand the technology because we weren't allowed to take one apart and attempt to duplicate it. We were just passengers to the Skrull crewmen who operated the vessel, not friends and comrades, so they didn't bother to explain it all to us. Every species in the Empire held their trade secrets very tightly.

As I understood the principal, the warp drive worked by generating a bubble of altered space around the ship. It didn't move the ship. Instead, it reshaped space around the ship. By making space thinner in front of the ship and thicker behind the ship, we were propelled forward in a manner similar to the function of an airplane's wing which provided lift.

Using this suction effect, the ship was drawn forward, which in turned moved the field and caused the bubble to warp space in a new area. The theoretical idea matched that postulated by Mexican physicist Miguel Alcubierre over a century ago—but we could only guess at the real details of the system's operation.

Since space inside the warped bubble was relatively normal, we weren't harmed and time didn't slow down for us. Months spent in transit matched the time that passed us by outside. The passengers and crew of the ship felt little sense of motion even when the ship effectively moved faster than the speed of light.

The one difficulty with the system was in observing the ship's surroundings. We couldn't see outside the warp bubble due to obvious conflicts in the laws of physics. How could you see the shine of a star if you passed it by at many times the speed of light? Instead of stars, anyone looking through the warp bubble saw only a diffuse, splattered light, as if we were inside a globe of gently shifting shades.

The observatory was our single exception. It didn't provide us with a real image of our environment as that was impossible. But it projected a computer-generated image of what was passing us by. The experience was exhilarating to me. I could see the stars, and if I watched closely enough, one could see them nudge in their positions ever so slightly. It was rather like watching the hands of a clock move, but I found it fascinating.

For the most part I kept my eyes forward, staring at the growing image of our destination star system. Zeta Herculis was bright by the third month, easily the brightest object in view. Behind us Sol was just a glimmer, one more star among countless others.

When we were within a day or two of reaching the target system, everyone began to feel tense.

"I thought I'd find you here," said a quiet voice behind me.

I turned to see Natasha. She was smiling.

"You didn't bring a date?" I asked her in a whisper.

"Not exactly."

It took me a second to figure that one out. When I did, I smiled back. I reached a hand toward her, and she took it, giving me a squeeze. Then she came to sit beside me.

The big chamber was kept permanently dim and lit only by starlight. There were benches laid out in a circular pattern with cushioned surfaces. Most of the observers were lying on these benches staring up at the passing stars. By unspoken convention, people only talked in hushed tones while enjoying the observatory.

I was lying on my back staring up at Zeta Herculis. It was an orange, K-class star that would eventually turn into a red giant before it died.

"What do you think it will be like?" Natasha asked me.

"I don't know. It was an early discovery as exoplanets go, which means it's kind of big. It probably has heavy gravity. It has lots of water, which is why we sent colonists. Probably very wet and humid too, like those tents where they tested our responses."

Natasha lay down next to me. She put her head on my shoulder, which made my eyebrows rise a bit. We'd gotten together in the past but not on this trip. There hadn't been any time for romance with my tight training schedule.

"Am I bothering you?" she asked.

"Not at all."

"You flinched."

I chuckled. "That's just my new muscles. They twitch all the time."

She ran her hands over my arms squeezing and gliding her fingers up to my shoulders.

"The skin's rough here, calloused," she said. "And your body hair is missing in patches."

"Sorry to disappoint."

She laughed quietly. "I'm not disappointed. You really have gained a lot of muscle. Harris is really working you hard, isn't he?"

"Like a rented mule," I agreed.

"James," she said a minute or so later. "If it comes down to it, what will you do if they order you to shoot civvies?"

55

That question took me by surprise. I managed to not tighten my arms which were around her by then.

"I won't do it," I said.

She nodded. "I didn't think you would. They might execute you for not following orders. You know that, don't you?"

I shrugged, making her head shift on my shoulder.

"I've been executed before," I said. "It's no big deal."

She giggled at that. She didn't know I was telling the truth. I had been executed before—put down by Harris under Turov's orders. It had been intended as a perma-death, too. But somehow, it hadn't stuck.

"Some of us were talking," she went on, "and we were betting a lot of the troops would fire. But not you."

I smiled. I guess if a guy had to have a rep it might as well be as the only man in the unit who wasn't a cold-blooded killer of innocents.

We didn't leave the observatory for about an hour after that, but by the time we did, we were arm-in-arm. We went up to the green zone and made love under a sugar pine tree. For me, that night was the highlight of the entire trip.

* * *

Things went drastically wrong sometime after four a. m. ship's time. Altogether, I'd spent over a year of my short life aboard *Corvus*, and in all that time, there'd never been an accident or hiccup of any kind. That was all about to change.

I rolled out of my bunk and crashed onto the cold, hard deck plates. It was a shocking way to wake up but nothing I hadn't experienced before. I looked around blearily, scrambling up onto all fours and expecting to find Veteran Harris had kicked me out of bed.

Instead, I was struck by a very large, hairy mass. Carlos had rolled out of his top bunk and landed on top of me. We grunted and cursed each other in annoyance.

When we got to our feet, we were unsteady. No, that was my first impression, but it was wrong. The *ship* was unsteady.

56

In all my time aboard the starship, it had never shuddered or thrown me around due to G-force manipulation. But today was going to be very different.

"What the hell...?" Carlos asked, getting to his feet beside me.

We had our hands out, reaching for the edge of our bunks in order to hold onto something. There was a deep vibration coming up through the deck into our feet now. It made my toes itchy.

"This crazy thing is going to blow up, isn't it?" Carlos demanded. "I knew it, I fucking knew it! I hate the Skrull. Alien bastards, they probably already jumped ship. We'll sail right into that Zeta star and burn up."

"Shut up," I said, and for once he did as I demanded. "Let's get our gear together."

Carlos watched me dig my armor out of my locker after thumbing it open. He did the same. Getting into heavy armor was much more of a pain than pulling on a light-trooper's vac suit had been. Instead of seconds, it took a full minute before we were mobile again.

During that time the ship continued to shudder, and an alarm sounded indicating we were to suit up and report to our rally point. Blue arrows flashed on the floor.

"Blue?" asked Carlos aloud. "That's the evac color. What the hell is going on? Are they honestly expecting us to launch in a lifeboat while in warp? We'll be torn apart before—"

"Just get your damned gear on. Pull my gauntlets up tight, and I'll do yours. Sargon showed me—it's faster that way."

He grumbled but did as I suggested. Carlos was a heavy trooper now, too—we all were. He wasn't a weaponeer so he didn't have a plasma cannon like mine. He only had to handle his laser carbines and the force-blades that could be extended from his suit's arms.

Less than a minute later, we were clanking down the passageways with the rest of our unit. The blue arrows split us up by number, and we gathered as squads at larger intersections. We stood there nervously looking every direction at once. So far, Veteran Harris and all the officers were absent.

There were only a few non-com specialists like me milling around, and we were as clueless as the grunts.

"The last time we did this," Kivi said by my side, "a wave of lizards charged in and ate half the unit."

"Correction," announced Carlos, "they ate everyone except for McGill, here. He got blown up."

I didn't appreciate those memories. My heart was pounding even though I did my best to look cool and calm. I really, really wished that Harris or Centurion Graves would show up and do their jobs.

Fortunately, the ship had stopped vibrating by now. Everything stayed still, and the lights were oddly dimmed. They were supposed to be like that during the night hours, but normally in emergency exercises they blazed into life.

"Is everyone vac-ready?" asked Centurion Graves' gravelly voice.

I was relieved to finally hear from an officer, and turned toward him.

"We're suited up, sir," I responded. "But we haven't been issued any oxygen tanks. What's the nature of the problem, sir?"

Graves cursed and walked out of the shadowy passageway. "You've got to get oxygen. That's an order, Specialist. You lead this team and find enough for the entire squad. Put your helmets on and lower the visors. The air in your suit will do for now, just keep opening it up to get a gulp of air when you can, and keep moving. Have you got that?"

"Yes, sir. Excuse me, sir, where's Veteran Harris?"

"Harris is probably dead. Now, move out dammit, and watch for enemy contact."

My jaw sagged in my suit. "Enemy contact? What…?"

"No time to tell you a bedtime story. I'm linking you into command chat. Listen and learn."

He left us then, presumably to organize other stragglers. He trotted down the echoing passages and didn't look back.

Having no idea what else to do, I put on my helmet, closed the visor and activated the suit radio. My ID had been fed into the command channel. I figured I could probably transmit on it as well, but I made damned sure I didn't do that by muting the outgoing voice on the channel.

All around me, my squad mates were demanding to know what the hell was happening—as if I knew.

I reached out and grabbed Natasha's arm, swinging her around to face me. "You're training to be a tech. Where are the oxygen bottles stored during transit?"

She nodded, giving me a worried look. "Yeah, sure. Near the mess hall. They'll be with all the non-weapons gear. Remember those little storerooms? They're up forward."

I didn't really remember the storerooms, but then I wasn't a tech. It was their job to manage all the equipment that kept a space-going force alive and fighting.

I put Natasha in the lead and we all trotted after her. I tried to ignore the complaints of the squad and focus on what I was hearing in command chat.

So far, it didn't make much sense. There was talk of an enemy force and damage to the bridge.

Damage to the bridge? Who could be dumb enough to damage the bridge of a starship inside a warp bubble?

We found the oxygen bottles right where Natasha said they would be. Handing them out, we plugged them into our suits and engaged the rebreathers. Our suits were pretty advanced. They would eventually run out of power, but until then, they could break down carbon dioxide and recycle it into oxygen again using only a small amount of fresh oxygen from our tanks. Unless we drained the power packs in combat, we should be good for days.

It's hard to explain how much better a space-going fighter feels when he knows he has a reliable source of oxygen. Space is a very unforgiving place, and a deadly environment doesn't require an enemy weapon to take a soldier out. Suffocation, heat, cold, or good old-fashioned radiation could do the job just as easily.

I had orders by the time we'd distributed the tanks from the command channel, and I led the squad to meet with Graves and the rest of the unit on the primary training deck. Those who hadn't brought their weapons found armament there—but only snap-rifles. I was the only man with a plasma tube in my squad.

Graves walked our line, checking our gear. He noticed that Carlos and I were fully equipped for battle.

"Who ordered you to bring your laser carbine, Ortiz?" he asked Carlos.

"McGill here. He's paranoid."

Graves nodded. "So am I. Ortiz, you'll stay with McGill. Your job is to keep our only weaponeer with a heavy tube breathing. Consider yourself expendable."

"Thank you, sir!" Carlos shouted. "I'll throw myself into the first enemy mouth I see, sir!"

"Unnecessary. And they don't appear to have teeth—not exactly."

I frowned. "What are we up against, sir?"

"Invaders. An enemy ship has attempted to block our passage to the target world. We'd have made planetfall a few hours from now, but they laid a trap and stopped us."

We looked from one to the other in concern. *A trap? For a ship in a warp-bubble?*

"There's good news, however," Graves continued. "The enemy took the bridge and killed the Skrull, but they only have a small force and obviously weren't expecting a full legion of heavily-armed troops to be aboard. We're going to retake this vessel, and the enemy will lose this battle by default. Tampering with a Galactic ship—they must be insane."

"I don't understand, sir," I said. "I thought we would be up against some kind of human colonists with delusions of setting up their own mercenary trade."

"We were wrong about that," Graves said. "Take a look."

He tapped at his arm then applied it to a nearby wall of the ship. The wall lit up immediately becoming a huge screen. It was a nice trick, but I'd rarely seen anyone do it. Only officers had tappers with high enough administrative permissions. Even the tech specialists weren't allowed to turn the ship into a video playground.

"Watch closely," Graves said. "You'll see a glimpse of the enemy. We downloaded this file from the bridge cameras before they knocked out the surveillance system."

We watched an empty corridor. For several seconds, nothing happened then shadows loomed—odd shadows.

60

"What the hell is that?" demanded Carlos.

For once, no one told him to shut up. We were all thinking the exact same thing.

A figure flickered past the vid pickup. It wasn't human—I was sure of that. It moved oddly, loping with an undulating motion. Due to the angle we didn't see all of it, only a portion of the body. There were thick snake-like appendages and interlocking plates shaped in diamond patterns.

"Something with scales," Natasha said, stepping closer. She lifted her hand to the wall screen as if drawn to it. "Very alien."

"Looks like a bundle of snakes tied together," Carlos said. "Whatever it is, it's frigging huge!"

"Not as big as a Jugger back on Steel World," Kivi said.

Carlos shook his head and chuckled. "Aliens. Freaky aliens. That's just great. Good thing they're morons. They must have no idea how the Empire operates. The Galactics will come here and fry the lot them. They've made our job easy. All we have to do is survive long enough to report this incident to the authorities. Take a last look at Zeta Herculis, people. The Galactics will erase it utterly when they hear about this. Soon, the enemy will be extinct. Hell, they might even put out the star itself. I hear they do that sometimes."

"You might be right," Graves said. "But it doesn't matter because the Battle Fleet could take years to get here. By that time, we'll be dead—or they will."

We stared at the monster on the screen as Graves replayed it over and over in a loop. It moved so strangely. I've seen my share of aliens on Steel World and in exo-nature vids back home. But these things were *weird*. There was no earthly equivalent. Just watching it made my skin crawl.

Everyone seemed to react the way I did except for Graves, Carlos and Natasha. Graves didn't seem to care. He was all business. Carlos was delighted with the idea the aliens had screwed up by attacking our ship. Natasha—she seemed fascinated.

Graves followed the vid with a little speech about how we were going to first encircle the command deck then close with the aliens when we had them boxed in. He sounded confident of victory.

I wasn't comforted. I couldn't stop thinking that we were facing unknown alien invaders who'd been smart enough to board a starship in warp and disable it.

We broke down into squads and advanced. *Corvus* was a big ship—huge in comparison to Earthly vessels. It wasn't like exploring a ship at sea; it was more like exploring a labyrinthine skyscraper. Fortunately, the Skrull were nothing if not efficient and logical. They'd laid out the vessel in geometric patterns. The command deck was surrounded by corridors that converged like spokes on a wagon wheel. Eight ways in—no more and no less.

All we had to do, according to Graves, was cover all eight of those escape routes. If we sealed the enemy inside, they couldn't come at us without facing a barrage of fire down a long passageway.

Our unit was assigned lucky passageway number seven. We marched up and encircled the entrance. The hatch was big, about ten meters in diameter. All the passages to the bridge looked that way. When we were in position, Graves moved to the panel and used his tapper to override the security. I was glad he was here. *Corvus* wouldn't have listened to any of the rest of us.

Before he opened it, he paused, receiving a message. I listened in as I was still connected to command chat. I made sure I didn't transmit anything. I figured Graves would revoke my permissions and kick me offline when he remembered he'd put me into the loop.

"Graves?" asked a female voice. "What's the situation on seven?"

I knew the voice. It was Primus Turov, our beloved cohort commander.

"We're about to open it up, sir," he said.

"Hold on that. We have a problem."

I looked at Graves. He was frowning now, but that was nothing unusual.

"May I ask the nature of the trouble?" he asked.

"The central torus has stopped rotating. There's no gravity in the aft of the ship, and we're having difficulty moving up to join you at your position. You beat the rest of us to seven."

"Standing by," he said.

Now that Turov's voice was no longer buzzing in his helmet, Graves looked around, gazing up and down the passageways. He signaled Adjunct Leeson, who was my direct superior and who'd brought the rest of my platoon to the party over the last few minutes. Veteran Harris and Weaponeer Sargon were with him, I was glad to see. Altogether, there were now better than a hundred troops jammed into the intersection. Gravity was light here, and we were holding onto the walls ten feet or more up. Like lazy monkeys, we relaxed and gripped rungs that were placed strategically all over the ship.

"Leeson, take your squads and spread out!" Graves shouted suddenly. "Move your people down toward the next junctions."

Leeson looked confused, but he didn't argue. He didn't even ask for clarification. Anyone who was in Centurion Graves' unit knew better. He waved to me, and I began to follow him.

"Hold on," Graves said. "Leave me with two weaponeers, McGill and Sargon."

A minute later, Graves had dispatched platoons in either direction down the curving passageway. They were only about a hundred meters away, but we couldn't see them.

Carlos came close to me and clicked his helmet up against mine. To non-spacers, this would have seemed like an odd action, but it was quite common when troops were suited-up. By pressing our helmets against one another, we could talk without the muffling effects of being englobed in armor. That way, neither party had to shout or use our radios. It worked especially well in vacuum where there was nothing to carry the sound otherwise.

"Graves is dispersing us," Carlos said. "That means trouble."

"Don't wet your suit," I said. "He's just being cautious before we open this door and confront the enemy. We're too bunched up here in the passageway."

I didn't tell him about what I'd overheard from Primus Turov. A delay in moving troops up to our position could mean nothing—or it could mean a lot. It sounded to me as if the aliens had realized we were coming and they were doing what they could to impede the counterattack. This might not be as easy a fight as we'd hoped.

When Graves had his troops set up the way he wanted, he contacted Turov again.

"Permission to open the doors, sir," he said.

There was silence. Nothing at all came over the line from command chat.

"Primus Turov? This is Centurion Graves. Respond please."

More silence.

I watched Graves. I stared at him through his closed visor. His face was flat, but I thought I saw his cheek twitch in irritation.

Why wasn't anyone responding? I thought of a dozen possible reasons. Communications failure was first on the list. Could the invaders have disabled the ship's repeaters, separating us from each other?

Graves tried once more, then looked up. "All right," he said loudly on local chat. "Listen up, we're opening these doors. Look alive, brace yourselves for a pressure change and ready your weapons."

We snapped lines to the walls and activated the magnets in our boots. Then we lifted our weapons and aimed them at the massive, concave hatch.

Graves applied his tapper, and the hatch swung open.

-7-

Up until that moment, I'd yet to fire my newly-assigned heavy weapon in a combat situation. I'd handled a belcher back on Steel World a few times, but I'd been an untrained recruit at that time, using it in a makeshift manner. Now I knew much more about the cannon that rested on my shoulder, and I had an appropriate respect for the weapon.

Plasma cannons were—weird. They didn't fire a pellet or an explosive. My trainers had told me to think of them as flamethrowers that launched a very brief, powerful gush of flame.

They were designed to release a lot of heat and energy in a directed cone in front of the Weaponeer who wielded the system. They could be dialed for long or short range, creating a tight beam or a broad area of effect. The range of the weapon lessened if you broadened the beam, but it could hit multiple targets that way and it was much easier to hit something.

Deciding how to adjust your cannon was the business of the weaponeer in question. Accordingly, I made a choice. Just as the doors began to open, I reached up and cranked the stiff collar at the muzzle to open the aperture two notches wider. At this setting, it would fire a cone about thirty degrees wide.

Sargon, who was on one knee beside me, tossed me a disapproving glance as I did this. I knew it wasn't standard procedure. The enemy was supposed to be at the far end of a long straight passageway that led to the bridge, and a narrow beam would provide the best reach in that case.

I felt myself flush slightly as I caught Sargon's glance. I was a rookie with my first cannon, and we both knew it. I also knew that he wouldn't have questioned a more experienced man. I wondered if I was making a mistake as he'd kept his beam very tight. There were good reasons for this. There were a lot of troops behind me in a cramped space. I wouldn't be able to fire my weapon without hitting friendlies if things got hairy.

Maybe I would have second-guessed myself after catching Sargon's frown, but I was out of time. Committed, I shouldered my weapon as the hatch yawned open like a giant's eyelid in front of us.

What happened next was a shock. A number of bizarre-looking hulks stood on the far side of the door. They'd clearly been waiting to greet us. Oddly, we hadn't heard a sound from them before now. Normally, we'd have seen them with the local cameras—but they'd wisely knocked out our surveillance systems. I wondered if they'd been listening to our lengthy preparations, counting us fools all the while.

The first thing I registered about them was their size. They were each larger than a man, perhaps three meters tall, and much more bulky. They looked like squids to me, with a dozen tentacles sprouting from the top of their bodies like incredibly thick strands of hair. These tentacles were thicker than a man's leg and they radiated from a central knot of flesh where I imagined their organs were. There were no eyes that I could see, nor faces of any kind. But in the center of that ball of muscle that connected those snake-like limbs together I did see something—a beak. That was the only way I could describe it. A mouth built of hard shell or cartilage. The tentacles themselves weren't soft and wet, either. They were covered in layered, metallic scales, each of which was the size of deck of cards.

There was definitely a quiet, predatory stance to these aliens. They weren't stupid; you could tell that instantly by the way they held themselves and the liquid grace with which they lunged forward.

There was no hesitation in them. We were surprised, but they weren't. They were hunting us, I realized. They'd turned off our security cameras, moved to this hatchway and then waited for their prey to open the door. Probably, they'd arranged things so our unit was alone up against them. Now that we'd finally opened the hatch, they were all business.

They rushed us. It was as simple as that. They had to weigh a ton each, but as heavily-built as they were, they still moved with a flowing grace. They ran forward on their numerous tentacles, manipulating them with perfect rippling synchronization.

Sargon fired first. I have to give him that. He took out the lead monster with a gout of energy that sliced right through it at point-blank range.

I fired a moment later, as they loomed right up into my faceplate. All I could see was a mass of tentacles with a silvery glint to them, shimmering and rattling as they rolled forward into the range of my suit lights.

When my weapon went off, the reflection from their scales blinded me momentarily. Two aliens reeled back, smoldering. The rest came on relentlessly. A wave of flesh plowed over me, knocking me onto my armored back.

When I could see again, I was being trampled. Sargon was down, too. One disadvantage of our weaponry lay in the slow firing rate of our cannons. You couldn't spam blasts at the enemy. The cannons had to cool down and recycle after every shot.

My mind tried to take in everything my senses fed me. A dozen thoughts ran through me. First on the list being that I was about to die. Second, I calculated that since we were out of communication with central, it could turn into a perma-death.

I tried to force myself to focus. I couldn't get up as more enemies were flowing over me, their massive limbs thundering with crushing force upon my breastplate. If I'd been in light armor, I'd have been dead already.

Then, one of them fell. A group of soldiers were all around it firing. Thick dark liquid resembling dirty motor oil oozed from the smoking holes in its scales. The two I'd shot were smoking, too. They weren't dead, but they were sagging and flopping. I felt a surge of relief to see I hadn't wasted my single discharge.

My unit was in confusion, struggling with the aliens in our midst. I saw two soldiers fly as an alien lifted them up and smashed them together. The monster seemed to know our faceplates were weak points, and it applied terrific force there crashing both troopers' heads into one another. The two helmets cracked. Blood exploded an instant later, falling like rain mixed with tinkling bits of starred plastic. The two troops had been rammed together with such terrific force their skulls had been cracked open.

Graves was somewhere in the midst of this nightmare, shouting a string of words over and over. I finally caught what the command was, as did others.

"Use force-blades!"

Every heavy trooper was equipped with a laser carbine, our standard long-range armament. But when things got close and ugly we had a backup weapon: beams of force that extended like knives from the arms of our suits.

While inside a spaceship, using force-blades wasn't always the best idea. They could slice through the metal hull of a ship as easily as they could an enemy. But Graves had given the order, so I engaged my blades and angled them upward into the press of bodies above me.

Only one of my two blades operated properly. The other flashed an orange fault light at me, and I cursed every tech in the unit. I used the other to cut off a tentacle. It took more work than it should have, with me sawing the flailing limb while it hosed out thick oily liquid mixed with blinding showers of sparks into my faceplate.

All around me, glowing blades of energy slashed and burned. The enemy didn't fall like cut grass, however. Their limbs were thicker than a man's leg and the metallic outer layer of scales seemed to resist our weapons, slowing us down. It took about two full seconds of sawing to remove a tentacle from an alien body while it thrashed about, smashing whatever got in its way. I was impressed as I knew human flesh could never have withstood a force-blade for that long.

In the end, we won the fight. Graves urged us to take a prisoner, but it was impossible. They never gave any hint that they were interested in surrender or retreat. They attacked with every shred of vigor in their massive, strange bodies until we brought them down and diced them.

I watched the last one go down with a soldier's foot in its beak-like mouth. The man was howling in fury and pain. He sawed at the central knot of flesh, but the beak wouldn't let go. It crunched down, sparking and rasping on his metal boot, *chewing* on it. Finally, we climbed on the shivering mass and stabbed our blades deep into it over and over until it stopped struggling.

The trooper's boot was mangled, and he said his foot had been crushed. A bio administered a sedative, then looked at Graves who had managed to stand up.

Graves examined the trooper's crushed foot, then nodded.

"Shit," said the man. He closed his eyes.

Carlos and I watched, gritting our teeth, as the bio used her tapper to activate the suit's survival systems. She pushed a button, confirmed it twice, and we all heard a snap and a crunch. The suit had amputated the man's foot. A sizzling sound followed and the wound was cauterized.

"Ugly," Carlos said. "Better than getting permed, though."

I told him to shut up, and for once, he did.

We counted our wounded and our dead. We'd lost eighteen troops and killed seven aliens. I didn't like the odds. We had no idea how many of them might be aboard.

"We have to have reinforcements, Vet," I told Harris.

He looked at me with wide eyes. His breath panted slightly in the transmitted reply.

"No shit? Is that what you really think? I was going to kill them all personally."

Graves walked up to me and picked up my cannon. "Your weapon isn't in your hands, Specialist," he said sternly.

He looked my cannon over carefully. I noticed that he paid no attention to the wounded around him. He was more interested in the status of my tube than he was in my health.

"This is one of only two working heavy weapons," he said, handing the tube over to me. "I want to keep it operating. It's worth more than any of us."

"How do you figure that, sir?" I asked.

Veteran Harris put his hands on his hips and glowered at me, but the Centurion took the question well enough.

"I know you didn't see much of that fight as you were resting on your back throughout most of it, but at range, these two tubes are the only effective weapons we have. Sargon took one down, you incapacitated two more. The other four aliens got in close and did a lot of damage. I'd rather take them out at range, wouldn't you?"

I nodded, conceding his point. I checked my tube and ran a diagnostic set of tests on it with my tapper.

"She's a little banged up, but she'll fire," I said.

Graves nodded and waved for everyone's attention. He had all the non-coms gather around the mess on the floor. He focused on the first alien we'd killed, the one Sargon had put a big hole into. He turned to Natasha, who was the only tech in the group.

"Tell me what we're facing here. Is this thing's outer skin organic or not?"

Natasha limped to us and dug into the alien flesh which shivered slightly at her touch. She didn't seem squeamish in the slightest. I recalled her interest in biological oddities. Once again, she seemed fascinated by what she saw.

"No," she said. "I'd say this is a polymer covering— something like a thick hose that forms a sheath over their natural limbs. See the layering here? The suit is tight, but I'm sure it's a suit."

I watched, impressed. She dug around inside the alien's smoking carcass like a pro.

"That's what I thought," Graves said. "What about these external scales?"

"A protective layer," Natasha said. "Light armor, I'd say. Maybe these aliens are wearing their equivalent of spacesuits. The material doesn't look smart, however. I'm not seeing any attempt by the fabric to reknit itself together. Nothing like an auto-healing system, either. It is a basic, protective spacesuit."

Graves stood up and put his hands on his hips. "No armament. No Galactic tech to speak of. I take this as a good sign. They're not all that advanced."

"Excuse me, sir," I said. "They did manage to penetrate a warp bubble and attack a ship inside."

Graves shook his head at me. "Negative. They jumped our ship as we left warp."

I must have looked confused because he chuckled.

"They're tricky, but they're not techno-wizards. We came out of warp when the Skrull sensed an uncharted field of debris directly in our path. Remember that a warp ship is still vulnerable to mines and the like. We shifted out of warp to change course—that's when they struck."

"No mines, sir?"

"No. Just an ambush."

I nodded. "A decoy. They faked us out like bandits on a highway."

"Exactly," Graves said. "Smart, strong and tricky, but not overly-advanced."

I was willing to accept his verdict, but Carlos wasn't.

"Sir?" Carlos said. "How'd they get out here? How'd they figure out exactly where and when this ship would show up?"

"We're not the first. We're on a known shipping lane. Galactic ships have come through the system before. The Galactics have been watching this system—but I think it was for different reasons than we'd previously assumed. In any case, these aliens must have known we'd arrive here and were lying in wait for us."

His thoughts asked as many new questions as they answered, but I decided to keep quiet about that for now. Were the aliens waylaying any ship that came into their system? That seemed ballsy. They'd been given the Empire's ultimatum. Join and submit, or die. Perhaps they didn't take it seriously.

"But, sir?" I asked. "What about the colonists who are supposed to be out here? Where did these aliens come from? How do they fit in?"

"What I want to hear from you is fewer questions and more answers. Let's focus on retaking the ship. We'll figure out the big picture later—if there is a later."

"Yes, sir."

What came next I should have suspected, but somehow, I was surprised.

"We're advancing up this passage to the bridge," Veteran Harris said. "Sargon, McGill, you're leading the way."

A minute later, I found myself moving down the tube-like passageway toward the dark, far end. I had my cannon on my shoulder, and I was sweating inside my suit. Every step, I expected massive aliens to spring out of the walls at me.

We reached the next bulkhead without further incident. I felt relieved, but this was far from over.

As troops clanked forward on my flanks and worked the next hatch, I directed my tube at the door. The scene was too familiar. I had to wonder if we were walking into another ambush. If the aliens didn't have ranged weapons, they'd be smart to keep attacking us when we were all bunched up at a hatchway.

Veteran Harris came closer to me as troops worked on the next hatch. They were having trouble of some kind.

"They'll have it open in a second," he said. "You still have that weapon dialed for a broad spray?"

"Haven't changed it, Vet."

He nodded. "I think that was a good call. Not to say Sargon's choice was wrong, but if they're hiding on the far side of this hatch, you'll be able to spray them in the face again."

Sargon knelt beside me and stared at the closed hatch with fixed concentration.

"Vet's right," he said. "I was worried, but you played that last encounter like a pro. I guess you're a heavy weaponeer now for real."

"Just doing my job," I said. Inside my helmet I smiled, enjoying the praise. I knew I'd have to make the most of it. In Legion Varus, a kind word was a rare thing.

We watched for about a minute—but the hatchway didn't open. Graves stomped forward, irritated.

"What's the holdup?"

"Stuck, sir," Carlos said. "The techs are working on it, but the hinges are jammed or something."

"So? Force it open."

Natasha joined the conversation. She stood near Sargon and I, who were still watching the hatch for any sign of an enemy

72

ambush. Anyone caught between our heavy tubes and that hatchway would be in a bad spot if the situation turned hot.

"Can't do that, Centurion," Natasha said. "This is Skrull tech, and we don't have the codes to override it or blow the hinges. If the hatch doesn't work, we'll have to go around."

"We could burn through the door," he said.

She shook her head. "Bad idea. These bulkheads protect the bridge. If they won't open, it's probably for a good reason."

Graves stared at her. "Are you suggesting there's active fire on the far side?"

"That, or hard vacuum."

Graves thought about it. "I don't care," he said. "We're breaking in."

"We should know what we're up against first, sir," Natasha protested.

"Then figure it out. Sargon, burn me a hole in that door, will you? Do all the damage to the bottom half."

"Stand clear!" Sargon shouted.

People scuttled out of the way—all except Natasha.

"I have a better idea," she said.

"Let's hear it," Graves said.

"Let me send in a buzzer."

A buzzer was a tiny snooping drone. Techs kept them in their bag of tricks on their backs.

Graves waved for Sargon to stand down.

"How will you get one past the hatch?" he asked Natasha.

Natasha produced a buzzer about the size of her thumb, which resembled a cockroach. It was a yellow metallic color, similar to tin.

She moved to the hatch control panel she'd been messing with and opened it. "There are conduits that lead to the far side. I'll set this one on a scouting mission and let him go—with your permission, sir."

"Do it."

The buzzer crawled from Natasha's hand and entered the panel. It soon vanished. She activated her tapper. I wanted to watch but stayed in position, aiming my weapon at the hatch.

"I'll pipe the signal to everyone's tapper," she said.

A moment later, a flickering, fish-eyed vid began to play on my arm. I put it low on the interior screens in my helmet so I could watch and keep my eyes on the hatch while it played.

The buzzer crept its way through a dark, crowded environment. Everything it saw was very small, but screws looked like pillars from its point of view.

Finally, it found its way out on the far side. The passage looked dark and empty. I saw its four tiny wings extend. They flapped and buzzed—but it couldn't take off.

Natasha looked back at us. "Vacuum," she said. "There's no air. It can't fly."

"That's it then. You sealed the first hatch behind us, didn't you?"

Natasha nodded.

"Brace yourselves, everyone," he said. Then he looked at me and Sargon. "Blow the hatch."

-8-

We burned through the hatch in less than a minute. When it finally breached, a screeching roar began. The air around us was sucked out of the punched-through hole we'd burned into the center of the lower steel leaf.

It took a while for the air to all be sucked away, and Sargon and I kept blasting. We'd set our weapons to lower yield with pulsing emissions. That wasn't optimal for combat, where you wanted to hit your target with a killing bolt of plasma, but for a stationary target like a hatchway it worked well. The beams lasted for several seconds each, then we had to recycle the units and let them cool down before firing again.

We kept working while the air around us leaked away. Everyone had their helmets on and the hatch behind us had been sealed, but there was still quite a bit of air that needed to escape from the long passageway.

As I worked to burn the hole larger, I wondered what we'd find on the far side. I could tell that there wasn't going to be any air pressure. This leak wasn't the mild hiss you got when two chambers were equalizing pressure. This was the all-out rush of gas that occurs when there's nothing but space—hard vacuum—on the far side of a breach.

Whatever we found, I was now certain we weren't going to encounter any living Skrull crewmen. They couldn't have survived this attack on the bridge.

When we had a glowing, orange-black opening the size of a manhole, we stopped firing. Two troops were ordered to wriggle into the dark chamber first.

We waited a minute or so, watching them as they struggled and grunted to get through. Then they walked around on magnetic boots in the cold chamber beyond. They transmitted back what they saw on their suit vid just as the buzzer had done.

One of the two was Kivi, and she did the talking as they reported on what they saw.

"Null gravity," she said. "No atmosphere. It's deserted in here, sir."

"Do a quick sweep," Graves said, "then open the hatch from the inside."

I glanced at him, wondering why he didn't just have them open the hatch right away and get it over with. The pressure had equalized, so there wouldn't be any explosive equalization. With the hatch open, we could support our two scouts if something went drastically wrong...

After another moment's thought, I finally got it.

"Right," I muttered to myself inside my helmet. Centurion Graves didn't want the hatch yawning open if there was going to be trouble. The heavies on the wrong side of the door would just have to deal with it alone, and we would be left with more options as to how to respond.

Possibly for the first time, I was glad I was now a specialist with a valuable tube and the skill to use it. The more expendable types were inside that dark chamber now, exploring.

We watched tensely. Kivi sounded nervous, but she was game. She'd toughened up since our first mission into alien space.

"Checking the corridors. Main power seems to be cut, Centurion. This module is running on auxiliary batteries as far as I can tell."

Graves didn't speak. He watched the vids intently. Most of the rest of us did the same. I noticed that Sargon wasn't watching the streaming transmissions. Instead, he'd repositioned himself to one side of the hole we'd burned

76

through the hatch. His weapon was shouldered and ready. I realized he was watching that hole like a cat hunting for a mouse. I joined him, thinking he was doing the right thing.

Graves flicked his eyes over the two of us. He didn't say anything, but he nodded in approval. That was a nice for a change.

Kivi made a sweep of the immediate area beyond the hatch, then opened the big doors. We tensed. After having been rushed by about ten tons of armored squids, we were nervous.

I took a look around as we advanced. We were in the Skrull living quarters—at least that's what I figured they were. Dead Skrull littered the place. Unfortunately, as we were in null-grav they were floating, not resting peacefully on the deck.

Skrull are a weird-looking species. They aren't very big, maybe a meter long from stem-to-stern, with wrinkled-up faces that are vaguely humanoid and hard shells over their central bodies. Several thin limbs come out of this shell. The limbs looked disturbingly like the arms of dead children as they drifted in frozen rifts of their own blood. They'd been killed then frozen by the hard vacuum.

"What do they call those freaky monkeys from Madagascar?" Carlos asked me.

I thought about it. "Lemurs?"

"Yeah. That's what these guys look like. Big yellow eyes."

"I was thinking of turtles with long skinny arms and humanoid faces."

"Sure, that fits too."

We hadn't seen the Skrull all that often even though we'd technically spent over a year in space with them. It struck me how you could live with another species and not really know them because each group stayed with their own kind. Now, they looked more like kin to me. Basically a peaceful, effective people, they'd been slaughtered wholesale like animals.

"This kind of pisses me off," I said as we waded forward, heading down narrow passages toward the central shaft that led to the control rooms.

As I spoke, I had to reach out and push away gauzy frozen mists of blood. The mists looked like crackling spider webs, breaking at the slightest touch.

"Why?" Carlos asked.

"I don't know. They weren't hurting anyone. They have red blood the same as us, too. I didn't know that."

Carlos laughed. "You're such a hater, McGill. Why not love those snake-armed killing machines? True, they aren't nice—but then, neither are we. Remember, the Galactics invaded their system and started giving them orders. You have to admit these giant armored squid-dudes have balls. They're fighting harder than we did."

I nodded thoughtfully. I didn't usually expect Carlos to have anything deep to add to a conversation, but this time he had pulled it off.

"You got a point," I admitted.

"That's enough chatter up there," Veteran Harris said, pushing his way past a few troops to get close to us. "Ortiz, stop distracting the specialist. We need his gun and his eye alert if you want to keep breathing."

"Would it help if I just offed myself right here, Vet?" Carlos asked.

"That would really, really make me happy," Harris told him, and I believed him. "But no, we need your sorry ass, too. Just shut the hell up."

Since the Skrull were smaller than humans and we were in heavy armor, the going was tough. I had to wonder about the enemy. They were comparatively huge. How had they managed to maneuver through these tunnels?

"Contact!" shouted a voice from the front line.

I was pretty sure it was Kivi. I pushed forward, but Sargon contacted me privately.

"Let the regulars engage first," he said. "You don't rush in when you have the only weapon that works."

I held back, but it wasn't easy. It went against my basic nature. I wanted to help Kivi—but at the same time I knew Sargon was right. He didn't always hold himself back, but this mission was too critical. We just didn't know what we were up against. Hell, if I died right now, I didn't know if I'd ever be revived. The rest of the legion where the revival machines were was still out of contact.

Sliding to the side and parking myself in an alcove, I let a few heavies drag themselves past me. They looked like they were climbing a ladder underwater. In null-G pretty much everyone moves like they're swimming, dragging themselves from one handhold to the next and kicking off from any handy surface. You couldn't just walk or crawl, as there was no gravity to hold you down to the deck and give you the grip you needed for such forms of locomotion.

Carlos was one of the troopers who rushed ahead of me obeying Graves and Harris. He thumbed his nose at me—or at least it was a close approximation. His faceplate got in the way of the full gesture.

My breathing accelerated as I rejoined the flow and moved forward. I was the fourth man as we emerged into a larger, more open area.

Kivi had called out "contact", meaning she'd found the enemy. But when I came out of the gopher hole that terminated the passageway, I didn't see any armored squids.

"Where are they?" I asked.

"Two o'clock," she said. "Look."

Kivi was hugging the aft wall. I saw she was staring and pointing her weapon toward an opening. It took me a moment to realize what I was looking at. There was a large rip in the hull of the ship. It was right there on the top dome of the observational deck of the bridge. The rip was about five meters long and maybe two wide, and it impressed me in more ways than one.

"I don't see any squids," I radioed, aiming my weapon at the rip. Flanges of dark metal drifted and I could see starlight beyond the rip illuminating the outer hull.

"I did," she said, breathing hard over the microphone in her helmet. "It was just a shadow, a fast movement. Something jumped over that breach up there."

Sargon and I put our backs against the deck and aimed up at the breach. If something did rush us, we'd have time for one good shot—that was it.

"Report, Sargon," Veteran Harris said. "Are we moving into the chamber or not?"

"Your call, Vet," he said. "There's been a sighting. There could be a million of them crawling on the hull or only one."

Harris cursed and kicked the decision back up the chain to the officers who were in the rear. They moved the rest of the troops up, apparently not liking their position any better than I had when I was in that hole. A few more of our troops came up onto the bridge.

Maybe that's what the enemy had been waiting for. I'll never know for sure. As our troops began surging up one at a time into the chamber, the squids made their move.

In space, humans are rather clumsy. We're used to gravity, and we don't operate well without it. Worse, we need air to breathe and a lot of temperature controls in order to be comfortable. As bad as I'd thought fighting on Steel World had been, it was a picnic compared to fighting in space.

Our opponents were not as disadvantaged as we were. They had many limbs, not just four. They could use any of them in any configuration to grip a wall or some other hold, anchor themselves and get leverage. In addition, they seemed to feel more at home in space. They *swam* in it as if it was water. I was immediately struck by this as they began appearing at the breach overhead and darting down through it like fish. I knew in that instant that they were at least a partially aquatic species. I'd thought they'd looked pretty agile loping on all those tentacles to overrun us the first time, but they looked even more graceful in null-G.

-9-

I didn't fire right off. Instead, I waited about half a second. Sargon, to my surprise, did the same. Then we both let go at almost the same moment.

Gouts of plasma leapt up in unison toward the dozen or so enemy. They withered instantly in response because both Sargon and I had dialed our weapons for broad cones of fire.

Only two of the monsters made it to us, but that was enough to do a lot of damage. My tube was plucked from my grasping gauntlets by the tentacle of one of them. The creature methodically raised and lowered the tube. I barely had time to shy away as the weapon crashed down upon my shoulder plate. If I hadn't been wearing heavy armor, I'd have suffered a broken collarbone at the least—perhaps I'd have been struck dead.

Fortunately, my armor held, but the tube itself was damaged. Despite my peril, I was more worried about my weapon than I was my own life. My body could be repaired more easily than the alien weapon, and others could wield it if I fell. The cannons seemed to be our best defense against these creatures, and I had no idea how many more we might have to defeat.

I reached for the tube and struggled to take it back before the thrashing alien clubbed more of us with it. I grabbed it and hung on.

Back home, I'd ridden mechanical bulls upon occasion, usually while seriously intoxicated. I wished I'd had a few drinks in me now. The squid didn't want to give back my tube, and that thing was *strong*. It lashed its limbs like whips, and I went flying with them. Only the power of my exoskeletal suit and the fact I'd managed to wrap my fist into the shoulder strap allowed me to hang on at all.

To tell the truth, the next fifteen seconds were a blur. I was whipping around like a ragdoll, vaguely aware of the rest of my unit engaging this creature and the other one that had made it in close. They stabbed the squids and slashed away their tentacles. They had a plan now, and the process went more cleanly this time.

By the time my squid stopped thrashing, my helmet was starred and my brains were a little rattled. Kivi made it to me first. She stared worriedly into my faceplate.

"Hi," I said.

"You're alive?"

"I think so."

She slapped my helmet, which made me wince. My neck hurt, but I managed to force a smile.

"Help me up," I said.

She did, and I managed to get my magnetic boots to clamp onto the deck. I stood unsteadily, glad my suit could almost balance itself. The world was spinning.

"Did you puke in that suit?" Harris asked, coming close and glaring into the faceplate at me.

"No sir," I said. "But I think I have a leak. Something's flashing on my oxygen supply meter."

"What's the reading?"

"Can't tell, sir. That part of the glass is cracked too badly."

"Crazy mother," he said, giving me a shake. He shouted over his shoulder: "Tech!"

Natasha came over and began working on my suit. She clucked and cursed at me in even proportions. Soon she had a glaze of fresh plastic crawling across the inside of my visor. I assumed it was a nanite repair kit she was applying. They'd heat up then remelt the plastic, forming a fresh glaze. It would be a little blurry but much better than a network of cracks. Best of all, my suit would be airtight again.

Graves came over to me next. He looked me over with a critical eye.

"Are you functional, Specialist?"

"Yes sir," I said in the strongest voice I could muster. "I'm doing fine."

Weakness was a bad thing to let on about in Legion Varus. If I couldn't keep up, it might be for the best for the unit to put me down. Normally, that wouldn't be such a bad thing because you'd get a fresh body an hour or so later. But today I didn't want to risk it. As far as I knew, we might never reestablish contact with the rest of the legion.

"You went for a quite a ride," Graves said. "Was that an accident? I noticed your gauntlet was caught in your straps."

"No sir," I said. "I didn't want the creature to have my weapon."

Graves chewed that over for a moment, then nodded. "Excellent," he said, and left.

I watched him through my visor, which was now slightly warped rather than nearly opaque. The nanites were dying off, having run out of power. Nanites didn't live long; they usually didn't have batteries that lasted more than a few minutes. A fine dust of metal tickled my nose and fell away like steel filings. They bugged my skin slightly, and the sensation was like the one I always had after a haircut. I knew I needed a shower to wash them away completely, but that wasn't happening any time soon.

Natasha watched me. "Use your tapper to evacuate the dust from your helmet," she told me. "You don't want that dust to get into your lungs. Dead nanites can be carcinogens."

I did as she suggested. The prickly sensation on my skin was still there but less intense. Within a few minutes, I no longer needed to sneeze.

While I was recovering, the rest of the team searched the bridge. I joined them when I could. All around the walls there were control systems and odd-looking perches with straps too short to support anyone larger than a child. The screens were dead, however, and the safety straps were floating in the void.

The scouts Graves had sent up through the rip in the ceiling came down as we looked around. They'd been crawling out

83

there, checking on the external hull. They gave us the thumbs-up, having met with nothing but vacuum and debris.

"I think we have a good idea of how the attack went down," Graves said, addressing the survivors a few minutes later. There were only about half of us left alive, I noted with some alarm.

"The aliens ripped open the hull and came onto the bridge directly into the control center. I would guess the Skrull were caught by surprise. They probably didn't expect an assault the moment they came out of warp. The vacuum probably killed them as fast as anything else. Not many bodies in the seats—they were probably sucked out into space."

I thought about it. I could see the attack in my mind: A sudden explosion, a gush of hot air out into the absolute cold that was space. The Skrull must have died in horror and anguish wondering what was happening to them and their ship.

"But sir," I said, "what was the enemy's ultimate goal? Did they hope to destroy the ship or capture it?"

"Doesn't matter much now," Graves said. "I doubt they expected stiff resistance. We amounted to an effective security force."

I nodded but wasn't satisfied with the answers he'd come up with so far. How had they pulled this off? I'd never heard of anyone attacking a starship before. I guessed that was because the Empire was too terrifying. No one dared.

"Do you think we got them all, sir?" Carlos asked.

Graves grunted noncommittally. "We'll find out soon enough. I want everyone to help Natasha get the power back up. Harris, get a detail on that rip in the ceiling. Use some emergency decking and patch it up."

"Are we going to repressurize, sir?" Harris asked.

"If we're lucky."

We got to work then. The enemy didn't attack right away, and for that I was very glad. I could still feel the bruises and scrapes my armor had created when that last squid had given me the ragdoll treatment.

We pushed the alien bodies out of the rip, one by one, but saved the corpse that was the least damaged. Graves explained we had to keep one for the bio people to dissect later on.

The whole process took several hours, but we managed to get the power up again. Very quickly, we had a com-link up to the rest of the legion in the main sector of the ship. I was happy to learn they hadn't all been killed in the attack.

Primus Turov spoke to us personally when we'd managed to get her on the line.

"I want to congratulate you all on a job well done," she began. "Graves, you'd just formed up that heavy unit, and I'm frankly shocked you pulled this off without help."

That statement could be taken as an insult or a compliment, and coming from Turov, I suspected it was intended to be a little of both.

Graves took it all in stride, however. "Thank you, Primus. Legion Varus always gets the job done."

"Exactly. Now I want to discuss with your team what we're going to do next. I'm going to report to the Tribune for the final decision, of course."

"Naturally," Graves said.

Inside my own quiet helmet, I translated the true meaning of her words. I was beginning to know my commanders and how the legion operated as a whole. What the primus meant was she would gather all the intel from us, then turn around and deliver it to the legion's overall commander, Tribune Drusus. That way, she could hog all the glory for a mission in which she'd avoided all personal involvement.

"Here's how I see it," Turov began. "There's only one explanation for this situation: We've encountered a new, unknown, definitely feral species. It's a worst case scenario, really. The Galactics probably knew they were here all along but hadn't gotten around to dropping the hammer on them. Sometimes a race of beings is so vicious, they can't be reasoned with. I've read about cases like this. Usually, a truly savage race would rather fight to the finish than give in to the Empire. That's their choice, and they invariably suffer the consequences. Humanity was considered borderline in comparison. We were *almost* too savage to become a civilized world. Even after our application was accepted and our viability as a trader of mercenary troops was proven, some factions within the Empire wanted us excised, predicting we would be trouble down the road. We were closer to being snuffed out right from the start than most people realize."

Her little speech impressed me. She had a better grasp of the situation than I'd thought , and I'd learned a few things along the way. In Legion Varus, we generally operated on a need-to-know basis. Things were safer that way. But with internal legion politics involved, lower-level people rarely got the whole story about anything.

"Does anyone have anything to add?" Turov asked.

Her holographic image was in the center of the dark circular chamber. Most of us had gathered around listening to her, but Natasha and several others were working on the ship's systems. The ship was designed to be operated by the Skrull, but most subsystems had been produced somewhere within the Empire and were built for default humanoid manipulation. Standard symbols and fittings were everywhere, and every member of the Empire learned how to handle Imperial computer interfaces almost before they learned to speak. The controls were very intuitive and largely based upon touch.

When I saw no one was going to speak up, I stood and addressed her. She looked at me expectantly. As we were still in a hard vacuum, I couldn't open my helmet. I realized she probably didn't know who I was. That was just as well, but I knew I had to identify myself.

"Specialist McGill speaking, sir," I said. "I'm wondering about the human colonists that were supposed to be out here—what happened to them?"

Primus Turov's expression darkened the moment she heard my name. I could tell right away she hadn't forgotten about me.

"That's a question, and it's not going to help with my report," she snapped. "But the truth is that the colonists are probably all dead. With a local nest of vicious aliens like these in the system, how could they have survived?"

"Are you sure that the squid-aliens came from this system?"

"It's possible," she said. "We really don't know. What we do know is that our mission here is complete and successful. We were charged with eliminating a threat to Earth's

86

livelihood, and we've done just that. Well—actually the aliens did the job for us. By attacking a Galactic ship they sealed their own fate. As soon as we can get *Corvus* operational again, we'll report what happened to the Galactics and the system will be slated for cleansing. Problem solved!"

I frowned, but nodded and sat back down. I didn't buy her theory concerning the colonists. They were our kin, after all, and some of them might still be around. I didn't like the idea of telling the Galactics they should erase all life from this system.

"Anything else?" Turov asked in a tone that indicated she didn't want to hear any more from anyone.

Natasha stepped up. She had a worried look on her face. "Primus, Centurion," she said seriously. "Navigation isn't responding. I think it's damaged."

"Well then, repair it!" Primus Turov said tightly. "We should leave this system before any more rapid aliens get ideas."

"That's just it, sir. I don't think we have enough time left to effect repairs."

"Explain yourself."

"The ship has changed course. I can only think that the invaders did it—or maybe it was the Skrull in a last ditch attempt to screw their killers...I don't know, really."

"What the hell are you talking about, Specialist?" Turov said.

"Sorry sir," Natasha said, straightening her spine visibly. "I will attempt to be clear. This ship is flying directly toward Zeta Herculis—the star itself—and I can't change course because the helm controls have been damaged."

"How long do we have?" Graves asked, joining the conversation.

"Seventeen hours according to the nav computer. Maybe twice that if we can get some braking jets to fire."

"Do what you can," Graves said. He turned and regarded the projected image of Turov, who looked stunned.

"This changes everything, Primus. I've just sent a priority code text to Tribune Drusus. He wants to talk to us in person."

Turov's teeth flashed. It wasn't a smile; it was more like a snarl. But she controlled herself, and her lips quickly closed into a thin line.

"Excellent. That's exactly what I would have done. Please move your unit off the bridge except for the tech. I've already sent our best people to help. They'll take over. With any luck, we'll turn this ship away from the star."

"Moving out, sir," Graves said.

After that, we were hustling down long, damaged passageways. Worried-looking techs hurried past us going the other way. They looked at the floating dead and frozen sprays of blood apprehensively.

I hoped for all our sakes they could repair the ship's systems before it was too late.

-10-

Natasha was a good tech. Too good. She'd called it down to the hour. By the time the rest of the techs agreed, we only had thirteen precious hours left before we slammed into the local star.

It was already getting hotter aboard ship. Fortunately, we'd started off somewhere around negative two hundred degrees Celsius. Now that we were moving closer and closer to the central star, the temperature was naturally rising. At first, this would feel good…but in the end we'd burn up.

There was nothing that the techs could do to change our course. The aliens had been very thorough and from all indications the sabotage had been deliberate.

"It makes a strange sort of sense," I told Carlos later when we reached the mess hall.

"How's that?"

We'd taken showers, been issued new inner smart-cloth suits by the dispensers, and then been sent clanking along the passages in full armor to get some chow while we could. We still had no idea how the brass was going to handle the situation. I didn't think they did, either.

"They attacked the ship as suddenly as they could," I said. "They took *Corvus* out fast and scuttled it. Maybe they figured the Galactics would never find out what happened and they'd get away with this violation."

"You think *that* makes sense?" demanded Carlos with a nervous laugh. "None of this makes any sense. It's crazy. The

89

squids are crazy, and our officers are crazier. Together they'll get us all permed in the end, you watch."

"What do you mean?"

Carlos put down his fork which had a chunk of pork and beans on the end. At least the food had been pressed into the general shape, color and texture of pork and beans. They hadn't quite gotten the taste right, unfortunately.

He leaned close to me and spoke in a rough whisper. "I mean, my challenged friend, that it's frigging obvious what we should do. We have to abandon ship."

"And just let *Corvus* crash into the star?"

Carlos shrugged. "Better than letting us all die."

"I've got a better idea," I said. "We should revive the Skrull and give them a shot at repairing the ship. After all, it's their vessel."

Carlos had picked up his fork again. He waved it at me admonishingly. "There you go, thinking up High Crimes again."

"Doing something to save yourself can't be a crime."

"Ha! Sure it can, dumbass!"

According to Carlos, if they ever put my brain into a monkey's skull the monkey would walk backwards. His natural personality was often amusing, but not when I was stressed. I struggled with an urge to throw my pork and beans into his face. If I'd thought it would get him to shut up, I'd have done it. The miserable food wouldn't have been a big loss.

When I'd controlled my thoughts of vengeance, I took a deep breath and asked him what he meant.

"We're talking about the Galactics and the Nairbs," he said. "The ultimate in government bureaucrats. As far as they're concerned, you can be dead and still legally perform a capital crime while you're sitting in your grave."

I thought it over, knowing he had a point. "I see what you mean. We don't have a license to use our machines on the Skrull. They haven't licensed the technology for themselves, either. It still seems wrong that we can't use machines we have on hand to fix our dire situation."

"There's more to it than that," Carlos said. "Let's say we're willing to chance an Imperial crime for the sake of a few of

90

these monkey-turtles. We can't do it anyway. Their bodies have never been scanned, never been backed up."

I leaned closer to him for a second. "I heard from some of the bio people we could still do it. With a dead body as a model, one that's flash-frozen, you can get a reading and copy them. All you'd have to do is edit out the cellular damage. Just think about it. Most of them were turned into popsicles when the squids opened the hull."

Carlos looked at me in concern. "Tell Anne Grant not to try it. Stay away from her, or together you two will mix up an entirely new stew of crazy and get Earth erased this time."

I frowned and started eating my food. Carlos was right in his assumptions, and that bothered me. The bio I'd talked to was indeed Anne. She was someone who I knew from experience was willing to go out of her way and even break serious rules to save lives. She was probably the most likely person on the ship to violate a Galactic law—besides me, that is. What bothered me most was knowing that if Carlos could figure out Anne was behind the crime, others could figure it out, too.

"Listen," Carlos said. "The Skrull are all dead. Leave them that way. Focus on the living."

"What about the colonists?" I asked. "There are humans in this system somewhere, and we should be helping them."

"Helping them?" Carlos snorted. "We're here to exterminate them, remember? That's why Turov was so happy. Her problem solved itself when those stupid squids attacked us."

I ignored him after that. I liked Carlos, and he was a good man to have in a trench with you, but he was the kind who could easily write off anyone who wasn't in his immediate vicinity. He'd risk his life to save a friend—but people a kilometer away who he didn't know personally would just have to fend for themselves.

That wasn't the way my mind and heart operated. As a soldier from Earth, I felt a need to protect all humans. I could probably get attached to an alien race, too, if I spent enough time around them. I don't know.

Chow time was over all too soon. We were sent to the armory next, and this had me worried. My suspicions were confirmed when our orders came in.

"Follow the arrows to yellow deck. Find your unit's embarking station. Do not vary or stray from the path. Stay with your units, and do not stop for extra gear."

A private contact came in from Adjunct Leeson shortly after that. "McGill? You fully operational?"

"Yes, sir!"

"Good. When you board the lifter, park your butt next to mine."

"Will do, Adjunct."

I was breathing hard during the short jog past green deck, then past blue. We were going all the way down to yellow deck where the lifters were stored when in warp. None of this sounded good to me.

Carlos contacted me, helmet-to-helmet as we jogged.

"What the hell is happening?" he demanded. "I saw your com-light flash. Who's talking to you? What are they saying?"

"Isn't it obvious?" I asked. "We're going on a little jog to digest that lovely meal."

"You're such a dick," Carlos complained. "How is our destination a state secret? Don't even try to stonewall me, McGill. There's no point."

I kind of agreed with him. It looked to me like we were abandoning the ship, and if that was the case, it hardly mattered if the rank and file heard about it or not. Legion Varus didn't believe in briefing their troops on details. They figured we weren't the most obedient bunch, and keeping us in the dark was their way of keeping us from giving them trouble.

"We're abandoning ship, if I had to guess," I said.

"Abandoning ship? To where? What about our stuff? Damn."

I snorted. Not ten minutes ago he'd been complaining that they hadn't ordered us all to jump ship, and now that it was happening he had fresh complaints. That was Carlos in a nutshell.

Another thought occurred to me as we jogged down passages under flashing lights following yellow arrows. Yellow meant we were in a possible combat situation. I guess that fit.

"That's why they aren't telling us," I told Carlos.

"What?"

"They don't want you loading up on personal effects. We're carrying full combat kits, and that's it. We'll board the lifters and we'll be flying as light as possible. That's got to be it."

The more I thought about it, the more obvious it seemed. Why not come over the voice net and give us a pep speech about why we had to move to the lifters and exit the ship? Why hustle us to the airlocks without much more than a final quick meal? Because they didn't want us to get any ideas, that's why.

I explained my thinking to Carlos.

"What bastards," Carlos said with feeling. "That makes too much sense. I had a lot of stuff in my locker—private stuff, you know?"

"Yeah. Stolen vid files and that weird collection of hair from the girl's shower drain, right?"

"Screw you, McGill."

I chuckled, and he finally stopped pestering me on the private line. We went down the null-grav tubes directly, diving head first and pulling ourselves along the rungs on the walls. They weren't even bothering with having us use the lifts.

I passed Veteran Harris at a junction. He took the time to shout: "Go! Go!" into everyone's faceplate as we passed while whacking the back of each trooper's helmet.

As a heavy trooper with a thick helmet, I could barely feel the impact of his gauntlet as it crashed into the back of my head, but it did create a ringing clang I could have done without.

"What's the bloody hurry, Vet?" Carlos demanded.

Harris didn't strike him again, as I'd halfway been expecting. His face looked a little worried.

"Don't know. Just orders. Get the hell to the first seat you find and strap your ass in. They aren't going to give you more than thirty seconds to stow your gear. Expect a hot release and drop."

Those words surprised me. *A hot release and drop?* Were we under attack? I couldn't figure it out. We still had more than ten hours before we reached the star's corona—the point of no return for all spaceships.

After the long jouncing run, I was rewarded with a small aperture to pass through. It was a small hatchway on top of the lifter we all had to wriggle through. Normally, the lifters were loaded one at a time in the bays designated for the purpose, but that part of the procedure had apparently been skipped this time. We were boarding through the top hatch because it would save time.

I opened a private channel to Natasha as I boarded and clanked down the ranks of huddled soldiers. Most of the troops on the lifter were heavies, as this was a heavy cohort. But the row I was passing by was populated by auxiliary troops—bio people, techs and other support personnel. They were in their pajamas, as we called smart-cloth uniforms. They eyed me in quiet concern as I crashed by them.

Most people didn't like to mess with heavy weaponeers. We had bad reps, lots of body armor, and like me, we were generally the biggest guys in the unit. The only reaction I got from most of them as I passed was a desperate effort to pull back feet so I wouldn't stomp on them too hard. My tube thumped into more than one unfortunate's ribs, and they glared at me, suspecting I was bullying them. In truth, it was hard to maneuver quickly in heavy armor with a full kit without slamming into everyone I passed them.

It took me a while to find the seat I was supposed to sit in. Adjunct Leeson had requested me to sit by his side, and I wasn't going to skip that invitation. I had a lot of questions about this entire exercise, and he might have answers.

I finally sighted Leeson with an open seat on his left. He waved me forward impatiently. I moved forward with purpose.

A girl's foot strayed, and I smashed it flat.

"Ow, you jackass!" raged the owner.

She rubbed her foot and glared up at me. She was blonde with a sharp nose and quick-moving eyes that reminded me of an excited bird.

"Sorry Miss," I had time to say—and then the world turned upside down.

Almost before I knew what was happening, I was lifted up and kicked down the row of seats. I could have sworn that Harris had finally lost patience with me and given me a boot in the rear—but Harris had long ago found a seat and strapped in.

I fell forward, armor sparking, plasma tube banging into helmets and knees as I hung onto it. The lifter was moving. We'd been dropped from the guts of *Corvus* and released into space.

Normally, launch wouldn't have initiated a series of violent maneuvers. But our pilot wasn't screwing around. The second we were down and out in open space, she'd gunned the lifter. I could imagine the plume of exhaust we were leaving behind us in space. Wherever we were going, we were doing it in a big damned hurry.

A gauntlet reached down and grabbed me by the air hose as I slid by. Fortunately, the hose didn't pop out.

Leeson hauled me up into the jump seat next to him.

"Quit screwing around, McGill," he said.

I strapped in as fast as I could. "Sorry, sir. Just couldn't pass up the opportunity to have a little fun."

"Does your tube still work?"

I checked it quickly. "Passes all diagnostics."

"Good," he said. "I have the feeling we're going to need it."

"Sir, could you clarify a few things for me?"

Leeson was a balding man with small, dark eyes. He gave me a hard stare. "I guess it can't hurt now. We're already underway."

"Thank you, sir."

"We're abandoning *Corvus*," he told me.

I almost rolled my eyes at him, but I controlled the urge.

"That makes sense, Adjunct," I said. "But why the hurry? I thought we had at least ten hours to go."

"Yeah, sure. We've had ten hours before we reached the critical point of no return and got sucked into the star. But did you stop to think about our position in this system? Once the

95

decision was made to jump ship, we realized we had to move as fast as possible."

I frowned. "So we have another ship we're trying to rendezvous with?"

This amused Leeson. "Right, sure," he laughed. "There're like fifty luxury cruise ships from the Core Systems hanging around out here circling this shithole frontier star in case lost troopships happen by."

"I take that as a no, sir."

"A big *no*, Specialist. We jumped off *Corvus* because the only places to run to consist of a few scrubby planets. Two of those are in the Goldilocks Zone. We're aiming for those worlds and we couldn't wait any longer."

After he said this, the race to get off the ship made more sense. I knew enough planetary astronomy to know that the Goldilocks Zone was the region of space around a star in which liquid water could exist on a planet's surface. Earth was in that zone as were almost all inhabited worlds.

"I get it, sir," I said. "The only place we could run to consisted of the local planets that are inhabitable. We'll need air and water to survive."

"Exactly."

"So, I'm assuming we're making planetfall on that ocean planet the colonists were sent to years back, right?"

Adjunct Leeson shook his head. "No, afraid not. That was considered and rejected."

"Why?" I asked, my heart sinking. I'd been entertaining visions of warm oceans and even warmer beaches.

"Where do you think those damned squids came from?" Leeson asked me.

I thought about it. "They did seem to be aquatic, at least originally. But are we sure they're native to this system at all?"

Leeson lost patience with my battery of questions. He'd never been a patient man. Competent, yes. Calm and collected, no.

"Look," he said, "I have no idea why they decided to bail out and head for the dust world instead of the water world. And I didn't order you to plant your butt next to mine so we could have this little bedtime chat, either. You're here for one reason."

He pointed at my plasma tube.

"I want that," he said, indicating my weapon. "I want you and your weapon as close as possible to my position. From what I've heard, only heavy weapons damage these squid things, and you've already had combat experience with them."

"That's true, sir. Just one more thing?"

"What?"

"You said something about a 'dust world'?"

"Yeah," he said. "The brass looked at all their options and narrowed them down to three. One was to try to invade the water world. That idea was dropped because those oceans are probably teeming with massive squids. The second idea was to hang around space and broadcast an S.O.S. That was rejected too, as the enemy would doubtlessly hear the signal and come to wipe us out—assuming we could even survive in open space long enough to be rescued in the first place. Fortunately, there's another world in the Goldilocks Zone in this system."

Dust World. It had a certain ring to it, I had to admit. Unfortunately, the name conjured up a vivid image—an image I didn't like in the slightest.

"Sir? What's this Dust World place like, if you don't mind my asking? I'd been kind of hoping to take a bath, if you know what I mean."

"Look," he snapped. "It's a frigging rock in space, okay? A dry rock with a little air, a little water, and a whole lot of dust. Maybe if you're lucky, you'll get to make mud when we land and you can take a bath in that. Now shut up. I'm listening in on command chat."

I fell silent and endured the Gs as the lifter maneuvered and rocked. I had time to ponder my choices in life, and I had to admit I was full of regrets today.

-11-

A banging sound on my helmet made me open one eye. I'd been sleeping—which wasn't easy to do in heavy armor aboard a lifter.

Adjunct Leeson's face stared into mine. Our visors were open, but we'd kept our helmets on. That was SOP in dangerous systems.

"Sir?"

"Let's go. I'm supposed to move forward and attend a briefing. You're coming with."

I didn't argue. I removed my straps and got to my feet, groaning. The internal joints of metal armor always created sore spots that dug into my flesh and cut off circulation. I was all but dragging my left leg behind me as I set off after the adjunct.

We traveled to an open ladder and hauled ourselves upward. The hatch at the top was tight for a weaponeer, and my kit scraped and banged as I slipped through.

On the upper deck things looked different—very different. I'd never been anywhere on a lifter other than down inside the troop pods. The upper decks were reserved for the crew and the higher ranking passengers.

The deck we stepped onto wasn't as big as the lower troop bays, but when compared with the rows of bare metal jump seats it was luxuriously appointed. There were swiveling chairs with actual cushions. These seats even had armrests with cup holders attached to them. Leeson directed me to an out of the way chair with a wave of his gauntlet. I settled into it happily even though my thick armor kept me from enjoying the upholstery.

Centurion Graves was there as were a lot of other adjuncts and centurions. Leading the conversation was Primus Turov. She strutted around a central planning table and gave everyone the evil eye. My visor was up, but I kept my face well back inside my helmet. I hoped she wouldn't recognize me.

"Let's get started," Turov said.

The rest of them stopped talking and took seats. There weren't enough to go around, and some of them had to stand. I felt self-conscious but didn't move from my seat in the back. Adjunct Leeson had ordered me to sit here. That was my story, and I was going to stick to it.

There were a few other non-coms in the room, but I was the only weaponeer. The others were veterans along with a few techs. The techs operated the planning table by working on their hands and knees around it, coaxing the system into displaying graphics that showed our position. I looked for Natasha among them, but I didn't see her.

On the planning table, our small fleet of lifters resembled a school of tiny green fish traveling in a slow orbit around the central star. The target world was represented by a burnt-orange ball. It didn't look to me like we had far to go.

"Here's the good news," Turov said, "we're going to make planetfall soon. There's no question of that. There's no sign of pursuit, either. The enemy fleet—if they even have one—isn't intercepting us. What we're here to do now is decide where on this Garden of Eden we're going to land."

Adjunct Toro, a woman who'd never liked me since we'd first laid eyes on one another, raised her hand.

"What is it, Adjunct?" Turov asked her.

"Sir? Is this really the only choice we have? Just about anything else looks preferable."

"I agree," Turov said. "I argued all along that our top choice was to bail out and stay in the space-lane to see if the techs aboard *Corvus* could pull a miracle and regain control of the ship. In fact, I wanted to put all our technical people on that task. But the Tribune felt it was too risky. He believes the enemy might be waiting to finish the job by ambushing us in space."

I frowned as I listened to her talk. I gathered from her statements that there were still techs aboard *Corvus*. The idea was alarming. People were on that ship, sailing into the star, still trying to fix it? If so, they had only a few hours left to live.

I checked the local roster of contacts on my tapper and my heart sank. Natasha wasn't on the lifter with me. That could only mean she'd been left behind on Corvus. I didn't want to think about how that was going to end for her.

Adjunct Toro seemed to be thinking along the same lines I was.

"But sir," she said. "Would it be wise to lose even more people in what's likely to be a fireball at the end?"

Centurion Graves stirred. He was one of the ones who'd been left standing. Turov signaled for him to speak.

"No one is going to get permed on *Corvus*," Graves said. "Not unless we all die. We copied their data to the lifters. If *Corvus* crashes into the star, we'll record the fact, then revive them after we land on the target planet."

This assurance seemed to settle everyone down. I was still alarmed, however. I couldn't stop thinking about Natasha. Things must be awful right now for her aboard that doomed ship. The techs we'd left behind were all sailing directly into a blazing star, knowing they'd been abandoned with nothing to look forward to other than cooking to death. The radiation alone would probably finish them before they felt the terrible heat.

"Now, back to the matter at hand," Turov continued. "Let's take a look at this rock we're supposed to land on. For the most part, it's a giant desert. There are a few places where life has been detected. Deep gullies exist—valleys that are essentially cracks in the surface of an endless expanse of blowing grit. Inside these valleys, water runs and the shade keeps the plants from burning up. By our best projections, the shaded regions are similar to tropical oases."

Turov proceeded to display the world on the planning table and show these rifts in the surface. Some were over thirty kilometers long, as wide as three kilometers and nearly as deep as they were wide.

"The valleys we're most interested in are those clustered around the southern pole. We've identified ten of them—one for each lifter—as landing zones. These valleys are sheltered from the sun and suitably temperate."

The briefing went on while I stared in fascination. I realized I was about to land on an unexplored world and perhaps be one of the first humans in history to breathe its air. I found that exciting, but it seemed like a wearisome chore to the rest of the assembled officers. Most of them were veterans of many campaigns on alien planets.

In time, the group settled on a green valley close to the pole itself. Due to the angle of the planet, the bottom of this gully was never in the direct sunlight. Our cohort's techs assured us the temperature would be quite comfortable and possibly even cool at night.

"We don't have a lot of time to find a suitable region where we can bivouac and survive until help comes," Turov explained. "The tribune ordered us all to choose a different valley—one for each cohort on each lifter—and to land there when we make planetfall. Once we're down we'll explore, compare notes and report in. The plan is to decide which of these holes in the desert is the most suitable and to gather all our people at that spot."

I could hardly believe what I was hearing. We were breaking up the lifters, each of which carried a single cohort? What if the enemy was down there waiting for us? We thought the squids came from the water world—but we could be wrong.

Several centurions moved about uncomfortably, but no one said anything. Finally, Centurion Graves cleared his throat.

"Yes?" asked the Primus.

"Primus, this seems like a poor strategy. Spreading our forces around the moment we land will weaken us if we meet resistance."

She nodded. "You're right, but we don't have much time. We're not going to engage the aliens if we meet up with them.

We'll cut our losses and fly out. Dead troops will be counted and revived later."

"What's the hurry, sir?" Graves asked.

Turov worked her lips thoughtfully as if considering how she should answer the question.

"We don't have much in the way of supplies, Centurion. Actually, we've got almost nothing. We don't even have enough water to last a month. We depended on *Corvus* for that sort of thing, and we had to leave the ship suddenly to make planetfall as we passed this world. We know nothing about this planet, but we're going to have to find a suitable spot to hole up until we're rescued. We can explore faster by splitting up."

Several others, emboldened by Graves' success, raised their own hands to ask questions. I wanted to join them but didn't dare.

Primus Turov lifted her own hands in a calming gesture. She looked worried. "I know, I know. You have a thousand questions. Let me give you a couple of facts instead. First, we need breathable air, potable water and hopefully a food source. We need them right now. Second, we might well be ambushed. We might even lose a lifter or two full of troops. But we've got the recorders running, and we'll capture all deaths as they occur. Any group that gets wiped out will be revived at one of the other camps. Problem solved."

I was stunned. This was just the sort of thinking that Legion Varus was famous for. If you didn't make it, they shrugged and made a copy.

Centurion Graves asked one more question. "How long will we have to wait on this rock, Primus? When can we expect a rescue?"

"Indeterminate. The Galactics are aware of this renegade frontier system. When *Corvus* doesn't come home, the loss will be reported. I would expect we'll have to wait no more than a year until another Skrull ship comes to investigate. Hopefully, they'll come before the Galactic Battle Fleet arrives. The warships may not bother to distinguish between legitimate castaways and feral local aliens."

As I heard this, my heart sank. Was I really about to spend a year on a desolate rock in space with no assurance that there would be a rescue in the end? I couldn't help but think about the events that would transpire when the Galactics finally arrived.

It was quite possible, I knew, that by the time the Battle Fleet darkened the skies of Dust World I'd have survived by scraping along for years only to be blasted to component atoms by a heartless maelstrom of interstellar ships.

The questions finally stopped and the group got down to the business of choosing a target valley. Turov made sure we all voted twice to choose the best possible option. In my opinion, she talked for too long. I was getting bored. We couldn't really make the best choice from such limited data, anyway.

The officers finally chose the biggest valley up around the southern pole. But after Turov selected it on the map, she quickly discovered it had been taken by another cohort. Then she selected our second choice, tapping at screen.

The computer map flickered orange, refusing to take the input. Frowning, Primus Turov became alarmed.

"Those bastards…" she muttered.

She quickly tapped at each of the other major valleys, one at a time. All of them had already been taken. There were ten cohorts in our legion and apparently the rest of them had chosen their destinations first and talked it to death afterward.

Turov scanned the map scrolling it this way and that. Finally, she found a small valley farther north than any of the others. I knew this place would be hotter as it was closer to the equator. But it registered as deep and wet.

"It's a crater, not a true valley," Turov said. "It's basically a deep lake with a sizable scrim of land around it. The sensors say it's circular, four kilometers deep and about six wide. I guess it will have to do."

I stared at the screen as her finger stabbed down. The outline of the valley turned green, indicating the selection had been accepted.

Adjunct Leeson walked over to me as the meeting broke up and gave me a grim smile. "Welcome to your new hole in the ground, McGill."

"Looks like home sweet home to me," I said.

103

"Now, here's the deal. When we deploy I want you right next to me. You understand that?"

"Yes, sir."

"Any questions?"

"Just one, sir. Why did you bring me up here to this briefing?"

"I wanted you to know the score."

"But why? You could have just briefed me later."

Adjunct Leeson's eyes slid around the room. After he was satisfied no one was listening in, he leaned closer to me.

"If these crazy squid-aliens of yours are down there waiting for us, I'm going to have you and your big gun front and center."

"That sounds like a real privilege, Adjunct."

Leeson snorted. "I'm not out to screw you over. You remember Cancri-9? When the lizards had us trapped at the spaceport?"

"I sure do. It wasn't our legion's finest hour."

"No, it wasn't," he said. "But it was *your* finest hour. You outlasted everyone. I like a man who can survive the worst a planet can throw at him. That's the kind of magic I want near me. I figured if you were here at the briefing it might give you an edge."

I nodded, finally catching on. "You want to live no matter what, is that it? That kind of attitude is almost unpatriotic in Legion Varus. Why not trust one of the other cohorts to revive us if things go wrong?"

"I don't trust my own mother when the blood begins to spray," he said. "But I trust a good weaponeer."

"Thank you, sir. I'll try to be worthy of your confidence."

Adjunct Leeson shook his head and chuckled. "Don't thank me until you hear the punch line. Our squad drew the short straw. We're stepping off this lifter first."

My face fell. "How exactly did that happen, sir?"

"Centurion Graves volunteered us."

My eyes swung to Graves. Leeson's did the same. We both stared at the Centurion grimly, but he didn't seem to care. He was having a private talk with Turov.

"You think he's over there volunteering us for some more special duties?" I asked. "Like repainting the lifter's hull after we land?"

Adjunct Leeson laughed. "I wouldn't put it past him."

-12-

About a dozen hours later, the lifter bounced through the upper atmosphere of the target world jolting me awake. All around me, troopers looked worried and a little green.

In the center of the aisle between two rows of seated troops was a vacuum-powered drain. When someone popped open their faceplate and leaned forward to puke, the drain turned on, whirring. It always seemed to know when there was work to be done. The rest of us tried not to watch. Vomit could become contagious during a rough reentry.

The pilot began to relay vid feeds from outside the ship to our helmets. I selected the input and displayed it inside my faceplate. The vid was distracting, for which I was grateful, but it wasn't comforting.

The arid planet we were hurtling toward was big and windy, but we couldn't feel that yet. We were just below the exosphere now and falling down into the thermosphere. Outside the ship, there was nothing to speak of in the way of breathable air at this point, and only enough gravity to pull the puke gently toward the drain under our metal boots.

But there was enough gas outside the lifter to bump us around. We hung on grimly, not talking much. What was there to say? We'd land then we'd get out and fight if we had to. I don't think anyone knew what we were getting ourselves into, not even the Primus herself.

Watching the vids, I saw snakes of dust crawling over endless dunes. I couldn't see any of the tropical valleys we were supposed to be targeting. What I did see was a constant parade of sandstorms rolling over the desolate landscape.

We began powering down and heating up with friction as we punched through layer after layer of the atmosphere. It never seemed to smooth out the way it did at the end back on Earth. I checked the surface temperature and sighed. It was about fifty degrees Celsius down there.

Carlos beeped my helmet. I answered his call reluctantly.

"What?" I demanded.

"Have you been checking out the travel brochure? Looks pretty sweet, doesn't it?"

"Maybe—if you're some kind of desert scorpion."

Carlos laughed. "Just like home," he said. "The Sahara Desert, that is. Highs in the upper fifties with bags of sunshine—wish you were here!"

I had no idea what he was talking about, but I didn't complain. Carlos often dealt with stressful situations by making jokes—even if they didn't make much sense.

Five long minutes later, the lifter heaved and then came to a final, thumping stop. It felt like someone had hit the bottom of my boots and the seat of my armor with a hammer all at the same time.

"At least they didn't make us jump out," Adjunct Leeson complained next to me.

We slapped off their buckles and got to our feet—at least, everyone in my squad did. The rest sat there watching us. Thirty troops took thirty seconds to arrange their gear and then a huge grinding sound began.

We all looked toward the exit ramp. A brilliant glare of light was expected—but we didn't see that. Instead I saw a cool, gloomy light. It was almost purple; the shade of twilight before the last rays of the sun are extinguished and night takes over.

"What's the temp out there?" I asked Carlos, who was still on a private line to my helmet.

"Thirty degrees C," he said. "Can that be right? That's like—reasonable."

I didn't have time to answer him. Leeson gave me a rude shove from behind. The servos in the auto-balancing systems of my suit whined in protest.

"Get moving, McGill. We'll be right behind you."

I pushed past the other troopers, who were all heavies in armor. My metal scratched theirs, leaving white lines on the burnished surfaces, but no one complained. They'd heard the adjunct's order, and no one wanted to take my place.

I marched down the ramp with my tube set for a long-distance shot with a narrow energy-spread. I figured there probably weren't going to be aliens waiting on the ground for us. It would probably take them a while to get to the landing site even if they'd been watching us come down.

When I came out of the bottom of the lifter and saw my surroundings, I was taken by surprise. The land was beautiful, not harsh and ugly as I'd expected. I'd been visualizing a desert, but instead what met my gaze were a thousand lush-looking plants. They weren't quite like plants from home, but you could tell they were full of water and life.

Most of them looked like some kind of huge flower. Thick stalks led up to massive growths that came in a riot of colors. Under the stalks of each plant was a spray of meaty-looking blue-green leaves. These leaves, stalks and even the flowers themselves all looked like they had a waxy coating on them. Maybe it was just their natural texture—I couldn't be sure. Whatever they were, I knew I wasn't going to be the first guy to touch one or, God-forbid, eat one. The bio people would have to run a load of tests before anyone dared to do that.

Besides the towering flowers all around the ship, there wasn't much else to see other than the canyon walls that surrounded us. Far, far above was a vast circle of glaring yellow light. The circle wasn't the star, however. It was only the hazy sky of the surface world, filled with dust. I was looking up from the bottom of a deep hole in the planet's crust.

Behind me, I heard clanking footsteps. The rest of the squad was on the ramp coming down to join me. We took up defensive firing positions among the flowers, but there didn't seem to be any need.

"No trees?" Carlos complained. "What kind of a jungle has no trees?"

"An alien one," I answered.

"What's that, McGill?" Leeson demanded. "Report, Specialist."

"Sorry sir. Nothing here. No enemy contact. No sign of civilization. There's nothing out here other than some really, really big orchids."

"Good."

Leeson finally appeared at my side along with Veteran Harris. Had they been hiding inside the ship at the top of the ramp?

"Nice of you two to join the party," I said. "Pick a flower— we have plenty."

"Keep your eyes on the horizon, McGill," Harris said.

I turned back to the scene encircling the ship. I couldn't see much. I noticed there was a fine layer of silt on the ground. It must filter down from the sky overhead all the time.

Carlos opened his faceplate. I think he was probably the first.

"Air checks out," he said when he saw us staring at him. "It tastes a little dusty, but all my monitors say it's breathable."

Harris, Leeson and I kept our faceplates closed. We watched Carlos closely, and I knew we were all wondering when he might keel over. Sure, the atmospheric sensors were glowing green, but they didn't always pick up airborne toxins.

Carlos investigated the environment while Leeson called down the next squad. He loudly claimed we'd secured the perimeter. I didn't think we'd done any such thing, but I kept my mouth shut.

"These leaves are waxy and coated with mucus," Carlos said, faintly disgusted.

Anne Grant came down to investigate. "That's sap," she said.

She had her faceplate up too, and I privately thought they were both crazy.

"Sap?" Carlos said. "Green plant-blood? I don't think so."

Specialist Grant investigated further. "You have a point. It seems to be moving over the plant, flowing downward. Look what happens when I let some dirt fall on this leaf."

We watched her experiment, but I tried to keep my eyes on the cliff walls which were alarmingly close.

"I'm developing a theory," Anne said, sounding excited. "This waxy, sticky coating flowing over the plant is an adaptation designed to protect it."

"Protect against what?" asked Carlos, yanking his gauntlet back and rubbing it on his armored legs.

"I'm not saying it's poisonous. The coating defends these growths against the endless sifting dust that falls from above. It works like the wet lining of your throat and sinuses, carrying away debris."

"What the hell for?" asked Carlos.

"There can't be much rain here, and they only get reflected light from the walls of the canyon. The water all comes from underground. If the dust constantly falls and covers their leaves, the plants must have trouble with photosynthesis. If the leaves became too dusty, they'd die, so they've developed a way to filter the dust away."

"That's an excellent theory, Grant," Centurion Graves said, joining the conversation. "But I don't really give a damn about the plant life. What I need to know is if we're alone down here."

"Sir, you'll have to scout the area for that."

Centurion Graves turned to Leeson. "Take a squad north. The central lake has to lie in that direction. I'll have Adjunct Toro go in the opposite direction to locate the canyon wall. If you find anything useful or dangerous, report in."

"Uh," said Leeson, "what about the rest of the cohort?"

"I'll give the all-clear and we'll disembark. I think it's pretty obvious we didn't land in the middle of an ambush. Our core force will set up camp around the lifter to defend it."

Grumbling, Leeson led Veteran Harris, me and the rest of the squad northward. The adjunct seemed to be in a sour mood.

"Graves must have it in for Leeson," Carlos told me quietly. "I bet his dog crapped all over the Centurion's lawn back on Earth."

110

Carlos' idea made me smile, but I didn't think he was right. Graves didn't need a reason to order a man to die. He just did it out of habit. If he thought your death was a good idea—you might as well accept what was coming. If a trooper's death would benefit the legion, even in terms of convenience or cost-savings, you were as good as dead. Even perma-death was negotiable.

Pushing through what amounted to a thicket of fleshy, sticky-leafed flowers was strange enough, but when we reached the lake's edge we were in for another shock.

"What in the holy hell are those things?" Carlos asked.

"Fish, I think," Anne answered.

Whatever they were, they were weird. They looked like floating rocks. They had no eyes or fins in sight. These creatures were all over the surface of the water, drifting up to the surface then down again. They varied in size and markings from little guys no bigger than my hand to monsters a full meter in length. At our approach, they moved slowly in our direction.

"They seem to know we're here," I said. "Maybe the rock-look is camouflage."

"You might be right," Anne said, standing next to me. She was clearly excited by the find and stared intently as the creatures approached us. "If they have adopted camouflage, that indicates they must have a predatory species that hunts them."

I nodded, watching the "fish".

"They must have some way of sensing us," I said, "and some kind of limbs underneath that rough-looking top we can see. They remind me a bit of gators in the swamps back home. But they don't have a uniform appearance from one creature to the next."

"Rock-fish," Carlos said, coming up behind us. "That's what they are."

"Who asked you?" I demanded.

"I named them first. That's how it works when you discover something. First guy to speak up gets to be famous."

Anne gave him a look, twisting her lips. "Rock-fish... All right. I'll enter it into my logs."

111

"Make sure you spell my name right," Carlos said, crowding close to her. "Carlos Ortiz. That's with a 'Z' at the end."

"Okay, enough admiring the wildlife," Veteran Harris said, slamming his gauntlets together. "Who's going to kill one and eat it first?"

Everyone looked alarmed. I pointed at Carlos. "He named them. He's the expert here."

"Hold on!" Carlos protested. "I don't know what they taste like. They might be poisonous."

"That's right," Harris said, grinning. "But our mission is to find foodstuffs. We're stuck here, remember? You might have saved the entire legion with your rock-fish if we can eat them safely. Now, quit being a candy-ass and catch one of those things."

Unhappy and complaining, Carlos lowered his faceplate and stepped into the water at a shallow point. The lake became deep quickly. He was up to his knees only one step out.

The rock-fish retreated at first, then came gently drifting closer again. They were like ducks, I thought, ducks at a park that were used to being fed.

Harris had a huge grin on his face. He came up behind Carlos and surprised him, with a heavy hand on his shoulder. Carlos swayed and we could hear the servos in his suit whining to keep him steady.

"Hey! Careful, Vet!"

I felt a bit sorry for Carlos. This sort of thing happened to him all too often. He had a way of making people want to kill him. I was sure everyone in the unit had at least fantasized about doing it.

Harris kept his hand on Carlos' shoulder.

"They say this soupy lake is over two kilometers deep," he told Carlos. "And it goes almost straight down from the edge. You're standing on a little shelf of sand—did you know that? Now, don't step out too far Ortiz! You'll sink like a rock in that armor—and you know how I hate to lose a good suit of armor."

"Yeah," Carlos said. "Thanks for the warning. I think for safety's sake I'll move to the shore."

"Nah," Harris said. He lifted his faceplate and spit into the water. Two rock-fish lunged at the spot then wallowed away disappointedly. "Catch me one. That's an order."

Carlos thought about it, then he did what I probably would have done—he shot one.

A hot beam of light flared and one of the rock-fish darkened and began to steam. It swelled up and rolled over.

The underbelly was unpleasant. White and wet, it revealed a dozen or so small flippers with little double-jointed arms to work them. We all watched with curling lips and wrinkling noses as the creature shook and hissed.

What happened next took us all by surprise, however. The other rock-fish lunged at the first one. Mouths appeared at the forward end of each fish, having been concealed just below the waterline. Every one of those mouths was full of triangular teeth that flashed like pearls. They tore apart their cooked comrade, pulling off the shivering fins first then taking chunks of meat away from the body. The water turned oily and slick on top with dark clouds of blood.

Carlos shot another one and this time reached out to grab it before the others could feast upon its carcass. He lifted the heavy lump of meat, grunting.

"Must weigh ten kilos," Carlos said.

"Vicious little bastards," Harris said in concern. "I bet you're glad you didn't go skinny-dipping, Ortiz."

"Metal armor for the win," Carlos said.

He threw his second catch onto the shoreline where it writhed and smoked. The underbelly was like that of a wet insect.

"Soup's on!" Carlos shouted enthusiastically, climbing out of the water.

No one went near the dying fish except Anne. In situations like this, bio people were the toughest among us. There didn't seem to be anything that could disgust them. I guess after seeing alien life on a dozen planets they had pretty strong stomachs.

"The top still looks rock-like, but scorched," Anne said, recording a vid for her report. "The upper layer isn't stone but rather an encrusted series of wart-like growths. I'm not certain if they've all been generated by the host creature or if they're parasitic creatures. They might be part of a symbiotic relationship where the parasites both feed upon the host and provide it with a natural defense at the same time."

She went on like that for quite a while. Whatever the fish was, I was fairly certain I didn't want to eat one after she was done poking, prodding and measuring it.

Except for the big flowers and weird fish, we didn't encounter any more interesting life forms. We reported all our sightings and were ordered to stay on point at the lakeshore.

We grumbled, and as night fell over the world far above, the sunlight that had reflected down the shaft from the surface world slowly died. We'd been in a shady, humid valley before, but as it became darker the canyon transformed into a clammy hole in the ground—which was exactly what it had been all along in my opinion.

Anne was the only one that seemed fascinated by the place we were in. She dissected her alien fish with gusto. Finally, about four hours after we'd caught it, she sat back with a grunt of triumph.

"It'll work," she said. "We'll have to careful, but we can eat these things. Not the plants, though. Only the fish."

Adjunct Leeson came near, and I stood with the two of them near the mutilated fish.

"Um…" he said slowly. "What exactly do you mean, 'we'll have to be careful'?"

"Significant portions of the animal are poisonous. It's about the proteins. Truly alien life forms aren't based on the same proteins we're based upon. Organic poisons are essentially proteins—venoms, that kind of thing. This planet has a drastically different ecology, and the life here is based on different chemical building blocks. We'll have to be careful. The main chunk of meat in the central muscle mass—the part that works those small flippers underneath—that's edible. We'll have to drain the blood carefully, and strip out all the organs and the cartilage—but we can eat the tail. It'll probably taste good."

Harris came up to join the party. "Whoa now, look at that! I've gutted fish before, but you do it right, lady."

"Who wants to toast up some of this meat and try it?" Leeson asked.

No one met his eyes, except for Harris, who looked delighted. He'd been wanting to poison one of us since we'd arrived.

"What are you grinning about, Veteran?"

"I've got the perfect volunteer for you: Carlos Ortiz. He's an avid daredevil."

Adjunct Leeson looked around at the nearby group. His eyes were calculating, and they fell on each of us in turn. I began wishing I'd found somewhere better to be.

"Carlos is an ass," Leeson said, "but he caught the thing. Grant is a bio—I need her. And she did the job of tearing it up and testing the meat."

Carlos let out a sigh of relief. Harris' face fell in disappointment. Then Harris followed Leeson's gaze, which had now fallen upon me. Harris began grinning again.

"An excellent choice if I may say so myself, sir," he said.

Leeson frowned at Harris. "I need McGill and his heavy tube if those squids show up. Let's see if your gut is as tough as your mouth, Veteran."

Harris froze. "What, sir?"

"You heard me, eat some fish."

Carlos whooped and banged his gauntlets on his knees. He rushed forward and began preparing the rock-fish. Leeson walked away to check the perimeter of our encampment, which filled a crescent of bare land at the edge of the lake.

"I think I have a lemon packet somewhere in my rations," Carlos said excitedly. "Maybe a little butter, too. I'll fry this right up for you, Vet. I'm good at cooking fish."

"Get the hell away from that!" shouted Harris, kicking him away from the fish. "It's my funeral. Let a man die with dignity!"

Carlos shut up, but his eyes were shining while Harris carefully cooked up the fish and tasted tiny bits of it.

"What's it like, Vet?" I asked.

He looked at me, eyes squinting. "Not that bad, really. Kind of like crab but with less flavor. I don't know...I'd say it tastes like crayfish."

115

He ate the damned thing. I have to give him that. He didn't just have a taste, either. He ate his fill, consuming a big serving of the white meat.

"How long do I have?" he asked Bio Specialist Grant.

"Depends," she said. "But if you haven't started puking by morning, I think you're in the clear."

"All right then," he said, and settled down to sleep.

Most of us camped in squads around the lifter. We watched Harris that night. We couldn't help ourselves. Every time he burped or shifted in his sleep, we expected him to vomit blood or something.

But by morning, the only reaction anyone could detect was some reddish itchy spots on his skin.

"He's got some kind of plague!" Carlos shouted.

"Shut up," Harris growled. "Probably just a bug-bite."

"Let's hope not," said Grant. She examined him closely. "No punctures. No bites. I'd say it was the fish. You had a slight reaction but nothing that a little shot of antihistamine can't fix."

"We can't eat the fish if we're allergic to it," I said.

"We can do a better job preparing it. In this case, we just tore it up and washed it with sterile water. With a little more processing...I think this could be a completely safe food source."

"Rock-fish!" Carlos declared. "The new Legion Varus staple. I'm going to come up with some recipes."

"You didn't even taste the damned thing, you chicken," Harris told him. "Shut up."

Anne worked over Harris as we all watched and ate rations. Secretly, I think most of us were disappointed the veteran didn't at least have a stomach ache.

"I've had time to do more chemical work on the meat," she said later on. Her expression was grim. "I'm detecting about six hundred parts per million of domoic acid."

"And just what in the nine hells does that mean?" Harris asked.

Carlos nudged me excitedly. "He's gonna die!" he whispered.

I wasn't so happy about it. If the fish was poisonous, that meant we didn't have a viable food source yet, and we'd failed in one of our primary mission objectives.

"Domoic acid is a neurotoxin," Grant said. "It's not uncommon on Earth, but it is dangerous. Causes brain damage at high levels over time and kidney failure at levels a thousand times lower than this. We can process it out, but it won't be easy."

Harris' face was twisted up into an enraged expression. "What I want to know is how you're going to process it out of *me*!"

Grant shook her head. "Your kidneys are trying to flush it out—that's how they get damaged by the toxin. I can give you an injection to help, but it won't be quick. It'll take some time. Don't eat any more fish."

"Don't worry. I'm not eating any more of that damned fish."

"Hey Vet, don't sweat about it," Carlos said. "I'm sure a quick regrow in the revival machine will solve everything."

Harris glared at him. There had been times in the past when Harris had given us just such sage advice.

Carlos moved a little closer to Harris. The veteran stood up, glaring at everyone.

"You want me to help out?" Carlos asked quietly, fingering his rifle suggestively.

I'd been wondering up until that point why Harris hadn't responded to Carlos' jibes. It turned out that he'd been keeping quiet to lure his tormentor in.

Suddenly, Harris lashed out with long arms, grabbed Carlos and slammed his gauntlet into the open faceplate. Carlos spit blood and staggered away.

Adjunct Leeson walked over to see what was happening, and Harris nonchalantly reached over and slammed Carlos' faceplate shut.

Leeson eyed the slurry of blood running down Carlos' breastplate.

"Is there some kind of a problem, Veteran?"

"Nothing I can't handle, sir."

"How's that fish doing for you?"

"Just like mom's cooking back home—but, there are some toxins involved. The bio says they can process them out, but we can't eat the stuff straight out of the water."

"Pity," Leeson said, eyeing the lake.

The rock-fish were back, looking at us with their invisible optical organs. We'd figured out with further observation that they *did* have eyes, but they weren't like ours. They were more like exposed light-sensitive nerve centers: Clusters of bulbous cells that allowed them to sense light and motion but didn't really give their brains a solid image the way ours did.

As we watched, one of the fish yawned. They did that from time to time, opening the forward third of their bodies to reveal neat twin rows of brownish, triangular teeth.

"If you can't keep up," Leeson told Harris, "we'll have to send you back to the lifter for reprocessing. I can't have a poisoned veteran on my line."

"Not necessary, Adjunct. I'm feeling fine."

"Good. Keep it that way."

After a breakfast of rations, the canyon warmed up and became dank. The heat increased steadily until it was oppressive. Everyone's suit air-conditioners were running, eating battery power, but we couldn't do anything about that. We'd get heatstroke if we turned them off.

The days on this planet were long—about twenty-nine hours long. When we'd landed, the sun had been setting and the environment had been cooling down. We hadn't yet felt the full heat of mid-day.

"New orders, people!" Adjunct Leeson said after reporting in. "We're to circumnavigate the lake."

A prolonged chorus of groans and curses swept the group.

"What? Were you guys planning on putting your feet up? Sorry to disappoint. Let's move out. Gorman, you take point. The rest of you stay awake. This isn't going to be a nature walk. Keep your weapons primed for discharge."

We began trekking around the lake, pushing through the ever-thickening plant growths. As we went, we discovered groves of plants that weren't flowering types. They were big things that looked like pineapples the size of barrels. I wondered if they might be another possible foodstuff but didn't dare mention it to anyone. I didn't want to be the next lucky taste-tester.

Anne walked with me, and she paused to take samples of the pineapple things. The meat inside looked juicy but was greenish rather than yellow. She noticed me staring and waiting for her. She hurried up, stashed her sample and walked with me again.

"We don't want the adjunct to get any more ideas," she said to me.

"Yeah," I agreed. "He'd poison half the squad before he's done."

We marched around the lake until we reached the far side sometime in the afternoon. It felt like the longest day of the year to me already, and it wasn't even close to over.

On this side of the canyon the water was closer to the cliff-like walls. Broken stones and dunes of dust had accumulated here.

"What I don't get is why this entire hole in the ground never filled up with sand," I said to Anne.

"I'm not sure about that myself," she said, staring at the soaring cliffs. "I guess the cauldron must erupt occasionally."

I looked at her in alarm. "Erupt?"

"Yes, of course. You do realize that we're inside the throat of a volcano, don't you? Every once in a while it hiccups and then fills back up with water from underground aquifers."

"Hiccups? As in it blasts lava into the sky?"

"Right."

I thought about that and found I didn't like the implications. She was saying we were inside a dormant volcano. That explained the sinkhole-like lake. And I understood that the water on this world was underground for the most part. But knowing that I might be consumed in a gush of fire at any second didn't do anything for my nerves.

A few minutes later I got the surprise of my day. I spotted someone—someone who wasn't part of our squad.

There was no doubt she was human. She was mostly naked, too. She had scraps of leathery cloth wrapped around the most important parts, but that was it. She was young, I could tell that. Full grown, but probably a little younger than I was.

I didn't shout, because I was stunned. I saw her crouching on a rock near the wall of the canyon, watching us. There was something in her hands, something which she lifted and directed toward me. There was a snapping sound.

For a brief second, I thought she'd thrown a stick at me. Then the crossbow bolt struck my armor and the point rasped and clattered, bouncing off my breastplate. If I'd been a light-trooper, I might have been killed.

I shouted an alarm and signaled the rest of the squad, but when I turned back toward the girl to point her out, she'd vanished.

-13-

At first, I don't think anyone believed me. But they examined the projectile the girl had fired at me, and they had to admit that none of us had brought a weapon like that from Earth.

"This is a big deal," Adjunct Leeson kept saying, over and over again.

He ordered us to close our faceplates and circle up, with our eyes turned toward the jungle-like plant growth. We did so while he stood in the middle and reported the sighting to the Centurion and then to the Primus herself.

"They want to talk to you," Leeson said. "I'm patching you in. Don't screw me by saying anything stupid, McGill."

"Uh…no, sir."

A moment later I was on the line with Primus Turov. She sounded agitated.

"What kind of stunt is this, McGill?" she demanded. "How can you possibly have found the colonists and then lost them again?"

"The colonists?" I asked, taken by surprise. But as I thought about it, I realized she was probably right. The girl must have been a member of the lost colonists we'd come to rescue or to exterminate, as the case may be. I'd been expecting astronauts of some kind not primitives.

"The colonists attacked you, I'm certain of it. That officially classifies them as hostile."

"It all might have been a misunderstanding, Primus," I said. "I don't think—"

"You aren't paid to think, McGill," she interrupted. "No reported sightings have come in from other canyons. None of the other cohorts have made contact. I need your team to communicate with them more meaningfully."

"Well, I can confirm that they aren't much of a threat," I said. "They can't fight worth a damn against our equipment using crossbows."

"You aren't qualified to determine what constitutes a threat," she snapped. "The colonists are a *huge* problem, but it seems they aren't a widespread one at least. I'm giving your squad new orders, effective immediately. You're to find their base camp and befriend these colonists. Do you read me, Leeson?"

"Yes, sir!" Leeson said quickly. He was patched into the conversation but had been keeping quiet. "We'll find them."

"See that you do. Turov out."

I was kicked out of the chat line then without so much as an over-and-out. I described the conversation to Anne.

"They've clearly regressed over the years," she said of the colonists. "What I wouldn't give to do a full write-up on them. Possibly the regression started while their ship was still in flight to this system."

"I don't care about studying them," I said. "They're human, they're in trouble, and they're just as trapped here as we are. We need to offer them our protection, not march around scaring them to death in metal suits."

"Well, I wouldn't go near that girl bare-chested," Anne told me. "She'll put an arrow through your sternum without hesitating."

"They're probably just scared," I argued.

"Look," Anne said, her face worried. "I know how you must feel. That girl looked young and harmless—but she's probably more like a wild animal than an Earth-girl by now."

"What are you talking about? Why is everyone so down on our own colonists?"

"First of all, they could get our species erased. If they screw up, we might get blamed for it. The Galactics don't care about the details. Humanity is like a school of fish to them. We're all the same. They'll remove us if we irritate them."

I'd heard this kind of talk before, and I'd become pretty irritated with the Galactics myself over the years. But I knew enough about legion politics not to say things that were against established policy.

"I get that part," I said. "But we aren't even trying to treat them like lost friends or like people who need our help. What about your oath to heal? Doesn't that extend to them as well?"

Anne looked troubled by that. "I suppose it does."

"And I don't know why everyone thinks they're animals. Maybe we just like thinking that so we'll feel less guilty about pushing them around."

"It's more than that," she said. "I've read up on the history of the colony mission to Zeta Herculis as we flew out here. The people aboard the ship itself were separatists—folks their own governments didn't want around. They didn't like the new way of things. They resisted worldwide government, and many of them were 'volunteered' to colonize the stars for precisely that reason."

I hadn't known about that, but it made sense. Even before the Galactics had shown up and annexed Earth, we'd been crunching down into blocks of nations. Currencies had merged, as had political entities. Many nations were only partly in control of their own destinies. My grandparents had protested the changes and been put on government shit-lists for years afterward.

"I studied the likely social progress of the Hydra mission in school," Anne told me. "It was part of every psychologist's dream to interview these people again, but it was assumed the mission was lost. Just think about it, James! They took off in 2041, just eleven years before the Galactics arrived and delivered their ultimatum to Earth. That's more than eighty years ago!"

"Yeah, so you're saying that none of the original colonists are alive, right?"

"Right, only adults flew. Even accounting for relativistic effects, I doubt there's a single colonist who can recall standing on their homeworld."

I thought about that, and I could see what she was getting at. These people wouldn't be like us. They couldn't be. Cut off and flying in normal space without a warp drive system, they'd traveled at sub-light speeds all the way out here. The long journey and the many subsequent decades they'd spent on this dusty rock would change them drastically.

"But they're *still* human," I insisted.

"Genetically yes, but not culturally. They might be barbarians now. After today's encounter, that looks very likely. Humans, but feral humans. Wild humans. People like nothing we've ever had to deal with before. The last truly wild humans on Earth died out a century ago."

We'd reached the jumbled pile of rocks that had formed at the base of the cliffs. Dusty and hot, I didn't find it a pleasant spot in which to be. We looked around, and it wasn't until our point-man, Gorman, fell into a hole and vanished that we figured out what we were looking for.

"They're underground!" I shouted. "Look for caves, tunnels."

When we found Gorman, he wasn't moving. We dragged him back into the sunlight and opened his visor. His eyes were closed and there was blood trickling from his mouth.

"Retreat off these rocks!" roared Veteran Harris.

He dragged Gorman with help from two other troopers. Our armored gauntlets whined and protested, giving us the strength to carry the man. Heavy troopers typically weighed in at over five hundred kilos in their full kit.

Specialist Anne Grant was there the moment we had him off the rocks.

"It was some kind of trap," Carlos said. "That has to be what it was. He just fell in and disappeared. The ground ate him and killed him. But there wasn't an explosion—couldn't have been a mine. Weirdest damn thing I ever saw."

"Shut up, give him some air!" shouted Harris.

Gorman's face didn't even twitch as Anne opened up his breastplate and looked him over.

"There's a wound here, at the base of the neck. My tapper shows his suit was breached."

"How?" I asked.

"At the joints. Something chewed its way in. Look."

We all did, and we didn't like what we saw. A small hole was right there in the black polymer cusps that formed the joints in the armor. Our suits weren't made entirely of metal. They had smart-cloth components inside and hard polymer interlocking tubes at the joints.

"Something cut its way in," Harris said, fingering a hole in the black tubing.

"Yeah," Carlos agreed. "Then it ate its way into Gorman. Could it be some kind of acid?"

"No vapor," Anne said. "No chemical traces, either. I'm not a tech, but I'd say it was a nanite swarm of some kind."

We frowned at one another. Leeson walked up and put his hands on his hips.

"Is he dead?"

"No, sir. Not quite," Anne replied. "I might be able to save him, but there's something burrowing into his skull right now. I've got it on my internal vibra-scope."

She showed the officer her instruments. I winced just thinking about it. The man had a worm in him—a metal worm of smart microscopic robots.

Leeson shook his head. "We're not screwing around with that!" he said. "I'm declaring this man dead. Call it in, Grant."

"But sir, he's still—"

Leeson pulled out his sidearm and discharged it into Gorman's face. He kept the trigger down, causing wisps of steam and smoke to rise up. He made sure that the probe digging into Gorman's suit was destroyed.

Anne looked pissed off. I didn't blame her. It was always hard to watch our officers kill one of our own. I imagined that for a bio dedicated to healing it was doubly difficult to take.

"That was unnecessary and counterproductive, sir!" she said.

"Yeah, well," Leeson said, "write up all your complaints and put them in your report. I'm not taking any chances out here. We've encountered resistance with sophisticated weaponry. I'm going to call this incident in, and then I'm going to blow this entire region of rocks to dust. From space it will look like a new sandstorm before we're done."

125

Carlos gave a little happy whoop. A few others echoed it. No one wanted to chase these colonists into the rocks and be eaten by some kind of nano-worm.

Anne was examining something else now. I looked it over, and I realized it was the arrow that had struck my chest. She eyed the point critically.

"This is made of the same material," she said. "Nanites, programmed to eat their way through any flexible soft points in armor—or flesh. You're lucky it hit your breastplate so squarely, James. It appears the arrowhead didn't activate."

"So these primitive colonists aren't so primitive," I said.

"Definitely not."

I thought about the encounter and wondered if the girl had really been trying to kill me. Maybe she'd been trying to warn me off. It was hard to say what her intentions were. But either way, I didn't feel good about the idea of blowing up these people without giving them a chance to explain themselves.

"Excuse me, Adjunct," I heard myself say.

"What is it, McGill?"

"I'm sorry sir, but I must point out that the Primus ordered us to make contact with these colonists: To befriend them."

Leeson laughed. He pointed down at the mess that had once been Gorman. Already our troops were stripping armor off the corpse. Heavy armor was valuable, and Gorman would need his suit again after he was revived back at the lifter.

"Does this look like they're in a friendly mood, Specialist?" Leeson asked.

"No, sir," I admitted. "But we're clanking around their home territory in suits of armor carrying military weapons. Historically speaking, that's not the usual way you make peaceful contact with a native population."

"What do you suggest?"

"I hereby volunteer to approach their tunnels. I'll strip off my armor and my weapons. If they kill me—well, I guess you can revive me back at the lifter."

"Don't let him do it, Adjunct!" Harris said, coming up to us. His eyes were big and bloodshot. I wondered if last night's dinner was starting to get to him after all.

Leeson glanced at Harris, then looked back at me with narrowed eyes. "Are you some kind of kiss-up?" he demanded. "Or are you just insane?"

"He's a little of both," Harris said.

"Neither, sir," I said. "I'm simply following the Primus' orders. I suggest you do the same, sir."

Leeson grumbled but waved me on. He pulled the rest of the squad back to the lakeshore where they could watch the show in safety.

"Could you move out of sight, sir?" I asked him. "I think it would be better if you were hidden in the brush."

"Is this some kind of a crazy dodge?" Leeson shouted back. "Are you planning to go AWOL on this rock? If you are you won't last a day, McGill."

"Nothing like that, sir."

After a bit more grumbling, the squad withdrew. They left me to face the hot rocks alone. I pulled off my armor piece by piece while I eyed the quiet rocks.

I had some second thoughts at that point. I found myself standing in a smart-cloth jumper in front of what had to be a nest of hostile people. All I had in my hands was a strip of white cloth I planned on holding up as a makeshift flag of truce. So far, these colonists had shot me and sprung a sophisticated booby trap. They were bound to have more tricks up their sleeves—if they had sleeves. I wondered what they were afraid of and why hadn't yet attempted peaceful contact. After all, we were as human as they were. We were the same species. Surely they could see that.

I hadn't moved a millimeter in over thirty seconds. My thoughts were interrupted by Leeson, who shouted at me from the plant growth to my left.

"Damn it, McGill! Get on with it!"

I sighed and began to climb those stark boulders. I felt the heat radiating from them and burning my hands right through my gloves. It was times like these that made me wonder if there was something wrong with my brain.

I picked my way over the hot rocks, staying on the large flat surfaces as much as I could. I avoided open areas of ground

127

and loose gravel, assuming that's where the traps were. I climbed until I was within fifty meters of the cliff itself.

Suddenly, I made contact. It happened fast, and it happened with smooth coordination. Six of the colonists—or hunters, or whatever you want to call them—sprang up from hiding places all around me. I wasn't armed, so I slowly put up my hands and stood there.

"Do you guys speak English?" I asked hopefully.

They didn't say anything. Up until this point they'd barely made a sound. They'd come out of dark cracks under the biggest boulders, sliding out from under their rocks like scorpions coming out of burrows.

None of them spoke or smiled. Instead they were crouching and staring. Their crossbows were loaded with dark metal bolts, and I had no doubt that a hit from any of those weapons would chew through my flesh. I'd be dead in less than a minute from a minor wound.

I kept my hands raised, and I glanced over my shoulder toward the lakeshore. I wasn't really surprised to find I couldn't see my comrades from here. There were a few key boulders between this spot and their position.

"Your littermates can't help you now," said one of the group. "We have your twisted life, and we will end it."

I thought I recognized her. She had long hair and even longer, tanned legs. She was the one that had shot me the first time.

"We don't mean you any harm," I said.

"You will die no matter what you say."

The colonists were a motley bunch. They had skins tanned a deep brown, hair that was pulled back in knotted tangles and bows held tightly. I could see their corded muscles outstanding on every arm and neck. They were very tense.

I lowered my hands and shrugged. "Well then, get on with it. Why haven't you killed me yet?"

"Your masters have trained you well," the woman said. "This is a new tactic, and I don't understand it yet. We hesitate, waiting for your trick to play out. We must learn so we can warn others. Your kind has invaded many valleys at once this time, but your purpose is unclear. Whatever it is, you will not be successful."

I frowned, not knowing what the hell she was talking about. "You sound like you've seen our kind before. We're the first to come here. We're from Earth, just as your parents were."

This statement seemed to surprise the girl. She gave a bark of laughter. The others hooted and bared their teeth in amusement. I got the feeling they weren't dumb, but they'd definitely lost some social skills somewhere along the way out from Earth.

"So strange," she said. "You do seem to be unlike the others. How can you know of Earth? How can you know of our name for that place?"

"Kill it now, Della," said one of the men suddenly. He was a hunched fellow with white wispy hair circling his head like cotton. His eyes were wide and staring. He moved his feet constantly, shuffling on the stones. Instead of a bow, he had a cocked and loaded crossbow trained on my back. He never shifted his aim away from me. My skin crawled as if it knew it had never had so many deadly weapons aimed at it at once.

"I'm in command, Stott," Della said. "I say not yet."

"Be sure, be safe," said another, younger male. He was maybe fourteen, and there was no pity in his youthful eyes. I took it that he was agreeing with Stott.

"Be sure, be safe!" they all muttered, as if saying a prayer. Even Della seemed compelled to repeat the chorus.

I looked around the group. They flinched as my eyes fell upon them.

"What are you people so afraid of?" I demanded. "Ever since we got here, you've been hiding, and now you're taking shots at us. We haven't killed any of your folk. Why kill us? We have ships and weapons. Don't give my commanders cause to harm you. We could wipe you out if we wanted to."

"It threatens us!" shouted Stott. He lifted his crossbow higher, sighting along the stock as if I was a kilometer away. "Della, we must kill it now before it learns more from us. Clearly, it is a spy."

"I'm not an 'it'," I said. I'm James McGill, a weaponeer from Legion Varus. I'm a soldier from Earth. If you'll let me, I'll help you."

"Now you sound like one from the litters," Della said. "Except you should not have a name. That's unnatural. Can it be that the cephalopods are trying to create beings that mirror our ways? You're so thin and small of stature. I don't understand you—how can you be the way you are?"

I shook my head. "I don't understand you, either. But you said something about cephalopods. That's a squid, right? Are you talking about the aliens? The walking squids?"

That was the wrong thing to say. They hissed and squirmed around me, clearly not liking any reference to space-squids.

"You see!" Stott shouted. "He's one of them! Don't be fooled! He's allied with them."

I was really starting to dislike Stott, but I decided it was best to ignore his outbursts and focus on Della, who appeared to be in charge.

"The squids attacked us," I said. "They attacked our ship as we came here from Earth. They damaged our ship, but we were able to escape on lifters—the smaller ships that came here to land. We landed in your valleys because they were the only places where we could survive. We didn't even know you were here. You were supposed to colonize the water-world."

"How can you listen to his twisting lies?" demanded Stott. "They've improved their techniques, that's all. He'll want you to mate with him. That's next. He'll turn you into a brood-mother, see if he won't!"

Della's dark, intelligent eyes swung to Stott, then back to me. "How did they teach you all this? Could you once have been a captive child? If so, you must have been raised since you were a pup, making it all the more odd. Small children don't have the ability to discuss space. The cephalopods themselves must have taught you this story."

At least Della seemed intrigued with me. She narrowed her eyes and stared at me as if I was some kind of deep puzzle. The idea that I was really from Earth didn't seem to be sinking in at all.

On a hunch, I reached into one of my pockets. They all tensed around me.

"Easy," I said. "I'm unarmed. I only want to show you something."

I drew out a knife. It was the one my dad had given me before I left home. I held it out toward Della.

"Take it," I said. "It's from Earth. Can you read?"

She snorted at me. "Of course I can read."

"See the inscription? It says made in the North America Sector. That's real, old-fashioned Pittsburgh steel."

She frowned at the knife and then at me. "You can't have this thing. No captive child would be given such a treasure from the old world. No littermate could have it, either."

"It's from Earth," I said. "My dad gave it to me."

I could see in her eyes that she was baffled but that she was starting to believe. I smiled at her.

That was a mistake. Stott, who'd been watching the interchange very closely, chose that moment to fire his crossbow. The bolt tore through my back and lodged itself in my ribs. I looked down, stunned. The head of the bolt was wet, dark metal. I could see a chunk of bone there as well.

I sank to my knees. There was a sick explosion inside my body, a cold feeling. Not pain yet—not exactly. It felt as if I had a new bone protruding outward from inside my chest.

The nanite head of the bolt activated then. It must have sensed the nearness of flesh, bone and blood. It crawled into my skin. I put my hand over it, trying to tug it out, but it was wedged in pretty well. I felt the head of the bolt bite my hand, and I tried to pull away but couldn't. I howled. My hand had been fused to the wound in my chest.

It was worse, I thought, to know what was happening. I envied dumb animals, creatures that just thrashed without thought, not understanding they were doomed.

The nanites invaded the palm of my hand and the arteries in my chest, digging into my body. I could feel them tickling and rasping in my bloodstream as my dying heart pumped them throughout my network of veins like hot poison.

I rolled onto my back, gasping.

"You were not to slay him," Della shouted at Stott. "You disobeyed."

"He was controlling your mind," Stott protested. "I saved you, Della. Didn't you see him smile? All of you! Speak truly! You saw it, didn't you? His smile was pure evil."

I used the hand that wasn't stuck to my chest to reach up to Della. I beckoned her closer.

"He'll strike like a water-slip!" Stott warned her. "Don't go near!"

She'd finally had enough of Stott, as had I. She kicked him in the face. I was impressed by the maneuver. She was quite limber, moving with the grace of someone who lives in the wild. Stott spun away, growling and spitting blood.

Della bent close to me. "What dying words do you have for me?"

I didn't smile. I'd learned my lesson there. Instead, I coughed some blood then spoke as clearly as I was able.

"When I come back here," I rasped. "I'll want my knife back."

I was rewarded with a confused, worried look from Della. I'd managed to freak her out a little. I thought to myself that she was quite pretty, in an unsophisticated way. As feral humans went, she was the best-looking one I'd met up with so far.

Then I lost interest in my new friends. Some trick of my nervous system decided to let me feel the full agony of the bolt in my back at this moment. I twisted and cried out, but that only made the pain worse.

Della leaned close and thrust her knife up into my skull. I'd been holding out a faint hope I might survive until that moment when all hope was lost.

In my final moments, I tried to absolve Della of the murder. I was sure she'd stuck me with her knife without malice believing it to be an act of mercy.

I heard the breath go out of my lungs in an elongated sigh. Then I died on that hot, flat rock in a sticky pool of blood and nanites.

-14-

The first thought that intruded upon the peace of my nonexistence was one of irritation. That Stott fellow had been a true bastard. He'd been jealous; angry to see Della talking to a rival male. Maybe she'd spurned him and he'd been a bloodthirsty prick ever since. I wasn't sure how I knew this, but I *felt* that it was true. The thought was clear in my mind as I came back to life. It was as if I'd been working on it during a long turbulent dream from which I was only now awakening.

I was naked, but I wasn't cold. In fact, I was too warm. Sweat rolled off my new skin pooling up on the steel tongue that I rested upon. My lungs spasmed, and I coughed wetly. Thick, choking liquids spouted, and I almost rolled onto the deck of the lifter's revival chamber.

I found I was restrained and couldn't fall. Hanging by straps, I spit on the floor.

"That's not normal. Give me some numbers."

"Ten-by-ten."

"Can't be."

"That's what it says, Specialist. Check it yourself."

There was motion around me, but I didn't feel like opening my eyes. I was prodded and needles were shoved into my arms only to be quickly withdrawn.

"His test numbers are good," said the bio specialist who was working on me. "My bad. He's an acceptable grow. Turn off the recycler."

I heard a whirring sound that was dying slowly, like that of a power saw when the switch was flipped off. I frowned and opened my eyes, glancing toward the sound. I didn't see a saw blade, but I did see a stained maw nearby. It looked like a chute of some kind, one that angled away from the revival machine itself.

The revival machine was behind me. Its mouth was warm and womb-like. Could that chute to one side of the chamber be where they sent the bad grows? To be *recycled*?

Had I ever been shoved into such a chute? Had a version of me with a very short lifespan been recycled and forgotten?

I made a growling sound and tried to rise again.

"Let me up," I said. "I've got to go get my knife."

This seemed to amuse the staff. "Did you lose it in the spine of one of the primitives?"

"No—and they're not primitives. They're just scared."

"Scared of what?"

"Cephalopods from space. They come here and attack them. I've got to report to my centurion. Get me into my uniform."

Their attitudes changed when I said this. They freed me from the steel tongue then helped me get my rubbery limbs into a smart-cloth suit. I was out the door and staggering two minutes later.

It was strange to be born again—to be back on the lifter, almost like I hadn't just been killed. I walked among groups of bored troops who sat in their jump seats. Some were trying to sleep while others played games on their tappers or ate sandwiches.

Those I passed by weren't green soldiers. They'd all seen a man fresh from a revive. They made room for me and let me pass. Some had pity in their eyes, but none of them said anything. They'd all been in my shoes before.

After passing two guardsmen without acknowledging their presence, I reached for the shaft that led up to the upper deck, where the officers held court.

A thick-fingered hand reached out and clasped my arm. I swayed and almost punched the guy, but I controlled myself.

"I have to talk to my centurion," I told them.

They eyed my insignia. "Graves is out of the ship. He's heading for the rebel camp."

"I have to talk to the primus, then."

The guard laughed. "You already died once today, McGill. Haven't you had enough?"

"No."

They shrugged and let me go. I could tell they were amused. "Your funeral, buddy."

I struggled to get myself up to the second floor. I wasn't one hundred percent yet. Normally, it took an hour or two after a revive for a man to feel like himself again.

When I finally found Primus Turov, she gave me a quick up-down look with sour eyes.

"What do you want, Specialist?" she asked.

"I've made contact with the colonists, sir," I said. "They aren't the enemy."

"I'll be the judge of that. You're not the only man they killed today—did you know that your unit mounted a rescue effort?"

I shook my head. I felt my heart sinking. This wasn't going to be easy.

"We lost six," she said sternly. "Only one of the enemy was taken down. It's embarrassing. I should demote Leeson when this is over."

Part of me hoped the dead one was Stott, and at the same time I worried that it might be Della. I took in a deep breath and tried to focus. This was important.

"Sir, I talked to them—"

"Indeed," she said, "I heard the details. It appears you managed to sweet talk them into killing you. Were you aware that your comrades could hear your screams all the way down to the water's edge?"

"I was following your orders, sir," I said. "Can I please make my report?"

She eyed me, then nodded.

I recounted the strange conversation I'd had with the feral colonists. She listened and frowned throughout. By the end, her expression became thoughtful.

"Do you believe them?"

135

"Yes. They've met up with the cephalopods, I'm sure of that. From the sound of it, they've had frequent violent encounters with them. That's why they live underground and employ traps and weapons designed to combat high-tech equipment. These nanite-tipped weapons would eat right through a squid's suit."

"All right," she said, "let's assume everything you told me is factual. What do you want me to do about it?"

"Call off the attack. Leave them alone and prepare to meet the real enemy instead. Who knows, maybe they can help us beat the squids when the time comes."

"It doesn't make sense," Turov said, pacing around the small confines of her office.

I eyed her as she walked away from me. I couldn't help it. I oftentimes figured that when I died for the last time, I'd do so while staring at a nurse's butt.

"What doesn't make sense, sir?"

"Why would the squids come *here*?"

"To kill humans?"

"Maybe. But if that was their goal, all they would have to do is drop a nuke in each of these little valleys. They have the tech, I'm sure of it. No spacefaring race could have missed the relatively simple feat of building a fusion bomb."

"I don't know," I said. "Maybe there's a resource here they need. Maybe they come to mine it and leave."

She snorted and shook her head. "Not worth it. Hostile locals, a thick atmosphere and significant gravity…no, any element they could get here they could get somewhere else in the system more easily. Even fissionables."

"Uh," I said, not sure why this mattered so much, but deciding to play along. "Maybe they want oil. This planet has life…maybe fossil fuels?"

She scoffed again. "Are you serious? Crossing a solar system for oil? You're not as bright as I thought, McGill."

I wasn't quite sure how to take this statement. It was an insult, but it also indicated that she thought I was *somewhat* bright, making it a compliment of sorts at the same time.

Irritated, I tried to come up with another reason. "Maybe they like to hunt," I said. "I've fought with them up-close and personal. I know these beasts don't eat seaweed. They're predators, I'd bet my last credit on it."

She stopped and narrowed her eyes at me, nodding. "Good thinking," she said. "That's possible. A hunter doesn't want to wipe out all the game. And a hunter will go far for unique kills or trophies. Could work."

"Uh, Primus?"

"What is it?"

"Why does all this matter so much?" I asked.

She looked at me for a moment, as if deciding something. "Because the techs aboard *Corvus* discovered something."

"They managed to regain control of the ship?"

"Partially. They managed to engage some of the sensor systems, but the propulsion and navigation units eluded them."

I frowned. "So is *Corvus* lost or not?"

"Yes, but it was a close thing. A valiant effort by the techs. The ship skimmed the corona of Zeta Herculis and cooked the last survivors. What matters is that they spotted something interesting. A single, large ship lifted off from the water world yesterday. I'm thinking there's only one reason for the cephalopods to launch a ship right now."

My eyes widened. "You think they're coming here?"

She laughed. "You just spent ten minutes convincing me of the fact! Damn, McGill, shake it off. Get your brain in the game. This isn't your first revive, soldier!"

"Sorry, sir."

"I'll call off the attack on your vicious, burrowing colonists for now. But if they give us too much trouble, or there's any hint Earth will be blamed for their misbehavior, I'll have to eliminate them. You understand that, don't you Specialist?"

"I guess so, sir," I said. "May I get back to my unit now?"

I moved toward the exit but hesitated when I thought of Natasha. She'd had been aboard *Corvus*, one of the many techs left there to attempt the repair work. I had been wondering if she was still okay or drifting out in space somewhere.

"Primus? If *Corvus* was burned, how did you get your report from the techs?"

"We revived them here, of course. Once we knew there was too much radiation aboard for anyone to survive, we approved the action."

"Right. But their minds…the backups would have to have been stored aboard the ship itself, which was lost. How can they remember what happened?"

She stared at me for a moment.

"You're a thinker, aren't you?" she said. "Don't ask the techs about that sort of thing. They'll get pissed off just the way the bio people do. They have alien equipment of their own that isn't widely talked about. Let's just say that the transfer from *Corvus* to our lifters occurred, despite less than optimal conditions aboard the ship itself."

Less than optimal conditions… That was a nice way to describe being bombarded by a million rads of gamma rays. No computer could function. No radio I knew of could transmit under those circumstances. Even if it could, a radio transmission would have taken hours to reach this world from the star.

I left her office wondering about Legion Varus' tech. We seemed to have gizmos no one else did. Another thought followed upon that last one: was all of it purchased with Galactic credits? Or were we stealing bits of know-how now and then and using it on the sly? That might explain the secrecy.

I filed these thoughts away in my mind and hoped that the revival systems would store them for me forever no matter where I was in time and space.

* * *

Since the attack on the colonist hideout had been called off and my unit was out on patrol, I spent the next hour looking for Natasha. There had been plenty of time for her revival, and she was part of the same unit as I was. I figured she was somewhere outside the lifter by now.

I felt bad for her. She'd been left aboard *Corvus,* working desperately to repair the Skrull ship. The techs had made a

138

valiant effort, but they'd failed and died in the end. I've died in some pretty bad ways, but I've never yet been cooked by radiation. That didn't sound like one of the best on the list to me.

It took me a while, but I finally located Natasha with my tapper and headed toward her coordinates without alerting her to my approach with a call or a text. Feeling sympathetic, I plucked a big-ass alien orchid the size of a basketball on the way and surprised her with it.

"Thanks," she said, taking the massive purple blossom from me and looking it over. It was waxy and thick, weighing about half a kilogram.

Natasha sat on a rock that was covered with a dry, blue moss. Most of the rocks close to the lake had similar patches of growth on them. We'd been worried about the strange-looking moss at first, but our bio teams had assured everyone it was non-toxic.

She wasn't totally living in the present yet, I could tell right off. Her hair was still matted by the slime of a fresh revival. Mine was too, of course. It hadn't been a good day for either of us. We were both wearing light uniforms and long faces.

"Don't sniff it," I advised her as she toyed with the flower. "They look good, but they smell like a gym sock."

Natasha eyed the flower contemplatively. Her eyes were slightly glazed as if she was in a thoughtful, distant mood. She was calm, but I could tell her mind was numbly pondering the horrors of her last minutes aboard *Corvus*. I'd seen that haunted look before.

"Do you want to talk about it?" I asked gently.

She looked at me as if seeing me for the first time.

"You died too, didn't you?" she asked. "About the same time I did. That means we're both fresh constructs of flesh. We've never truly met before, James. Have you ever thought of that? We *remember* having met, having made love, but those were different bodies that have long since decomposed."

I grimaced. She was going through a bad one, I could tell right away. Harris always said that the best thing for a revived soldier was to go right back into combat. That way, they didn't have time to think about what had just happened to them.

I reached out and touched her.

"There," I said. "Now we've touched. Now we're real."

She rewarded me with a wan smile. "Is that all there is to it?"

"I could arrange more…when I'm off-duty."

Her smile swelled and transformed into a quiet laugh. I smiled back, feeling relieved. I didn't want her to freak out on me. Occasionally, troopers had to be sedated or even restrained after they were revived.

I sat beside her, and she went back to eying the alien orchid I'd given her.

"It went badly in the end, James," she said suddenly, quietly. "They let us fry up there. We knew we couldn't save the ship after a few hours. It was obvious. But central didn't even try to let us escape. We were ordered not to take any of the lifeboats or the emergency pods. But a few of us tried anyway when we reached the corona. Do you know what we found?"

I opened my mouth, closed it again, then shook my head.

"They'd launched them all before you fled in the lifters. There was never a way for us to survive. We were left there to fix the *Corvus* or to die trying."

"Are you sure you should be talking about—"

"Don't worry about your suit recorders. I'm wearing a jammer I built myself. Most of the techs have them. They're against regs but it's so easy to build one, and even the tech officers look the other way. I guess it's a perk of being in charge of technology—we get to turn it off when we want to."

I thought about that, and it made sense. The computer people back home on Earth had always lived apart from the rest of us. They were the watchers, and we were the watched. Only they could avoid that fate.

I sidled close to her and put an arm behind her. Not anything intrusive. I just wanted her to feel supported. She leaned back against my shoulder without thinking about it.

"Okay, tell me the rest," I said. "What really happened up there?"

In truth, I didn't want to hear her story at all. I was already pretty sure I would be pissed off and disgusted by the end of it. But I knew she wanted to tell me, so I let her.

"We freaked out a little," she said. "Discipline broke down. We're techs, you know? Like the bio people, we don't always have to play by the same rules as everyone else does."

Pretending to know what she was talking about, I nodded my head.

"We switched off the neural transmitters first. That way when they were revived, they wouldn't remember the final hour."

I frowned. "Who is 'they'—who are you talking about?"

She shook her head. "Doesn't matter. I'm talking about the last of us. The techs who didn't want to fry. The ones who were the most upset about being consigned to death."

"Okay…" I said slowly. "What did you do then, when your minds were no longer being transcribed?"

"I don't remember what happened, only what we planned up until that point in time. My mind wasn't stored after that either. But I know there was a group of techs that weren't going to break ranks. They were all smug and self-sacrificing. They thought it was their duty to die horribly if that's what the Primus wanted. Others thought differently when the final moments came. We didn't think it was fair, and—well, I guess we lost our minds a little. Part of that might have been due to the growing radiation, heat and fear."

The picture-perfect listener, I didn't move a muscle or a make a sound. Internally however, my guts were crawling. I hated imagining what it would be like to be trapped in what amounted to a giant microwave oven.

"We had a plan to stay alive. It wasn't in the script, but we thought it might work. By separating the modules of the ship, we could give each part of the ship a jolt of lateral thrust, just enough to send one part of the ship away from the star. There would be radiation and heat, but we *might* have survived."

"Sounds like a plan. Why didn't the others go for it?"

"Because central command had already set the plan. We were to be copied as soon as *Corvus* burned up. If some of us got off the ship inside the corona, we wouldn't be able to report back whether we'd lived or died. It might have taken a long time to get the word back to the lifters that they'd made a mistake—that the bio people on Dust World had made copies too early."

She looked at me then, and I began to figure out what she was talking about. There would be *two* Natashas if that scenario had played out. One out there in space, clinging to life, the other coming out of the revival machines here on this dusty rock.

"That would have been a violation of Galactic Law," I said.

"Yeah," she said. "It would have been. But we were going mad. You know what I mean. Sometimes, the urge to live is too strong in a person. Even if they know intellectually that they'll come back in a new body, it's hard to give up on the old one."

She was right. I knew that feeling well.

"So," I said, "how did it play out? I mean, obviously you failed and were revived here."

She looked at me strangely. She gave me a tiny shake of her head.

I froze. "You don't mean…"

"I don't *know*," she said. "I don't remember all of it, but that's because the neural transmitters were switched off. I do remember the plan: we were going to kill those who demanded to die on the ship. The plan was to reprogram their own buzzers remotely—to kill their masters. I mean, they wanted to die anyway, we thought we'd help them along a little. Then we would try to escape the corona. That's all I know, because my memories stopped in the planning stages of the mutiny."

My mouth hung open and I stared at her. I lowered my voice to a whisper even though I knew it wouldn't help if my suit was somehow recording my conversation despite her jammer.

"Are you saying there might be *two of you*?" I asked. "One here, in my arms, and the other one out there—lost in space and still alive?"

She nodded and turned her attention back to the orchid I'd given her. She plucked a petal from it and peeled it back. Thick greenish sap ran like syrup from the stem.

142

"What will they do if they figure it out?" I asked. "I mean, which one of you is the valid, bona fide, genuine, Tech Specialist Natasha Elkin?"

"You mean, which one will they execute? Probably that poor, desperate, murdering bitch who disobeyed orders and did her utmost to survive."

I heaved a big sigh and hugged her.

"Stop worrying," I said. "I can understand why you'd be upset, but it's all for nothing. There's only one Natasha, and I'm hugging her right now. You couldn't have survived. No one could have."

She looked at me gratefully. "You really think so?"

I nodded my head firmly. "Absolutely. I saw diagrams of your flight path. There's no way out of a gravity well that big when you are so close to a star. You had a bad death, that's all. Just let it go. Would it be better if you'd been permed?"

"I guess not," she said, giving herself a little shake.

She hugged me back and one thing led to another. We'd only made love a few times before, but this time, there among the alien orchids on the mossy lakeshore, she had a new fire in her.

The sex was good—but I was a little freaked out. Could there be another Natasha out there, still alive and screaming in space? I had no idea. I'd lied to her about seeing diagrams and flight paths. That was pure, grade-A, Georgia bullshit. And I didn't know anything more about surviving in the corona of a star than I did about the rock-fish in the lake nearby—I probably understood the fish better.

Sometimes, it's better not to know all the details when bad things happen. Was Natasha a murderer? Or had she chickened in the end? I prayed she'd never find out what had actually happened up there aboard the *Corvus* in those final, desperate hours.

Keeping my thoughts to myself, I loved her, held her afterward, and I got her through the malaise that sometimes lingers in a soldier after a bad death.

-15-

I woke up with Harris' boot crashing into my side. I swear that man must creep up on sleeping troopers just to indulge himself in this kind of sport.

Scrambling awake, I automatically reached for my hand-beamer, but Harris' foot was already planted on it. Then I recognized him, and cursed aloud.

He chuckled at me in return. Then he looked over Natasha's kit, which was lying nearby.

"A jammer, huh?" he said.

She snatched her clothing and her ruck away from him and pulled her uniform on. She threw her shirt over her bare back like a shawl. The smart-cloth flaps found each other and knitted themselves together to cover her skin.

Both Harris and I watched this happen while she glowered back at us. Modesty was a funny thing in Legion Varus. You might take a shower with a girl, all the while chatting her up and enjoying the view, and no one thought anything of it. But if she'd been caught doing something she wasn't supposed to— like screwing in the bushes on an alien planet—she got all prudish on you for some reason.

"You could have said something to warn us," she complained.

"And spoil the fun?" Harris asked, chuckling. "Two sleeping love-birds in a nest of mossy rocks—I'm a sucker for that kind of cuteness. I took a few pics, hope you don't mind."

Natasha gathered her kit and left in a huff, disappearing into the thick fleshy leaves that surrounded us. Despite her angry exit, I felt good about her behavior. She seemed to be back to normal. At least she wasn't wondering about her hypothetical twin, who might or might not be cooking out in space somewhere at this very moment.

"Get rid of that jammer, Specialist!" Harris called after her. "You know it took me more than half an hour to find you two? This isn't the Garden of Eden, this is a damned war zone."

She shouted something back, but I didn't catch it. Harris reached down and hauled me to my feet. I wanted to push him into the lake but restrained myself. His sense of humor didn't extend that far.

"Sorry Vet," I said. "Won't happen again."

"Bullshit. I know your kind, McGill. You latch onto every piece of tail that comes into range. Now, get your ass back to the lifter. We're gathering up the unit and marching on the colonist stronghold tonight."

We began the trek back to the lifter. As we walked, I began getting worried.

"You said something about a war zone," I said. "No one's attacked the colonists yet, have they? No reprisals, no diplomatic incidents?"

I looked at him meaningfully as I knew he was perfectly capable of causing a diplomatic incident if he was in the mood.

"Nope. That's your job, McGill."

"What are you talking about?"

"You made contact the first time, remember?" he said, grinning at me. "The Primus nominated you for round two. We're sending you in to negotiate surrender conditions with the colonists."

"What happens if I can't do that?"

Harris' grin grew a fraction wider. "Then it's boom-time for our little arrow-shooting friends. No more mantraps or picking off patrols. They're a menace, and they've got to learn who's in command on this rock. The Centurion will tell you all about it."

When we got back to base camp around the lifter, I met up with Centurion Graves. He waved me close and walked away from the rest of the troops who'd built up a firebase with a perimeter of low puff-crete walls. We didn't have a lot of extra material for a really big wall—those supplies had been lost with *Corvus*.

"McGill, you're just the man I want to talk to. Where the hell have you been?"

I glanced back at Harris who made kissing faces at both of us.

"Ah," said Graves. "I get it. Pretty ballsy of you to pull a stunt like that right after a revive. You feeling up for a new mission?"

"Would it matter if I wasn't?"

"Not in the least."

"I'm operating at one hundred and ten percent, sir."

"Good," he said. "Let's go over the game plan."

As he spoke, he walked me out of ear shot of the rest of the unit. Harris lost interest and went to harass Carlos, who was trying to catch more rock-fish with a nanite string on his finger. He'd gotten one of the techs to make a wriggling lure which he'd attached to the end and now was reeling them in every few minutes.

"What's my mission, sir?" I asked Graves.

"You're going to penetrate their defenses, as you did before. They speak English, right?"

"They do, sir. But with an odd accent."

"Good. You're to deliver the ultimatum and return to our unit which will be in hiding about a kilometer from that shitty rock pile they like to hide under."

"What's the nature of this ultimatum, sir?"

"Simple enough. They must march out of hiding and surrender their weapons by dumping them on the beach, then walk to our lines with their hands on their heads. After that—"

"Sir," I said, interrupting. "I've talked to these people. I think it's highly unlikely they will—"

"I'm not going to candy this one up," he said, cutting off my protest. "The orders are unreasonable. In fact, I think they're damn near impossible to execute."

I stared at him, trying to recall an occasion when he'd candied up anything. My mind drew a blank.

146

"But you're a smart boy," he continued. "You've already figured out that you're *supposed* to fail. If you want, you can walk up there, hide in the boulders for half an hour or so, then run back to our lines. I wouldn't blame you. The results will most likely be the same either way."

I straightened my spine. "No sir, I'll deliver the message. But I have to point out that these people are civilians. They're human civvies, and we should be protecting them, not threatening and killing them."

"They seem human enough, I'll give you that one. But they aren't officially citizens of Earth—they're *wild* humans. Out of control and unaware they live in the shadow of the Empire. Look, you have to understand what's at stake, and you have to try to explain it to them if you want to save them."

"I've heard that line of reasoning before. Why do we have to mess with them at all? Let's just leave them alone. When a rescue ship comes, we'll leave and forget about them."

"It won't work that way, soldier," said a voice in the growing darkness.

Graves and I turned to see a man wearing a cloak walk up to us. He didn't wear full battle armor as I did, but he did have on a breastplate and an ornate sidearm.

"Tribune!" Graves said. "You honor us with your presence."

"Take a walk, Centurion."

Without another word, Graves turned on his heel and headed back toward the shimmering lake and the scattered campfires. Men were toasting up rock-fish and dousing the meat with alkaline solutions to leech out the toxins.

"We can't just leave them alone, McGill," Tribune Drusus told me. "The Empire will blame us for whatever these people do once they've been discovered—and they will be discovered when the Galactics come to pick us up. We had to report the attack upon our vessel to regional command. When the Galactics return, they'll come in force."

"The Battle Fleet?" I asked in awe.

Drusus nodded. "Perhaps not right away, but a violation of this magnitude can't be ignored. They'll have to come and expunge all disobedient life from these worlds. The

147

cephalopods are as good as dead even if they don't know it. Knowing what's coming, our mission has changed. Instead of worrying about putting down a possible rival, I'm here to ensure that Earth isn't going to be somehow blamed for what's happened here."

"I understand that, sir. Maybe if we took our time and talked to the colonists gently, we could win their trust over a period of—"

"Hours," Drusus finished for me. "That's how long we have. The Galactics have military-grade warp drives. They might be far from here, but we can't take that chance. Really, we should pulverize these warrens with an immediate bombardment, but I've decided to give them one last chance."

"Hours? But the Galactics aren't likely to come that fast. They'll probably take months to arrive."

"Yes, but then again, they might not. It is imperative that we have this situation resolved before they arrive."

"You're willing to kill an entire population of your own people just because the Battle Fleet *might* be nearby? May I remind you, sir, that these people don't have revival machines? Every one of them we kill will be permed."

"I know that. But I also know the Galactics are as heartless as the stars themselves. The threat they represent forces my hand. I have to protect the Legion and I have to protect Earth."

"Can I ask one more question, Tribune? Why me?"

"Because you at least managed to talk to them for a while before they became violent. I think it was the adaptation of removing your armor that saved you. Can you explain that choice to me?"

I thought about it. "Yes sir. I didn't want to look threatening, so I stripped down to look more like one of them. They seem to fear armored men. They said something about me having 'littermates', and they doubted I was even human at first. I didn't know what to make of it."

"Strange. Maybe they've developed superstitious beliefs. They've been cut off from Earth for quite a while, and they've obviously diverged from the rest of us culturally."

"Am I to understand that I'm the last attempt we're making at diplomatic contact?"

"Yes."

I mulled that one over for a second. I didn't like the situation at all. I'd never considered myself to be good at diplomacy—except possibly when it came to getting myself laid. Other than that, I'd always failed miserably at negotiating anything. Most people found me abrasive and difficult to deal with. Maybe that was the real reason they were sending me—I was expected to fail.

I didn't see any way out of my situation. The colonists were slated for death, and I had to do what I could to help them. The poor bastards probably had no idea what an Earth legion could do to them.

"I understand, sir," I said at last. "I'll do my best."

"I know that you will."

The tribune left then, vanishing into the dark. Most soldiers wore identifying lights around the camp at night and used lamps to see, but not Drusus. He walked like a ghost among the rest of us.

An hour later I found myself picking my way through loose gravel toward the hulking boulders in the dark. I shed my armor and left my cannon at the base of the first big rock I came to. I then went on with only a shoulder-lamp and my sidearm. Going completely unarmed would probably have been best, but I couldn't bring myself to do that. I'd already decided that if that rat-faced guy Stott showed up with his crossbow I was going to kill him if at all possible, diplomacy be damned.

For a while, I felt like I was grunting and climbing among the boulders alone. But I knew that this time there were buzzers nearby. There were insects on Dust World—plenty of them— but our buzzers sounded different from the native species. Their black polymer wings made a tiny clicking noise that I found distinctive.

The legion techs were watching me. Natasha herself was probably playing the vid feed inside her helmet.

Feeling a little self-conscious, I came to the area where Gorman had bought the proverbial farm. I stepped carefully from there on, staying on top of the widest, flattest rocks and avoiding loose dirt.

I heard another kind of click about a hundred meters farther in. It was a sound that made my skin crawl. It was the sound of a crossbow string being drawn back and loaded with deadly bolt.

Halting, I put my hands over my head.

"I'm here to talk," I said loudly.

"You people don't learn, do you?" asked a female voice.

"Della?"

She stayed quiet for a second, then I heard a soft thudding of feet as she circled around me. She was almost invisible in the rocks. I tried not to flinch, and I almost managed it as she brought the tip of her weapon under my chin.

She reached out and turned my shoulder lamp upward to shine upon my face. She gasped.

"You *are* a littermate!" she exclaimed. "I didn't believe they could do this! I didn't *want* to believe!"

"Hold on," I said, sensing that she was about to shoot me. "Can you at least tell me what a littermate is? I don't have a clue."

"Pretense of ignorance will fool no one. I've patrolled these stones since I was little. I know them better than anyone alive. You can't fool a scout. I'm surprised you would even try."

I sensed she was proud of her accomplishments and her title. I filed that information away, trying to think fast. I had no desire to be revived twice in a single day. It would make Harris far too happy.

"Look," I said. "I'm no littermate—if you mean I'm some kind of clone. If I was a clone, how would I know your name? You killed me last time, remember? How would I know that?"

She circled and I sensed indecision. "You made a mistake coming back here, whatever you are. Abominations will always die in Happy Valley."

"Happy Valley?"

"That's our name for this place—as if it matters to you."

"Look, Della, I just came back for one thing. Give it to me, and I'll go."

She didn't speak for a moment. "What is it you want?"

"My knife," I said. "Remember? My dad gave it to me. I told you I'd come back for it."

-16-

I stood with my hands on my head. I wasn't even looking at the girl that stepped around me like a bobcat circling a rabbit hole. I didn't dare.

"You can't have your knife," she said. "It isn't possible that such a valuable thing is yours. You've stolen it. Taken it from our ship, perhaps."

"Your ship? Where is it?"

She moved, and the tip of her crossbow bolt came up to touch my neck. I pulled away fractionally, but she pressed it closer. I knew the tip of the bolt was made of nanites that twisted and churned in a locked pose, wanting to break their formation as a sharp point and transform into a swarm that would dig through my flesh.

"I'm no child," she said. "You will get no information from me. Not even if you were the one with the bolt at my throat."

"I'm not here to spy on you," I said trying to sound as nonchalant as I could.

"Then why do you come here?" she asked a moment later, almost sounding exasperated. "Why do you torment me at my patrol spot? Why not attack or ignore us? Always before, your kind has done exactly the same thing. You march from your ships, you line up, and you hunt for game. Nothing else. Why talk now?"

I glanced at her not knowing what she was talking about. She still seemed to think I was someone else. I wondered if there might be another group of colonists that preyed on these people. That would explain a lot.

"I'm talking because I'm trying to save you," I told her. "There's a great threat, and you don't have long to live if you don't listen."

She laughed. She shook her long, fine hair, and I felt it brush my arms.

"I'm the one who holds your life in *my* hands."

I shook my head. "You can't kill me. Not really. I'll come back. Again and again."

"How do you do that?"

"We have a machine aboard our ship. It has the power to rebuild our bodies after we die. Our cells are copied, our minds too, and we live again."

Della moved in front of me and her head cocked to one side. I could tell she was intrigued.

"Your lies are complex and bizarre. Let's pretend I believe you have the power of a god. Why does a god care about me?"

"My name is James McGill," I said. "I'm a specialist, a weaponeer to be precise, in an organization called Legion Varus. I'm part of Earth's space-going military. I know who you are. All of your people are descendants of colonists from Earth. A lost people who—"

Della grabbed me by the ear then. I couldn't remember the last time a woman had done that. I think it must have been my grandma after I'd painted her cat with some varnish I'd found out in her barn. Being dragged by the ear hadn't felt good as a kid, and it didn't feel good now.

I was pulled along by her, stumbling over the rocks. She kept her crossbow aimed at me, and I had to admit, it made me nervous. One slip of her finger would send that bolt right through me. Even if she just bumped the point into my flesh, the nanites might go crazy at the taste of blood and worm their way into my organs to feed.

Della dragged me to a spot I thought looked familiar. I eyed the place, and I recognized the wide dark stain on the flattest part of the rock.

"You know what that is?" she asked.

"My blood?"

"Your life was spilled out and taken from you."

"Where's the body?" I asked.

She looked at me with narrowed eyes. "You want to see it? Why? Are you a sorcerer who will bring it back to life? If so, I'll kill you both again, and I'll use your own knife to chop up the pieces."

"Won't matter," I said. "I'll come back anyway."

Puffing with anger, she dragged me again. I knew I could take her this time. She was getting a little careless. I'd never shown her any of my moves, and I knew if I could push away the crossbow, I'd be able to throw her off her feet. She couldn't weigh more than half what I did. With any luck, I'd put her down before she could react. It would be a risk, but I was becoming annoyed with her attitude.

I felt my body tense up, my mind planning my moves. But I had to stop myself. This was supposed to be a diplomatic mission. I had to put up with her nonsense to win her trust. Tripping her onto her face and sitting on her would be satisfying, but it wasn't going to win me the Nobel Peace Prize.

We finally halted. Together, we stared at a corpse that lay face down on a large, flat rock. He was a tall guy with blond hair and a hole in his back. A great deal of blood had leaked out of the body, and the clothes had largely been stripped away.

My skin crawled to see myself dead at my own feet. I'd never had that experience before. I'd died several times, but I'd never had to bury myself. For the mental health of our troops, it was a general rule that legionnaires were excused from dealing with their own dead bodies if at all possible.

"That was me," I said. "It's weird to see myself lying there. I've never looked at my own corpse before."

Della watched me.

"You don't mourn?" she said. "You don't pray?"

I shook my head. "We only do that when we've been permed. When we've died somehow and can't be returned to life."

"How many times can you come back from death?"

I shrugged. "How many times can you make a new crossbow bolt out of nanites?"

She narrowed her eyes and looked at the tip of her bolt. "Until we run out of nanites, or our fletchers die, or our lathes no longer work."

I nodded. "It's the same with us."

Della reached down between her breasts and into her tunic. She fished around in there, and I got the feeling she had a pocket inside to stash objects. I tried not to be obvious as I stared at her tanned breasts, revealed in flashes, but she didn't seem to mind or even be aware of my scrutiny.

She pulled her hand back out and held my knife in her palm, still in its sheath. She handed it to me.

"No one has ever gone through so much to retrieve something so small," she said. "You've earned this—before you are slain again."

I took the knife. "Thanks. As I said, my dad gave it to me back home."

"Home," she said slowly. "You still claim to come from Earth?"

"Yes. From Georgia, North America Sector, to be exact."

"You profane Earth with your lies. You come from a brood-mother. You are artificial, bred by the cephalopods in vats. We know these things to be true. Whatever your real purpose is, know that you have failed, creature."

Bred in vats? I found this idea confusing, but I didn't have time to mull over it now. I'm not an intuitive man, but I sensed that things weren't going my way. She was thinking about killing me again.

"Look," I said, "why don't you just come down the hill to the lakeshore? Talk to my commanders. We won't harm you. We want peace with your people because you are *our* people. We want you to rejoin your own species."

"You might even believe what you say is true," she said, almost wistfully. "And in truth, I find myself attracted to your mind and body. You're not like the other men I've known. But you'll not lure me away from my post. The idea is absurd."

I sighed. "Then I've failed. I'll tell you what's going to happen next. Heavy weapons will be brought up. They'll have explosives and maybe gas. Drones will be sent in and men in armor. You'll all die here, and hiding in your tunnels won't save you."

"You threaten us? After all this talk of peace?"

Her weapon, which had strayed a fraction off target, now began to move back toward my neck. I decided to act. There wasn't going to be another chance. I slammed the crossbow away.

We struggled for an instant, and she bit my shoulder. I reached down and pressed her finger on the trigger of the crossbow. The bolt fired off into the sky, hissing.

A quick sweep of my leg under her ankles brought her down. She looked up at me, stunned. I leaned forward.

"You'll kill me now," she said, "proving your words were all lies. Why did you bother to try to fool me?"

"I wasn't lying, and I'm not going to kill you. I'm your last chance for life, in fact. Come with me, and we'll talk further."

A blade appeared in her hand. The metal edge had a black, wet look to it that I recognized from the tip of her bolts. I sprang away.

She scrambled to her feet and fled, crying out for her comrades. I looked after her, but knew I couldn't chase her down. There were too many mantraps, and her friends were sure to kill me the second they saw me pursuing her.

"Della!" I shouted. "I'm sorry! Run out into the desert when the bombs come. Maybe they'll miss some of you!"

I turned then, and ran downhill the way I'd come. Rocks shifted and slid from under my boots, and any second I expected to be consumed by a patch of innocent-looking gravel to die screeching in the dark, like Gorman.

* * *

"Command isn't easy, McGill," Graves told me. "It's best that you learn that right now."

I didn't even look at him. I didn't care about his subtle hints at promotion. I didn't want a promotion. I wanted the colonists in this little green valley to survive to see another morning.

155

"In light of your recent actions," Graves said. "I'm not sending you on the mop-up mission. You're to report back to the lifter under Leeson's command. Keep that ship safe for me. All our supplies are aboard her."

I scoffed. I knew I was being shunted aside. I wondered what kind of whining Harris and Leeson had done to get out of attacking the rock pile themselves. Probably, they feared going in there to clean the place out. Bombs and plasma grenades could only do so much. We didn't have a single heavy artillery piece from the arsenal. We'd left the big stuff on *Corvus*, and it was certain we'd be down to poking around in tunnels up-close and personal by the end of this disgusting mission.

"Permission to head to the lifter, sir," I asked.

"Get to your platoon and tell Leeson to move out. And one more thing, McGill."

"What's that, sir?"

"Quit moping like someone ran over your puppy. This is our job. Legion Varus never gets the easy missions."

"I've got that clear in my head now, sir."

"See that you stay on target. Dismissed."

I trudged away, not even having the heart to grumble. I found Carlos—or rather, he found me.

"You nailed her, didn't you?" he asked, studying me.

"What are you talking about?"

"The wild chick with the crossbow, who else?"

I didn't say anything for a second, keeping a poker face. I knew this would set him off.

"I knew it!" Carlos exclaimed, extending an accusing finger. "I could see it in your eyes! These colonist chicks are cut off from real men. They've got to be hot for it. I knew it the minute I heard about this place."

"So why aren't you up there in those rocks making your play?" I asked him. "Go up there naked, they like that best."

Carlos didn't seem to be listening. He shook his head and chided himself.

"This just proves it," he said. "My problem is I don't act on my hunches as fast and as naturally as you do. I'm not ninety-percent animal. I'll be the first to admit it—and I think that's my greatest character flaw. I salute you, McGill. For a farm boy, you have all the right moves with the ladies."

I didn't feel like explaining anything about what had really happened on the rocks, so I went to find Leeson instead. I relayed Graves' orders.

Leeson was all smiles. Retreating to a defensive position had to be what he'd wanted all along. Why sweat and fight crazies hiding under rocks when you could sip green fizzies in the shade of the lifter ramps?

We set off immediately, heading back along the lakeshore toward the lifter. I barely had time to put my armor on.

It was pitch dark, and we only had our night vision systems and a few suit lamps to go by. On Dust World there was no moon to light up the sky. When night fell it was as if you had a thick blanket pulled over your eyes. The effect was intensified by the fact that we were a few kilometers down in a hole below the desolate surface. Very little starlight penetrated from the distant skies above.

Our night vision systems were helpful but less than perfect. We stumbled over objects that didn't register as solid to the computers inside our helmets. Carlos fell flat on his face in front of me at one point.

I laughed but then hustled forward when he didn't get back up.

"You okay?" I asked, grabbing his shoulder.

He didn't answer. Instead he shivered, his entire body spasming. I let go of his shoulder and unlimbered my weapon.

"Man down!" I shouted over the unit channel. "I repeat, we've got—"

"Make for the lifter!" Leeson ordered. "We're under attack!"

I heard a series of snaps and whistling sounds. I knew what they were, and I began running up the lakeshore. I didn't like leaving Carlos, but he was probably as good as dead.

Ahead of us, the lifter was a dark hulk. It was slightly greenish in my night vision face plate as the ship had a hotter heat signature than the vegetation or the stone cliffs behind it.

I wondered if I'd reach the ramp before I was shot in the back. I wondered, too, if Della was among those who were attacking us.

-17-

The colonists had decided not to wait around for us to attack them. They'd gotten ahead of us and reached the lifter somehow—I suspected they had tunnels worming through the rock walls of this canyon and had been watching us all along.

Running toward the lifter in my heavy armor, my boots sank into the sandy soil along the lakeshore with every step. Clumps of earth and vegetation squirted from under my heavy tread as I crashed along. Being a heavy trooper was kind of like driving a very small tank. You felt isolated from your surroundings but not invincible.

At least once a bolt spanged off my armor. It didn't find a crease or joint to penetrate, fortunately, and the nanites dribbled off. They couldn't eat through solid steel.

When I came to the ramp, I was horrified by what I saw. A dozen dead legion regulars lay around the foot of the massive tongue of steel. I knew this was a very bad sign. Normally, the first action the crew would have taken would have been to button-up the ship. But the ramp wasn't moving, and there were no signs of life.

Gauntlets struck my back and shoved me. I stumbled forward, servos whining.

"Get up that ramp!" Harris shouted. "We're exposed out here. I can't see the enemy. They must be cold-faced bastards."

I jogged up the ramp, holding my weapon at my hip. I adjusted the spread to form a broad cone and stepped into the gloom at the top.

Lights—there should be lights. Someone had shut them off or smashed them all.

Harris and Leeson were right behind me, breathing hard. About a dozen more troopers came up behind them.

For me, the combat situation was an odd one. I'm accustomed to fighting aliens. My experience came from Cancri-9—Steel World—where the enemy were all in the form of very large lizards. These were men I was fighting against today, and this wasn't a drill. I was on their planet, and despite their lack of armor or heavy weaponry, I knew they could effectively kill my kind.

I turned my suit lamps up to full power and disengaged the night vision. Clearly, the damned infrared input wasn't working.

What I saw then was shocking. We were surrounded. They were all around us. Some crawled on all fours on top of the jump seat racks. Others hid behind the rows and were even coming up behind us on careful, padding feet.

They wore green-black outfits. That was something I hadn't seen before. I didn't know what they were at first, but the way their suits moved and shifted—they had to be smart-cloth.

Nanites, I thought. Of course, if the colonists were masters of a single technology, it was nanotech. They had tight-fitting suits which concealed their bodies even from infrared signatures. The suits must cool the exterior or operate with some other chameleon effect. All I could see were their eyes. The rest was pure green-black.

In a way, the fact that they startled me helped out. I didn't hesitate. If I'd been given time to think, I might have delayed my fire for a fraction of a second, and that moment of indecision might have been fatal. But I didn't. I sprayed those that were in front of me, sweeping them with a broad cone of plasma like violet fire.

"They're all around us!" I shouted, as those in front flickered in flame and withered away to smoldering corpses. I swept to the right and left, singeing the enemy that hid behind the rows of jump seats. Harnesses, gear and even seats

160

themselves caught fire, burning and producing black, oily smoke.

I heard a great deal of commotion behind me, but I didn't have time to worry about that. The survivors in front of me rallied and charged. They were brave—I had to give them that. I'd read up a bit on the colonists we'd sent into space last century. They'd been hardy souls. They were people who were bright, tough and who'd also apparently been irritating enough to the gathering world governments to warrant being shipped out into the unknown.

Three of them rushed me. They couldn't have known that I was unable to fire my weapon again so quickly, but they came on anyway. I dropped my cannon as there was no time to cycle up the next blast. I flicked on the force-blades in the arms of my suit, and these weapons met the nanite-edged black weapons of the enemy.

It was one type of high-tech blade against another. Mine had more reach, but theirs were no less deadly. The first man who came at me did so without finesse. He howled and cut at me. I met his twisted blade with my own beam of force—and his disintegrated. My left arm thrust upward and swept high, a classic follow-through movement I'd learned on my first day of heavy-infantry training. His head popped off and flew away, steaming.

Witnessing this fight gave the other two colonists pause. To their credit, they didn't run. They came on with greater caution trying to feint and jab at a distance. They didn't want their blades to touch mine. They wanted them to touch my armor.

Fighting two enemies at once isn't easy. I was far from a master with force-blades, but I liked to think I knew what I was doing.

The guy on the right sprang close, jabbed, then hopped backward. I made the mistake of going after him—and then the second fighter made her move.

She slashed at my chest, which was lucky for me. The nanites left a long streak of dark metal as if she'd hit me with a charcoaled stick. They dribbled and bubbled there, trying in vain to eat their way through my armor.

I pulled a move then that neither of them was expecting. I extended my right force-blade. Force-blades aren't made of anything physically tangible. They are mass-less energy, plasma-fields that can reach out ten feet or more.

Instead of a short wand, I suddenly possessed a lance. I thrust it through the retreating man and cut him down.

I'll never forget the look on his blacked-out face. His eyes were so wide...I realized as he fell that he was a real person, a man who believed he was fighting terrible invaders. Worse, he was right.

The woman howled and came at me, slashing and cutting. I didn't have the heart to gut her as well. I crashed my fist down upon her head and she crumpled. She was hurt but alive. I kicked her nanite weapon away from her and turned around.

The scene behind me was shocking. Leeson was down, but Harris, Kivi and two others had survived. They hadn't seen their attackers at first and had let them get in from the sides. Hacking at the joints, the enemy had managed to kill most of the platoon.

Veteran Harris looked around and realized he was in charge.

"Damn," he said. "Looks like the last of them have run off, but we have to be more careful, people. How did you spot them, McGill?"

"Just turn off your night vision. They're using it to hide from us. They're more visible with suit lights and regular optics."

We made the adjustments, and we pressed forward.

"Stay on point, McGill," Harris said. "We have to head up to the bridge. We can't let them take this lifter."

In my opinion, it was pretty clear they'd already taken the ship, but no one was asking me. I pressed ahead, and we swept the hold. There was nothing left alive.

"Crazy ninja bullshit," Harris complained. "An entire unit was stationed here to protect the ship. They must have crept in while we had our pants down and slaughtered everyone."

"The revival unit will be working overtime," Kivi said.

"Yeah," I agreed. "If they haven't captured it."

Harris' eyes bulged at the idea. "We can't allow that. Let's roll, people. Retract that ramp so they can't come in behind us then we'll clear the rest of the ship."

We grouped up and passed over bodies, banging our steel boots down as we tried not to walk on them. A few injured people moaned. We had no time for them, friendly or otherwise. We had to get control of the ship.

We headed to the tube that lead up to the crew quarters. I only hesitated for a second before climbing up there. I figured there might very well be a full squad of "bullshit ninjas" up there waiting to cut off my limbs, but hesitating wasn't going to save me. I was on point, and the enemy had to be defeated.

The last few feet, I threw myself upwards, heaving into view on the deck above. I'd hoped to surprise whoever might be up there, but there was nothing to see…except the dead.

A vicious fight had occurred on the upper decks. That was clear. There were dead bodies everywhere, many still locked in fighting positions. As far as I could see, no one had made it out.

Harris bumped up after me. He looked around grimly.

"They must have fought to the finish. No way out up here. The emergency exits are all on the first floor. They sealed the tubes and swept the command deck. Clearly, the colonists won, and the survivors ambushed us as we boarded."

"Why didn't they signal for help?" Kivi asked.

"Com system is down in the ship," Harris said. "Check your tappers, people. We'll have to fix that. If these colonists know how to sabotage a ship, they're smarter than I thought they were."

I had to agree with him. I walked to the hatchway at the end of the main passageway.

"Don't tell me—" Harris said as we pressed inside and looked around. A stream of curses followed.

I didn't blame him. The room contained nothing but corpses. Anne Grant was among the dead, as were several other bio specialists and a few colonist fighters.

But the worst part was the revival machine. It had been stabbed and cut with black blades. The interior guts of the machine looked damaged to me.

"This is bad—really bad," Kivi said.

No one argued. We knew she was right. We needed our revival machines more than any other piece of equipment in the legion. Without them, every death we suffered was permanent.

"We've got to copy everyone to the other ships," I said. "They're all as good as permed otherwise."

"Hold on," Veteran Harris boomed as people began working on the com gear. "Kivi, you call this in to the Tribune. McGill, you take the rest of them and sweep this deck. I don't want to see any other ninjas jumping out of the shadows at me."

We split up and looked around. We soon determined that, except for the wounded, we were alone on the lifter.

We captured the wounded enemy and secured them in jump seats. We made our own people as comfortable as possible.

I picked up one of the black blades and showed it to Kivi. Her lips pulled away from her teeth as she eyed that twisting edge.

"It's like this blade is alive," she said. "Such a nasty way to fight. They use metal poisons to kill us."

"Can you blame them?" I asked her.

She frowned at me. "Whose side are you on, McGill?"

"I'm on humanity's side. We're all the same species. You understand that, don't you?"

She nodded and looked down. "Yeah, but it's hard not to hate them even though this is their world. Our people might be permed. Our entire unit, James! And the lifter crew, too. Their data was on this ship, and odds of recovery aren't looking good."

"Well, it's like Graves says: if you don't like getting hurt, don't start a fight."

We were all upset. This wasn't supposed to happen. We were Legion Varus, and these people were a crowd of colonists. We didn't like killing them—but we liked dying even less. The thing I was most surprised about was the ability of these colonists to fight. How had they learned the art of warfare and become such tough fighters?

164

We swept the lifter twice but found nothing. Outside, everything looked quiet until shells began to fall on the cliffs on the other side of the lake.

Turov's bombardment began with a growing series of flashes on the shoreline. They lit up the water with wavering reflections in a display I might have found pretty if they weren't heralding destruction.

I knew it was only light artillery, as we hadn't had room to bring the heavy stuff on the lifter during our hasty exit from *Corvus*. But our light guns were enough to do the job. They wouldn't level a town, but they hit much harder than my shoulder-mounted plasma cannon.

The shells arced upward at a forty-five degree angle then performed a right angle turn high in the air and crashed down into the cliffs. Each impact resulted flashes of blue light. The shells were both guided and independently smart. What they lacked in punch they made up for in accuracy. Under normal conditions, they were designed to hit armored vehicles from above. Today, they were being used to go over the jumbled boulders and crash down upon defenders hiding behind them.

Each salvo shot up then slammed down again like a spiked volley ball a second or two later. The impacts created booming reports that echoed across the valley. In the lake, great numbers of rock-fish surfaced to watch with their wart-encrusted optical organs.

After careful examination via the lifter's outside scopes, we saw no sign of the attacking colonists.

"The enemy must be ducking and trying to ride this out," Harris said at my side.

"I agree Vet. We should stay buttoned up, too."

Once we were sure the lifter was free of the enemy, we all got to work repairing vital systems. We reported our status to the Primus, who was out marshaling the cohort at the base of the cliffs on the other side of the lake. Harris gave me the job of reporting—I think because he didn't want a disaster of this magnitude associated with his name.

"Primus Turov?" I said, making sure I wasn't talking to a flunky.

"Who is this?" she snapped. "I'm in the middle of an assault, a priority call had better be worth my time."

"Sir, this is Specialist James McGill. I'm at the lifter, and I have bad news."

"McGill? Where's your commander?"

"Our officer is dead, sir."

"Then get off this line and put on the lifter's pilot."

I took a deep breath. "I'm sorry, sir. The lifter crew is dead. So are the bio people and the ship's garrison."

There was a brief pause. "What are you talking about?"

"The colonists attacked the lifter just before we hit them at the cliffs. They took it but with heavy losses. Leeson's platoon was able to retake the ship, but we're down to a handful of effectives."

"Are you telling me you're the highest ranking survivor on that ship?"

I glanced up at Veteran Harris, who was watching closely while he pretended to work on the ship's alarm system.

"Uh, no sir. Veteran Harris survived. He's repairing the ship's warning system to—"

"Put him on!"

Veteran Harris winced and worked his tapper in resignation. He joined the channel.

"Primus Turov?" he asked. "Has McGill reported our situation—"

"Silence!" Turov shouted. I could tell she was at the end of her patience. "I'm transferring you up to the Tribune. Make your report to him."

Harris and I looked at one another in alarm. We waited, and a few minutes later Tribune Drusus joined the line. The instant he did, Turov disconnected.

"I'm going to ask questions," Drusus said. "I don't want any excuses, just data."

"Understood, Tribune," Harris said.

"Are you under attack now?"

"Negative, sir. The enemy—"

"Next question: is your revival unit operating?"

Harris hesitated. "We have a tech working on it. The unit was damaged by the enemy."

166

"Damaged? How?"

"They appear to have stabbed it, sir. They have these—I don't know—black swords with nanite blades. They can cut through our armor if they hit the non-metal components. Once a little of that metallic glitter is inside your flesh, it eats away at you."

"Interesting," Drusus said. "I'm surprised these isolated colonists have tech like that. It's an expensive import—but of course, they don't know about imports and exports. They just make whatever they want and to hell with the regulations. Their list of violations must be incredible."

I thought about what he was saying, and I quickly realized he was probably right. In the Galactic Empire, a planet couldn't produce anything that other member worlds also produced and sold without going through a rigorous procedure to prove the new product was better than anything produced by the current patent holders. The truth was, Earth hadn't invented much in the way of new tech since the Galactics had come to our star system. Maybe that was the way they wanted it.

"McGill!" shouted Drusus suddenly, bringing me out of my thoughts. "Are you on this channel? My tapper says you're here, lurking."

"Yes, sir," I said. "I'm here."

"You are hereby ordered to get that revival unit working. Stay on the lifter, and work with the tech until it starts popping out fresh troops."

"But, sir?" I asked. "I don't know how to operate the system, and all the bio people are dead."

"Figure it out. Grow a bio first and get their help."

I must have looked sick at these orders, because Harris was grinning at me.

"Harris!" Drusus barked.

"Sir!"

"Keep the enemy off that lifter. I'll have Turov send a unit back to support you. Hold out until they get there. Do you have any questions?"

"Tribune?" I asked. "What about the other valleys? How are things out there?"

"We're holding out," he said noncommittally.

"How long until we can expect relief, sir?" Harris asked.

"You're on your own for now. Expect nothing from the other cohorts. I've grounded all the lifters."

"Can I ask *why* that's the case, sir?" Harris asked.

Drusus was quiet for a second. "There's a ship coming. The techs we left on *Corvus* spotted it, and now we have as well. The configuration is unknown. I don't want to fly any of our lifters up out of these valleys until we know the score. Our landing ships don't have much in the way of weaponry."

Harris nodded grimly, twisting his lips. I could tell he was worried. The tribune signed off and the connection broke.

I looked at him. "Another ship?"

"That's what the man said."

"Who do you think it is?" I asked. "Squids? Galactics?"

"I have no idea, McGill. If the Tribune wanted us to know, he'd have told us. Now, we need to—"

I got to my feet.

"Where the hell are you going?" Harris demanded.

"To help Natasha. Those are my orders."

He grumbled but let me go. Left with only two able-bodied grunts, he had a lot of bodies to sort through and a lot of equipment to check.

I headed straight to Natasha's side, where she was working on the revival machine. She jumped up and came around with a pistol in her hand when I pushed the hatch open. Fortunately, she recognized me before firing.

"Sorry," she said. "I'm jumpy. These bio machines—they creep me out."

"I don't blame you," I said, stepping carefully over the gory deck to her side. I poked at the biological innards of the revival machine. To my surprise, it shivered at my touch.

Revival machines are probably the strangest things I've ever encountered. They looked sort of like old-fashioned pot-bellied furnaces on the outside. But instead of producing heat, they formed flesh out of raw materials. They were metal on the outside, with a data entry panel over the primary exit maw, but inside they were as fleshy as the people who came back to life inside them.

"How does this damned thing work, anyway?" I asked.

"I don't have a clue," Natasha admitted. "This isn't our kind of technology. Human technology is pretty much machine-based. We have some bio-tech, and can handle things like viruses, medicines and surgery. But this—this is like understanding your own reproductive system and having full conscious control over every aspect."

"It seems to be alive," I said.

"Yes, these units are very hard to kill. I used a small EMC blast to kill the nanites and I've been using flesh-printers to heal the wounds, but the unit is in shock. The internal nervous system is giving me nothing but warning lights. I've tried to get it going by charging all the plasma bays and injection ports— but they still register empty."

I looked the machine over carefully. I couldn't help but curl my lip in disgust. If you've never worked in a slaughterhouse with animal guts all over the floor, you probably can't imagine the smell and the mess.

"I still don't get how it can make any person it wants to," I commented as I tried to help her.

"Controlling biological output isn't new," Natasha said. "Some species on Earth can control their biological output, you know," Natasha said as she poked and prodded, trying to get the machine to operate. So far, most of the indicator lights were a cautionary yellow, and a few were red.

"Like what kind of animals?"

"There are hundreds of mammalian species in which the female is capable of manipulating the sex of her offspring."

I looked at her, my eyebrows upraised in surprise. "Why would they do that?"

"Strategic reproductive reasons. For example, a strong female that's likely to produce an attractive male will select sperm that will grow into a male. But weaker females play it safe and are more likely to produce female offspring."

My jaw sagged a bit. "Really? Can *you* do that?"

She blushed and turned away.

I smiled and went back to tapping around under the dripping innards of the machine.

"It would be a neat trick if you could," I said. "If you want to give it a shot, I'd be willing to donate—"

"Just shut up," she said. "Forget I said anything."

I did shut up, but I found forgetting her words to be an impossible task.

"Ants can do it too, can't they?" I asked a minute or two later.

"What?"

"A queen ant—she can decide to make soldiers if she needs them. Or drone males, or even new queens."

"Yes, they have that ability. But this tech is so far beyond anything of that kind. I suspect it's done through extremely long organic molecular chains. Through programming, essentially, that can grow cells to order by creating DNA and allowing natural cell division to take place. Compared to our bio tech, it's as advanced as a computer is to a shovel."

"I get that," I said. "I can understand how these machines could build a cell to order and start incubating it. What I don't get is how they work so damned fast. It takes less than an hour for a full-grown human to come out of one of these. I don't see how that's possible."

Natasha frowned at the machine. "That's been puzzling me as well. But I think I know the answer. They use time dilation. There's some kind of stasis field that operates to speed up time inside these units. It's the only answer I can think of."

"If you're right, these machines are incredibly advanced."

She nodded. "Any luck down there?"

I came out from under the machine and wiped away goo. "Not really. I suggest we take a tried and true approach."

"Name it."

"Let's cycle the power—turn it off and on again. The system needs a reboot."

Natasha shook her head worriedly. "That might not work," she said. "What if we kill it? They have an internal source of power, and they never get switched off. You can't just stop a person's heart and start it again without knowing what you're doing."

"Well, what do you suggest then?" I asked.

She heaved a sigh. "I think we're just going to have to wing it. We're going to have to operate the machine despite the fact every indicator is scrambled. A few are green now, but most of them are still yellow."

I stared at her for a long second. "I don't like that idea, but I have to admit we're less likely to kill the thing by accident that way."

"Should we contact the other bio people and inform them of our plan?" she asked.

I eyed her, then shook my head. "I don't think so. They'd totally freak out. They did everything they could to get me permed the last time I messed with their equipment."

"I know they're a little jealous of their tech," Natasha said. "But this is a matter of life and death."

"They'd just say we should wait until an authorized operator got here," I said. As soon as I'd spoken those words, they sounded like pretty good advice to me.

Natasha's face became stubborn. I realized then that she wanted to run this machine. She was tech not a bio, but she'd built her own life form in college and been punished for it. She had a streak of curiosity about technology—any kind of technology.

"Let's just *do* it," she said quietly, as if whispering a secret. "The Tribune ordered us to. We'll stand on that."

I wasn't sure that would fly with the bio people. Some of them could be downright crazy. But I was game to give it a try anyway.

I stood up and approached the data terminal. That was the one piece of this monster that looked familiar to me. The aliens who'd made this contraption had sewn an interface on it that we humans felt at home with, and I, for one, thanked them for their thoughtfulness. I wouldn't have enjoyed the experience of stimulating its nerve endings manually to get it to do what I wanted. Instead, there was a touch screen, a keyboard and even a few buttons.

Cracking my knuckles, I reached for the terminal. Natasha put her hands on mine and pulled me away the way a mother might have removed a toddler's hands from the knobs of a stove.

"Let me do it, James," she said gently.

I nodded. She was the tech, after all.

"Who are you going to revive first?" I asked.

Natasha licked her lips. "No choice there, really. I'm going to have to bring back Specialist Grant."

I grimaced. The choice made sense, of course. Anne was the one who would have the best chance of repairing the machine and getting it back to normal. But I didn't like the idea of doing that to a friend.

"What if—what if it goes wrong?" I asked Natasha.

"You mean, what if she's a bad grow?"

I nodded. We were both speaking with lowered voices. We weren't bio people. We still had hearts and stomachs that were built of flesh, not iron.

"Don't think about it," I advised her. "Just do it. We don't have any choice, really."

Natasha reached for the controls and began to tap at them. I watched with a growing sense of unease.

-18-

Anne's revival took many long minutes. The alien machine gurgled and hissed as it suckled on tanks of liquid and sent up odd vapors that lingered near the ceiling.

During that time, the bombardment along the cliffs had shifted. The Primus wasn't getting the results she wanted, I figured, and was now walking her cannons across the walls of the valley blasting apart rock where she imagined the enemy might be hiding. For their part, the colonists weren't reacting. They hadn't made any more attacks—but they hadn't surrendered, either.

When the revival machine finished its strange incubation process, the primary maw yawned open. I hunted around for the scoop you were supposed to insert to help slide the body out.

Natasha gave a little shriek, and I turned back in alarm. She was crouching in front of the steamy maw looking inside. She shined her flashlight into the dark opening.

"I can see her feet in there!" she said with a noticeable degree of fascination in her voice. "Bare feet—and they look normal."

"Aren't babies supposed to come out headfirst?" I asked. "Maybe we've screwed up already."

"Just get the shovel-thing. We have to get her out of there, or she might suffocate."

I realized right then we had absolutely no idea what we were doing. We were criminally incompetent. Without a bio to help out, we might as well be two cavemen trying to operate a computer—only in this case a human being's life depended on us.

I approached with the shovel-like tool extended in front of me. It looked like one of those things they use to take pizzas out of ovens. It had a handle and a flat metal scoop in front. But this tool was longer and had a tip that was wrapped in soft polymers. I imagined this was to prevent tearing up the soft internals of the machine—or the newborn human.

Sliding that scoop in there was a teeth-gritting experience all by itself. Natasha tried to help, lifting Anne's bare feet with her hands and saying: "Careful! Careful!" about thirty times in a row, while I worked the scoop into the opening.

I finally had it all the way in and started to withdraw the scoop.

"She's not coming out!" Natasha said. "She's stuck!"

"Well, pull on her feet for God's sake!"

A few moments later, Anne came loose. She gushed out with the scoop. There was a lot of fluid and other stuff—I didn't even want to look.

"Oh my God!" Natasha said. "She's got an umbilical cord!"

I felt my stomach heave a little, but I tried to keep it together.

"So far so good," I said. "First, let's check her vitals."

"Heart beating—but I don't think she's breathing. What are we going to do, James?"

"Uh…hold on."

I wrestled Anne's flopping, nude body onto a gurney. The umbilical cord was pulsing, still beating with purplish blood. I had to wonder what was at the other end of that hose-thick blood vessel. Did the machine have a heart of its own beating somewhere inside?

I tried not to think about that—I tried not to think about anything at all. I tilted Anne's head to one side and fished in her mouth.

"There's like a plug in here—something rubbery."

"Rip it out!"

I did it. I'm not sure if I've ever had to do anything worse, but I did it. A lot of liquid flowed out, but I didn't see any blood.

Natasha pushed her fingers on Anne's chest. Anne's small, perfect breasts shivered.

"I think she's dead," Natasha said. She bent forward and gave her mouth-to-mouth.

"Keep trying. I'll try to figure out how to work the defibrillator."

Fortunately, I never had to shock Anne with the defibrillator. I'm sure that if I had, I'd have jolted myself to death somehow.

"She's breathing now!" Natasha said. "We've got a pulse and breath. I think we did it."

"I don't know," I said. "She looks a little green."

"That's just the afterbirth."

"Maybe."

Anne started to cough then. She wheezed, spasmed and shifted into a fetal ball. I felt for her. She'd been revived by two amateurs and spit out of a broken machine. If there was any possible way we could have screwed this up—we'd probably done it.

Natasha and I looked on helplessly while Anne's eyes fluttered open. She coughed with a deep, lung-ripping sound.

"Anne?" Natasha said gently, running her fingers over Anne's face to push back the lank, wet hair that was plastered to her forehead.

"What the fuck are you two doing in here?" Anne gasped, then went into a fresh round of wet coughing.

Natasha and I grinned in relief. Her heart was beating, her lungs were working, and she could talk. We felt like proud parents at that moment.

A few seconds later we weren't so happy. Anne slipped off the gurney head first. She'd passed out.

We lifted her limp form as gently as we could and put her back onto the table. We tried to awaken her again.

"Anne?" Natasha kept saying. "You have to tell us what to do. What's wrong, Anne?"

Anne's mouth worked, but she didn't say anything intelligible. Natasha bent close to listen.

"She's talking about the cord," she said.

I looked and immediately noticed that the umbilical had grown dark and was no longer pulsing.

"I bet it's killing her," I said. "We have to cut it. Get the flesh-printer!"

I reached for my father's knife and drew the blade, quickly wiping it on my suit. I didn't have time to sterilize it or even to think about what I was doing.

"She's going, James," Natasha said urgently. "Do it."

I began to saw at the cord. It was slippery and tougher than it looked, but the blade was insanely sharp. A surgeon's scalpel couldn't have done a better job. A moment later, Anne looked like she had a pumpkin stem sticking out of her belly.

Just as with a newborn baby, the cord had a valve in it that prevented heavy bleeding. We pinched it closed anyway and sprayed fresh cells over it like there was no tomorrow.

After another minute or so, Anne was conscious again. She wasn't happy, however.

"You two shouldn't be here. Where are my people?"

"They're dead," I told her. "All of them. The tribune ordered us to revive you. We're supposed to get you started on reviving the rest of our troops."

Anne looked around in confusion until she saw the bodies that still littered the deck.

"The colonists..." she said, then turned an accusing eye toward me. "You said they were harmless peasants hiding under rocks! They came in here like a pack of wolves! They tore us apart!"

"I never said they were harmless," I said. "And they don't have much in the way of tech, just nanite-blades and tools.'"

"That was plenty. They came at us so suddenly... The drones and trip-lines on the perimeter around the lifter didn't work—there was no warning. You techs failed us, too!"

Anne wasn't being reasonable, but I knew how she felt. I often came off the table fuming after a bad death. The fight that ended your life was often still fresh in your mind.

One of the odd things about revival technology was the fact you could often remember your own dying moments. Our neural connections were constantly recorded whenever we were in range of the legion networks. Updating a person's mental state wasn't as data-heavy as it sounded because the system only recorded *changes* to your synapses and neural pathways, not your entire mind. Like many large databases, the system saved only the parts of the mind that differed when compared to the last refresh. Most of the contents of any human brain were fairly static, such as long-term memories and basic skills. Only our most recent memories needed to be stored on a continuous basis.

Our bodies were even easier to work with. Once the entire DNA sequence was input, only a few alterations had to be recorded. For example, a person might have had their wisdom teeth removed when they first joined the legion. It wouldn't be helpful to revive such a person with a fresh toothache that would have to be surgically fixed every time, especially during a campaign. Using DNA blueprints to map out the basic design of the body, then storing changes that resulted naturally from age and artificially from repairs such as surgeries, the machine was able to reproduce a copy without the injuries that killed the person in first place.

This had the side effect of being able to make a person younger after they died and were revived. If there was no good reason to save a person's body, the system didn't bother. The revival units just grew a new body that was often years younger than the original and put the freshly-copied mind into it.

Anne finally noticed she was nude and climbed slowly down off the table. We held her up, but she slapped our hands away. Moving painfully, she got a fresh uniform wrapped around herself and let the flaps close and seal over her skin.

"I need a shower," she said. "Why am I so coated in slime? Oh, I get it. You clowns didn't even drain the machine's underbelly before you pulled me out, did you?"

We shook our heads.

"Amateurs! This is embarrassing. I'm probably operating on a bad grow. I think I have a fever. What about—?"

177

Anne broke off and sucked in her breath in a horrified gasp as she finally took a good look at the revival machine itself.

"What did you *do*?" she demanded. "Are you idiots or vandals?"

"A little of both, I guess," I admitted.

Natasha wisely chose that moment to duck out of the room. "I'm going to report in," she said as she vanished. "Drusus needs to know we've been successful."

Anne glared after her with baleful eyes. Then she turned her reddened orbs toward me.

"The colonists damaged the machine during the battle," I explained. "We came in here and killed them all if it makes you feel better."

"It does, a little," she said. She walked to the machine and ran her hands over it, then reached inside and pulled something out. A gush of liquid flowed out of the maw and ran into a drain in the floor.

I'd never been invited into a hospital maternity ward, and at this point I hoped I never would be. I had to remind myself that babies were supposed to be small, and this alien machine's efforts were probably more disgusting than a normal birth would be. Still, I wanted to get out of here.

"If you're okay," I said, "I'll be—"

"Forget it," Anne snapped. "We're the same rank, but I'm your senior. I need help. You know that by now. Start recharging the plasma tanks. These are no good anymore—you can't leave the fluids hot and under pressure for hours. They turn septic."

That was how it went for me. I was in for the long haul. I resigned myself to my fate, and together Anne and I began reviving people. We started with Leeson, as officers usually came first.

While I worked, I thought about the power these bio people really had in our legion. They decided—quite literally—who lived and who died. They could bring back whomever they pleased in the order they pleased.

But the reality of this power was muted by the nature of the work. We weren't playing god in this chamber—we were working our asses off. It was a hot, disgusting and thankless

178

job. Almost always, the newly-reborn people were pissed off, sad, depressed or just plain stunned to be alive again. I couldn't recall getting a single thank-you from any of them.

After we'd revived about thirty people, everything changed. The first hint came when the bombardment outside on the cliffs halted.

For the past several hours, we'd been listening to the steady snap-whine-*boom* of continuous, pounding fire. But it finally stopped.

I looked up, sweating and fingers goopy. Anne didn't seem to have noticed anything. She was pulling on a pair of feet and shouting for me to help.

"They stopped," I said.

"Don't you ever have your mind on the here and now?" she demanded. "I'm glad you aren't an orderly, I'd write you up as the worst failure—"

I reached past her, grabbed a foot and pulled. To my surprise, I recognized the body that flopped out. It was Carlos.

"Ew," I complained.

"He's no worse than any of them," Anne said.

"Yeah, yeah he is. He's a lot hairier than average for one thing."

"Just get him onto the damned table."

I did as she asked. She frowned at Carlos, looking into his eyes and ears and checking out his vitals with various instruments.

My attention wandered. "I'm going to have to go up and check this out," I said.

"Stand your post, McGill," Anne ordered in a commanding tone.

Technically, she outranked me, but I had no formal orders from an officer to keep reviving people with her. My place belonged with the combat arm of the unit if something had gone wrong.

"Sorry," I said. "If you need help, revive a trained orderly next. I'm checking this out."

I left her as she fussed over Carlos. She wasn't happy, but she understood. She didn't try to order me to stay again—which was best for both of us.

I had to admit to myself, I had mixed reasons for exiting that chamber. I'd had about enough of regrows and recharges for one thing. But I also had an aching curiosity about the battle outside. Had the colonists waved the white flag? Had Della been killed?

When I reached the ramp to the lifter, I was surprised to see it had been lowered. Leeson stood at the head of it looking down into the bluish light of dawn. I realized with a shock I'd spent half the night in the lifter, working that damned alien machine.

"McGill?" Leeson asked, seeing me. "Is everyone back on their feet?"

"No, sir. I came out to see what happened. Why did the primus stop hammering on the cliffs?"

"I don't know," he said, looking worried. "The tribune called for a ceasefire. There's something going on."

I dared to brighten. "A ceasefire? Has peace and sanity broken out on this forsaken rock?"

He shook his head. He had the attitude of someone listening. I stopped bugging him, realizing he was concentrating on the command channel. As an adjunct, he wasn't really expected to say anything on officer chat, but he was allowed to listen in.

Suddenly, he looked at me with wide eyes. "Go out there," he said. "Take your weapon. Look up, and tell me what you see."

I shouldered my belcher and marched out into the cool dim light of early morning. There was no direct sunlight, but at least the pools of shade all around the valley weren't impenetrable to the eye.

Gazing up, I couldn't believe what I was seeing. I'd expected something unusual, but not anything this shocking. There was a looming object lowering itself down silently from the skies.

The ship was huge. It wasn't any configuration I'd seen before, either. There was a dish-like silver structure at each end. These rippled with a quiet, powerful, amber light of some kind. I didn't know what to make of it.

180

But then I thought that maybe I did. I contacted Leeson.

"Sir? There's some kind of big ship out here—it must be a kilometer long. It's coming down right next to the lake between us and the rest of the cohort."

"I'll be damned," Leeson said.

Right then, I realized he was still up at the top of the ramp while I was outside. I was exposed to possible incoming fire, but I figured it didn't really matter. If this monster decided to lay a salvo down on top of our lifter, there wasn't much we could do. We'd be obliterated.

"What do I do, sir?" I asked.

"I don't know. No one does. The commanders are all talking about it. We're relaying the imagery to all the lifters."

I used the rangefinder on my cannon to sight on the ship. It had to be about five kilometers off. That was too far for me to damage it from here.

"Could it be that the Galactic Battle Fleet has arrived? Is this what they look like?"

"There's a lot of talk about just that possibility. We don't have a record of a ship with this configuration—at least, when we last saw Battle Fleet 921 this type of vessel wasn't recorded in orbit over Earth. But that was nearly a century ago. Maybe the Galactics have updated their vessels since the last time they came to this region of the Empire."

"Sir?" I said. "It's down now."

I watched as the rippling amber effects around the two dishes stopped strobing. Beneath the ship, countless massive waxy flowers had been crushed.

I heard footsteps coming down the ramp behind me. A hand pushed my tube down. I looked at Leeson.

"Were you about to shoot that ship, McGill?" he demanded.

"It had occurred to me," I admitted. "But it's out of range."

"Don't shoot anything without orders! If this is a Galactic vessel, you might screw up everything. Notice that they haven't fired a shot at us yet? Whoever they are, they look peaceful. We're not to take any chances."

Shrugging, I put the rangefinder back to my eye. "Safety's on," I said. "Just to be sure though—shouldn't we abandon the lifter?"

He shook his head. "I don't have any orders in that regard."

I looked at him. "The brass is going to be pretty upset if we lose the ship *and* the revival machine inside."

That got through to Leeson. In Legion Varus, we were all pretty much expendable. Even a permed unit was less important than just one of those precious revival machines. We couldn't replace equipment like that, especially now that Earth was hard-up for Galactic Credits.

"Yeah," he said, nodding half to himself. "We've got to take precautions. Let's get that machine out of there. We'll use the drones to help carry it and stash it among the rocks to the south."

I immediately thought of the colonists who liked to haunt the rocks all around their home valley. But I didn't bring it up. Leeson looked worried enough. I knew his orders were to protect the lifter and the revival unit. He didn't want to lose them both at once, no matter what happened.

Leeson tramped back up into the dark lifter and disappeared. "Stand watch out there," he said. "Tell me if anything happens."

I watched the ship, feeling uneasy about it. The design was so alien, so different. I'd made a study of local shipping in the Empire as had every schoolboy from Earth. This thing didn't look like anything I'd seen before.

The ship didn't do anything for several long minutes. Finally, a door opened on the side of the vessel. I stepped from foot to foot in anticipation. What kind of creatures would be manning a real Galactic ship? Would the crew consist of the spidery-looking guys I'd met before on Cancri-9?

I watched for several long minutes and was disappointed when I saw a delegation of what appeared to be humans walk down the ramp and halt at the bottom. They moved with precision and it was clear they were soldiers. Nine of them stood in a perfect square, in three ranks of three. They wore what looked like armor, but it was black and shiny like the carapace of a desert beetle.

Straining my eyes and adjusting the scope on my rangefinder I was able to see them with greater clarity. I had to go up the ramp a ways to get enough height so that my view wasn't inhibited by the towering flower-like growths between them and my position.

Then I began to frown. The flowers—could they be smaller over there next to the ship than they were here at my position? I stared, and my heart began to race. The men who had marched down the ramp and now stood motionlessly at attention were *tall*. They were about as tall as the flowers themselves.

"Adjunct Leeson?" I called. "Something's happened all right. A squad of men just marched out of that ship."

"Men? Did you say men?"

"Yes, sir. Well, not exactly normal humans. They're about three meters tall, all of them. At least, that's what it looks like. It's hard to tell."

Leeson came running down the ramp to stand beside me. He pulled out a scope of his own and stared into it.

"You're right," he said. "They're big, and they look human. They can't be, though. If it's a Galactic ship..."

"Maybe they're using some other race of humanoids from a distant star system for troops," I suggested.

Leeson looked baffled. "I'm reporting this. Keep watching. I've ordered the techs to send buzzers over there. We'll have more info shortly."

"What about the revival machine, sir?" I asked.

"Here it is now."

Several grunting troops in battle armor struggled and heaved a very large object down the ramp. One of them was none other than the freshly reborn Carlos. He looked at me in disgust.

"This was your idea, wasn't it?" he asked. "It has to be."

"Yeah, pretty much," I admitted.

"Where are the pigs? Aren't they supposed to be helping?"

Our biggest drones, or pigs, often helped with heavy lifting.

"Not this time. I guess they're doing something else," I said.

"Great. Where are we supposed to drag this monster?" Carlos demanded. "Grant is going crazy. She'll recycle us all next time around, just for fun."

I chuckled and shook my head. Carlos and the rest dragged the machine down the ramp and off toward a sheltering circle of boulders. Leeson had to join in to finish the job. The group returned a few minutes later.

"We've got it stashed in a safe place for now," Leeson said, coming up to me. He was breathing hard. Everyone had to strain when carrying the revival unit. Even with exoskeletons to help out, it was heavy.

I turned back to the strange visiting ship, and as soon as I sighted on the ramp I knew things were heating up. Previously there had been a squad of nine giants standing outside the ship. Now, instead of a single squad, there were at least a dozen squads. Each group stood in a perfect square of nine. Another group marched down in locked step order as I watched. Their gait was so carefully timed, if I hadn't known better, I would have thought they were robots of some kind.

"Sir?" I called to Leeson. "There are about a hundred troops at the base of the ship now."

Leeson came back to my side and stared through his scope. "That's weird. According to command central, these intruders have made no attempt at radio contact. They're not listening to any attempts to hail them, either."

For perhaps the first time, I felt a little nervous flutter in my guts. Something was wrong. These guys—whoever they were—weren't operating like Galactics or humans.

Something occurred to me then. What if the giants were human colonists of a different variety? What if the local people that we'd been trying to blast out of these cliffs had more advanced kinsmen? I just didn't understand the situation. The intruders might be on a rescue mission to save the local population from us. Or it might be that Della and her crew were really hunted like rats, and another group of aggressive colonists had come here to wipe them out.

I wasn't sure which hypothesis held water or if any of them did. But I was sure that the situation was a strange one.

The procession continued and became even odder as it progressed. The troops stopped marching out of the ship and began unloading equipment instead. Huge boxes, taller than the giants themselves, were carried down and deposited on the ground. When there were about twenty of these lined up outside the ship, I heard a sound I didn't want to hear.

A hissing sound passed my faceplate. I saw the bolt flash by me. It struck the support-arm of the lifter, uncomfortably close to my nose.

I reached up and slammed down my visor. Turning in a crouch, I aimed my plasma cannon in the direction I thought the bolt came from. I scanned the foliage—but only briefly.

A figure stood at the edge of the forest. She had a slip of white cloth in one hand which she was waving wildly. In the other hand was a crossbow which she'd just used to shoot at me.

I knew the woman by this time. It was Della.

-19-

Any thinking man would have melted that little witch down without hesitation, but I held my fire. I looked for her friends but saw no one. Of course, that didn't mean they weren't hiding somewhere nearby.

I thought about contacting Leeson, but I was worried he'd freak out. I'd taught this girl what the white flag meant, and she'd now decided to use the technique on me. Would it be right to take revenge now?

Heaving a sigh, I decided to take a chance. I knew I'd probably take another trip through the guts of that damned revival machine for my troubles, but for the sake of peace between the colonists and Legion Varus I lowered my cannon and walked toward her.

Della withdrew a few feet into the flowers. I walked up to her and flipped open my visor so she could see my face clearly.

"You are McGill?" she asked, staring at me warily.

"You know who I am," I said.

She extended a long tan arm toward the alien ship.

"Your littermates have come for you. Are you happy?"

"I don't know who those people are," I said. "And I'm definitely not pleased about them crashing this party."

She stared at me oddly, turning her head this way and that, as if she was listening to my words and trying to understand if they were true or not.

"How can you not know what they are?"

"You've seen them before, that's what you're saying?" I asked.

"Of course. They're marauders from the stars. They come here on off-years when the planets align. They capture as many of us as their ship will hold and fly back into the heavens. We kill some of them—but they always come back, and they always take more than we can kill."

I frowned. "Is that right?"

Looking at the ship, I got a creepy vibe from it. "Are you telling me these guys aren't related to you? They aren't your people? They look human enough."

She laughed bitterly. "They *are* related to us, but in a perverse way. They're bred from our bodies. They're twisted and unnatural, like plants that grow in neat rows under the earth, nourished by lamps rather than sunlight."

I was beginning to catch on. "You told me about this before, right? You said they were littermates. Are there nine in every litter?"

She nodded, staring across the lake. "For this variety, yes. The armored ones always come in nines, and they always march with their brothers. There is some humanity still left in them, I think. If you kill one of the brothers, the rest go mad."

"That sounds encouraging. I thank you for the warning. I'll pass the information on to my superiors. Do you think they'll attack us?"

"No," she said. "They never harm anyone unless you harm them first. But they will come, and they will take your weapons from you and destroy them. Then they will place rings around your arms and touch them together like this."

She crossed her wrists to demonstrate. "Then you will never be able to separate your hands from one another again until they will it. Once bound, you will be herded into the ship and carried away.

At first, it's said that many of my people didn't fight. They thought it was better that way. They didn't believe in violence. But all those people are gone from this world by now."

"Only the fighters are left, huh?"

"That's right. For each individual, the choice is clear. Fight and die, or hide and live—maybe. Or submit and know you will live on in a different place."

"Don't worry. We'll all fight. Every last one of us."

Della looked at me suddenly. Her eyes flashed with a fire I'd seen there before. She was a killer, I could see that. A killer, through and through.

"Good," she said. "Perhaps there is room for talk between us. You killed my people on this ship, did you not?"

"Yeah," I said. "Sorry about that. They didn't give us any choice."

She laughed. That surprised me, as I didn't think anything about the situation was funny.

"You had a choice," she said. "A man always has a choice. You chose to fight, rather than to die."

"Well, yeah. I guess so."

"Never apologize for struggling with an enemy who attacks you," she said, almost as if she was quoting a proverb. "That is the path to slavery."

"Okay…" I said. "How about we make a deal? You don't attack us, and we won't attack you. Not as long as this ship is here. We'll all fight these invaders instead."

"Why should I choose one intruder over another? They only want to enslave us. You are trying to kill us."

She had me there. I thought hard for a second.

"Would they offer you a deal to kick us off the planet?" I asked her.

"No," she said, shaking her head. "They never offer deals. You obey them, or you die. There's no room for anything else in their minds."

"Okay then," I said. "Call a truce with us to improve your situation. It's easier to fight one enemy at a time than two at once. Accept my deal so that we both have a better chance of winning in the end. We'll kill them first then decide what to do about each other afterward. The odds of victory will improve for both of us."

"I will not stand at your side. I do not trust you. Your bombs…to us, you're worse than the littermates! You have destroyed homes carved in stone that have stood safe and cool for decades."

I lifted a hand, and she retreated back a step as if I were threatening her. I dropped it again quickly. These were very suspicious people.

"No alliance," I said. "We're not expecting any direct cooperation. All I'm saying is that both of us will fight only these intruders, not one another. When they leave or are destroyed, then everything goes back to the way it was."

Della nodded and then flashed me a tiny, tight smile. I think it was the first smile I'd ever seen on her face. "I can get the others to agree to that," she said. "But don't ask for more."

"I wouldn't think of it," I said. I was proud of that lie. From her expression, I could tell she believed me. It had been smoothly told, and it was for a good cause. That's the best kind of lie a man can tell.

Naturally, I wanted more than a truce. But outright peace wasn't going to come easily, especially not after the Primus had bombed-out their homes so relentlessly. We had to earn their trust and this sounded like a good first step.

"Watch the skies for the little things that waver in the air," she said, pointing over the ship toward the cliffs. "They have aircraft that will drop canisters. The vapors will render the strongest man unconscious."

I turned toward the ship and stared above it where she'd pointed. I thought I saw something up there—something like a black leaf with a triangular shape to it.

I turned back to ask Della if that was what she'd meant— but she was gone.

* * *

Explaining the deal I'd arranged to my superiors wasn't an easy task. I was only a specialist, a non-com, and a junior one at that. I was told by Leeson in no uncertain terms that I lacked the authority to do what I'd done. He kicked the connection up to Graves, who rumbled something about me having larger genitals than was normal on a human being. I took this as a compliment, but I wasn't sure if he'd meant it that way. He kicked me up to the Primus, connected the two of us and then quickly exited the channel.

When I made my report to the Primus, I was met with outright fury, rather than mere disapproval.

"You did *what*?" she demanded. "Who the hell do you think you are?"

"I'm Specialist James McGill, sir," I said evenly. "And I was following orders."

"Whose orders?" she said quickly, guardedly.

I'd been referring to her orders. She'd instructed me to talk to the colonists and make contact. Sure, she hadn't indicated I should arrange any deals, but I'd seized the opportunity that had presented itself.

By her tone, I knew right off she wasn't thinking about her orders. She was wondering who else might have given me leave to operate independently. In the past, I'd been given private orders by the Tribune himself. I'd executed those orders, and the Primus had gotten herself into a lot of trouble by interfering in the matter. I decided to bluff my way through.

"I think it would be best, sir, if you pass me up to the Tribune himself," I said, knowing that she'd been reprimanded for not doing so in the past.

"You're a red-assed bastard, McGill," she commented, then connected me to the Tribune.

"McGill?" Drusus said. "Why do I know that name so well, Specialist?"

"I'm not sure, sir. But I've made contact with the enemy."

"Which enemy?"

"Uh…the ones hiding in the cliffs, sir. The wild colonists."

"Good," he said, sounding amused. "Now, what was the nature of your contact? Is the legion being sued for paternity, or—?"

I knew he was joking, of course, but I was alarmed. Did I have that kind of reputation all the way up to the top? The thought was disturbing. How could a man hope to succeed with the ladies if he was infamous?

"Nothing like that, sir," I said. "I talked to a leader who called herself a scout. I understand she's a military officer of sorts. Anyway, we agreed to halt all fighting until this new threat is dealt with."

"We're not connecting clearly, McGill, you and I," Drusus said dangerously. "Are you saying you negotiated a ceasefire with an enemy combatant without orders?"

"No, sir!" I shouted. "I'd never do that. Primus Turov ordered me to make contact with them yesterday. I was to see if I could get them to talk peace. Well, I managed it."

"Hmm," he said. "A day late and a dollar short, as they used to say. But, I think we'll honor your unsanctioned ceasefire. You do realize that you were operating without authority on this?"

I swallowed and hesitated. I could bullshit most people—ask anyone, especially my parents—but I had known right from the start that Drusus wasn't just *anyone*. He always seemed to know what I was thinking almost before I did.

When caught red-handed, there are only two moves a man can make. You can deny everything in the face of the facts or confess utterly and try to look dumb or at least harmless. Drusus wasn't going to fall for a lie so I chose the latter strategy this time.

"Yes, sir," I said, and left it at that.

"Good. I want no misunderstandings on that point. If there is future diplomacy to be done, let me do it. But I'm willing to take the opportunity to improve our tactical situation. We're in a bad spot, McGill. I'd like to fly the other lifters to your valley to repel the enemy, but I don't dare now. The lifters are unarmed, and they are our only ships. They'll be destroyed if I try to come to your position. Your cohort is cut off—we all are."

I didn't like to hear that. I'd had in the back of my mind the assurance that the rest of Legion Varus could always back us up if things went badly here.

"We'll stop shooting at the colonists as long as they stop shooting at us," Drusus went on. "At least until these new arrivals demonstrate their intentions."

I explained to him then what Della had told me about the invaders and what I'd seen with my own eyes.

"Very strange," he said. "And alarming. If true, this isn't a Galactic visitation. It's either an off-shoot of the same colonists, a separatist group among separatists—or these giants are in league with the cephalopods."

"After talking to Della, I think it's the cephalopods, sir," I said.

"That's worrisome news. If they're behind this, we can claim innocence when order is restored to this system—but it might not matter. The Galactics might well blame us for something our own species has done, even if it was done by specially-bred human slave troops. I'm liking this entire situation less and less."

"What are your orders, sir?" I asked.

"Obey your officers. Man your cannon. And above all, McGill, try not to get us into a fresh war of some kind."

"I'll do my best, Tribune."

A quiet, tense stand-off began after that, which lasted for several hours. The invaders from above didn't seem to be in any kind of a hurry. They'd first unloaded about a hundred littermates, then began unloading a great pile of other stuff. Natasha and I watched them from the ramp of the lifter, excited about whatever it was they were doing.

"Just imagine the tech they must have," she said. "An entirely alien species unspoiled by Galactic influence. It's moments like this that make first-contact situations unpredictable and memorable. I hope I'm allowed to collect some scraps of it. We'll have to steal a few pieces before the Galactics blast it all to fragments. Are you with me, James?"

"Yeah, sure," I said, bored and tired. I was, in fact, trying to take a nap. Natasha was cute and all, but she liked to talk too much and was overly interested in what I considered to be a pile of alien junk. My only interest in it was whether it could kill me or not.

"We'll have to do it after these aliens march into the catacombs and try to fish out the colonists," she said.

I looked at her and frowned. "Do what?"

"Go up there and steal a few pieces of their equipment. I'm flying buzzers toward it right now—they don't even seem to

192

care. I'm getting such good vids. Should I share them with your helmet?"

"If it makes you happy," I said, shutting my eyes. I could see things flash and flicker on the other side of my eyelids. Damn, I was tired.

I passed out for a time after that. When I woke up, Natasha was standing next to me. Her foot withdrew, and I realized she'd kicked me awake. That wasn't as bad as it sounded. Wearing heavy steel armor protected us from things like a friendly kick. The thumping had probably awakened me rather than any sensation, as I could barely feel her boot slamming against my hip.

"What's up?" I asked, coming awake with a groan.

"I can't believe you can sleep at a time like this. They've reached the catacombs. Our units are falling back from them, letting them march forward. Check it out."

I stood up wearily and dialed up my scope. Things had indeed shifted on the battlefield—if that's what it really was. The ship had unloaded a great deal of equipment. Most of it I couldn't even recognize. There were big crates, small ones, a few in between. They had devices that were conical, spheroid and even flat black planes that were left lying on the ground.

Around me there was more activity as well. Most of my unit had been revived and was now guarding the lifter in an expanding circle.

Anne Grant had set up the revival machine in a secluded spot away from the lifter. In retrospect, it seemed like that precaution was unnecessary now that the colonists weren't attacking but, on the other hand, keeping the revival unit safe was even more important now that our cohort had been cut off from the rest of the legion.

"Look!" Natasha said, pointing across the lake. "They've reached the fallen rocks. Our people aren't fighting yet—I wonder what they're waiting for?"

I frowned in concern. I looked back and forth from the ship to our line of retreating troops. I could tell what was happening.

"The Primus is pulling back," I said. "She's going to let the aliens march right into the caves the colonists set up."

"Yeah, so?"

I made an exasperated sound. "She's screwing them!" I complained. "They made a deal with us, and she's double-crossing them."

"No she's not," Natasha said in concern. "We agreed to stop shooting at them. That's all. If the invaders want to attack them that's their problem."

Technically she was right, but I wasn't happy. I'd hoped this arrangement would lead to open fighting with the invaders on one side and our troops standing with the colonists on the other.

"First off," I said, "the Primus bombs holes in the colonists' cliffs exposing them to fire. Then she backs up so the enemy can roll right in. She's screwed them. They'll die like rats in there."

Natasha looked at me. "Isn't that a good thing?"

"No," I said.

"Why not?"

"Because the colonists are *our* people. We shouldn't be killing one another. We should team up and chase these freaks off the planet."

Natasha stared at me critically for a while. "You know what I think?" she said. "I think you're in lust with that half-naked wild girl you've been talking to. I think she's warped your thinking."

I felt a pang. Was it guilt? Outrage? A little of both, I guessed. I went with the outrage as it was a better cover.

"Jealousy?" I demanded. "Now? There are hundreds, maybe *thousands* of lives at stake here, Natasha. These people are just defending their home, where they've lived all their lives. What if these three meter tall pricks landed in your hometown tomorrow? Wouldn't you want a little help?"

She lowered her eyes. "Sorry," she said. "Too bad we can't do anything about it."

I didn't answer. I was scanning the scene. The enemy, marching in their perfect squares of nine, were climbing up the fallen boulders now, where I knew there were mantraps and ambushes every meter. Now I knew why the colonists had built such an elaborate defense.

Then I panned upward, higher and higher, searching for the wobbling little craft that Della had pointed out to me earlier. I finally found it in a new location. It was hovering over the lifter.

"Well, I'll be a son of a bitch," I said, looking almost straight up.

"What?" Natasha asked, craning back her neck and staggering to look above us.

"There they are, watching us. They're probably wondering what the hell this lifter is doing here and whether or not it's a threat to them. I can see three figures riding up there. What a strange little ship. Seems unstable in the air. It flutters, falling and rising again."

"Maybe it was built with underwater travel in mind," Natasha said. "After all, they come from a planet covered in oceans."

"You know, I think you're right," I said, sighting on the craft carefully. "Natasha, would you like to get a good look at that aircraft?"

"Oh yes," she said, sighing. "I've never seen true alien tech. I mean, the Galactic stuff we can buy seems so well-known and generic."

I reached up and cranked the aperture on my weapon to its narrowest setting. The lenses inside shifted with a tiny whirring sound.

"Could you turn on that little scrambling unit you used earlier?" I asked her.

"What for?"

"Just to make me happy."

Frowning, she activated her jammer. I knew it didn't have much range, so I stepped a pace closer to her. It was supposed to scramble the vid output from our suit cameras as well as making us untraceable on the net.

"What are you doing, James?" she asked.

Such innocence. She was the kind of girl I'd always dreamed of back in school. Smart—but still a little bit on the sweet side.

"I'm going to give you a closer look at some alien tech," I told her.

195

I fired my weapon without further delay. The beam punched a hole into the bottom of the odd, wobbling aircraft above our heads.

-20-

My beam lanced up from the ground to stab right through the aircraft overhead. I could tell right away that the crewmen aboard her were surprised. Two of them fell off, spinning and twisting all the way down until they splashed into the lake.

Twin white fountains of water shot up, such was the impact of their fall. One of the figures vanished in a churning spot of bubbles that quickly subsided. The other, however, seemed to be alive.

I was impressed by the hardiness of the enemy. If they could live through a fall like that—it had to be a five hundred meter drop.

"James? What did you *do*?" Natasha asked. Her voice sounded like she was out of breath.

"What did I do? I fired on an enemy combatant that was threatening our lifter."

"You didn't have orders to do that!"

"Sure I did," I said. "Leeson told me to guard this ship. I've been standing on guard duty out here for hours. I recognized a threat, and I eliminated it."

Natasha looked up. "It's not falling. It's leveled off."

I sighted on the ship again. It was harder this time as the ship wasn't holding still. It was flying in a circular pattern, directly above the lifter.

Before I could get another clean shot, a smoking object fell from the aircraft. I frowned at it. The object looked like a glass sphere full of a pitch-black substance. A spiraling tendril of gray smoke trailed behind it as it fell.

"Incoming!" I shouted over the general unit channel.

"McGill?" Leeson's voice answered. "What's going on out there?"

"Close visors!" I shouted. "I think its gas, sir!"

I fired my weapon but missed. The glass sphere fell nearby and popped. Roiling vapors exploded in every direction, obscuring my vision. My visor was down, as was Natasha's.

Not all our troops were so fortunate. Caught by surprise, a few of them slumped, crawled then stopped moving entirely.

The fluttering aircraft moved away then, scudding back toward the enemy aircraft. I fired twice more and got lucky on the last shot. I missed the aircraft, but I hit the last of the three crewmen. He pitched off the platform. Unguided, the craft slid sideways and slammed into a cliff face. A gush of orange fire brought a smile to my face.

A heavy gauntlet slammed down onto my shoulder. I half-turned and was hauled around to look into Harris' bulging eyes.

"What did you do, Specialist?" he roared.

"I brought down an attacking aircraft, sir. It was an amazing shot, if I do say so myself."

Harris looked out toward the cliffs, where a spot still burned brightly. Then he eyed the vapors that were hugging the ground stubbornly, refusing to disperse.

"What about the enemy crew? Any survivors?"

I pointed out to the water. We all looked, and my mouth twisted into a grimace.

The pilot who had fallen into the water wasn't having a good time of it. The rock-fish had gathered around, sensing an injured, helpless victim. I could barely see the man anymore. He looked more like a hump of wriggling flesh. The rock-fish, with their wart-encrusted bodies glinting wetly, were feasting.

"How can he still be alive?" Harris asked.

I lifted my weapon again. "Permission to put him out of his misery, Vet?" I asked.

"Since when do you ever ask permission to fire your weapon, McGill?"

198

I just looked at him.

"All right," he said, sighing. "Do it."

Fire lanced out of my tube, and the water steamed. The splashing stopped until fresh, living rock-fish came up to finish the task their dead comrades had begun.

"Guys, look," Natasha said. She had a scope out and was examining the far side of the lake. We both joined her.

The situation on the rock-pile had changed. The troops that had been laboriously climbing the stones and occasionally falling into mantraps had halted and reversed themselves. They were now marching toward the verdant line of flowery growths along the west side of the region.

There was a moment of calm—then Legion Varus did what they had to do. They fired upon the advancing enemy.

I watched with interest as the armored squares of troops rocked backward, taking the shocks in stride. The laser rifles the legionnaires were equipped with didn't seem to be having much effect. Each hit staggered a trooper—but a moment later he was back in perfect stride with his brothers.

"The primus shouldn't play around with these boys," I said. "They look pretty serious."

"Why don't you call her and tell her how to handle it, McGill?" Harris suggested. "I bet she'd like that."

"She's got to use her mortars, or at least her plasma cannons. I'm just saying."

As if I was a fortuneteller, my fellow weaponeers stepped up the assault. Lasers weren't penetrating, so heavy beams lanced out taking down troopers with each shot. Sometimes, two fell to a single beam. They rarely got back up.

At that point, the battlefield shifted again. I got the feeling both sides had been hesitant, feeling out each other's capabilities to inflict harm. Now, the littermates were convinced.

Just as Della had intimated to me, the armored enemy didn't take kindly to watching their brothers die. They changed demeanor suddenly and completely as if a switch had been thrown.

They'd been marching in precise order, lockstep, almost methodical in their movements. Now their calm melted and turned into wild rage. Their slow, measured steps became sweeping bounds. Their limbs, once quiet at their sides, came up and formed gauntleted claws.

"Holy shit," Harris whispered at my side.

The troopers charged. It was a berserker thing and an astounding rush of metal-encased flesh. The beams coming out of the flowery embankment ahead of them increased to an almost frantic level of fire. Energy beams were released steadily but struck the ground as often as armor, forming glassy patches on the sandy soil and smoky holes in armor.

At the last moment, a line three ranks deep of our own heavy troopers rushed forward. They carried the banner of the wolf's head emblem, and Legion Varus' best rushed to meet the maddened enemy.

The two lines crashed together. We were too distant to see the details, but I could tell our men were using force-blades for the most part. They were sawing and hacking limbs from their larger opponents. The enemy was not helpless, though. They had large pistols, which they used to great effect at close range. In hand-to-hand, they wielded heavy sabers to hack and hew. I wished I could have been there with my comrades.

Outnumbered four to one, the massive berserkers could not win. But they did reap a terrible toll. Before the struggle was over, dozens of our silver-armored legionnaires lay in the mud.

"Not one of them broke—did you see that?" Harris demanded. "Not one of those big bastards would turn tail and run. They all fought to the death. They fought until they were chopped apart."

I didn't say anything. Neither did Natasha.

Harris hit me then, slamming his fist into the back of my helmet. The blow didn't really hurt, but it did cause my head to ring.

"Did you want to add something to that, Vet?" I asked.

Harris glowered at me. "If I find out that you started this fight, so help me McGill, I'll kill you myself."

"You'd be well within your rights, Vet," I said calmly.

"Don't think I won't do it, McGill. I've done it before."

"You have indeed, Vet. I haven't forgotten."

For several long seconds, we had ourselves an old-fashioned stare-down.

"I've been tired of your bullshit for nearly two years now," he told me. "I can't wait until you muster out."

"Haven't you heard? I'm re-upping. Planning to become a lifer."

Cursing and muttering, Harris disappeared into the ship leaving Natasha and me at the bottom of the ramp.

Natasha looked after him in concern. She put a hand on the back of my helmet.

"He dented your helmet," she said.

"That's legion property, too."

She gave a small, nervous laugh. Then she spoke with me in a hushed, worried voice.

"James, what if he finds out what you did?"

I shrugged. "I don't think he will. I think he'll have plenty of better things to worry about from now on. Look."

She followed my arm and gasped. Fresh troops were marching down from the huge ship. These new enemies looked different. They weren't all standing in perfect nines, either.

"Are those—squids?" Natasha asked.

"Looks that way."

A group of cephalopods had emerged for the first time. They were the same size as the human troopers they'd bred for war. I realized that now. I wondered if they'd tried to make them in their own image, growing them and altering their genes so they were the same size and weight. There was something creepy about that. This species was a cold one, and I found I liked them less with every passing hour.

"They might have made a mistake," I said hopefully.

Legion Varus hadn't been slow to react to this new threat. They fired a barrage of heavy beams toward the cephalopods. But the beams didn't reach the enemy. Instead, the energy splashed and flickered as each beam was intercepted by a shimmering field of force.

"They put a shield up!" Natasha breathed. "A shield big enough and strong enough to cover their entire ship."

I nodded thoughtfully. The squids had just moved up a few notches in technical prowess in my estimation.

"How are we ever going to get through to their ship if they have shields with that kind of range?" Natasha asked.

I didn't reply because I didn't have an answer. I watched as the squids calmly rummaged in the equipment they'd piled outside their ship. No wonder they hadn't worried about protecting it from fire. They were in no danger from our weaponry now that they'd shielded the region.

While we looked on, the fresh troops kept flowing down the ramps. Before they were done, there were twice as many as there had been. They all stood in calm, perfectly-formed squares of nine. Their black armor gleamed like star-studded space.

As we watched, a protuberance began to slowly lift from the crown of the great ship. It was oblong, sleek, and quite large. By my estimation, it was at least thirty meters in length.

"What the hell is that thing?" Natasha asked.

"Looks like a big weapon," I said. "Or it could be a sensor of some kind."

As we watched in growing concern the object began to swivel, coming around slowly.

"It's got to be some kind of cannon!" I shouted.

I reported in—but it was hardly necessary. Half the people in the valley had seen it. The threat was unmistakable.

Across the lake, the legionnaires who'd been busy removing valuable equipment from their dead comrades stood up and bolted into the forest of flowers. I heard the tactical chatter and tuned into my overall unit chat. They'd been ordered to withdraw and scatter.

For several seconds, as the giant turret traveled, I felt certain it was going to fire on the troops who were fleeing certain death. But it didn't.

The big weapon kept turning, slowly, coming around until...

"Run!" I shouted. Natasha was right behind me. We didn't really have anywhere safe to go, so we ran to the lakeshore. I leapt out into the water just before the air grew blindingly white and a tremendous beam of power flashed out.

The beam cut into the lifter and tore it apart. There was no chance for anyone aboard to escape. I was sure of that. Harris, Leeson and whoever else was still aboard—they were all dead.

Natasha and I got separated in the confusion. I knew as I crouched in the water, pushing away rock-fish that kept yawning, trying to get a grip on my armor, that Leeson was going to be mighty upset when he was revived. Nothing made a man feel like more of a loser than dying twice in the same day.

-21-

"Good thing we pulled the revival unit out of the ship when we did," I said to Carlos when he came staggering back to camp after his revival.

He was still dripping wet. He reached for his armor with numb fingers. I helped him with the leggings. That was always the worst part when a man was fresh from a revive. Your balance was one of the last things to start working right. The bio people said it was due to the excess liquids inside the sinuses, which clogged the inner ear. It took a while to drain out and clear our heads.

"No it isn't!" Carlos complained. "If the cohort's revival unit had been destroyed, I could have been revived in another valley—one where I wasn't up to my ass in space-squids."

I chuckled. "Most of them seem to be some kind of genetically-altered mega-humans," I pointed out.

"Is that supposed to make me feel better?" Carlos demanded, leaning on me heavily. "And how come you're looking so smug?"

"What did you want?" I asked him, "a kiss on the top of your head?"

Carlos was quite a bit shorter than I was, and he always hated it whenever I brought up this obvious comparison.

"That's all you've got?" Carlos demanded. "Smartass remarks? I died at your hands—*again*—and I don't even get an apology? Nothing? Zip? Some friend you are."

204

"I didn't fire that big beam," I told him somewhat defensively. "The squids blew you up, not me."

I'd been getting accusations like this all afternoon. The platoon was looking at me like I'd personally executed them. I knew it was partly because I'd survived and they hadn't. The guys who got lucky and lived through a bad fight always seemed like dirty, lucky pricks to the ones who'd died.

"You might as well have blown up the lifter," Carlos retorted. "Yeah, yeah, I know, they attacked us first. But I heard about what you did."

I eyed him coolly, trying to hide my concern. If Carlos knew that I'd shot down that enemy aircraft—well, I might as well broadcast vid of the event to the entire legion. There were many things Carlos was capable of, but keeping his big mouth shut wasn't one of them.

"What are you talking about?" I asked.

"Don't play dumb with me, you freckle-faced cracker," he said. "The role of village idiot suits you, but it doesn't fool me. I know you talked to that crazy little chick with the crossbow— that's treason right there, did you know that? You arranged some kind of alliance with her, didn't you? And now, all of a sudden, the aliens are shooting at us. What a surprise. Before, they'd been content to play slave-driver with the colonists, but noooo, you had to go and mess that up and drag us into this crap-stew..."

I stopped listening to his tirade around then. Carlos kept complaining, but I didn't hear a word of it as I helped him into his armor. He was right, of course, but if he didn't know *how* I'd pulled it off, it didn't really matter. Suspicion wasn't in the same league as evidence.

Internally, I breathed a sigh of relief. Natasha seemed to be the only one who knew the full story. She'd seen me shoot the alien aircraft personally, but I was pretty sure she would keep quiet. After all, we already had a few secrets between us.

Carlos finally shut up when I put his helmet on. He lifted the visor and stared at me.

"You aren't even listening, are you?" he asked.

"Nope."

"I totally hate you."

"I kind of figured. Close your faceplate, the enemy is using gas."

Grumbling, he did as I suggested.

We got moving then, as Leeson was calling on all his able-bodied people to assemble. We were to advance and recon the enemy ship. Carlos wasn't happy about these orders—no one was.

"This is just total bullshit," he kept saying as we pressed our way through the thick, waxy leaves. We ran into a patch of different vegetation every now and then, stuff that looked like chard or spinach, but which was as tall as a man.

"We could make a nice salad with all this greenery," I commented.

"Be my guest and eat some of it, McGill. I double-dog dare you."

I chuckled and kept moving forward. Leeson wasn't happy with me, either. He'd put me on recon and given me a three-man team. Naturally, the adjunct let the rest of his troops fall behind and linger. With me were only Carlos, Kivi and Hudson. None of them were smiling when they realized the four of us were getting close to the enemy ship alone.

Finally, Carlos kicked me in the ass. I turned around, my servos whirring. I straight-armed him, and he almost fell down.

"You left a gouge in my armor," I complained.

"It was an accident, Specialist."

We glared at each other for a second. Kivi and Hudson caught up, and Kivi rolled her eyes at us.

"You boys going to fight again?" Kivi asked. "Don't be pussies this time. Use force-blades. You might both die that way."

Carlos stopped glaring at me long enough to look at her. "Both of us, huh?" he asked her. "Aren't you pissed at McGill? He got you killed along with the rest of us. And don't pretend you don't know it."

Hudson took a step forward, but before he could speak I lifted a hand to silence the group. I was only a specialist, but I outranked all of them. They paused to look at me.

I could tell morale was low. That wasn't unusual in Legion Varus, but I didn't like being the cause of it.

"Look," I said. "We've had a bad day, but we're marching in the right direction now. We're going to kill these squids and their pet freaks, not colonists from Earth."

"That was your plan, wasn't it?" asked Carlos, squinting at me. "I see it all now. You're not just having fun—you're on a crusade. Well, count me out. I don't want to be involved with another of your lost causes."

"You sure?" I asked him. "I've seen the colonist girls, you know. They're pretty hot. They'll be grateful if we save them all."

Carlos chewed on that one. I knew he'd been having fantasies about innocent colonists all the way out here in *Corvus*.

"They don't seem very friendly," he said.

"Let's find out."

I turned and kept marching. The rest fell behind me. They were still grumbling, but at least no one was kicking me in the butt. I hoped we'd pull together before we made contact with the enemy.

My hopes were dashed when we reached the top of a rise and bellied up to have a look. I could see the ship and, at this close range, the shimmering shields were visible to the naked eye. The shields looked like a shell of rain that fell endlessly over the ship but never touched it.

"Turn on your suits and transmit," I said quietly. I needn't have bothered. Everyone was working their tappers, taking stills and transmitting vids.

Something strange loomed up among the thick foliage directly to the east of us. It wasn't anything I'd seen before.

Impossibly tall, thin and man-like, the creature had dangling limbs with oversized hands and feet. Naked except for a flap of leathery cloth wound around its narrow midsection, it had no weapons that we could see. The face was even odder than the body. Nostrils the size of credit-pieces quivered in a nose that was as large and protruding as a normal man's elbow. Red-rimmed eyes like coals stared at us over that nose.

I think it was as surprised to find us as we were to meet it. When it first appeared it had been walking on all fours, but it reared up when it encountered us, standing a dozen feet tall.

Kivi's force-blades sizzled into life extending from her wrists. I lifted my tube, but a huge hand lashed out and smashed it down.

The creature was skinny—but strong! My plasma tube went whirling away.

Kivi struck at that arm, quick as a snake. The oversized hand flew free with a spray of dark blood which splashed the foliage with a sound like falling raindrops.

The creature galloped back from us, scrambling and using its stump as well as its other three limbs. I went for my plasma cannon—but never managed to reach it.

An intense beam leapt out from the direction of the alien ship. It slagged my cannon and then swept toward me, melting earth and withering the giant flowers.

I raced back toward cover. I turned my head to see how the fight with the tall, skinny freak had gone—instantly, I knew all was not well for him.

The cannon had shot the freak down, and he'd been left quivering, slumped on the ground. I felt a pang of sorrow for him. He hadn't seemed too bright. He'd been enslaved since birth, I felt sure of that, and the aliens in that ship didn't seem to give a damn if he lived or died.

My recon group ran farther into the brush. Whooshing, crackling sounds ripped through the plants over our ducked heads setting fire to the crowns of a hundred flowers with blossoms the size of umbrellas.

When we found a shallow depression and hunkered down inside it, Kivi spoke first.

"What was that thing?"

"Some kind of specially-bred human," I said.

"Bred for what?" asked Carlos. "Reaching the top shelf?"

"I don't know, but it was sniffing around. Maybe it was patrolling the area for stray humans. They're here to collect slaves, remember."

"Yeah," Carlos said thoughtfully. "Yeah, that's it. He's like some kind of skinny tracking hound. He's a slaver who runs people down after sniffing them out. I can see how that would be useful when they're trying to dig people out of their caves."

"A slaver," I said thoughtfully. "As good a name as any."

Carlos seemed to puff up with pride. He liked naming things and took credit for such honors whether he deserved it or not.

The beams from the ship soon stopped coming. We reported in via our suit radios, and it wasn't thirty seconds later that the enemy found us again.

I think it was our transmissions that had screwed us. We'd forgotten these weren't low-tech lizards in a forest. Whatever they were, these squids knew their tech.

This time, there were six slavers, not just one. They carried nets that crackled and sparked in gloved hands. With an odd, croaking series of cries, they sprang up all around us. I wouldn't have thought such large creatures could move with such stealth. I swore later, as did the rest of my team, that they hadn't made a sound or disturbed a single leaf.

The nets launched, spread and floated down toward us. Electricity flowed in each metallic thread. I could see the nets spark and flash, arcing with everything they touched. The nets floated downward slowly—as if they were made of feather-light material.

The look on the faces of the slavers was one of triumph. They seemed certain of victory. I guess that's because they'd never fought with armored humans before. A group bearing crossbows and wearing leathers, like the colonists, would have surely been in serious trouble.

My team circled up and we put our backs together. Carlos used his laser, beaming away at the face of the one nearest him. The eyes smoked, and the man-thing fell back, screeching and clawing at its face. Hudson and Kivi followed his example by trying to burn the other slavers. But they'd been warned and hunkered back, hiding behind the fronds and stems of nearby plants.

The lasers still found them and burned smoldering streaks across their leathery chests. But they lived, even if they were left screaming and thrashing.

I didn't have my cannon, so I went with force-blades. Looking back, I realized this was the right choice and probably saved my life. I directed the beams upward and squeezed my gauntlets, depressing the studs in the palms.

Twin blades shot upward, and I kept squeezing, reaching for maximum extension. I'd realized that these guys were *tall* and I had to have as much reach as I could get to fight them on an even footing.

Before I could thrust my blades into the slavers that circled us, I heard a screech—a human sound.

I glanced to my left and saw Kivi sink to her knees. One of those falling, gossamer nets had touched her armor, and she collapsed under it, paralyzed.

Without even looking up, I slashed over my head with my force-blades. They crackled and snapped as they cut through the strange fibers of the net that had almost reached me.

The slaver in front of me plucked his shredded net in confusion. I'm sure he'd never seen a man defeat it before. His overly-long fingers reached out—but he didn't get them back. I cropped all of them from his hand with a smooth slashing motion using my left blade. Then I cocked the left blade over my head to act as a guard. The right blade I thrust with, and its length pierced that skinny stack of ribs, opening up the slaver and spilling his organs over the mud. Twitching the tip upward, I ended his life, and he collapsed in a shivering, bony mass.

Two pairs of hands gripped me from behind a moment later. As I was dispatching the slaver closest to me, the others had leapt and grabbed me from behind.

They warbled and hooted in excitement. I felt my body lift from the ground. I had a hand as big as a basketball blocking my vision almost completely, as it had been placed over my faceplate. More hands had me under the arms of my armored suit, and with a grunt they lifted me. I was amazed they could manage it. They were strong, like apes, with muscles that jumped and rippled under their stretched skins. More hands had each of my wrists, holding them out so I couldn't cut them with my force-blades.

I struggled, but a second later I was lifted like a child by a kidnapper. I realized I was aloft and bouncing. They'd lifted me up and were carrying me away toward their ship, no doubt.

Visions of slavery on a strange world sprang up in my mind. I quelled panic. I had to keep myself in as cool a frame of mind as I could. I wanted to shout and call for help—but I resisted the urge. The recon team was too far from the rest of the platoon. No one was going to come to my aid in time.

As calmly as I could under the circumstances, I radioed Leeson and reported my situation.

"Sir, we've been overrun. We killed two tall, skinny guys, but I'm the only man left conscious."

"What are you saying, McGill? Where's the rest of the team? I'm only seeing your suit on my display."

Squeezing my gauntlets, I shortened the force-blades. As it was, they'd been cutting through the forest of growths like twin scythes. I figured I might as well save power.

"Sir, they've been captured in some kind of metallic netting. Maybe it interferes with radio contact. We're all being carried to the ship. We've been captured, sir—all of us."

"What? By a bunch of naked freaks? Kill them and free yourself. That's an order, McGill."

I rolled my eyes as the channel closed. I tried to think, but it was difficult. There had to be something I could do. They were smarter than I'd assumed, and when they got me to their ship I was pretty sure they'd dismantle my suit and pull me out of it as a man might rip an oyster from its shell.

In the meantime, the slavers weren't idle. They must have noticed my force-blades had withdrawn. They forced my arms forward, and I strained against them—but not too strongly. I didn't want them to know just how powerful my exoskeleton could be if I diverted all power to the enhancement systems.

That was a mistake on my part because they touched my wrists together, and I heard a loud, metallic click.

The huge hand that had been over my visor retreated. I was able to see my situation clearly. My wrists each had a circle of metal around them. Two black rings that touched one another. I tugged, but my wrists would not come apart.

I recalled then what Della had told me: *They will place rings around your arms and touch them together. Then you will never be able to separate your hands from one another again until they will it.*

I stared at those rings around my wrists for a long second, then cranked my neck around. We were heading toward the ship just as I'd thought. I saw Kivi, Hudson and Carlos were all netted and being dragged behind the other slavers. My comrades appeared to be helpless, paralyzed by the effect of the nets.

I wondered then if my first command was going to go down in Legion Varus history with a footnote declaring it a record-breaking failure.

We'd made a sorry showing. We'd only killed two of our attackers, and they'd captured my entire team. As the only man who could still act, I was determined to put up more of a fight.

The first thing I did was relax. I let the slavers transfer me to one of their group, who carried me on his back at a loping run toward the lowered ramp. Being carried like captive prey by tall skinny guys that were twice my height had to be the oddest ride I'd ever experienced. I felt like a little kid—something I wasn't at all used to.

We reached the force shields that encircled their ship. I felt the screens tingle against my skin as we passed through them. The slavers were forced to slow down and edge their way through. As we pressed into the shimmering zone of stilled molecules, I felt a chill pass through me, which was a side effect of shielding.

The slaver carrying me on his back made a mistake then. He let go of my clasped wrists. His huge palm, a webbing of bones and skin, reached up to press against the screens. It was a natural enough thing to do. People normally tried to push away the screens, as they felt odd against the face like a mass of breaking cobwebs. Putting out your hand to brush them away never helped end the sensation, but people did it all the time anyway.

Biding my time, I waited until the very moment we passed through the shielding. Force-blades didn't operate properly inside a shield wall.

Once we were through, the slaver's hand came for my wrists again. I grinned inside my helmet. I squeezed my fingers closed inside my right gauntlet, and a shimmering line of force sprouted like a unicorn horn out of it.

The slaver must have known what was coming. His red eyes widened, and I thought I heard a croak of dismay. I thrust my, short, thick blade home. The slaver crumpled, his legs

212

going limp, and I crashed down five feet or more to the hard ground.

I grunted, rolled onto all fours and struggled to my feet. Ahead of me, Kivi, Hudson and Carlos were all being dragged away. I reached for my sidearm, but it was gone. The slavers had been bright enough to disarm me.

Glancing toward the shield that shot up into a high dome at my back, it occurred to me that I should be slipping back through it and running for the forest. Don't think for a moment that this thought didn't impinge strongly—it did. But standing against my desire for self-preservation was concern for my teammates, who were even now being carted toward that strange, looming ship. I stared after the slavers, watching my friends bang against their legs in sacks of metallic webbing.

What would happen to Kivi, to Carlos? I didn't know Hudson that well, but I knew he didn't deserve this fate.

The key problem was that they couldn't be revived if they were captured. One of the chief nightmares of any Legionnaire was exactly this situation. There were few fates worse than being held captive and incognito on an alien world. Without a confirmed death, the legion couldn't legally revive you— probably a good thing, in my estimation. Who'd want to try to live a normal life knowing that you had a copy of yourself screaming in a cell lightyears away, circling a distant star?

"Ah, crap," I muttered, and started after the trio of slavers. I cranked my exoskeleton to full power and diverted most of it to my legs. With leaps and bounds, I raced after them.

They spotted me before I reached the ramp. The slavers were at the foot of that vast tongue of metal. Just the ramp by itself was impressive. It had looked small at a distance, but up close, I realized it was *huge*. The size of a basketball court at least.

Above that tongue was a black mouth that yawned open. There was darkness inside, punctuated by brilliant points of white light. I didn't know what they had in there, and right now I didn't want to know.

I concentrated on one thing: getting to my friends before they were dragged into that ship and forgotten forever.

Very aware of my situation, I saw the big gun on top of the ship catch sight of me. Like a bird of prey, it tracked and swiveled. Could it have nothing better to burn than little old me?

To give it something to worry about, I ran into a pile of crated equipment. The operators would have to make a decision; was a single man worth damaging their stockpile?

The gun kept tracking me right up to the point where I set foot on the ramp. It never fired, and at that point shifted away toward more distant enemies. I didn't have time to breathe a sigh of relief, however.

In front of me, the three slavers turned around. They looked surprised to see me sprinting after them—even amused. Behind me, a squad of nine littermates who'd been standing in a perfect square like switched-off robots suddenly came to life. They turned together and approached. I imagined that someone in the ship had activated the squad to deal with the lone human inside their perimeter.

It didn't take a genius to realize I was trapped and screwed. The nine at my rear shouldered huge rifles, but the slavers lifted hands and chittered at them waving them back. They must have been happy to see a new captive who seemed intent on delivering himself into their vast hands.

The trio dropped my friends like sacks of meal. Then they stepped apart, moving to flank me.

This was it, I realized. It was time to do—and to die.

Moments like this come to legion troops more often than old Earth armies. Knowing you're going to come back to life after a fight changes a man's calculations. Sure, plenty of times in history men have made the decision to go down fighting, to take as many of the enemy with them as they could, but with foreknowledge of resurrection, I think we were a little more likely to choose such a path.

Legionnaires didn't fall to their knees and beg for mercy from our alien foes. We didn't embrace capture as a way out. Instead, we feared it as one of the worst possible fates.

Knowing I was about to die freed up my mind and my body. I wasn't afraid anymore—not exactly. I was intent on doing damage, as much as I could, before they brought me down.

The slavers didn't know any of this, naturally. They knew I could fight. They knew I was dangerous, but they couldn't know they had a suicidal maniac charging toward them.

I veered left, letting the center man maneuver to circle behind me. The man on the far right huffed and ran forward, not wanting to be left out of the capture.

Take down one at a time, Veteran Harris had always said. *The others guys can wait. Finish your target and move on only after you're sure the first one is in the bag.*

To my pleasure, I noticed a hint of doubt in the expression on my targeted slaver's ugly face. The tall, skinny monster on the left side of the ramp didn't look as happy as the other two.

Still, he postured himself gamely enough. His knobby knees flexed and bent. His arms flew wide—impossibly wide. He had a wingspan that would have made a condor jealous.

Instead of extending two force-blades, I extended only one. After all, my wrists were still clamped together. I couldn't work two weapons effectively if I couldn't move my arms independently.

I slowed down in the final moments of my charge. I leveled one long blade like a lance. Shimmers of dusky orange, magenta and neon green ran the length of the blade like electric flames. The colors reached the tip, then chased themselves back again to my gauntlet.

Thrusting for the slaver's midsection, I was surprised by his agility. He bounced backward, squirming in the air. I thrust and missed again, while he retreated farther.

His strategy was immediately clear to me. The other two were circling and closing in. They'd pull me down from behind, just as they'd done before.

With a snarl of frustration, I shifted right toward my three helpless comrades. The slaver I'd been stabbing at gargled something in his throat and advanced to follow me.

That was the move I'd been waiting for. I whirled back and thrust for him again—but this time I stabbed downward, lancing his foot. I pinned it for a brief second to the ramp itself.

He struggled with a cry of pain and pulled away the smoking remnants of his injured foot. My blade flicked upward again—and this time he couldn't dodge and hop away. I gutted him and left him flopping on the ramp.

I turned with barely a second to spare. The center man, who'd been coming up behind me, closed his massive hands. His fingers enveloped each of my arms.

It was a losing strategy for him. Force-blades don't get pinned. They may take a few seconds to burn through a tough substance, but they always go through in the end.

I cut the second man in half, from crotch to skull. Those big hands that gripped me fell away as lifeless as dead autumn leaves.

The third and final slaver lost heart then. He pointed at me and turned toward the nine that stood in perfect formation at the foot of the ramp. He was obviously declaring me *persona non grata*. I couldn't blame him for that.

The front rank of the nine dropped to the ground, the second rank went down to one knee, and the three in back stood tall. Once in position, they lifted their rifles and sighted in unison.

I hadn't waited around while they created their own miniature firing-square. I ignored the last slaver and ran to my three friends.

My force-blade sank first into Kivi. It was a hard thing to do, let me tell you. I've slept with Kivi, and I've fought with her and died at her side. To kill her, to drive my lance into her back while she lay there helpless and paralyzed—I never wanted to do it again.

Three quick strides brought me to Carlos next. He was lying in a different pose. His face plate was open and his brown eyes stared up at me. Even though he was watching, I found it a little easier to kill him—don't ask me why.

The first volley caught me then, knocking me from my feet and tossing me ass-over-teakettle right up the ramp. I was broken, and my armor had at least four smoking holes punched into it.

I'd taken nine massive slugs, but I struggled to my knees and approached Hudson, the last of the captives. I can't tell you how much pain I was in. I'm not really sure anyone can when they're already dead but still moving. My body was functioning to some extent, not having shut down completely yet, but for the most part I was numb.

The last slaver made whooping noises. I'm not really sure if he was cheering on the gunners, or impressed by my performance, or just plain happy to be alive.

Crawling, I reached Hudson, but I didn't get my blade into him. I tried, oh Lord, how I tried, but my body just wouldn't obey me anymore.

I rolled onto my back, going limp. The sky above was lit by the harsh light of Zeta Herculis, but there was no beauty in the sight for me.

A weight fell upon my wrists then. A vast, impossible weight. I saw with fading consciousness that the last slaver had come and placed his foot upon my wrists, to keep me from cutting him. Cautiously, curiously, his face loomed over mine.

He asked me a question then, something in his strange warped tongue. I didn't understand it, but I knew that I'd intrigued him. He looked into my dying eyes with a squinting, uncomprehending gaze.

"Maybe," I rasped, "I'll get a chance to explain things to you later on, freak."

And then…I died.

-22-

The next thing I knew, I was lying on my back in a bunker that the legion had dug in the midst of a stack of boulders. The bunker gave people a chance to recuperate after revival, but I knew its critical function was to protect the revival machine itself. Nearby, the revival team worked feverishly to revive everyone who'd been lost on this very long day.

"Are you insane?" demanded Carlos. He was standing over me, glaring down at my naked body on a makeshift cot.

I blinked, barely able to process his anger. I barely knew who I was yet—but memories were drifting back to me.

Dying and coming back to life was kind of like waking up suddenly in the middle of a dream. Sometimes you weren't quite sure how to sort through the stuff that had actually happened, and the stuff that was only ghostly echoes inside your head.

"You're saying you killed me so I wouldn't be captured?" Carlos asked after I'd explained my decision to him. "That's just unreal. I don't buy it—not for a second, McGill. You're either full of shit or certifiable. Maybe both."

"Of course that's why he did it," Kivi said. She was sitting on a rock nearby dressing herself.

Anne Grant, overworked and haggard, waved at the two of them irritably. "Take McGill out of here. He's a good grow—get him dressed and out of my bunker."

"Kicking us out already?" Carlos asked. "I thought you were sweet on him. At least, that's what he says."

Anne growled at him and pointed toward the exit. I followed her gesture, and a white square of light hurt my freshly-grown eyes. It was strange to think these eyes had never experienced sunlight before.

A few moments later, I stumbled out into the open with Carlos and Kivi on either side of me propping me up.

"I was hoping you'd come out with a bad grow," Carlos complained. "I was going to volunteer for the grim but very necessary duty of recycling you, you murdering sack."

Getting tired of him faster than usual, I shook his hands off my elbow.

"I had to kill you," I said, slurring my words slightly. "I had to, and my only regret was that I didn't get to poor Hudson fast enough."

"I still don't buy it," Carlos said. "You forget, McGill, I saw your face. I was looking right up, and I saw a bloodthirsty leer as you drove that force-blade through me. I felt it, too. We were paralyzed, but we could still see and feel everything!"

I frowned. "Sorry about that."

"You enjoyed it, didn't you? Some little part of you has always wanted to kill me. You saw your chance, with an excuse all lined up, and you went for it. I saw your eyes."

"I don't remember," I lied.

"Bastard."

Kivi put her head against my shoulder.

"Well…" she said. "I'm glad you did it, James. What if that ship takes off right now? What if everyone aboard is hauled away never to be seen again? They'll be captives forever in some vile prison, warped into those monsters that have been bred from human flesh. I don't want to be forced to have children and to watch them grow into genetically-modified slaves."

"You're welcome," I told her.

Carlos made a farting sound with his mouth and stomped away. I didn't care. I knew he'd get over it eventually. He always did. He knew I'd done the right thing—he was just upset that it had to happen at all. Carlos always had to blame someone when things went badly—anyone other than himself.

219

He was a good enough friend when you really needed one, but I hoped he never made it into the officer ranks.

I liked Kivi's reaction much better. She gave me a little kiss and helped me into a fresh suit of armor, talking as she did. I learned we'd been ordered to report to Graves himself the second our bodies were operating normally.

To my surprise, the first thing Graves did was order us back to the bunker with the revival machine. We'd been tasked with escorting the machine and its operating staff on a circuitous route around the lake. Fortunately, we didn't have to carry the thing by hand. It weighed over a ton, and even with our suits it wouldn't have been easy. We were provided two drone marchers which up until now had been kept in reserve. Most of the drones were in other valleys assigned to other cohorts. These two, however, had been aboard our lifter from the start. They'd been used to transport the revival machine off the lifter, and had thus been spared when the ship blew up.

I marched with the rest of the revived group ahead of Centurion Graves and the bio people. We took the long way around the central lake so as to avoid the alien ship on the other side.

The drones were four-legged machines that resembled thick-legged pigs. We called them "pigs" or "piggies". They had a barrel-like central torso, four heavy legs and no head at all. They navigated with a mix of input from high-frequency sonar and scanning cameras in cages along the sides. Once in a while, I heard a little singing sound, which I knew was the sonar. But for the most part, I had to listen to their engines and those churning legs, which put up quite a racket.

We were all glad to have the piggies with us even if they were kind of noisy. They carried the revival machine strung up between them like it was no big deal. The only clue they gave concerning the tremendous weight they were bearing was the depth of their footprints. The pads on the bottom of their feet were about as big around as that of an average elephant, but they sunk into the soft ground anyway. When the drones pulled those feet back up and out, there was a terrific squelching noise.

After about two hours of marching through the odd growths on the west side of the lake, we were within sight of the rest of the cohort. They'd taken the time to build up a small fortification—puff-crete mostly hidden behind a ridge in the landscape. From here, they couldn't be hit by direct beams from the ship.

For their part, the aliens had stopped coming after Legion Varus. When we'd retreated from the area of their ship, they seemed to lose interest. They were now scouring the cliffs again searching for captives among the colonists.

Reaching picket lines posted in the forest, we identified ourselves and were hustled through to the main camp. The piggies picked up the pace, almost as if they knew they'd be allowed to rest soon.

The camp was on full alert. I could tell the cohort hadn't been idle. They'd been digging and building. Puff-crete bunkers were everywhere, buried in the soft dark soil around the lake. We delivered the revival unit, and a team of bio people took over. They hustled and heaved, carting the machine down into the black, gaping mouth of a bunker they'd built specifically for this purpose. To me, they looked like ants dragging a kill down their hole to be consumed.

Afterward, we formed up with the rest of our unit. I felt relieved. I'd never liked being off on my own with just Leeson and a few troops defending the lifter. Now that the lifter had been destroyed, the commanders had decided we'd all be better off here in one central encampment which couldn't be hit by the enemy's big cannon. I wasn't so sure about that, but I was happy not to be in a smaller group.

"McGill," Graves said, waving me to come closer the moment he saw me.

I stumped over, and he eyed me critically.

"You're one crazy son-of-a-bitch," he said without humor or anger. "I heard about what you did right there on their doorstep."

"Uh…thank you, Centurion."

He snorted. "It wasn't meant as a compliment. You killed your own men *after* killing most of the skinnies that caught you? Did I get that right?"

221

"Skinnies? You must be talking about those tall, freaky-looking guys, right? We've been calling them slavers. They seem to specialize in capturing humans. They can sniff us out wherever we hide."

"Skinnies, slavers—whatever. Nasty freaks, no matter what you call them. But let's get back to the part about killing your own team, shall we? That's not exactly in our standard playbook—you know that, right?"

"Yes, sir. I'm aware that I didn't follow regs. But I wanted my people to be revived and to come back into the fight. If we'd all been dragged aboard that ship, we might have been transported into space and end up on another planet indefinitely."

"So...no regrets on your part?" he asked, narrowing his eyes.

"On the contrary," I said. "I have plenty of regrets. I wish I'd killed all the skinnies right off—that would have been a much better outcome. And sometimes I wish I'd signed with a different legion: A legion that doesn't specialize in such deadly missions."

Graves rewarded me with a rare, rumbling laugh. "Such a bullshitter. I'm talking about killing your own team. No regrets there?"

"That? No, sir. They're happy with the outcome too—just ask them. My only regret in that regard is that I didn't make it to Hudson in time to finish him along with the rest. I can't imagine what the aliens are doing to him even now inside the guts of that ship."

Graves' eyes drifted toward the vessel in the east. We couldn't see it directly, as the ridge was in the way, but we all knew it was there. It didn't take much imagination to think of Hudson, shivering and miserable in some cage, trapped within that vast ship.

Graves turned back to me and clapped me on the shoulder. The metal of his gauntlet rang against my epaulet.

"That's what I wanted to hear," he said. "No regrets. Well done, McGill. In my opinion, you made the right call. But I'll have to edit your after-action report slightly just in case the brass gets nosy."

He walked away, and I frowned after him. Edit the report? Did he think that anyone higher ranked than he was going to read it? I hadn't even considered the notion.

But then, I hadn't been thinking about Primus Turov. She was always looking for a good reason to take a shot at me. I'd thwarted her plans a year back—and she wasn't the forgiving type.

Shrugging, I went back to my platoon and met with Leeson. He looked me over as if he didn't quite know what to make of me. After he gave us a briefing on the planned morning action, which involved attacking the slavers as they searched the caves for colonists, he beckoned to me.

I moved to his side, and he stood with his back to the others so no one could listen in.

"I don't want you thinking you can pull that kind of shit whenever you want, McGill," he told me in a hushed tone.

"What specific variety of shit are we talking about, sir?"

He glared at me. "You know damned well what I'm talking about. Don't think for a second you can get away with driving a force-blade into my throat and walking away a hero afterward. I'll erase you when I get revived—that's a promise. Legion Varus won't even have a record of your existence by the end of the next day."

"Don't worry. If these freaks manage to get their gentle hands wrapped around you...well sir, as far as I'm concerned they can keep you."

I smiled and walked away. I could feel Leeson's eyes burning into my back, but I didn't care.

That night I slept with Kivi. Killing a girl had to be the weirdest way to turn her on that I'd ever heard of –but it had worked out for me this time. I doubted anyone else had ever tried it, and I sincerely hoped never to experience such a situation again.

The sex was great, don't get me wrong. Of all the girls I'd been with in Legion Varus, she was the most intense—and probably the most experienced.

I'm not sure what it is about the nearness of death that causes the human brain to turn to quick intimate contact—but the effect is undeniable. We were alive again after having died so utterly, so helplessly. The reprieve, the second chance, it seemed to kick over something in our minds. We wanted to live life to the fullest and didn't hold anything back.

In the depths of the night, which was several hours longer than I was accustomed to, I heard a stealthy sound.

One would think that I would have slept right through it. After all, going through a revival and enjoying Kivi's companionship in my tent had pretty much worn me out. But some part of me lit up, and I awakened anyway.

Sucking in a gulp of air and sitting up suddenly, I groped in the darkness. I found a wrist, and clamped onto it with my hand. The wrist was a thin one, but it tried to pull away with surprising strength.

I held on, and my bleary eyes adjusted.

"Della?" I asked in a whisper.

"Let go of me," she hissed back. "I have a blade."

I saw now that she did indeed have a weapon. It glimmered in the light coming from the vertical slit she'd carefully unzipped to let herself in.

"What the hell are you doing in my tent?" I asked.

"I came to talk to you."

I gave my head a shake to wake up and let her go. I glanced over at Kivi. She was frowning and twitching in her sleep but hadn't awakened. I could tell she was dreaming, her eyelids were shifting.

Then I noticed something else. A tiny, open vial lay near Kivi's face. There was a dark red dust under her nose. It looked like cinnamon, or chili powder.

"What did you do to Kivi?"

"She will sleep. Come with me. Your mechanical birds will find us soon."

I frowned at her, but I followed her out of my tent. I was trying to wrap my mind around what was happening. How had Della gotten into our camp? We had drones, guards and sensors. The techs were seriously screwing up, and I didn't buy the idea Della had sprinkled sleeping powder under *everyone's* nose.

The answer came soon thereafter. She led me to a thicket of alien growths that looked like bulbous cacti—but these cacti had feathery leaves rather than spines. In the middle of these plants was a collection of boulders. One of them shifted at her touch. A dark opening stretched about a foot wide.

"Follow me," she said and began to slide into the opening.

I looked dubiously into the crack in the earth. I walked up to it, crouched and stared into the darkness. I couldn't see much other than Della's shapely legs and butt disappearing into it. When she was gone, I grumbled to myself thoughtfully.

Why me? I know that's the sort of question a fighting man should never ask himself, but I did it anyway.

"Della?" I called down the hole.

There was no answer. I was alone.

There was no doubt in my mind about what I should do then. I should stand up, walk back to my tent and call my unit commanders. Hell, I wasn't even wearing my heavy armor— not that it would fit into that slit in the ground anyway.

Doubting my sanity, I went back to my tent, grabbed a small ruck with a sidearm and a few supplies, and prepared to leave. I took the time to check Kivi's pulse, which was strong, and to take the vial away from her face. I didn't want her to overdose on whatever that stuff was.

As an afterthought, I stoppered the vial and put it into my ruck. One never knew when such a substance might come in handy.

When I returned to the spot where Della had disappeared, I couldn't find the crack in the rocks. I cursed and shoved aside underbrush and dead leaves. It had to be here, right here.

I found it at last. Could it have narrowed even further? I slipped my fingers inside and pulled at it, stretching it wider. The hole was triangular, and it looked like a sliding section of rock—but it was clearly something fashioned to resemble rock.

When it was wide enough, I shined a light inside. There wasn't much to see other than a narrow stone tunnel.

A buzzer swooped nearby. I flicked off my light and stashed it in my bag. I sat next to the opening and yawned. Whoever was running that buzzer took a good, long look at me. I wondered if it was Natasha herself. I pretended to be oblivious to the attention and soon the buzzer wandered off.

The best way to avoid surveillance, I've always found, is to be as boring as humanly possible.

The second the buzzer left, I felt a sharp pain in the back of my leg. I gritted my teeth, holding back a shout. Standing up, I flipped my light back on and peered down into the hole again.

There was Della's face, staring up at me. I realized she'd jabbed me with something, but as I wasn't dying, I figured it hadn't been a nanite-tipped weapon.

"Are you coming or not?" she asked sharply. All I could see were her brown, almond-shaped eyes. There were streaks of dirt and sweat on her brow, but somehow she was still pretty in a rustic sort of way.

"Yeah," I heard myself say.

What happened next was hard to credit, even to me, but I climbed down into that hole. I seriously doubted my mental capacities as I did it. I had to wonder if those psych tests they'd given me long ago back at the Mustering Hall had been right all along.

-23-

The tunnel slanted downward, then leveled off. As best I could tell we were headed toward the nearest rocky cliffs, away from the lake. That was good, as far as I was concerned. I didn't want to risk drowning under the lake and out of range of the legion's sensors.

The passage widened, narrowed then turned wet and dank. We splashed through regions of still, oily water.

"Where are we going?" I asked Della.

"To the Verge," she said, as if that explained everything.

I grumbled and kept after her. "Why did you come to me?"

"I don't trust any of your kind," she said. "But I can't deny that you're fighting the slavers. I saw you die on the ramp—that was a brave thing. Few warriors have ever defeated even a single slaver."

"You saw that? How?"

Della glanced back over her shoulder, eyeing me with a calculating glance. There wasn't much in the way of a light source in the tunnels. The walls glimmered faintly, just enough to keep a man from ramming his nose into them. She carried a chemical light in the form of a tube around her neck which illuminated her face from below with a wan, yellow-green glow.

"We have tubes drilled through the walls of the cliffs," she told me. "There are lenses and mirrors inside. We can see most of the valley. Guiding wires allow us to direct our scopes and focus on distant objects. We installed the system to watch our enemies years ago. If you ever find one down here, be careful, however. They're dangerous when the ship fires light at the walls of stone. Your eyes will be burned from your head. My people are careful never to look through the tubes at the wrong times."

I nodded thoughtfully, and she turned and trotted away. I followed.

The system of scopes and the network of tunnels I toured over the next ten minutes were an impressive engineering effort. The tunnel system represented a low-tech solution and a clever use of resources. These colonists were admirable in their own way. They were determined and obviously tough survivors. I'd always thought we'd had it rough back on Earth over the last century or so. But compared to these people, Earthers like me lived in the lap of luxury.

"Where the hell are we going, girl?" I asked after we must have jogged and slogged twenty minutes or more. "Isn't this far enough for a private talk?"

She halted and looked back at me, cocking her head in the same way she'd done the first time I talked to her.

"A private talk?" she asked.

"Yes. I've been assuming you wanted to discuss our alliance, to talk about what we're going to do next. No one can hear us down here."

"I'm taking you to speak to the Investigator," she said, as if this explained the situation with perfect clarity.

"The what?"

"Our leader. The principal. The one in charge of this valley."

"Oh, okay. What does he want?"

"I don't know, but I'm sure it will be important. You've decided upon your course of action, we understand that. But we've yet to decide ours."

That was all she would tell me. We spent thirty more minutes in the tunnels, during which time I became hopelessly lost. We'd jogged upward and downward, taking various forks, twists and turns. I was trying to keep a mental map, but there were no landmarks to differentiate one tunnel from another.

228

At one point, we passed a glimmer of light from outside. A pale circular beam played along the left wall. I stopped and searched the right wall for an aperture. When I finally found it, Della came back to see what I was doing.

"I found one of your little spyglasses," I said, peering into a conical tube about the size of a water glass.

"Careful," she said. "You never know when they might shine their great weapon. You'll be blinded."

Deciding to take the chance, I put my face to the cone and swiveled it. Pulleys squeaked and grit shifted. My field of view was limited, but I could see a slightly blurred, dusty version of the valley at night.

Stars overhead played like pinpricks in a velvet blanket. To my left, the ship was visible only as a darker hulk in a pit of umber. To my right, there were lights scattered over a circular region.

"That must be our camp. So far down—I hadn't realized we'd climbed inside the cliff walls. We must be two hundred meters up and a kilometer from the camp. We're right between both armies now."

"You see much for an untrained eye," she said.

"We have devices like these, but they fly and carry cameras."

She nodded. "The intelligent insects. We know about them."

"Tell me, Della," I said. "What will the aliens do next? They must know we're going to fight them. Will they come at us, or will they keep trying to capture you in your tunnels?"

"They'll do whatever they find to be the easiest. They only want slaves. If we make it too difficult and delay them long enough, they will eventually go away. That is our goal."

I nodded thoughtfully. "Have you ever considered anything more drastic?"

Her eyes narrowed. "You'll have to talk to the Investigator about that."

She clammed up then, and I was left following in her wake. By the time we reached a large open cavern, I figured we must be getting closer to the side of the valley where the ship was than my own side.

The main cavern was a surprise. There had to be hundreds of people in it—maybe thousands. I couldn't see them all in the faint light.

Unlike the dusty, crumbling holes I'd been traveling through, it was well-kept and airy. There were exhaust ports in the roof—could they be natural chimneys? Fresh air came in from someplace else. They even had a row of fires along one wall for cooking and the like.

Along the far wall, up a series of ramps and stairways, was an area apart from the rest of the cavern. This upscale region was set upon a shelf of flat, fine marble. I could tell right off that was where the important folk spent their time. Instead of crude furniture built of sticks and canvas, there were real chairs and even tables carved from polished stone.

We passed people performing odd operations. There was something that looked like a forge—but not a primitive one. Men with goggles handled lead-shielded pots, pouring hot molten metals. My rad meters jumped on my tapper when we passed this operation, so I gave them a wide berth.

Della led the way to the base of what appeared to be manufactured steps built with tubular steel. I frowned at them as I followed her to the top.

"These steps…" I said, pausing. I looked around, noticing the even, regular shape of the cavern. The walls were ribbed, in fact, with heavy curved supports.

I looked at Della, and she eyed me quietly.

"I think I figured it out," I said. "This cave—this isn't a cave at all. It's what's left of *Hydra*, isn't it?"

She stepped close to me. "Pretend you don't know. People will not trust you with the knowledge."

"Right," I said, looking around. It was obvious now that I thought about it. Sure, it was dusty and decrepit. What must have been decks had been turned into open floors. "Looks like you guys cannibalized much of the ship to build stuff. You must have removed a lot of the metal and—where are the engines?"

Della pursed her lips in annoyance. I don't think she was happy that I'd figured out their little secret.

"*Hydra* was a colony ship," she said. "The vessel was built to be dismantled and used to start our colony. But, as I said, it's best you don't talk about it."

"Okay, I'll play dumb. You have to tell me one more thing, though: how did you bury it in solid rock?"

"When we found the system was occupied, we decided to hide ourselves here, in the wall of this valley. We used the engines to burn into the cliff and let the rock fall outside to cover the entry point."

I nodded thoughtfully. It was quite an engineering feat. My estimation of these people and their technical skills had risen another notch. It almost made me sad to think that Earthers had been such amazing engineers before I was born. We hadn't done much of anything on our homeworld to advance ourselves for several generations. I guess that was part of the grand design of the Empire—to prevent frontier worlds like ours from creating new technology and eventually becoming a threat to the Core Systems.

Following Della, I found I was in for a further surprise. I'd been expecting a scene of wealth, at least compared to the lower class folks who lived on the ship's belly and outer hull. But although I did see better materials and living conditions on the upper deck, I was struck by the number of scientific instruments they had as well.

There was a region of batteries fed by clattering generators. Past that, following the black and red wires, we reached a wide variety of machines. There were computers, medical equipment and even a full machine shop. Labs, enclosed presumably to keep the dust out, lined one wall while extra equipment sat closer to the edge of the deck. There were a lot of people here, some of whom wore old-fashioned lab coats of various colors. I was impressed by these people the most. They eyed me seriously, but without the same mistrust as the simpler folk downstairs.

"What's this place?"

"The Verge," she said in a tone that indicated I was some kind of an idiot for asking.

"Ah," I said, looking over the edge of the railing. "The Verge is the upper deck. What's its purpose?"

"This place keeps us all alive," she said with a hint of pride in her voice. "All that we know, all that we learn, comes from here. Our tools are fashioned here as well with the raw materials smelted below."

Nanites, I thought to myself. This place was the source. They had retained some of the equipment and obviously had been very busy creating effective weaponry against the slavers.

At last, we came to a lab unlike the others. It was full of vats of colored, bubbling liquids. Most of the liquids were yellow or red—or a tainted mixture of both.

I hesitated at the entrance. I'm not sure why. I think it was the smell of the place. It was a distinctly organic odor. Not rot, or offal—more like a tannery, or a slaughterhouse.

"This must be the stranger," said a voice. "Hello stranger. I'm the Investigator."

I stepped into the chamber and turned toward the voice. Taking in the man and the scene around him, I have to admit I recoiled in horror.

Standing not ten feet from me, was a big man with a scalpel the size of a butcher's blade in his hand. He had long, salt-and-pepper gray hair that hung down past his armpits in an unruly mass. That wasn't what freaked me out, however.

What I had trouble accepting, what my eyes latched onto and couldn't escape, was the body on a cold marble slab in front of this blade-wielding Investigator. I would recognize that dead man anywhere. I'd seen him in my dreams a thousand times. His hair was sandy blond. His eyes—carved lidless—were as blue as the Georgia sky.

It was my own dead body on that slab, and it had been carved up into bloody pieces. I stared at it, frozen in place.

"Can it truly disturb you?" asked the Investigator, his sonorous voice both gentle and commanding at the same time. "I hadn't thought that it would."

I opened my mouth, then closed it again. I took a breath, but almost choked on the cloying scents that intruded into my lungs. Was I smelling my own death?

"Yes," I said, looking away from the thing on the slab. "It disturbs me. It would disturb any thinking man."

"Tell me, star man," he said, setting the big blade down and walking a step closer to me.

Della, who stood at my other side, watched the Investigator approach with a mixture of respect and worry. I got the feeling that she was comfortable in his presence—but not completely.

"Tell me what year it is back home," he said.

I met his dark eyes and knew I was taking a test. I've never been good at tests—ask anyone who's ever had the displeasure of administering one in my presence.

"Uh…" I said. "It's 2122, sir."

"A correct answer, but you hesitated!" said the Investigator, turning away from me and walking toward a computer that was set upon a shelf on the far wall of the laboratory. "Is that because of time-dilation? What year did you set out to come here? Really, you must have moved very quickly. You can't have gotten our signal before you left. Do you realize that you're more than twenty years earlier than we expected?"

I blinked at him, chewing over what he was saying. The presence of my own torn-up corpse, not ten feet from my left hand, was distracting to say the least.

To help myself think, I shifted on my feet so that the body wasn't in my field of vision—at least, not most of it. I could still see those cold bluish-white feet out of the corner of my eye.

"Sir," I said, "I'm not quite sure I'm following you. I know you sent your message indicating you'd arrived here on Zeta Herculis about thirty years back. You're correct if you're saying that we only just got your message on Earth not six months ago."

The Investigator made a strange sound. "It's not possible. What you're saying—not possible."

"What's that, sir?" I asked, truly curious.

"You're saying that you came from Earth, but you only got our signal a few months ago. The speed of travel that suggests—it defies logic."

"Ah," I said. "I get it now."

What was it that Natasha and the other techs had explained to me at one point?

"Have you heard of the Alcubierre drive, sir?" I asked him.

His dark eyes fixed upon me. He nodded slowly. "A fable. We tried to make it work. We had theories, mathematical models, but to build such a thing… Are you saying Earth has managed it? That you've uncovered the secret of warp drive?"

"Yes, in a way."

"In a way," he echoed, and his face took on a haunted look. "I've dissected your corpse, sir," he said. "Surely, you must know that I know you better than you know yourself: The foodstuffs and the micro flora species in your gut. Also the protein levels, trace radio-isotopes and even the lead content of your bones. They all match up. You *did* come from Earth."

"That's right," I said. "I'm from the old state of Georgia, actually, North America Sector."

"You said, 'in a way'," the Investigator said suddenly, walking toward me and halting at arm's reach. "What did you mean by that?"

Normally I'm a straight-talking fellow, but I found myself wanting to hide things from this man. He was clearly highly intelligent and dedicated to science. But he also seemed mildly insane. At the very least, his brain and mine didn't work on the same frequency.

But despite my hesitation, I decided to tell him the truth. I'd already blown his mind partway. I figured I might as well blast it apart completely.

"We, meaning the people of Earth, didn't exactly figure out how to make the warp drive work, sir. We had help. Well, more than that. The truth is we bought passage on an alien ship to get out here. We didn't build the ship. We've never managed to build a warp drive, either."

"But…" he said, trying to take it all in. "If you've been in contact with aliens with superior technology…what year?"

"What, sir?"

"What year did you make contact?"

"2052, sir. They came to Earth in 2052, and they had so many ships we could scarcely make out the stars between them."

The light of madness in the man's eyes flared brighter.

234

"That makes it all useless," he said. "Everything we've done here—a waste of time. We're jokes, forgotten and laughed at. My life's work, my mother's work before me…"

"Well now, hold on," I said. "It's not quite like—"

"Why didn't you come sooner?" he asked suddenly. "Why did you leave us here to rot on this rock beneath an alien sun? Why did you allow the cephalopods to torment us for half a century? Can there be an excuse for such cruelty?"

I opened my mouth and raised my hands to answer him, but he was already answering himself. He was up and pacing now, not even looking at me.

"The answer can only be political," he said, his haunted face searching empty years and trillions of empty kilometers as if they stretched out before him as far as his mind could see. "We were exiles, my mother always told me. Whoever hated us so much must have stayed in power: The Social Synthesis, the nation-blocs. You said something about North America Sector—not the United States."

"You have part of the answer," I said, getting a word in edgewise at last.

He loomed close to me. "That's it, isn't it, star man?" he asked. "Your masters hated us, feared us, and wanted us to stay forgotten. What other answer is there, really? I don't even know why I'm asking you. The answers are in the facts as they've been laid out before me. I hadn't wanted to believe—"

"Sir," I said suddenly, loudly.

He looked at me with white-rimmed eyes.

"Sir, you don't understand it all yet. Yes, the situation is a political one. But your old enemies are gone. Long gone. It's the politics of the Galactics that matter now. In fact, that's all that has ever really mattered throughout human history. We just didn't know it."

I proceeded then to explain to him what every kid on Earth learns in elementary school now—about the layers of government all the way up from Local, to District, to Sector, to Hegemony and finally to the distant uncaring halls of the Galactics themselves. I explained the deal we'd made to stay alive and the reality of living under the watchful eye of aliens who cared not one whit if we all lived or died—as long as the rules laid down millennia ago in the Core Systems were strictly followed.

The Investigator listened closely, and I think he got it. He really did. I might have explained this to anyone else on the planet, and it would have failed to penetrate, but this man was ready to listen. He'd dug inside my corpse and seen the light of truth there. We were human, we were from Earth, and we'd gotten here faster than the speed of light would allow. What was even more amazing to him was my regeneration. Our talk turned to that topic once he understood the basics of the Galactic Empire.

"All right," he said, waving away my windy words. "I understand what you're saying although the details are vague. How are you able to come back to life—not once, but over and over again?"

"I'm a copy of the original," I said. "I didn't *really* come back to life. But if you trace every synaptic connection in a man's mind, and you have his DNA as a roadmap to rebuild his body, well, effectively I live again. I have my old memories in a new version of my body. Actually, I'm better than before. I'm younger and stronger than when I died. Injuries aren't copied."

The Investigator put a bloody glove to his bearded chin. For some reason, this made me wince. Maybe it was because it was my own blood that now streaked his face.

"So strange," he said. "And so much information all at once."

Della spoke up then. "Then you believe him, Investigator? I thought him mad at first, but he convinced me he was not a simple littermate like the others. I feel better to know I'm not a fool."

"No, my young scout. You're no fool. You were wise to bring this man to me." He waved a hand toward my previous self and chuckled. "More than once, in fact!"

"Let's talk about something else then," I suggested. "We plan to attack the littermates and slavers when they come for you again. When they try to dig into your, uh, cavern, we'll hit them from behind."

The Investigator narrowed his eyes. "Why? That will only provoke them."

"I think, sir, that they have provoked us. We're Legion Varus. We're one of Earth's space-going armies. What's wrong with protecting our fellow earthmen?"

"Hmm," he said thoughtfully. "You described yourselves as mercenaries. Swords sold to the highest bidder. Who then paid your freight out to this distant star, soldier?"

Finally, he'd touched upon the one topic I didn't want to talk about. After all, we'd come out here to solve a "problem". That "problem" had been the colonists themselves at the time.

As a teen, I'd become an almost professional liar. I could tell in an instant that my hesitation was becoming too long, and he was growing suspicious. The Investigator was many things—but he wasn't stupid.

"Sir," I said, pulling upon my bag of tricks. "Let me explain. The aliens in this sector—the cephalopods—they aren't part of the Galactic Empire. They're operating in space without license, and they attacked a Galactic ship in this system. That isn't acceptable to the Empire. Eventually, they'll come here and correct the situation. In the meantime, we're here. We're local, and we're combat-ready. We didn't know exactly what we'd find when we got here, but now that we've arrived, we're ready to render assistance."

For the first time, the Investigator looked worried. "The Galactics will come? Here? To...*correct* the situation? Can you be more specific?"

I squirmed. "That's the part that might go badly," I said. "They aren't very understanding. They might blame your people, mine, the squids—anyone and everyone for what happened. We're going to try to sort that out in our favor, of course."

"Of course," he echoed. "By that, I take it you mean you're going to try to blame it all on the cephalopods?"

I nodded.

He smiled then and laughed aloud. It was a hearty laugh, and it made his body heave with the force of it.

"What a grand joke!" he said. "These Galactics will come with so many ships that you can scarcely see the stars? That is

237

what you said, isn't it? The cephalopods have only one that we've ever seen. I will weep with joy the day the Galactics arrive."

I tried to laugh with him but found the best I could do was smile thinly. I had no idea who the Galactics would blame when they got here. They were good at punishment, sure—but justice wasn't always their strong suit.

-24-

After we broke up the meeting with the Investigator, I found myself on the Verge with Della.

"Hold here a moment, James," she said. "I want to talk to him privately."

She left me there. I looked after her, wondering what she wanted to talk about. But I soon became too interested in my environment to worry. The equipment—such well-kept, exquisite antiques!

I'd seen computers like these in museums. They were entirely electronic with nothing organic inside at all. What was even stranger was the way they warmed up your hand when you touched them. Computers in my day were usually as thin as a slip of paper and gave off no heat at all like the tapper inside my arm. I could scarcely imagine what it would be like to lug around something that weighed a man down.

Before I could do more than poke at the antiques, Della popped out of the door behind me. She smiled when I looked at her with questioning eyebrows.

"I'll take you back to your camp. The Investigator would like to arrange a proper meeting with your leader. Perhaps greater cooperation would benefit both sides."

"That's good news," I said.

I followed her down the stairs, across the smoky sward where most people slept huddled on the cool stone floors and across a sandy region that eventually led to the winding tunnels. Once in the tunnels themselves, I tried to keep track of the route, but it was difficult. Convincing Della that I was only idly curious, I paused now and then to look through the conical tubes that showed me events on the valley floor below.

The true purpose of my investigations was to track my position, of course. If I could use the tubes, I could find my way back here, should I ever have the need, just by taking occasional glances through these tiny scopes.

I was surprised to see that the nearest tubes were close to the alien ship itself. We were right above it, almost within the shimmering dome of its force field. The thought was an alarming one. If the aliens knew exactly where to concentrate their fire, surely they could blast their way through and kill everyone huddling inside the guts of *Hydra*. Even the lab coat types working with their obsolete instruments on the Verge itself would be in danger.

On the way back, we seemed to be taking a circuitous route. I frowned, noticing that the tunnels were becoming moist and warm now rather than cold and dank.

"Della," I said, slowing down. "Where are we going? This tunnel…we've not been here before."

"Follow, this is a shorter path," she said without looking back.

I stood still and waited. She walked ahead a dozen steps. When she realized I wasn't following, she returned with an odd expression on her face.

"You're as suspicious as a tunnel-stinger," she said.

"I have good reason to be," I said, eyeing her. "Why are you taking me some place other than my tent?"

"It's the girl, isn't it?" she asked. "The one we left behind. She's your mate?"

"My…no, not really. We're friends."

She scoffed. "Do you have many such 'friends'?"

"As many as I can find," I admitted.

She plucked at the sleeve of my smart-cloth suit. The fibers retracted from her touch like slow elastic.

"Arrogant," she said. "Overconfident—but also very capable. You disgust me as much as you attract me. I can't understand my thoughts. Perhaps it is as they say—that a man from a distant valley is always more interesting."

"Uh…did you say you find me attractive? Is that what this is all about?"

"I killed you once. You bested me in a fight the second time. I've never had such experiences with a male before."

I sized her up, and I can't say that I was entirely comfortable with what I saw. She was lovely and strong and there was a definite look of odd excitement reflecting in her eyes. I wasn't quite sure if she wanted to screw me or cut my throat. To be honest, I suspected it was a little of both.

"Where are you taking me, Della?"

"There's a place ahead of us. There are pools in the caverns. Warm pools that bubble under the earth. Would you like to see it?"

"I really need to get back to my unit, they'll be—"

Wham! She'd slapped me, just like that. Her hand had flicked out and caught my jaw.

Then I saw that her small fist was closed tight. It took me a second to realize that she hadn't slapped me—she'd full-on punched me in the mouth. What's more, she was pulling back her arm to drive her knuckles into my face again.

I caught her wrist before she could punch me a second time and twisted her around, grabbing her other wrist. She struggled, but I was much stronger, heavier and better-trained. I held her from behind, one arm around her neck, both her arms straining against mine with hysterical strength.

Della raged and snarled, stomping on my feet. My boots took the abuse stoically.

"How about we settle down a notch," I suggested, putting my face to her ear.

She banged her head into my mouth, and my lips stung. I don't know why, but this pissed me off. I've always had a slow fuse, but once I get going, things can go badly.

She'd already dropped her crossbow, and I took this moment to toss aside her knife. Disarmed, I threw her on the ground in front of me. I stood with my fists balled up, but controlled myself from doing anything else.

Lying at my feet, she stared up at me in the dim light. We were both breathing hard, and neither of us was saying anything. I waited for her to make the next move; to give me a sign.

What she did surprised me. She scrambled up and ran down the passageway. I shook my head and almost laughed—but then I thought about all the twisting tunnels behind me. Sure, I might find my way back out of here, but it would take hours. I hadn't even seen any more of those little observation scopes for the last kilometer. Concerned that she was ditching me in the tunnels, I ran after her.

I've got long legs and am in shape, but she gave me a good run for my money. Fortunately, she still had that glowing ring around her neck, and I followed it doggedly. Once in a while, I thought I'd lost her, but then I would hear crumbling dirt or catch a flash of that wan, green light, and I was off again after her.

The tunnels became positively steamy after a while. Wherever we were headed, it was definitely somewhere new. When I was beginning to get tired, the tunnel widened and became a low natural cavern.

It was lighter here, but not much. White growths lined the walls and the open pools of bubbling water. A sulfurous smell met my nose. It wasn't entirely unpleasant, but I suddenly felt like I'd entered a geothermal steam bath in a volcanic region.

Della had stopped running and stood by the pool's edge. She began stripping off her leather tunic. I watched, pleasantly surprised. She didn't even look at me. When she was naked she stepped into the pool and sank down into it, hissing in pleasure.

Confused, I walked to the edge and looked around suspecting every shadow, stalactite and boulder to be hiding a team of assassins.

"You have got to be the weirdest chick I've ever had the misfortune to meet," I told her.

She laughed.

"Twice you should have killed me," she said. "Twice you stopped yourself. There's only one reason a man would restrain himself. Stop lying to both of us, and get into the baths with me."

I don't know why, but her logic seemed unassailable to me. I took off my clothes, climbed into that hot, hot water, and

242

made love to a certifiable wild-woman. She turned out to be a screamer, too. I wasn't in the least surprised about that part.

When we were done, she escaped my arms and climbed onto dry land immediately.

"Getting out so soon?" I asked. "What's the hurry? Veteran Harris probably has me down as a deserter by now. We might as well enjoy ourselves."

"I must exit the water," she said, lying on her back, naked and steaming. "It might interfere with conception."

I don't know what I'd expected her to say next, but that wasn't it. As hot as that water was, a cold chill ran right through me. I climbed out and stood over her. She lay there, looking up at me curiously.

"Conception? Are you talking about what I think you're talking about?"

She appeared quizzical. "Why else would I have mated with you? Why else did you chase me through the tunnels?"

"Uh...where I come from, most ladies have birth control of some kind. All female legionnaires have it built-in when they sign up."

"Birth control? What's that?"

"Drugs, implants—you know, to stop conception."

She lifted her pretty face and frowned up at me. "You speak of immorality. Every child is precious. None of my people would dare interfere in the process. I've been shunned for years because I've selfishly waited for so long."

My jaw opened, and it didn't seem to want to close up again. "You mean you're honestly trying to have my kid? That's crazy. You hardly know me!"

"The Investigator thought it was an excellent idea," she said. "I asked for his advice while you waited outside."

I nodded slowly. I hadn't known what they were talking about, but I never would have guessed this scheme.

"Della," I said, "I'm not going to be able to be much of a dad if your plan works out."

"I've thought about that," she said seriously. "Every child needs a father to look up to. Fortunately, I have many suitors who I've long spurned. I'll allow one of them to help me with the child when you've left us."

243

"Whatever you do, don't make it that asshole named Stott who shot me in the back."

She laughed. "Don't worry, I would never allow that man near me."

I didn't know what to say after that. A young man like me spends a lot of mental and physical energy on the process of getting laid, but we spend precious little time pondering the possible results. Sleeping with the sterile women in the unit had left me in a state of mind where I was particularly unprepared for this situation.

Not knowing what else to do, I put my clothes on and waited for her to do the same. She took her time about it, as she wanted to give my seed the best possible odds of impregnating her. Was this a curse, a blessing, or just sheer madness? I had to admit I had no idea what to think.

Before we'd gone a hundred meters back up the tunnel leaving the baths behind, Della halted and put a hand up to touch my mouth. I dragged out my sidearm and stared into the darkness ahead.

I saw the sandy dirt shift and heard the tiny splash of pebbles in a puddle. What was it, a lizard? I wasn't sure, but I was willing to follow her lead. After all, she lived down here. I was just a visitor. She crept forward in a crouch, and I followed, senses straining.

When we came to a twist in the tunnel, one of many, we heard an unmistakable sound. It was a snuffling noise, like a hunting dog might make—but this creature was larger, heavier. The sounds reminded me of a bear following a scent to a food source.

I wrapped both hands around my pistol and the snuffling stopped. Della had frozen in place, so I did the same. We were waiting, hoping the slaver would turn and go another way. I didn't even know how it had managed to get down here. The tunnels seemed too narrow for one of their kind. But then I remembered just how lanky and thin they were. They'd been bred for work like this.

What happened next took both of us by surprise. A distant hooting sound echoed through the tunnels. Whatever was around the corner from us stirred, sending sifting grit down

244

onto the tunnel floor. Then we heard what could only be a stealthy retreat. Footsteps padded away.

I heaved a gentle sigh and edged forward. Della was hung back, tense.

"We're good, I think," I whispered to her.

She shook her head slightly, so I waited longer. Finally, in the silence, I became restless. I walked around the corner with my pistol extended in front of me. If I so much as saw a—

An object flew out of the dark and struck my hands. I thought for a moment a rock had fallen from the ceiling. My hands hurt, and—

A black, ape-like shape unfurled itself from the ceiling of the tunnel. In shock, I watched it reach for me.

Della charged around the corner and clawed at the thing's eyes. My vision was filled by those red-rimmed eyes, ear-flaps and huge puffing nostrils. Saliva ran in strings from the slaver's mouth. I wondered if our scent made them hungry.

Deciding she was an easier catch, the creature sprang upon Della, letting its weight fall from the roof of the tunnel and crush her down.

We were both now unarmed. I'd already wrestled with several of these creatures, and I knew how strong they were. We didn't have a chance without weapons.

I knew what I should do, of course. I should turn tail and run for it. But that just wasn't in me. Instead, I reached down to pick up a rock.

Holding Della down on her back with one knee planted on her chest, the creature turned its attention toward me when I bashed it on the head. It looked annoyed, rather than dazed or hurt.

An incredibly long arm snaked out to pull me closer. I let it happen. My hand was fumbling in my pocket, digging out the tiny vial of powder that looked like cinnamon.

I popped open the vial, held my breath, and as the slaver snuffled me happily, I gave it a snoot-full.

The reaction was quick and would have been amusing if we hadn't been so close to death or capture. The slaver went into convulsions, coughing and flailing. Della screeched in pain as its knee shifted more weight upon her.

Then, the slaver finally sank down, weakening, I grabbed hold of him under an armpit and heaved, roaring with the effort. He must have weighed several hundred kilos, and Della was being crushed to death.

The stink of the slaver's unwashed skin was strong. He was scarred with what looked like burns that had ridged his skin. Did they beat them, or had this one already been singed by our lasers? I didn't know, but I was certain there wasn't any deodorant being used on his homeworld.

When at last I had the unconscious form stretched out and off Della's body, I found my pistol and helped her stand.

She shook me off and pushed me away, coughing.

"I'm fine," she said.

"How'd they get in here?" I asked her.

She looked at me with frightened eyes. "They can't possibly—they can't know the path."

"Well, I think they do."

"Then all is lost. We must save ourselves."

"What are you talking about?"

"*Hydra*—they'll find it. They'll follow our scent, backtrack. For them, scent is like vision. We've left a glowing trail fresh on these rocks. Once they know the way, my people will be forced to fight them in our sanctuary."

"Surely your fighters can beat a few slavers."

"We can. But that won't be the end of it. They'll mark the spot, and the ship will begin boring in through the walls. That's what they've been waiting for, you see. They've been searching for our core living area. They want our young, our pregnant women. They prize them above all."

I was torn as to what to do. I could go back up the tunnels and fight the invaders—that was my first instinct. But I also knew I couldn't do it alone. If they blasted holes in these walls, the littermates would be marching in their tight squads. They were far more deadly than any skinny.

"I'm going back to my unit," I said. "I have to tell them what's happened. I'll try to get help."

She nodded, eyeing me seriously. "I think you're telling the truth. I'll lead you to an exit. But I can't go with you. I must try to warn the others. I might be able to beat them to *Hydra*. We must hurry, McGill."

"Call me James," I said.

"That is your secret name?"

"Uh…yeah. Just for friends and mating partners."

Della smiled at me and gave me a kiss. After that, she was all business. She led me to an exit, and I wriggled through. Deeper back in the tunnels, I could hear the sounds of conflict. The skinnies must have met up with some of her people.

I reached down and grabbed her arm. "Hold on," I said. "You should come with me. Your people must know about the invasion by now. You'll be safer in our camp."

She shook her head. "My place is with them. As yours is with your unit."

I heaved a sigh, knowing she was right. I handed her my laser pistol.

"Use this then. Short bursts—don't burn out the diode."

She thanked me and vanished into the darkness.

When I managed to get out onto the surface of the world again, I couldn't believe how cool, fresh and open it seemed. The sky was bright pink overhead, and I enjoyed the dawn winds that lightly ruffled my hair.

My eyes widened. *Dawn?* We were supposed to attack the ship at dawn. I set off toward the camp at a run.

-25-

They almost shot me as I approached the base. It was a close thing. I was out of uniform, unarmed and too tall for their liking.

"Halt!" boomed a voice. "Identify yourself!"

They didn't even wait for me to comply. Skittering and flailing, I threw myself down as a bolt sizzled in the air over my head.

"McGill, James!" I shouted. "Weaponeer, 3rd Unit!"

The firing stopped. I quickly worked my tapper, synching it up with the local network again. I'd forgotten I'd turned it off in order to make sneaking away easier last night.

"Advance, hands on head."

I did so, and when they recognized me, they cursed my name. As I made my way past the pickets, a guard drove the butt of his rifle into my back. Under different circumstances, I would have grabbed that rifle and twisted it around—but I didn't have the heart. After all, the guards were right. I shouldn't have been running around outside the camp all night long.

I didn't make it ten feet farther before I was arrested and hustled back to 3rd Unit. Graves ran his eyes over me, shaking his head, and Leeson snarled—but Veteran Harris—he went ape.

"What in the *hell* do you think you're doing, McGill?" he roared. "Are you aware that we're gearing up for an attack not twenty minutes from now?"

"Yes, Vet! Sorry, Vet!"

I was on my knees. My hands were still on my head, as I hadn't been given leave to lower them. I stared ahead, hoping that this would be over soon—one way or the other.

"I should execute you on the spot. You know that, don't you? I'd be perfectly within my rights. AWOL on the battlefield. No weapon in hand. Not only that, you look like shit."

"Sorry, Vet," I repeated. "I was—"

"NO!" he roared. Spittle landed in my hair. "No, I don't want to hear it. If I didn't need you on the line this minute, I'd put you out of my misery right here, right now. And no one— frigging *no one* would give me any crap for doing it."

"Are we done here, Vet? I have to get my kit on."

"You should be in the brig. Now, get your ass to your tent. Don't be stopping to shower and eat—you gave that up for whatever little romp you had in the bush."

I smiled a little. I couldn't help it. Harris must have seen my smirk, because he kicked me in the side. The armored boot hurt more than usual, even though I'd been half expecting it. I got up and staggered away, feeling my ribs. None of them seemed broken.

"This isn't over, McGill," Harris called after me.

Instead of responding, I scrambled into my tent, pulled on my gear, shoved a protein bar into my face and began to chew. I was dead tired, but battles rarely waited for a man to get his beauty sleep.

Being a heavy trooper isn't always better than being in a light unit. One problem is the length of time it takes to put your gear together. I shoved my feet into the bulky leggings, cursing and fumbling. The chest piece I managed to pull over my head, but the two halves didn't seem to want to knit up. Cursing and struggling, I tugged and slapped at locks and smart-gels that were supposed to find one another and cinch up.

"Here," said Kivi. She'd followed me into my tent. "You've got something stuck in the hinge."

I cranked my neck, and looked into her face. Her eyes didn't meet mine.

249

"Are you okay?" I asked. "I left when you were sleeping. I—"

"Yeah, I figured out where you went, James. Save it. We all looked at the vids."

She still wasn't looking at me. I felt a burning sensation on my face. I was surprised to find myself feeling a little embarrassed.

"So you guys saw her, is that right?"

"Of course we did. The buzzers picked her up, followed her as she went sneaking around the camp. Didn't you even hear them?"

I did recall the sounds of a buzzer or two passing by as we were sneaking into the tunnels.

"I thought they'd missed me."

"They don't miss anything. The techs don't miss anything. We aren't an outfit of complete morons, you know?"

She was cinching up my armor now, tapping at the smart-gels until they activated. I felt a cool touch at each side of my abdomen as they began easing the armor closed. Like a turtle-shell with two halves, the breastplate closed over me and clicked into its locked position.

"Thanks for the help, Kivi," I said, feeling bad as I realized she must have known I'd left her lying in the tent and gone off for the night with another woman. "Sorry about leaving you."

She finally looked me in the eye. I could tell she was hurt. "What I said before—I was wrong," she said, suddenly becoming angry. "There is a moron in this outfit: it's me."

"Ah, now, don't go there Kivi."

"First, you kill me. I understood that. I'm glad I wasn't dragged into that alien ship. But like a fool, I felt grateful. What I forgot was that you don't care. It's all just fun for you. Kivi is a fun-bot, just like back home…but I'm not plastic, you know?"

I groaned inwardly. Kivi was an odd sort. She was promiscuous but could get hurt and upset and jealous about relationships anyway. This was one of those special occasions. It was easy to see that I hadn't treated her well. I'd run off without a care and pretty much forgotten about her.

"I'm sorry. I was trying to make contact with the colonists—and I did."

"Yeah, I bet."

"I'm not talking about that," I said. "I meant I talked to their leader, in the tunnels. They might help us directly against the aliens now. The slavers are infiltrating their base."

"That's great," she said. "You care more about the colonists than you do about me. For all you knew, that bitch had killed me with poison."

"No, you were breathing. I checked before I left."

Kivi's eyes were a little red. She glared at me for a second. "Why'd you follow her? Just for more tail? Just for seconds? I think that's bullshit."

"No," I said with conviction. "I negotiated the ceasefire with the colonists, remember? I wanted to keep that going. That was all I was thinking about when she came into the camp."

"But you did end up screwing her, right?"

I put my helmet on and didn't say anything. It turned out to be the right move because she swung a steel-gauntleted fist at my head. I'm not sure if she would have done it if I hadn't put my helmet on—but she might have, and I might not have been in any condition to move out with the unit if she had.

"Hey, don't scratch my gear," I protested lightly.

She growled and exited the tent, throwing it aside so hard that the flap ripped. Smart-cloth tabs sought one another in vain looking like two blind vines trying to touch. They kept squirming, but the tear was too wide and they would never patch up.

I stared at them, then after Kivi. I felt bad, really I did. The night had been a strange one even by my standards.

Heaving a sigh, I gathered up my plasma tube and hustled to Leeson's platoon rally point. Veteran Harris was already there, but he wasn't even looking at me.

"On the ready-line, on the ready-line," he shouted. "Let's move, people. I want you to show me how much you love Legion Varus today."

I moved up and joined the crowd on the line. There was a glowing nano-active paint line all along the ridge where we

251

were, just out of sight of the enemy ship. Up and down that long row I could see troops organizing and standing on their lines.

"This is going to be a straight-out charge," Harris told us. "Three waves—and lucky us, we're in the first!"

A groan went up from the assembled troops.

"Why don't they just recycle us all right now?" Carlos complained.

Harris swaggered over to him with a predatory grin. "In your case, I'm willing to make an off-script exception, Ortiz."

Harris had his sidearm out and he directed it into Carlos' face. Carlos turned his attention to the line, and Harris stalked away.

Leeson walked the line with Harris. Both of them were checking kits and hitting people in the head if they didn't like what they saw.

"Keep focused, people!" Leeson said as he walked the line. "We'll get the signal soon enough. We've got nearly two kilometers to run, so I want you to use every gram of your suit's artificial muscle in this effort. You're to make a full-burn charge all the way to the ship's force field—if we can get that far without enemy contact."

"What if those armored giants are waiting out there for us?" Carlos asked.

"Then we kill them. We're expecting to run into enemy troops. They're marching out of the ship and toward the tunnels they've been blasting open all day. We're going to roll in behind them as they try to get underground. We're hoping to catch them by surprise and pin them down. The second wave is going to rush the ship, get inside, and take it."

I was impressed. It was a bold plan.

"What about third group, sir?" I asked.

Leeson fixed me with a stern gaze. "They'll watch our progress. They're operating as reserves. They'll back up whichever group they figure needs help."

I nodded. Legion Varus was made up of ten cohorts, each about a thousand strong. There was only one cohort in this valley, and we were getting all the action. We had nine units in our cohort that were really combat troops. The last unit was made up of auxiliaries, mostly bio people and techs.

Looking up and down the line on the ridge I saw three full units in armor. Three waves of three hundred men each. It was going to be quite a show of force.

"They'll never know what hit them, sir," I said.

Leeson didn't smile, but he nodded. "Okay, the Primus has just given me the final warning. I'm signaling green. If you've got a god or a mama, send some happy thoughts into space for me and the rest of us. We're doing this in three…two…"

I never heard him say "one". Instead, a roar swept the line and everyone charged. I joined them with my bulky plasma unit banging on my shoulder.

When set for a dead run, a heavy in a suit can make an amazing spectacle of himself. We bounded across the land, smashing through the wilted vegetation and splattering mud along the lake shore. We tried to spread out and ended up forming a ragged line that wouldn't be easy to take out all at once.

My heart pounded, and my helmet rang with battle cries from the hundred throats of my unit. There's something about a long charge across open land that isn't quite like anything else a man can experience in combat. I can't recommend it—but it is unforgettable.

My suit was in command now; my legs were moving but almost without meaning to. It was like running down a steep hill—it was all I could do to keep from falling on my face.

As my bounding legs propelled me almost painfully fast, I had a moment to think about charging lines of troops in years past. During World War One and prior to that, this sort of thing was a standard of warfare. Heavy armor and faster infantry had brought it back into style.

The ship loomed ahead like a beached black whale. The gun on top of it took notice of our approach. It rose, swiveled with an almost intelligent motion and took aim at our right flank—the unit plunging along closest to the lakeshore.

My unit was on the left, and I was relieved not to be the first group that the massive cannon turned its wrath upon. The tip brightened and the shaft rippled with released gasses. I could hear and see 1st Unit trying to scatter. Some fell back while others plunged forward, running faster. I'm not sure how much of a difference it made in the end. The ship's big gun fired, and a dozen or so heavy troops were caught in that invisible beam of destruction.

When you're hit by a high-powered beam, the effect isn't just a matter of heat. The blow is a physical one, spinning around the victims and blasting them flat. In a fraction of a second, a thousand pulses of energy are released and delivered to the target. The effect was explosive, as if the victims were suddenly all individually hit in the chest plate by their own personal grenades.

The lake hissed and exploded into steam, which billowed up in a white cloud. The lakeshore under the stricken soldiers was slicked into a crusty mass, having been instantly slagged into smoking glass.

In response to the blast from the big gun, our own people back on the ridge fired at the gun itself. In order to release that big bolt of power, the shield had to come down for a split-second. In that moment, everyone behind us tried to knock out the cannon.

From what I could see, they had little effect. At this range, even the heavier weapons didn't have enough punch to damage the big cannon. They did strike it, evidenced by little pockmarks rippling the sleek black canopy and the sub-shields that protected it. But they didn't score the kind of hard, direct hit that would take it out. The dome-like shield shimmered closed again. The gun began to travel, seeking a new target.

I turned away from the scene out on the beach. I had my own problems, the biggest of which was keeping up with my unit. That wasn't easy, as I was carrying more weight than anyone else. A weaponeer's bane was always his massive tube and the hump-like power source on his back. I felt like I was lugging a set of trucker's tools into battle.

The big cannon charged up again and struck at our center next—2nd Unit. They took it hard. I don't think their commander had expected to get nailed. It didn't make much sense to strike one unit then another on the opposite flank. But then, I wasn't an expert in squid psychology.

The beam took out nearly twenty men. *Twenty!* I couldn't believe it. At this rate, we'd be half dead before we even reached the dome.

But as it turned out, I didn't have to worry about that. The enemy troops that had been sent to root out colonists had been recalled, and they now engaged us from the broken rocks long the bottom of the cliffs to our left. They fired guns that sent heavy pellets into our midst. To me, they looked like huge, high-tech muskets.

"That's it, people!" Graves shouted over the unit-wide channel. "Split up by squads and charge left. Get into cover and engage those troops. We can't let them get back to the ship."

Eagerly, we obeyed. At the very least, it would take us out of the hellish face of the cannon. I was almost fantasizing about a good, old-fashioned, stand-up fight with the littermates by now.

-26-

All three of the charging units veered left to intercept the enemy that was coming out of the rocks and heading back toward their ship. We'd managed to get in between them and their goal. I understood the plan, but this wasn't the spot any trooper wanted to find himself in.

As we scrambled toward the rocks, the huge ship with its deadly cannon still fired slow, ponderous bursts into our formation. I don't know how many died. I'd lost count and interest. All I cared about was reaching the line of boulders that formed a wall like worn teeth in a skull in front of us.

Behind every boulder was an enemy soldier whose job seemed to be to make our lives as difficult as possible. Their muskets cracked and boomed. They had a slow rate of fire, but they hit hard. Even in full armor, men were spun around and knocked flat. Usually, they got back up and limped forward rejoining the charge. But sometimes they'd taken the round right in the visor, or at some weak juncture in the armor, such as where the shoulder cusp met the breastplate. When that happened, they were taken out.

Despite everything, we charged on. We didn't have much choice. When we finally got in close to the enemy clustered among the boulders, the big cannon stopped burning us down. It swung away, no doubt to punish the next wave of three units which had been sent forward in an avalanche of flashing steel toward the ship. I didn't wish the next three units any harm, but by damn, I figured it was their turn to take a few hits for the team.

When we reached the boulders the enemy stepped forward in almost stately calm. These guys were funny in the head if you asked me. I'd seen them fight before, and it was the same this time. They operated like they were on parade until they took losses—then they went absolutely ape. It wasn't normal.

As we'd been trained, we spread out so we could fight without taking a neighbor's head off. This stretched our thinned lines. I tried not to think about how many of us had fallen on the charge to get here. It had to be close to half.

This was one of the moments where an Earth Legion really shined. When we took hard hits, we could still keep going. In history, there weren't too many armies that could withstand the kind of losses we did without breaking. Morale figured differently in my era. We knew that we'd come back to life if the worst happened. We didn't *want* to die—far from it. But we were more likely to keep on fighting if there was any reasonable hope of victory. Like any force, we could be broken if it was utterly hopeless. If any sane person knew it was time to run...well, we'd run, just like the next guy.

Smashing into the enemy line then was both a relief and a new terror. I knew the big cannon couldn't fire into our midst without killing their own troops. I also knew, however, that these littermate guys were slightly insane.

Breathing hard, I ran right into a boulder at a trot, letting it slam into my armor and halt me. Then I geared down the exoskeleton, broadening the power distribution. During the charge, everything had gone to the legs, and already my power reserves were down nineteen percent.

I gritted my teeth as the last few muskets boomed and we finally plunged into the rocks. I extended my force-blades and set them for standard, close-quarters fighting. Both my blades rippled with energy, each about a meter in length.

"Turn off those blades, McGill!" screamed Leeson, slamming into the rocks beside me.

I turned my armored bulk to look at him. "They're hiding in these rocks like ticks, sir," I said. "I don't want to go farther without my blades out."

Leeson shook his head and pointed upslope. "See that guy? The one poking his nose out with a big gun in his hands? Take his head off with that tube of yours. With any luck, they'll come to us. We won't have to dig them out."

I caught on to the tactic he was suggesting, and I thought it was a good one. I retracted my force-blades, unlimbered my belcher tube and laid it over the top of a handy scorched rock. A moment later, I took down the monster that seemed to be aiming right back at me.

"Got him!" I shouted as he toppled back.

Leeson and I grinned at each other, and I swiveled my tube to the right planning to play sniper. Their muskets weren't as powerful as our weapons, and they didn't have armor that was as effective. This might not be the hell-fight I'd been expecting.

My fantasies soon vaporized. Before I could even take a second shot, the littermates rose up in a fury.

I saw their eyes—they were impossibly wide. I found large men with the whites of their eyes bulging out in red-ringed circles intimidating.

Slam! Leeson hit the back of my helmet. "Aim and fire! Piss off another group!"

Breathing hard and uncertain now, I did as he ordered. I have to confess, I didn't aim particularly well the second time around—I was a bit nervous. Instead of a clean shot, I'd have to say I got lucky. A second enemy head was left pulped and smoking.

The first group had abandoned their sniper positions. They were now up and charging across the tops of the boulders, taking huge leaps toward me. I knew in my heart that my second shot had tipped them off. I'd alerted them with the first round, then firmly placed myself on their radar with the second. The second group went mad a moment later, and soon it seemed like they were all charging down over the rocks.

I can't tell you what it's like to have a pack of thundering genetic monstrosities bounding like mountain goats over boulders toward you, especially when you know they're out to get you and no one else.

Laser rifles from my comrades flashed and burned them as they came. Headshots worked best, and our troopers took advantage of this, taking down half before they reached our line. When the berserkers got in close, our troops, who'd infiltrated the rocks a dozen meters or more, fired and slashed upward cutting them from below. Maddened warriors lost legs and were spun around with burning gouges in their chests and faces.

But most of them came on. They were all wounded, I think, by the time they got to me. Leeson was screaming something, but I didn't honestly have any clue what he was saying. I was in full-automatic panic-mode, knowing I was in an all-out fight to the finish. I'd already counted myself dead, but I meant to deliver some more pain before they got their revenge.

Dialing the big cannon into a broad cone, I burned the first two that got close. A few curses and screeches came up from my own people who'd caught a whiff of my final blast on the back of their armor. I was sorry about that, but any weaponeer will tell you, a plasma cannon is far from a surgical instrument of death—it's more like a blowtorch.

I dropped my cannon. I don't think Leeson liked that, and he got into my face. But I knew the cycle time on my own weapon, and at the rate these gentlemen were approaching my position, I didn't have time for another shot.

Perhaps I shouldn't have shoved Leeson to one side, but I did it anyway.. I'm a firm believer in the concept of allowing a man to choose his own death when it's a foregone conclusion. Not everyone in Varus agrees with me—but frankly, they can all screw themselves.

Squeezing my gauntlets, my twin blades extended with a sizzling sound. I lifted them both and put up my guard.

Not a second later, the first of the psychotics reached me. His eyes were still white-circles, bulging. I doubted they'd closed or blinked since he'd first spotted me, and I knew somehow that even if I killed him those eyes would track me until the last drop of blood ran out of his burning brain.

In his hand, lifted high over his head, was a razor-sharp cutlass of sorts. The sword looked as long as a fencepost, and the edge shone with the unnatural precision of an enhanced blade. It made a glittering arc as it chopped down toward me.

I assumed a pose designed to meet a charge from high ground. My left arm was up guarding my helm and my right was low ready for a thrust at the gut. It was a textbook stance, one that had been drilled into me over the preceding months.

I was almost surprised that it worked as well as it did. The berserker's sword came apart when it touched my force-blade, sending most of its length skittering harmlessly over my head. Then I thrust, and the monster lost a leg.

Side-stepping, I let him crash down where I'd been standing. Such weight! It was like having a Clydesdale thrown at you. An unarmored man might have been killed just by having one of these guys fall on him.

I drew a long line down his gut with one blade as he fell and was stunned that he still flopped and twisted, trying to get back up despite the fact he should have been stone dead.

"McGill!" Leeson screeched nearby.

I barely turned in time. I'd forgotten about the rest of the berserkers for a fraction of a second. That had been a mistake.

They launched themselves, one, two, and three. I couldn't believe it. There had to be several tons of flesh hurtling airborne over those rocks. It was the second group, the second litter, whatever. My comrades had cut down the first pack that had charged me, but these guys had made an equally dramatic effort.

Bracing my feet and crouching low, I put my blades up and extended them toward the enemy. I didn't have much choice. I didn't have time to dodge or hide. Even if they all died this second—they were going to land on me.

There was triumph in their eyes. I saw it just before they hit me. I could tell they were happy. They'd done their best, charging and hewing down troops as they came. But that didn't matter to them. All of their hate, all of their ferocity, had been focused on one James McGill.

The first guy was torn apart by my blades and Leeson's combined. It was about time he'd helped fix what he'd ordered me to create. Some part of the first one slammed into my back—I think it was a dismembered arm—but I stayed up.

Less than a second later, the next two stomped me flat. They howled in victory, a strange, deep sound that no normal human could have produced.

I think, looking back, that the only thing that saved me was they'd gotten tangled up on top of me. They couldn't get their swords into play. Either that, or maybe they thought I was dead when I went down under them.

Whatever the case, before they could get organized, my comrades ran to my aid and stabbed and hacked with blades sizzling. A wild melee began right on top of me, with my arms pinned under a half-dozen heavy boots from both sides.

People think that combat back in the olden days—the days of knights and charging horses—must have been cleaner and more chivalrous than more modern methods, which generally consisted of pecking away at one another at long range. But I can tell you, those romantic notions are dead wrong. There's nothing more bloody and vicious than a battle with blades.

Before the last two littermates went down, they managed to cut off a few limbs of their own. Carlos was one of the unlucky ones. He'd been trying to help, but he came in too close. He took a smashing blow on the helmet from the hilt of one giant's sword. Before he could recover and get his guard back up, the other one thrust through his visor. He sagged down, dead.

The whole fight had probably taken no more than three minutes, but to me, it had seemed like a very long time. Leeson and Harris dragged bodies from the pile, checking for life.

"Sir?" I said from underneath the shivering form of the last enemy in the pile.

"You're *alive*, McGill?" Leeson said in disbelief. He loomed over me and stared into my broken visor.

"Right as rain, sir," I said. "But I could use a little help getting this elephant off my chest, if you don't mind."

"Weaponeer, you shouldn't have drawn your blades. I ordered you not to."

"Yes, sir," I said. "You did that. Are you going to put me on report?"

Leeson gave me a hard stare. He tried to look stern and pissed off, but he couldn't keep it going. He shook his head and laughed. "You're an ass, McGill."

261

"Thank you for noticing, sir."

The fight was pretty much over by the time I was up on my feet again. Really, it had gone well. The enemy had a critical flaw in their makeup. They'd been conditioned to go into a rage when one of their brothers fell, and I could see how that would work well as long as they held the upper hand. But the minute they were in a bad fight, one where they had to use careful tactics to win, it had become a disadvantage.

All along the front line, we'd teased them by taking out one member of each group of nine. That caused a general charge, and our trap had been sprung. I found out that I was the only fool lucky enough to get two charges at once—the only fool that had survived the experience, that is.

After the last of the littermates died, the big cannon swept toward us and began slamming us with heavy beams. Boulders cracked and smoked when the invisible beams of heat struck them.

I craned my neck, looking down toward the lakeshore. Where had that charging group gone? It took me only a second to figure it out. They'd shifted their course and charged into the rocks with us. They'd taken heavy losses, just as we had, while covering open ground. Now six of the cohort's ten units were battered and hunkering down in the area of broken boulders.

"We're pinned down," Graves said, conferring with his unit commanders. "Leeson, you're the last adjunct I have left standing in this unit. Harris, you and the other vet are going to have to double up in the command area. Assume you're in command if you don't see anyone of higher rank within earshot."

"Sir, yes sir," Harris said.

I noticed he didn't sound happy with his instructions. He wasn't a man who sought promotions. He didn't want to distinguish himself. He wanted to live to see the sun in the morning—that's it.

"We've learned a lot about this enemy," Graves continued, gathering what was left of our unit around him. "We lost some good people, but they'll be happy to know we won the day in the end. Now, we're going to reorganize the six units we have here in these rocks. We'll charge up our suits and be ready move out within an hour. With firing support from the three reserve units back at the ridge, the forward six will make that last short charge. We'll assault the ship and take it."

A groan went up. I couldn't blame them. We were tired, half-down on power, and many of us were injured. Voices rose as everyone discussed this so called "plan".

Graves threw his arms up. "Listen people! Listen…*SHUT UP!*"

We quieted. Complaints dropped down to the level of grumbling. I took a moment to look around. Kivi was still standing, but she looked away from me when I glanced at her. Natasha had been left back at the camp; we'd only taken combatants on the charge. But Carlos and about a third of the rest hadn't made it this far. Most of the other units were in even worse shape. All in all, I'd have to say we were half-dead and really wanting a break. If we charged the ship now, I doubted we'd have three hundred effectives in all six units combined, and we still had no idea what was inside that ship to greet us.

"I know you want to hide in these rocks and give it a rest," Graves said. "I understand that. But that's not going to happen. Not this time. There were over a hundred of their troops in these rocks, and we took them out. That means we've probably destroyed their ground forces. Command thinks we have the enemy on their heels, and we're not going to stop pushing until they break or we do. Just remember, they only have a limited number of squids and freaks in that ship. We can reproduce every one of you that falls. We'll win through attrition, if nothing else."

No one was happy with his speech, not any part of it. "Winning through attrition" meant we would get the joy of dying over and over again, hoping each time to take down one of the enemy. With luck, we'd break through and finish them. But that ship looked big and mean. There was no telling what they had in there to oppose us. We hadn't even fought a single squid yet.

I raised my hand, waggling my fingers. That always seemed to work for Carlos.

Graves glanced at me, but waved my hand down.

"Save it, McGill. We're going in."

263

"Sir?" I asked. "I'm not going to argue about that."

"What *are* you going to argue about?"

"Sir, I think I have a way of getting us aboard that ship—without everyone out here dying six times in the process, that is."

Graves stared at me for a second, then he heaved a sigh. "I know I'm going to regret asking, but what the hell are you talking about, McGill?"

Everyone looked at me. I smiled slowly and began to explain.

I was sure there was a tunnel complex underneath our feet. I'd seen the locals come crawling out of here in half a dozen places. Since the area had been heavily shelled, the tunnels had to have been damaged, but I was equally sure some had survived.

"We need to get a few techs up here with equipment," I said, "or at least some of those buzzers specially equipped with sonic sensors."

Graves, Harris and Leeson were all listening to me. Harris rolled his eyes. Leeson looked pissed. Only Graves seemed to be taking me seriously.

"Let's say we get into these tunnels of yours," Graves said. "How the hell does that get us into the ship?"

I cleared my throat. "I've been down there in the tunnels, sir. They go everywhere. With a decent compass to follow, all we have to do is find an exit that's close to the ship. We go into the tunnels, find exits close to the ship, and then we come out like a horde of gophers rushing the ramp."

"You've got to be kidding me, right?" Leeson demanded. "You don't have a map. You don't have any idea where these tunnels go and where they don't. You're asking us to duck underground into some rabbit-warren full of booby-traps and hope we can find a way out?"

"Well, sir," I said. "If you'd rather charge that force-shield, getting nailed by a cannon the size of a submarine at close range every step, I guess that's up to you guys."

Leeson's face had turned from red to purple during my little speech. I knew I was mouthing off to an officer. He was only two steps ahead of me in rank, but he *was* my direct commander.

I opened my mouth again to apologize, but I never got the chance. Harris had seen his opportunity, and he'd jumped right in. He smashed me one on the head. A white light flashed, but I didn't fall or pass out.

Legion Varus operated to some degree like the Roman Legions of ancient times. Back then, any officer could execute a soldier for disobeying or disserting. Punishment was often physical including flogging and the like. I knew and understood all that, but I felt like killing Harris, anyway.

Harris knew it, too, but he didn't back down. He didn't apologize. He stepped up and gave me that crazy stare of his.

"You settled down yet, kid? Because if you haven't you can just try it. I can see it in your eyes. I can—"

"Harris," Graves said. "Step back, gentlemen."

I had respect for Graves. I had respect for Harris, too, even if he did piss me off at moments like this. Both of us sucked in a breath and took a step back from one another. I realized I'd been visualizing Harris' next death at my own hands. That sort of thing wasn't good for morale.

Graves looked from me to Harris and back again.

"You know," he said. "You two have always been annoying to every officer I put in charge of you. Did you know that? They complain every time. Now I can see what they mean."

Harris seemed surprised. "Just doing my job, Centurion."

"Yeah, I know," Graves said.

"Sir, can we just investigate the tunnels?" I asked. "We're in a relatively safe position here. The boulders are stopping the enemy's heavy gun. We have a little time."

"But that can't last," Leeson said suddenly. I think he was worried that Graves might listen to me. "We'd just be giving them more time to set up their defenses."

Graves was busy with his tapper while we argued for a minute or so. When he finally looked up, his face was unreadable.

"I just texted McGill's idea to the Primus," he said. "She told me I have half an hour to try it out. After that, the general attack begins."

Leeson and Harris were stunned. I tried to look cool, but inside I felt triumphant—that was until I heard the rest of what Graves had to say.

"McGill, you're going in. I can't afford an officer, or too many troops for that matter. But I need someone senior to vouch for what you find. Harris will handle that. He's in command. Take three regulars who can walk and head into the tunnels. Remember, you have thirty minutes—or at least you did three minutes ago. Hustle up, people!"

I think Harris was in shock. His mouth hung open. He wanted to argue, but he'd just received a direct order, and he was too much of a soldier for that.

Graves had a hint of a smile on his face. "A little time together in a hole might do you two some good," he said. "You might bond or something."

Or something. I was still thinking of murder—and I knew Harris was doing the same.

When Graves moved off to organize his remaining forces, Harris snarled at me and slammed his shoulder into mine as he passed by. Walking along the huddled lines, he tapped three regulars announcing they'd just volunteered. The last "volunteer" he selected was Kivi.

This pissed me off. I figured he'd tapped her just to irritate me. He had to know Kivi and I had an informal thing going on—everybody did. He figured that if he had to go underground with me, he would damn well bring along my girlfriend, too. Probably if Natasha and Carlos were here, they'd have been picked next.

We gathered up our kits and made our way uphill into the highest boulders up near the cliffs. I was in the lead, as I'd seen the colonists vanish into these rocks with my own eyes.

"It was up here when I first saw them do it," I said, crouching and scanning the rocks.

267

Harris nosed up next to me. "Isn't this where that hot little number shot you in the face?" he asked, as if eager to hear the story again.

I looked at him, and he grinned at me.

"She finished me with a knife, but yeah, that's about right. They came up out of slits in the rocks right along here. See those shadows under the boulders? They aren't just shadows. They're narrow tunnel entrances."

Harris scoffed, eyeing them. "How the hell is a fully-kitted heavy trooper supposed to get into that weasel-hole?"

"Like this, vet," I said, sliding toward it feet-first.

I almost got stuck, but I made it through. I had to shed my power-pack and drag it along with my weapon behind me, but I made it inside.

"Don't go running off to make out with some tunnel-slut, you hear?" Harris shouted loudly.

Kivi was right there at his side, not looking at either of us.

Grumbling to myself, I flipped on my lights and had a look around. The tunnel was tight, and it rambled off in several directions. I investigated while the others came down after me one at a time.

My algorithm for searching the tunnel complex was simple enough. I took whatever route seemed to be going downhill, explored until I met a dead-end, then turned around and searched the next branch. When we spotted smaller side-passages, we sent in one of the others to scout.

In the first ten minutes, we had only one bad moment. A fresh-faced legionnaire named Perez found a booby-trap.

I'd been of the opinion that the traps were only in the rocks above, set to catch invaders before they entered the tunnel network—but I'd thought wrong. Perez was jabbed right in the butt with a black-tipped stick. The nano-metal was black and shaped like an arrow or maybe a small spear.

Heavy troopers have armor over their butts just like the rest of our bodies, but the same weakness existed there that existed at our shoulder joints. The tip penetrated the polymer joints at the hips and sank in just enough to graze her skin inside.

Hungry nanites flooded her bloodstream. Our suits have good medical systems and can even perform life-saving operations, such as amputations, if necessary, but Perez was struck too close to her vital organs. The nanites quickly coursed through her blood to her heart and consumed her.

Perez shivered and gagged. She said it was like having ants inside her guts—huge metal ones.

Harris did the honors, frowning. He put his sidearm up to the woman's chin. Perez nodded. We couldn't do anything else other than leave her. We didn't have time to wait around until she hemorrhaged and died.

"I'll see you next time, girl," Harris said, almost gently. This kind of surprised me, as I'd generally thought of him as a heartless prick.

His beam glowed, and Perez relaxed, eyes glazing. The nanites were still busy in there, hollowing her out, but at least she didn't have to feel it.

"Nasty people, these colonists of yours, McGill," Harris growled at me.

"They aren't *mine*, Vet," I said. "And remember, they laid these traps for littermates and slavers. Not for us. We're new in town."

Harris waved for me to get moving. I went back to exploring the tunnels.

About seven minutes later, I was ready to give up. With less than ten minutes left, we had lost a good fighter, and we still hadn't found anything.

Then I saw something new. Something I hadn't expected, but I knew the second I saw it that I *should* have expected it.

I saw a pair of eyes down one long, dark tunnel. They stared back at me from the darkness.

"Vet, hold up," I called over my shoulder.

"What have you got, McGill? Is a snake eating you for dinner now?"

"Just hold your position, please."

Harris and the others grumbled, but they stopped moving and stared after me.

I waved at the eyes in the darkness. They blinked, but didn't move. Taking a chance, I scooted closer—but not too fast.

The eyes vanished, retreated. I spotted them again a little farther away. I chewed my cheeks for a second, considering.

"Hey," I said in a loud whisper. "I know you. Talk to me."

The eyes appeared again. They were narrow and suspicious. "Why are you here?" demanded the owner.

"You're Stott, aren't you?" I asked.

"You don't belong here. I should kill you—again."

Hmm. My hand slipped to my sidearm. I knew we had a truce going with these people, but here was that same weaselly little bastard who had shot me in the back, bringing on the first death I'd experienced on Dust World. The temptation to return the favor was strong.

"We're allies," he said suddenly, as if following my train of thought. Maybe a lot of people dreamt of killing Stott. If they did, I couldn't blame them for it.

"Stott," I said. "Show me the way out. Show me a path close to the ship, and we'll leave. We only want to get closer to the ship so we can attack."

"That's a bad idea," he said.

"Do you have a better one?"

"Yes," said Stott earnestly. "Give them people. Give them a few hundred of your best wives and children. Once their hold is full, they will fly. They won't come back for a long time."

I frowned at him. "Yeah, that's great for you, but what about our people? The ones we send off into slavery?"

Stott sidled a little closer, but he was still far out of reach. I sensed that he could dart away any moment if he wanted to.

"That's the center of my plan," he said. "You don't care about your people. You can just make more. When the littermates and their masters leave, bring the lost ones back to life."

I had to admit, it would probably work. Stott made me feel a mixture of disgust and pity. Submission, hiding—these were the keys to survival among a beaten people.

I shook my head. "We can't do that," I said. "We can't make a copy of a person unless we know they're dead."

"Ah, that's too bad...but wait! Just tell them to kill themselves. Nothing could be easier aboard the great ship. All you have to do is disobey enough times and they will end you. Staying alive is much harder than dying."

"Yeah? What do you know about it?"

He sidled closer. I could almost grab him—almost.

"I've been aboard," he said in a whisper. There was a slightly mad gleam in his eyes. "The last time the great ship came. I was found unsuitable and dumped from the ship after failing their tests of the flesh."

Tests of the flesh? Did they check genetics, and reject the losers? I guess it made sense. How else could they have bred such specialized versions of humanity?

"What's it like on the ship?" I asked.

"It's madness. It's like the worst of dreams where you can't awaken."

I nodded. "Well, Stott, I'm sorry to disappoint you, but we're Earthmen. We fight, we don't surrender. If someone tries to capture us, it is the same as trying to kill us. Either way, we fight to the death. Just tell me how to get close to them, and we'll leave you alone."

Stott looked thoughtful. "You experienced Della, didn't you?" he asked me.

"Uh…"

"She told me you did. She said I would never be considered again and to stop asking."

"Yeah…well…Look, are you going to help or not?"

A strange light came into his face. "I think I will," he said. "I came here to kill you, you know. But that was before I knew what you wanted in my world. Now that I understand, I have a better fate for you than the screaming death."

"That's great. Listen, I have to—"

"Don't go that way!" Stott whispered, as I turned to continue my exploration.

"Why not?"

"That way lays the next trap. I set many of them. You'll never get out of here without my help."

I stared at him. "*You* set traps? Inside your own tunnels?"

He nodded slowly.

271

I pulled out my gun. I should have shot this bastard the second I'd seen him. He'd managed to kill me once and now Perez. He didn't deserve to live.

"I see you understand," Stott said. "But you don't *fully* understand. I don't want you to find my traps now. I want you to find the ship. I want you to go inside. I want you to be tested and taken from this world and never brought back to life.'"

Stott was right. I did finally understand him. He wanted me to find the way to the alien ship. He wanted me to do it, so I could be tormented and abused the way he had been at some point.

I pointed my gun at him and gestured with it meaningfully. "Lead the way. Show me how to get to the ship."

"I will find the closest exit. I know them all. Better than most."

"Stott," I said as I followed him and called for Harris and the others to follow me, "if you screw me, I want you to know, I'm going burn you down before you can get away."

Stott laughed. It was a weird, haunted sound. "Don't worry! I don't have to harm you. To kill a fool, all one has to do is lead him to a cliff. You're a special fool, since you demand to be guided there."

I followed him through dark tunnels for several minutes. As I went, I dropped beepers: small devices that marked the path for the rest of the troops I hoped would follow soon.

Stott occasionally giggled, and he crept along on all fours as often as not. As I followed him deeper, going downhill toward the giant ship, I had to wonder which of us was the crazy one.

I didn't trust our guide. How could I? The man had shot me in the back only a few days ago. I'd caught him planting booby-traps that had already killed one of my comrades. What's more, he knew about Della and me. Our little get-together in the hot springs had become front-page news. That alone might be enough for him to try his luck at killing me again. Who knew? Maybe it would stick this time around.

But I didn't have much choice in the matter. We had to find a way out of these tunnels that reached closer to the ship— either that or my commanders were going to send us on an

272

insane charge right at that shield. We'd squeeze through the dome of force, dying as we went, and probably finish up on the ramp in a heap of fried meat.

I knew Stott might be leading us to our deaths, but I felt like I had to take the chance. Hell, we were all about to die anyway. At least this way, I figured there was hope.

So, I led the way. I didn't tell Harris about Stott—who he was, and what kind of a sneaky little psychotic bastard he really was. I figured they might turn around if I did, and I wouldn't have blamed them for it.

We pressed ahead into the darkness. Every time dirt sifted down from the crumbling roof of the tunnels, dribbling onto my helmet or armored back, I figured that was it. The cave-in was finally letting go, and I'd screwed up royally.

But instead, the tunnels just went on and on. When I was just about to give up, and Harris was reminding me we only had a few minutes left, Stott halted. He felt around in the dark. I cranked up the beams on my helmet lights and tried to peer past him, but I couldn't. The tunnel had ended.

"What's this crap?" I demanded.

We were down on our hands and knees now because the ceiling was low. I scrambled up to Stott and grabbed him around the throat with steel gauntlets. He began keening, sounding like a rabbit in a snare.

"Hey, hey," Harris said, coming up behind me and giving me a shove. "What the hell is wrong with you now, McGill?"

"He led us into a dead end. There's nothing here."

"Why the hell would he do that?"

"He hates me. I—"

Kivi came up to us then and kicked me. "You screwed his girlfriend, didn't you?" she demanded. "That's why he's here. That's why he came looking for you in your crazy love tunnels. This is all bullshit, Harris. We've got to get back to the surface and rejoin our unit. The attack will come soon, and we'll be stuck down here."

I pushed Kivi off me. "It's not that way at all," I said. "But I do think he's screwed us over."

"This is just like when you came down here to find your new girlfriend," Kivi went on. "Why die in battle if you can have a little fun in the dark instead? I thought you were moving kind of fast—I bet you were trying to lose the rest of us in this maze. Admit it!"

Kivi wasn't always a reasonable person. When she got jealous, every butt in sight got a dose of her foot.

Harris pushed the two of us apart.

"Shut up!" he roared. "Look up, you fools!"

We did and gaped at what we saw. There was a crack, not much more than a slit, in the limestone ceiling. Stott had jammed himself into it and was squeezing upward as we watched.

"He's getting away," Kivi said.

Harris bashed her one on the helmet. "Who cares? That's got to be the way out. Kivi, you're the smallest. Get up there after him. Scout and report. You've got one minute. McGill, unlimber that cannon of yours. We can't get out through this exit if it's so small. I'll report in. If Graves approves, we'll melt the walls back a little and make more room."

"You really think he's found it, Vet?" I asked, incredulous.

He gave me a quizzical frown. "Was Kivi right, boy? Were you really down here looking for booty the whole time? Of course he's found it. What the hell else are we doing down here?"

"Right," I said, pawing at my kit. I had to clear off the dust, connect the cables and test-fire the unit. I checked the power-levels…they looked good.

In the meantime, Harris used a guide-wire we'd left in our wake to talk to Graves. Radio didn't seem to want to penetrate these stone walls.

Kivi crept up the hole after Stott, cursing and squirming.

"I'm stuck," she said, sending down a cascade of dust into our faces. "Oh, shit, I'm stuck!"

"Calm down," Harris said. "What do you see up there?"

"Uh…not much. There's light ahead. Must be daylight. That colonist weasel is gone."

"Follow him."

"I won't be able to get back!"

"That's an order!"

More squirming, churning and dust: I could tell she'd turned on her exoskeleton and goosed the power. Her limbs churned with strength she couldn't have mustered otherwise.

"I hate you, McGill!" she called down.

"Join the club, girl," Harris answered. "Any progress?"

"Yeah. I'm up at the top. I'm under some kind of big rock. We can't charge out of here. We won't be able to move fast enough. They'll nail each of us as we come out once they figure out where the exit is."

"What about our guide?" I called.

"He's—ah, hold on, I see him. They've got him! I think he tried to run, and two slavers ran him down. Permission to fire, Vet?"

"Denied," Harris said firmly. "We can't give away our position. We aren't ready."

I shook my head. Despite my dislike of Stott, I felt a little sorry for him. His worst fears had been realized. He'd been caught and dragged into that ship of nightmares again. Whatever he'd done in the past, I knew he had only one life to give. He'd played us fairly.

"Vet, we've got to go after him," I said.

"You crazy?" Harris asked. "I thought you hated him anyway."

"Yeah, but he's a civvie. And he did what he said; he played his part."

"Okay then. You want to go up there, McGill? Be my guest."

I stood and shoved myself up into the tunnel. It really was a tight squeeze.

Harris yanked me back down. "I was kidding, fool. The only way you're getting your little buddy back alive is when we take this ship. Focus on that, and stop with the suicidal heroics. Man, if there is anything I can't stand, it's a goddamn hero."

He fumed and complained like that until Graves called back with the verdict. Harris listened, and his face fell.

"You sure, sir? Absolutely sure? It's just that I can't advise…yes, sir."

"What?" I asked him.

Harris looked depressed. "It's a go. Start burning this tunnel wider. Graves is sending our whole unit down here and two more behind it. They figure it's a better shot than charging across open land. We're going to storm your ship, McGill, using this pathetic gopher-hole. I hope you're happy."

I smiled at him. "Actually, Vet...I am."

-28-

The next few minutes stretched into twenty, then became an hour. By the time we were prepped and ready to go, I figured we might as well have dug our own tunnel to the ship.

What really helped finish the job was a drone team that had come along with one of the units in the second wave. They had to crawl on their bellies, to burrow through the tunnels.

When they came to a spot that was too narrow, their usefulness became even more apparent. They could dig. We usually used drones to move earth, build bunkers, or carry heavy loads over rough ground. But with careful instructions and operators who knew their business, they could be used as tunneling machines.

The walls at my end of the tunnel were already as slick as glass due to countless bursts from my plasma tube. It had helped, but wasn't an elegant solution. Digging with a cannon was kind of like—well, digging with a cannon: Messy, dangerous and only half-effective.

The mechanical pigs did a much better job. They could really tear apart loose earth and softer types of stone. Fortunately, Dust World's crust seemed to consist of little else. I'd come to believe there wasn't much in the way of hard granite on this planet. Whatever wasn't sand was sandstone, limestone or clay.

The aliens in their ship above us plotted and waited for us to come out of the rocks they'd cornered us in. They thought they had the upper hand. Rather than attack us, they were waiting for us to make the next move. As we geared up to explode back out onto the surface, I sincerely hoped the aliens had no clue as to how we planned to hit them next.

The only good thing about the delay was that it gave me time to recharge my pack and replenish my ammo. After about ninety minutes of digging and massing up in the tunnels, Graves finally made a fateful announcement.

"Good news, people," he began. Honest to God, the man's voice sounded like he really *did* think he was relaying good news. "3rd Unit has been given the honor of going in first! The entire cohort will follow up on our charge. The Primus herself insisted our unit was to lead the way."

"That bitch," Leeson complained in the dark nearby.

I had to agree with Leeson's assessment. Going first up a ramp into an alien ship full of vicious squids and their slave troops didn't sound like an honor to me.

Harris clapped his gauntlets together, making a ringing sound that echoed painfully from the tight walls of the tunnels.

"Listen up!" he boomed.

Adjunct Leeson sidled forward like a crab and crouched in the middle of our platoon. There were less than twenty of us left. I found myself wishing Carlos had survived long enough to see this thing through to the end with me.

"This is do or die, people. Maybe both. We're going up and out of that hole above your heads. The buzzers have reported back that there is a handy circle of rocks, and we'll probably be under the firing cone of their main gun. The second you see daylight, spread out and head for cover in every direction. Our initial mission is to set up firing positions. We'll be playing overwatch for the rest of the troops as they come boiling up out of this anthill behind us."

We gave him a ragged cheer, as he seemed to be expecting it. The sound was lackluster, but he didn't make an issue of it.

"Now, this next part is important: If the enemy doesn't seem to notice our movements, don't fire on them. I repeat, *do not engage* unless we're attacked first. Command is hoping for surprise. We want every trooper up on the surface before we hit them, if possible."

"Sir?" I asked. "The buzzers didn't show there was enough room in that circle of rocks for all the troops."

Leeson looked at me with dark eyes. "Yeah, I would agree. But you have your orders. Just set up and cover everyone coming up to the surface."

"But sir," I said, pressing the point. I'd been watching the vids from the buzzers for nearly an hour now, having had little else to do. "A fast strike might be a better—"

"For the sake of every legionnaire that ever died on an alien rock like this, I want you to shut up and follow orders, McGill. Shock us all, just this once."

"Glory hound," said someone off to my left. I thought it might have been Kivi, but I hoped not. She knew me better than that.

"Yes, sir," I said with a sigh.

A timer beeped a thirty second warning in my ear. My tapper had been engaged remotely and was counting down the seconds until we were to make our first push up to the surface.

I had to admit, I was feeling a little keyed up. Maybe it was sitting down here in close quarters—or maybe it was the complete insanity of what we were about to do. I'm sure men had felt like this throughout history while gearing up to storm a beach, charge up a fortified hill or drop onto an alien world. You couldn't help but sense your heart hammering in your chest until it felt like it was coming out of your mouth.

Finally, it was go-time. Everyone's beeper sang, and we were all up and rushing through the fresh-dug tunnel to the surface.

I was about the seventh man to reach daylight. We hadn't dared to put scouts up ahead of time, relying on the vids from our buzzers to do that job. The whole point of this exercise was to catch the enemy off guard.

My legs were stiff from crouching for so long, but I forced them to work when I reached the surface, goosing the power in my suit and transferring it to the legs. I had my cannon on my shoulder, bouncing and clanking. Seeing a pile of loose rocks about as big as a house, I broke left and rushed to cover, putting the stones between me and the ship.

The enemy wasn't caught napping, unfortunately. I don't think they knew we were coming, but they figured it out in two minutes flat. A squad of slavers was nearby, and they set up a screeching, warbling sound. They lifted their huge hands to their pursed mouths and called toward the ramp of the ship which, I now realized, was a fair distance away.

The only good news, as I saw it, was that we were inside the force dome, and it looked like their main gun couldn't dip down enough to hit us here so close to the hull.

I threw myself flat and set up my weapon, cranking it to long range since there didn't seem to be any immediate resistance. Behind me, troops kept bubbling up out of the ground at a rate of one every three or four seconds.

Harris came close and threw himself down beside me. He looked at what I was doing with a suspicious frown.

"McGill, have you seen any incoming shots fired yet?"

"No sir," I said. "But those slavers over there have seen us. I'm sure of it."

He gave me a hard stare, then looked at the enemy in question. There were four of them in a cluster. They were standing tall, looking like meercats straining and sniffing the air.

"They don't see us yet," he said. "They probably smell us, though."

I sighted on the closest, most exposed man. At this range, I couldn't miss with a tight burst.

Harris bashed my shoulder spoiling my aim. "What the hell are you doing?"

"Preparing to fire, should the need arise. Could you get your gauntlet off my pack, Vet?"

Harris clearly suspected me of all sorts of craziness. I felt wronged. Sure, I'd gone off track now and then, but to assume I'd disobey a direct order right off—that didn't seem right.

"Okay," he said, digging out his scope. "I'll sight for you."

That happy period of cooperation lasted about a minute longer. After that, events changed on the battlefield around us.

Two more ramps extended silently from the ship. One was far off to our left. The other was closer to amidships on the huge vessel.

280

It was immediately clear to everyone present that the enemy had noticed our position and was responding to it. They'd decided to up the ante.

Down each of these three ramps came six squads of heavy troopers. The littermates marched in strict box formation with their lockstep, easy pace.

But it was the immense creatures that followed the littermates that surprised us. They were true giants. There's just no other word one could apply to these monsters. They were twenty feet high and almost as broad as they were tall. They moved like sumo wrestlers and carried huge guns that were grafted onto their arms.

Staring at these three beings, one of which had emerged from the ship at the top of each ramp, I realized the giants only had one serviceable hand each. The other had been removed and replaced with a weapon that dwarfed my own plasma cannon.

"Giants," Harris said, staring. "They bred *giants*. I don't frigging believe it."

I didn't either at first. But there they were, blinking and yawning with wet mouths full of jagged teeth.

"Hold your fire!" Graves roared in my earpiece.

All up and down the encircling rocks, troopers were now aiming their weapons toward the enemy carefully. Almost everyone aimed at the giants. They were terrifying.

"I see a white flag," Graves said. "Let's give them a chance."

I craned my neck and, sure enough, the team of slavers that had first scented us came galloping forward on all fours. The leader, who I'd been targeting had a white flag up, and it whipped in the wind as the group of four approached us.

Such strange creatures. They disgusted and intrigued me at the same time. Did they think like we did? Did they experience feelings like love and sadness, or just rage? They were like specially-bred dogs, but molded by direct genetic manipulation rather than selective breeding. Anne Grant had told me there couldn't have been enough generations for the squids to change a human's physiology so drastically. They must have spliced in the traits they wanted artificially to produce these abominations.

Flapping ears spread wide, then drooped as they gathered not a hundred feet from my position. The leader of the slavers stood taller than the rest, rearing up on his hind legs while the others moved restlessly behind him on all fours.

"We speak!" shouted the leader. "We speak!"

I looked up and down the line. Who the hell was going to…but then I saw him. Graves rose up from our line and marched calmly out to meet the skinny who called to us. I was proud to see he didn't cower. He looked as if he were taking a stroll in the park. I doubted I could have looked so self-assured, and I was doubly glad it was Graves who had stepped forward rather than me.

"I'll talk to you," Graves said. "Tell me what you want."

I glanced over my shoulder and smiled. While Graves talked peace with these freaks, our troops were still coming out of that hole. We were starting to get crowded among the rocks, and our pigs were already throwing up fresh barriers at the open spots by tilting up boulders to block laser bolts and other incoming fire—just in case this little chat went badly. Watching all this, I understood Graves' motivation. He was playing for time.

"You must drop your stingers," said the skinny with a fluting voice that was strangely high-pitched for a being of his size. "Stingers not allowed in the ship."

"Stingers?" Graves asked mildly. "You mean our guns?" He drew his sidearm but didn't point it at the slaver.

In reaction, the slavers squirmed and milled uncomfortably.

"Stingers must be cast aside. It is commanded, and it must be so. Otherwise, you will not be allowed stay alive in the ship."

Graves smiled. "What if we don't want to live in your ship?"

"Wasteful," said the slaver, suddenly spitting a gob of juice on the sands. "Unpleasant. Hopeless."

Graves shook his head. "We enjoy our freedom. We will not throw down our weapons. We will not walk aboard your ship like sheep."

The slaver tossed his head and looked at his fellows who made chattering sounds. I realized they were amused. The leader turned back, and his face suggested he was speaking to a lost child who did not yet understand the way of things.

"There is no freedom. You live here only because the masters allow it. Today is the day your herd must be gathered and taken home again. Do not waste your lives—you are of value to the masters only when you serve them."

"I see we don't understand one another," Graves said. "We will never give in to your demands. We are not native to this world. We are from outside this star system. Our Empire is vast, much greater than you or your masters can imagine."

More twittering and grunts ensued. Finally, the slaver turned his attention back to the tiny man at his feet. "The masters know of your Empire. It is sick and weak. You are to be *our* slaves, now. Not theirs."

For the first time, Graves didn't answer right away. I was stunned as well. Could these aliens and their slaves know about the Galactics? If so, why didn't they show the proper fear and respect that extinction should rightly instill in any thinking being?

I turned to look at Harris, and he glanced back to me. We were both frowning, but we didn't say anything. Either these aliens were crazy, or they knew something we didn't.

Graves decided to make another attempt. "Be that as it may," he said, "let's talk about the here and the now. We are strong, not weak. We are also your brothers, tall man. Look at me. I'm human, just as you are. Your masters have changed your form, but I suspect there is a strong heart beating in your breast, a brave heart."

The towering slaver eyed Graves curiously. "Your talk is pointless. What must be is preordained. The will of the masters is beyond question. I know you and I are similar beasts—but we are still beasts, nothing more."

"No," Graves said firmly. "We're much more than that. We're brothers. I've listened to your demands. Now, you must listen to mine: turn around, board your ship, and rebel against your masters. Use the giants that stand on the ramps. Command them! Take this ship for your own. We will help you kill your

283

masters, and we will all be free. You can have valleys here to live in if you want."

All the slavers generated blatting sounds with their overly-large noses. Their ears flapped and splayed. I could tell they were shocked.

"I will attempt to explain again," the leader said carefully, as if Graves were a slow child. "First, you must lay down your stingers. Then you will be allowed to board our ship. If you do not do this, you must all be killed."

I thought Graves had demonstrated a great deal of patience up until now. But I could tell he'd had enough. He shook his head.

"Go," he said. "Go back to your ship before we kill you!"

The face of the slaver darkened. "Insulting beast!" he said. Then his great hand lashed down and struck Graves.

My centurion had his visor lifted to talk to the enemy more easily. The blow caught him full in the face. Graves tumbled, almost doing a backflip.

That was enough for me. I fired. My beam caught the slaver in neck, and his head popped off and splatted down into the dust at his own feet, smoking and steaming. The tufts of curly hair circling his head caught fire briefly, filling the air with an acrid smoke.

The other three broke and ran off. Harris and Leeson, along with the other officers, stood up and roared for calm. No one else fired.

I didn't wait to find out what my commanders thought of my action. I rushed up to Graves, grabbed him under the arms and dragged him back to the protective line of rocks.

His head was lolling, and I could tell right off his neck was broken. He was having difficulty breathing, but his eyes rolled around to stare at me.

"Did you kill him?" he rasped.

"Yeah," I said.

Graves chuckled, coughed wetly, then managed to control it. "I knew it was you who shot him."

With that final comment, my centurion died.

I fully expected Leeson, Harris and the rest of them to chew me out for firing my weapon without authorization—but they didn't. They didn't say a word. I think they were all secretly happy I'd done it.

The truce lasted about two more minutes. We watched the enemy delegation of skinnies reach the ship and vanish. The giants at the top of the ramps went into motion then, tromping to the bottom. The heavy troopers moved to cover, staying in their tight groups of nine. They encircled our position, deploying as we watched.

"Are we going to do this or not?" I demanded of Harris.

He shrugged hopelessly. We were way off the game plan, and no one seemed to know what to do next. Our chance to "surprise" the enemy had long since faded.

Adjunct Leeson walked to my position and crouched beside me. "McGill, you trigger-happy cuss. I've got a suggestion for you."

"What's that, sir?"

Leeson gestured toward the enemy line. "Why don't you go nuts and poke a hole in one of those giant bellies? I almost feel sorry for those big bastards. They look scary enough, but they're really just walking targets."

I frowned. "Is that an order, sir?"

"No. But you're always pulling crap like that, aren't you? I'm hoping you *feel* like doing it."

"Why aren't we all attacking?"

He grunted in disgust. "The Primus became overjoyed by the idea that we might end this fight with the aliens peacefully. The surviving centurions have reported back to her that the effort to talk to the freaks failed, but she hasn't given the go-order yet. She's still hoping."

I looked back over my shoulder. The distant ridge that hid our main camp was about two kilometers away. I figured the Primus was back there second-guessing everything we were doing up here on the front line.

"I get it," I said. "You want me to go rogue and take the blame for starting this battle. Is that it?"

"Exactly."

I turned away from him and sighted my weapon on the closest giant, but I didn't fire.

"Forget it, sir," I said. "Man-up and do it your damned self."

Leeson cursed me and kicked dirt on the back of my armor. I smiled inside my helmet.

"Shit, McGill. You're even annoying when you're following orders. Fine!"

Leeson drew his sidearm and shot the nearest giant in the belly. It was a nice shot, actually. I could see the impact point perfectly.

But, instead of a burning hole that revealed red guts inside, the laser bolt splashed and split apart into shimmering flashes of color.

"I'll be damned," Leeson said. "The giants have body-shields."

He didn't have time to say anything else because, after that, all hell broke loose.

-29-

When we had power to spare, any heavy trooper's suit could generate a thin body-shield. They weren't really useful in prolonged firefights, however, as they drained your reserves too fast. We couldn't use them when we were charging across a field, either, because we needed every kilowatt to operate our motor systems.

Although we hadn't used shields much in this conflict, it was still a shock to see the enemy had the technology at all. These squids weren't losers, I had to say that for them. As far as I could tell, they didn't have revival machines, but they had pretty good tech otherwise.

After Leeson discharged his weapon and lit up one of the giants, there was about a two second pause—and then it seemed like everyone on the field began hosing the other side with indiscriminate fire.

The giant he'd hit initially looked down stupidly at his belly, which was undamaged but sparkling. He touched the area, then his quizzical expression turned to one of dark rage. He lifted the heavy projector attached to his arm and blazed power in our direction.

Rocks popped, and sand melted to glass. We hunkered down as the beam swept over us, and no one died immediately. The moment the beam had rolled by, I took aim and fired my cannon back at the enemy lines.

Leeson was right, of course. I did want to burn these freaks and run them off the planet. This was the moment I'd been waiting for. But I'd gotten tired of being the only guy who took drastic action and catching hell for it later, so I'd let the Adjunct go first this time.

"Firing center!" I shouted, warning the troopers around me. Plasma cannons had a serious back-blast and more than one legionnaire had been crisped by trotting behind a weaponeer at the wrong moment.

My beam didn't splash against the giant's shield. I'd decided to light up the squad of littermates at his feet instead. I nailed one full in the chest, slagging his armor and dropping him right there on the ramp. I have to tell you, it was the best feeling I'd had all day.

The other littermates immediately went ape and charged. That was enough to change the tune of the officers around me. They'd been shouting orders to hold our fire—except for Leeson. They recalibrated their minds in a hurry when they saw those crazed heavy troopers bounding across the short span of sand between our makeshift defensive position and the ship's ramps.

All of a sudden, the air was alive with bolts of power mixed in with a few heavy projectiles. A missile-launching team on our side let loose from the middle of our circle of rocks, and they aimed in the same direction I had.

The very giant that had started all this was hit hard. His shield buckled, going burnt orange and flickering. He was knocked flat by the blast—but he got up again. I was stunned. If a direct hit from a portable missile battery couldn't take one of these guys down…this was going to be interesting.

All nine squads of littermates were in the fight at this point. Most of the squads were advancing at a stately pace, as if they were taking a stroll in the park. They fired their weapons sporadically, spanging bullets off our rocks. When one of those explosive rounds hit one of our men square-on, it took him out as often as not.

But as we poured back fire into their advancing squares, eventually we knocked out one of them, and the rest predictably charged. After that, we took most of them down before they reached us. When the survivors did manage to make it to our lines, a desperate melee began. I watched as troopers on both sides were cut apart and gutted in their shining armor.

I stood up and fired my cannon point-blank. I took out a charging, bug-eyed berserker who was knocked on his smoldering ass, stone dead.

There wasn't any time to congratulate myself. It seemed that the sky had darkened.

I turned and gaped upward. One of the giants had arrived, towering over my clump of rocks. He had a sword in one hand, which he used to thrust and cut. I saw men get hit by that thing—it was like being struck by a blade the size of a car. Limbs were shorn off, and troopers fell, howling.

The giant's projector swept the scene methodically, burning victims as they crawled away. An idiot's grin rode his face, as if he was enjoying his butchery. His personal shield sparkled, like it was in a rainstorm, deflecting dozens of light, incoming fire.

Staggering backward, I shook my cannon and cursed at it. The recycle time on these units seemed like an eternity when you were about to die.

Finally, a green indicator LED flickered on, and I shouldered my weapon. Somehow, I think the giant sensed I was about to take him out. His sword arm swept forward—

I fired. I think I'd been holding the trigger down, in fact, for several long seconds. Finally, the chamber cleared and the weapon released a fresh gush of energy.

Getting hammered by a plasma cannon isn't like being hit by a laser pistol. Still, I thought it would have been less effective if the giant hadn't been recently hit by a missile. These force fields were touchy, and it took a minute or two after a hard strike for them to settle down, turn glassy, and be fully integrated again.

The field collapsed, and my beam made it through. I held the trigger down, ignoring overcharge warnings and heat indicators. I had to keep the beam going until the job was done.

The giant's chest was a smoking ruin before I let go of that trigger. He toppled backward scattering a group of my comrades who'd been trying to come in behind him to hamstring him. They never got the chance. He was dead before he hit the rocks.

A heavy hand clapped me on the shoulder. "Good job, McGill," Harris said. Leeson walked up and surveyed the scene.

The enemy charge had been broken, and they'd been killed down to the last man. On our own side, we'd lost about fifty troops.

"The revival machines are going to be busy tonight," I said.

Leeson shook his head seriously. "No, I don't think so. The enemy took out our machine."

"What?" demanded Harris, his voice cracking high in alarm.

"That's right. Remember that flying platform? Another one of them just swooped down and nailed the camp a few minutes ago. Maybe that's why the enemy was standing around here waiting. They seemed to know just where to hit us, and they took out the medical bunker."

"But sir," Harris said, looking around in alarm. "Can I assume we're synched up with the other valleys for revivals? We just lost a lot of people. We can't have all these troops permed."

Leeson looked at him. "Don't worry, Vet. I'm sure the techs are working on it. Now, let's talk about taking that ship."

He pointed toward the yawning ramps. They were all still fully extended. Inside, the ship looked cavernous and black.

"Shouldn't we wait until the revival machines are—"

"No," said Leeson firmly. "We're moving out now. Graves is dead, so I'm assuming command of what's left of this unit. We're not going to fold into the other units right now. There isn't time. We have to take advantage of the situation."

Harris began to argue, but I could see Leeson's point.

"That's right, sir," I said. "The squids might wise up and close their hatches any second now."

Leeson nodded. "Here, McGill. Take this."

He handed me a new plasma cannon. For a second, I didn't understand why he'd given it to me, but then I noticed that the indicator lights on mine were locked red. The unit had overloaded during that last blast and hadn't recovered. It would take a tech hours to fix it—if it could be done at all. The new weapon had a few dents in it, but it looked serviceable.

"Where did this come from?" I asked.

"Sargon died with it in his hands," Leeson said. "I'm sure he'd be happy to know you had it now."

I wasn't so sure he'd be *happy*, but I took the weapon anyway and discarded my own unit. I plugged it into the grid, slapped in a fresh cartridge and gave Leeson the thumbs up.

"Come on, at a trot now!" Leeson shouted. "Advance!"

Harris and I followed. We moved toward the nearest ramp. The other two Centurions had teams of their own heading toward the ramp as well. If I had to guess, I'd say there were less than two hundred of us left alive.

I had to wonder what was going on back at camp. If the enemy had attacked the camp and taken out the bio people, it was certain we weren't going to be seeing any reinforcements up here at the front.

The ramp was so huge it looked unreal. It must have been a meter thick and made of pure, black metal. The hull of this thing was dense and dull in color.

"This is bullshit," Harris complained. "*Total* bullshit! We should fall back and hold our position, waiting for fresh troops."

"They might seal the ship by that time, Vet," I said.

Harris didn't seem to hear me. "Hell, they could be flying them in from the other valleys by now," he said. "If the Tribune really wanted to win this fight, he could do it now. I don't get the brass sometimes. I really don't."

Harris went on like that as we mounted the ramp and clanged into the interior. I knew what he was really upset about, of course. He liked dying even less than the rest of us. But the idea of dying without a revival machine waiting for you back at camp—well, to a member of Legion Varus, that sounded just plain wrong. Getting permed was a fate for some other loser, not for one of us.

Once we reached the top of the ramp and entered the ship itself, a cool gloom closed over us. Dozens of troopers hustled in behind me.

291

I think every one of us slowed down when we actually stepped into the ship. It was hard not to.

The ship was...*different*. You just knew, looking around, that your tiny little human ass didn't belong here. The ship had been built by true aliens—aliens so utterly different from us that they didn't have much in the way of recognizable features on the distant walls or the high ceiling. There were no markings, no lights, and no flashing symbols.

Instead, there were sweeping streaks of glimmering reflections on the floor of the ship. I hadn't seen the phenomenon in the ramp itself, but here in the dim interior it was unmistakable.

"Is that writing of some kind?" I asked Harris.

He frowned at me, then frowned at the deck. "Looks like various metals all mixed together."

"I think it's more complex than that," I said. "The metal is reflective—various tones of silver and dark gray mixed in flowing streaks."

"I know what the hell it looks like!" Harris snapped. "I'm trotting along next to you. Don't you think I have eyes? Forget the damned floor, McGill. Look for targets!"

He had a point there. I lifted my eyes and peered into the vast, dark chamber we were marching farther into every second. The place was strange. It seemed to have a closeness to it even though it was obviously huge.

"Mists," I said, waving my hands at the air that seemed to coalesce and move around me like thick, silvery smoke. "The atmosphere in here—"

I broke off as a screeching sound began. I turned to see who was in trouble. A trooper was down right behind me. I grimaced realizing it was Kivi.

"Back up, give her some air!" shouted Harris.

I could see Kivi's face. She was in agony, and her visor was up.

"No!" I shouted. "Close her visor! She doesn't need air, she needs to keep her visor shut!"

Harris finally got what I was suggesting. He reached down and closed Kivi's faceplate. I could see her in there, still squirming in pain and dying. It was too late for her.

"Leeson!" I shouted. "Nanites, sir! We've got clouds of nanites in the air. I think they're on the floor everywhere, being activated as we walk by. Close all vents and faceplates!"

"Do it!" shouted Leeson.

Six more people went down before we'd all buttoned up our suits. While troopers milled around and tried to help their stricken comrades, I cranked my weapon, broadening the beam to its widest setting. I fired an experimental cone into the air. Leeson was all over me after that.

"What'd you see?" he demanded, staring upward.

I pointed at the deck. "Look, see that fine grit? Those are dead nanites. They look kind of like graphite dust."

Leeson stared. Finally, he got it. He passed the word on. Soon, we were marching behind a line of weaponeers who were hosing down every centimeter of the ship's hull and even the air around us with broad blasts from their cannons. But that was costing too much power. We halted our advance and retreated a hundred steps.

I looked over my shoulder toward the open door behind me. Outside, the sun blazed.

"We haven't made it very far into the ship," I said. "I think these nanites are like watchdogs. Maybe they know friend from foe."

Leeson shook his head and conferred with the other centurions. They weren't sure how to proceed. I went out into the sunshine again and stood on the ramp looking around.

Harris came out to join me. "This is a charley-foxtrot," he said, and I had to agree with him. "Look over there," Harris said, pointing. "There are those colonist buddies of yours. They're probably having a good laugh at our troubles."

Surprised, I followed his jabbing finger. He was right. A few colonist fighters were in the area we'd come from, squatting on some of the same rocks.

"They're unusually brave with us in front of them," I said. "You mind if I go talk to them?"

"Suit yourself," Harris said. "But don't go running off down any of those rabbit holes with them. I won't cover for you if you do."

293

His statement baffled me. I couldn't recall Harris covering for me on any occasion—or for anyone else.

I walked up to the colonists calmly, with my weapons and hands down. They eyed me with flat stares. No one waved or shouted a greeting. I guess I would have to count myself lucky they weren't shooting at me with their crossbows.

I saw they were in battle gear as I drew near. Rather than the near-naked state they'd been in while underground or hunting, they were in black, loose-fitting clothes. Their faces were painted with cooling paint that would hide their heat signatures. They held their weapons loosely, but I could tell they were ready to snap them up and fight if I made a wrong move.

"Hello!" I called when I was about ten meters away. "Can you guys help us out?"

They looked from one to the other and shook their heads bemusedly. I thought I might have recognized one or two of them. I'd hoped Della would be among them—but she wasn't.

"We've found hostile nanites inside the ship," I said. "They seem to be all over the place, killing our troops if we go inside too far."

One man broke ranks and stepped up to me. He was short in stature but had wide muscular shoulders and a sure-footed stance. "Those nanites are not ours," he said.

"Yeah, I figured that. But do you know how to switch them off? To get past them?"

"Yes," he said. "You must strip away all your gear. Find manacles and apply them to each wrist. Cross your arms so they clasp firmly and can't be pulled apart. When you are naked and helpless, the nanites will let you pass and join your new masters."

I didn't like his explanation or his attitude. I nodded to him.

"Thanks a lot for that valuable information. Too bad none of you are brave enough to enter this ship or smart enough to figure out a way to pass the nanites. Don't worry, we'll do the job for you. Go back and hide in your holes. You might get a sunburn or a bug-bite out here. Wouldn't want that to happen to civvies."

The short guy's smile faded. I think he understood that I'd insulted him. This made me happy.

As I turned to go, he called me back.

"What is this you call us? What is a 'civvie'?"

"Civilian. A non-combatant. Someone who must be protected from harm by real soldiers."

The colonists looked from one to the next. They were all frowning now.

"I'm a scout," said the short guy. "This is my team. We're not civvies."

I laughed. "Really? Then come on inside the ship with us and end this fight. Put up or shut up—civvie."

I walked away without bothering to look back. If there was one thing I couldn't abide it was a mouthy, arrogant bystander who complained behind your back and didn't have the guts to join the fight himself.

Harris looked at me quizzically as I mounted the ramp and returned to his side. Leeson walked over to join us as well.

Leeson gestured behind me. "You want to introduce your new friends?" he asked.

I turned in surprise. The colonists had quietly followed me up the ramp. They didn't look happy, but I could tell they were game. There were seven altogether, and their eyes roved around the interior of the big ship. I was impressed by their bravery, as I knew this vessel had come straight from Hell as far as they were concerned.

"Yeah," I said. "These are *warriors*. A scout and his crew. What is your name, sir?" I asked the short guy.

"Alders," he said. "My name is Alders."

"Scout Alders," I repeated to Leeson. "He's the toughest of their fighters. Think of them as native guides."

Harris and Leeson looked at the colonists suspiciously.

Alders, for his part, had swelled up with pride during my introduction.

"Where is the Investigator?" Leeson asked. "If you are helping us, what has he been doing?"

Alders looked surprised. "Do you not know? We'd thought that with your instrumentation—well, it doesn't matter. I'll tell you now: the Investigator is keeping this ship grounded."

295

Leeson's eyes widened. "How?"

"By manipulating fields. The ship uses twin dishes for propulsion when close to our planet. Surely you've seen them at either end."

We nodded, listening closely.

"Those dishes generate the energy field surrounding the ship. They also propel it. We've interfered with those emanations, forcing them to stay on the ground. We've prepared for years for this day—we might have taken their ship by now if it hadn't been for your arrival and interference!"

"I think you're talking big, short guy," Harris said.

Leeson promptly whacked him in the chest with his knuckles. It did my eyes good to see that.

A few things clicked for me as I thought over what Alders had said. I realized this ship *should* have been leaving.

"If I was this ship's captain," I said, "and enemy troops were wandering into my hold, I would take off."

"All right then," Leeson said. "You're doing your part. That's great. How can you help us capture the ship?"

"Alders and his crew are going to get us past these watchdog nanites," I said.

"Yes," Alders agreed. "We can do that...I think."

-30-

Alders and his crew had opened up vials of dust and were carefully sprinkling it ahead of them as they edged forward.

The nanite watchdogs had lain down in silver rivers all over the deck when we'd retreated, but now that new alien nanites of a darker shade were detected, a strange battle took place.

Twin swarms rose up in a whirlwind cloud. There was no breeze, but they flew in a deadly embrace anyway. The colonist nanites seemed superior. I don't think they'd been programmed to fight other nanites. They had been designed to tear up flesh that didn't match the configuration they'd been built to recognize, and that's it.

We watched the battle from a safe distance. Steadily, the dark nanites of the colonists ate up the silver swarm the cephalopods had left as a trap for the unwary.

"Where did you guys get this technology?" I asked Alders. "It seems so advanced."

"The Investigator and his students have bred these metal creatures," he told me. "They did it in the same manner the cephalopods manipulated our flesh, bending it to their purposes. These tiny constructs are our greatest achievement. We've been working on them for years, preparing for the next visit."

Leeson stepped up, fascinated. "I'm impressed," he said. "You copied the tech, didn't you? You stole the cephalopod design and made it your own. These nanites are similar, but they're a breed apart."

"Essentially, yes."

"What powers them?" I asked.

"Sunlight, flesh, heat: Various things, depending on the breed. This particular type of creature feeds upon emissions from the ship."

A tech happened by, and I realized it was Natasha. "These things are amazing. Can we have a sample?"

Alders eyed her critically. "I would like to trade."

Natasha gave him a replacement tapper and a few power cells in trade for a tube of nanites.

"Are they dangerous?" she asked.

"Only if you are a rival nanite," Alders said, smiling.

The battle in the hold was soon over. The nanite swarms died down, one group having destroyed the other. I had to wonder what these things would look like under a microscope. I suspected they'd resemble insects made of metal.

We pressed ahead, knowing that the enemy wasn't beaten yet. It didn't feel good, walking into an alien ship full of unknown traps.

The squids were orderly; you could at least say that about them. There were literally thousands of tons of equipment in the hold. Foodstuffs, weapons, cages—this last surprised me, but I guess it shouldn't have. We'd found thousands of man-cages. About two meters square, they were built with thick lusterless metal and outfitted with receptacles for both feeding and elimination.

Just looking at those cages gave me a sick feeling. How many of my fellow humans had spent their lives inside them? All of them were empty—where had the occupants gone?

Our expedition paused again when we ran into a blank bulkhead. We'd figured out by that time that we were in some kind of central hold. Probably, invasion forces gathered here before sallying out down the ramps.

We had no answers, so we took a right turn and followed the walls to a ramp. The ramp led upward into hanging darkness.

"Let me guess," I said to Leeson who stood at my side. "Weaponeers first?"

He looked concerned, and glanced back toward the other officers. They had a little huddle and decided to send up a few grunts instead. The last weaponeers had been deemed too vital to the mission to waste them on this particular duty.

Four heavy troopers marched up the ramp ahead of me, looking like scared rabbits. I wondered if I'd looked so nervous when I was leading a team into what could be a deadly situation. I hoped not.

"Don't piss yourselves all at once!" I called after them.

All I got for my trouble was a finger flicked up from a single gauntlet. I chuckled—but my amusement was cut short.

Just as they reached the top of the ramp, long tubular things reached out from both sides. Like elephant-trunks, twelve tentacles snaked out and snatched the troopers from our view. Three grappled each man and retracted. It happened so fast, so methodically, the team barely had time to react.

One man in the group managed to get his force-blade out and use it effectively. A single tentacle was lopped off and fell, writhing and flopping. It rolled down the ramp toward us.

I didn't wait for orders. I rushed forward with my weapon at my shoulder, priming up. I'd already cranked my tube's aperture wide open, prepping it for short-range fire.

Leeson was calling after me, saying something. There were shouts and tramping feet—I didn't get what he'd said, but I didn't much care, either. I knew I was one of the few who could do anything serious to these damned squids.

The first one I saw loomed directly ahead about ten meters away. He was at the top of the ramp. I halted to sight on him, a grim smile darkening my face.

I squeezed the trigger—but to my shock, I squeezed it on nothing. The weapon had been snatched from my grasp. What happened next made me a little sick.

Another squid had been hiding out of sight on the right side of the ramp, sitting in ambush on the next deck of the ship. They had an amazing reach and could do things with any of their eight arms we mere humans couldn't manage with both of ours.

Once I'd been disarmed, a total of three squids launched themselves down the ramp. They knocked me down on the way past, almost throwing me off the ramp. But I hung on and stood back up. The charging squids ran into our line of men, and a wild melee began.

The alien who'd taken my weapon now dipped down into plain sight hanging over my head like a spider on a wall. He had my tube.

I reached for it, but he held it out of range. Depressing the firing stud with the squirming tip of his ropy appendage, he fried my comrades.

A cone of burning plasma enveloped half a dozen troopers. The beam was too diffuse to burn through our armor, but we all had weak points. One was our visors, which cracked wide. A fraction of a second later, the human faces behind the protective barrier smoked, then bubbled.

Screaming, one man reeled and threw himself off the ramp. He fell at least twenty meters to the deck below. Two others did the same, while the rest dropped and rolled down the ramp, crashing into those who ran to give aid. Sporadic fire erupted from the lower deck, splattering energy onto the squid above me.

The squid wasn't looking too good at this point. He'd taken a dozen hits. He must have known that his move would expose him to our weapons, but maybe he'd thought it would be worth it.

He also didn't seem to understand our weapons very well. He kept the firing stud on my cannon depressed hosing down the line of approaching legionnaires with a continuous stream of energy. After about two full seconds, it overheated, and the gas chamber ruptured. It sort of popped, sounding like a big light bulb, and stopped operating.

By that time, I'd gotten my force-blades out and was stabbing the monster repeatedly. I thrust and cut. It took long seconds of chopping at it before the thing finally slid down and rolled away down the ramp as dead as a fish in a barrel.

The rest of the unit behind me got their act together then. Harris was the first man to reach me. I honestly misread his eagerness. Silly me, I thought he might be happy I'd taken one out.

Instead, he bashed me one and pointed at his blackened shoulder.

"See this, McGill? You stupid cowboy son-of-a-bitch! That squid murdered half a squad. And he did it with *your* weapon, McGill!"

"Yeah," I said, "I didn't see that coming."

"Open your visor, Specialist," Harris said.

I could see more than a little crazy was going on in his eyes.

"Uh, why Vet?"

He pulled out his sidearm. "Specialist McGill, that was a direct order. Are you disobeying a direct order?"

I flipped up my visor, and he punched me. I managed to turn my head a bit, so he didn't break my nose, but my cheekbone felt like it had been smashed with a hammer.

"Happy?" I asked, but it came out sounding funny. I realized then that my teeth had been driven into my upper lip. His gauntlet had caught more than just my cheek.

I lowered my head and reached up with my fingers to tug at my lips which were now stuck on my teeth. Harris lowered himself into a crouch so he could look me in the eye.

"No, I'm not happy yet," he told me. "I'll tell you when I'll be happy, hero. The next time I see you die on this little bug-hunt."

I wanted to hit him. I really did, but I sort of understood his rage. I'd advanced without orders. The squid had gotten my weapon and taken out a number of my own men. We'd won the fight, but quite possibly we could have done it with fewer losses.

Leeson loomed over me.

"Specialist? Are you still functional?"

"Ready and able, sir," I said as clearly as I could.

I got to my feet, trying not to sway. I thought that Harris had messed me up worse than the squid itself but kept quiet. I knew that if I wasn't able to fight while on a critical mission like this, I might well be giving my superiors just cause to recycle me. They wouldn't want to simply leave me behind while they advanced. If they did that, I might be captured and

301

thus not be a candidate for revival. Not being able to revive a heavily-trained specialist would inconvenience the legion.

Leeson looked me over critically, then eyed Harris. He knew what had happened. It was obvious.

"Up the ramp," he said. "A weaponeer without a weapon is just a slow-moving heavy trooper. You're on point, McGill."

Unsurprised, I marched up the ramp to the top. I didn't want to die—but I cared less than usual right now if I did.

There were no squids at the top of the ramp. The deck was different, however. It was full of heavy equipment and machines that were alien to me. We marched past generators the size of houses and other, bigger machines that I couldn't begin to identify. Maybe they were engines, or maybe they ran the life support systems. I thought they powered the big cannon on the top of the ship. Whatever they were, we didn't damage them. It was just possible this ship could be useful to us if we could take it from the present owners.

What came to my attention as we mounted the next ramp upward was a serious stink. I'm not talking about an easy-going stench like one might find at the local landfill, sewer farm or dairy. I'm talking about the sharp, finger-up-the-nostril stench that only a concentrated amount of human waste can produce.

I closed my visor, of course, but it was a little too late for that. We had come to the living space of the beings we called littermates.

The evidence was unmistakable. Groups of coffin-like boxes had been arranged into sets of nine. These coffins thronged the deck. We counted them, and they came pretty close to the number we'd slain.

"Looks like we got them all," I said. "Maybe the ship is empty."

"Don't bet on it, McGill," Harris told me. "Ain't no way you're living through this to the end."

Despite his prediction, I was beginning to feel upbeat. There was only one more ramp and one more deck to go.

Before we reached the last ramp, we found the captives. They were locked up in rows upon rows of stacked man-cages. The people inside were dark-eyed, haunted. None of them spoke. The one man who was still game was Stott. I found him and released him. He scuttled off into the shadows without even saying thank you.

We found Hudson on the last row, on the bottom of the final stack. He'd been abused horribly. There were burns all over his naked body. His eyes were gone—and I mean *gone*. They'd been burned away. All that was left was fresh scar-tissue and dripping fluids.

"Hudson?" I asked when I found him.

"Is that you, McGill?"

I rattled at the cage, but it held firm.

"We've got to get him out, sir," I told Leeson.

"Yeah…we will. First, can you answer a few questions, Hudson?"

"I'll try, sir."

"You're in bad shape. Why are the colonists looking so much healthier than you?"

"They aren't as dumb as I am, sir. They kept quiet and did as they were told. I tried to provoke these squids—the colonists call them 'masters'. Can you believe that?"

"Yeah…" Leeson said, his face screwing up in disgust as he looked Hudson over.

Harris and Leeson exchanged glances that Hudson couldn't see. They both shook their heads.

I knew what that meant. Hudson was too injured to recover in any reasonable fashion. He had to be recycled to heal up. Basically, he needed a whole new body. It would be a mercy, really.

Leeson drew his sidearm and crouched in front of the cage. I worked on breaking the lock, but it wasn't easy to do.

"Talk to me, Hudson," the adjunct said. "Why are you so messed up? Was this done in reprisal for our fighting outside?"

"No, I don't think so. After they captured me and brought me to these cages, I asked the other prisoners how I could escape. They said you could only escape through death. So I tried to piss them off enough to get them to kill me. Other colonists managed it. But the squids really didn't want to kill me. They burned me, but they kept me alive. I think they wanted to take me home and really go to work on me to find out what makes our kind different."

I looked around at the dull-eyed prisoners. I thought I understood why they were so quiet, so resigned. They'd given up. The fighters among them were already dead.

"Anything else you can tell us about the enemy?" Leeson asked.

"Not much. I think the squid stronghold is one floor up. By that, I mean their quarters and the bridge. They usually came from up there when they wanted to prod me."

"Right, thanks for the input. You've done well, soldier."

"Sir? Could I ask one thing?"

"What's that?"

"Could you have McGill do the honors? I saw him do the rest of our team when I still had eyes. I wanted him to get to me, but he didn't make it. I was the last man alive on that ramp, and now I truly wish that I'd been lucky enough to die with the rest of them."

Leeson looked at the gun in his hand. Hudson knew it was there even if he couldn't see it.

Leeson looked up at me, squinting. I must have looked pretty long in the face because what he did next surprised me.

"All right," Leeson said. "McGill, do it." Then he raised his pistol and shot Hudson in the head.

I knew it was an act of kindness. First off, Hudson had been seeking a way out of his current life for days. He'd been tortured and now had finally managed to die. We all knew he'd get a new body this way. Maybe he'd even get lucky and some of the memories of his final days in this cage would be lost, as he'd been isolated from the group and our recording systems.

Secondly, Leeson had done the job as a favor to me. He'd taken on a grim burden that I clearly didn't want weighing on me.

I thought better of Adjunct Leeson after that.

-31-

The squids made their last stand on the ship's bridge. We could tell that the Investigator's efforts hadn't been in vain, as they did their damnedest to get the ship flying right up until the end.

"We've got to take them now," I told Leeson, who'd called a halt just out of range of the enemy. "What if they fix this ship?"

"They won't. Alders said that Investigator guy took care of it."

Strangely enough, Leeson was in command now. Out of three full units of a hundred troops each, we'd lost all three of the centurions. Graves had died first, and the second centurion hadn't made it into the ship. The last one had died on the ramp when the squids first ambushed us. That had left Leeson in charge, as he was the most senior adjunct left. That wasn't good, because he wasn't the most decisive man in the legion.

"Sir? Can we trust this situation to continue unchanged? If this ship manages to launch while we're waiting around with our fingers—"

"Don't give me that look, Specialist," Leeson told me. "We've had a tough time of it, and we're going to do the last part by the book. We'll wait here for the next three units. The Primus is in contact with me through relayed buzzers and nanite wire. I've got her approval to hold here until relief arrives. We don't know what their final defenses will be like on the bridge."

I twisted up my lips, which hurt, as Harris had torn them up with his punch. They were starting to swell now.

"Sir," I said, "I'm going to give you my private opinion, then I'm going to shut up."

He grinned at me. "That'll be a first, McGill, and I'm going to hold you to it."

"Look, sir, what if they manage to get this ship to fly right now? We don't know anything about how the colonists sabotaged them. If they lift off with us trapped in here, well…"

I saw the Adjunct's eyes light up. He finally got it. He was risking all our skins on the hunch that the colonists knew what the heck they were doing—and the squids didn't. That was quite a bet in my book. I knew why he wanted to wait for back up. It was the safer bet. Why take any more losses when we could gather up hundreds of fresh troops and do it without further bloodshed on our part?

But it was just too risky. Flying off into space—that could get a man permed, and we both knew it.

Leeson stood up and straightened his kit. He addressed everyone on the general com channel.

"Troops, we've got one more job to do. We're going to finish this—one way or the other. Gear up and advance. I want a squad on each flank and remember not to mass up in the center. We'll hit them fast with a steady advance, firing as we go. Oh, and try not to hit their equipment if you can. Force-blades in close, shorten up the length and be sure of your targets."

We were on the move again less than a minute later. Harris and the other vets screamed at anyone who didn't get up fast enough. Laggards were roughly propelled toward the enemy. I thought the vets might have figured out the score on their own.

When we finally got to the bridge, we found it was only lightly defended. There were only about ten aliens left alive. Still, squids are tough, and they gave us plenty of trouble despite their small numbers.

The aliens that had survived and now awaited our long march through the entrails of their vast ship were injured and desperate. I saw them at the controls as we approached. They were still working at them with tools and flaring lights that must have been welding torches of some kind. They hadn't given up on effecting repairs—but time had run out for them.

They fired on us the second they spotted our approach. That's one thing I'd come to understand about the squids: they weren't big on peace talks. Their only attempts to communicate had been made through their littermates, all of whom were now dead.

A wobbling, black projectile was sailing toward our advancing line. I knew it was gas, as did everyone else. We dived away from the impact point, but I don't think anyone was dumb enough by this time to have their visors open in the face of this enemy.

We pressed ahead, marching out of the coiled mists of gas like ghostly warriors. For the first time since I'd met the squids, I sensed a hint of fear in their behavior. This pleased me. Up until now, they'd been arrogant, self-assured and merciless.

After a brief, vicious fight, the last of them laid quivering and leaking fluids all over the deck. They hadn't asked for quarter—at least, not in any way we could understand—and we didn't offer them anything less than death. It was butchery by the end, but I didn't have a qualm.

The bridge was aquatic in nature. The rest of the ship had been filled with a breathable atmosphere, but the bridge was enclosed in a shallow tank of water. I figured this was probably a luxury for the squids. They were an aquatic species who were able to function well on land, but it hadn't been comfortable for them.

Encircling the central pool of liquid were banks of instruments. They weren't designed the way we would have done it. The controls were large, and most of them were disk-like knobs without labels. I thought such a control system might be easier for a race with tentacles to operate than buttons, touchscreens or levers.

Six of them floated in the middle of the control panels in their pool of dark water. I eyed the corpses, intrigued despite myself by these aliens.

How many years had these creatures been enslaving my kind? It was bad enough that we'd abandoned our colonists out here. These aliens had put an extra twist into our callous handling of exiles. I thought that killing the monsters which had tormented our people for so long was the least Legion Varus could do for our long lost cousins.

The road had been long, but victory was finally ours. When we finally were certain we'd taken the entire ship, there was a ragged cheer from the units but not much more. We were exhausted both emotionally and physically.

The celebration, if you could call it that, rapidly degenerated into troops stretching out on their backs and gasping like beached fish. We were so glad it was over. A battle like this one seemed like an interminable grind.

It wasn't only the marching around and fighting that tired us—it was the tension that had filled our every step. We'd feared for our lives ever since we'd dared walk into this ship. Knowing that we'd made it to the end of the campaign, and that we'd probably get to live and sleep and eat proper food again was a great relief, but it also meant all that nervous energy and adrenaline abandoned us. I saw men staring at nothing and even snoring on the decks just a few minutes after the all-clear had been called.

* * *

About two hours later, a delegation of VIPs arrived. Among them were Graves, the Investigator and even the Primus herself.

As usual, the Primus looked like she smelled a cat-box that needed cleaning. Graves didn't seem to have any emotion—but he did give me a nod of greeting. I nodded back, then leaned against a control module that was shaped like an octagon and was about the size and weight of a fireplug.

"Who gave the order to attack the bridge?" the Primus asked, staring around her. She had her hands on her hips and her lips were twisted.

It took me a moment to figure out what her problem was. A group of techs were with her, and they had buzzers out—the kind that took movies of everything.

When I saw her standing on the deck loaded with alien carcasses and floating camera-drones, I finally understood that she'd wanted to be present when the final push was made. She'd hustled up out of camp to be here, and she wasn't happy that the party was all over before she arrived.

Finally, with obvious reluctance, Leeson walked up to her.

"Primus," he said. "I led the final action."

She stared at him, looking him up and down for a second. "One of Graves' team, I see. Figures. Not one of you can follow a simple order. Any reason I shouldn't put you on report?"

Leeson looked befuddled for a second. "On report?"

"You were told to hold your position and wait for overwhelming force. You ignored my orders. Explain yourself."

"Uh, we were fighting all the way up here, and the enemy was effecting repairs on the ship. If I'd waited around, they might have flown off with it. I didn't want such a valuable prize to be lost, sir."

"Bullshit," she said. "You attacked to save your own hide: To make sure the enemy couldn't carry you off into space."

Leeson was finally getting angry. It wasn't good for an adjunct to mouth off to a primus, but he did it anyway.

"So what if I did?" he demanded. "That's better than risking lives to grandstand at the final moments of a battle."

The two glowered at each other. Graves stepped forward, making calming motions with his hands.

"Let's not lose sight of the important thing: we've won. The ship is ours. I would suggest you report this information to the Tribune personally, Primus Turov."

She nodded and took Leeson with her to act as a tour guide. Together they stalked away to make their reports to the Tribune. Techs followed her, with their buzzers continually recording and transmitting everything. She wouldn't get the glorious pictures she'd wanted of herself striding in during the final moments, but she could at least pose with the big pile of alien bodies and equipment.

The Investigator stepped forward in her absence and addressed Graves.

"Beastly woman," he said, indicating Primus Turov.

Graves was bemused, but it barely showed. "She's in command," he said.

The Investigator eyed Graves coldly. "I overheard something disturbing," he said. "Did you tell your commander that you were now in possession of this ship?"

"I believe I did say something to that effect."

The Investigator shook his head. "You were mistaken. This vessel and all her contents belong to us. Without our help, you could never have taken her."

Graves frowned slightly. "Investigator—is that your title?"

"Yes. I'm the Principal Investigator of the Hydra Mission. There is no higher authority on the planet. Using antiquated words, you could call me a planetary governor."

Graves nodded. "Sir, you would be well served to grasp certain realities. This ship isn't under your control because we're the ones with military units inside it."

While Graves spoke, the Investigator's eyes roved and landed on me. I was standing nearby listening, while trying to appear as if I wasn't doing so.

"You there. You've been to my labs. Come forward, soldier."

I approached reluctantly. I could recognize trouble when I met up with it.

"Hello, Investigator," I said. "Enjoying your victory?"

"What exactly is that supposed to mean?"

"I mean these cephalopods have been enslaving and tormenting your people for a generation. Surely you must feel relief to see they're all dead at your feet. You've been saved, man."

The Investigator eyed me as if I were speaking in an alien tongue. But slowly, his expression shifted. He nodded at me.

"Well said," he replied at last. "You're right. Gratitude is in order. This victory was achieved through cooperation. It's best for both our factions to accept that reality. I'll tell you what, Graves. Let's co-occupy the ship. We know these beings. We've studied them for decades. We have labs and equipment you military types lack. In turn, I'm sure that your people have technology we don't possess. Together, we can study this ship and mull over the findings. I've often found that if done properly, scientific methodology results in answers that become obvious to all."

Graves looked from me to the Investigator. "I take it you two know each other?" he asked.

"Yes," said the Investigator. "We've met."

Graves shook his head and chuckled. "All right, I'll try to play it your way. It makes sense. But that doesn't mean it you'll get away with it, because I'm not in charge. You see that woman over there?"

Graves indicated Primus Turov, who was taking a victory lap around a severed tentacle that still twitched now and then as her team filmed it.

"She's going to be your biggest problem," Graves continued.

"Then I must convince her with unassailable logic," the Investigator said, and took a step toward the Primus.

Graves and I both moved to stop him.

"Bad idea," I said. "Listen to the Centurion for a minute."

The Investigator paused and looked at Graves curiously.

"Fortunately, she's not in charge of diplomatic matters," Graves said. "We have a higher authority. The leader of our entire legion is Tribune Drusus."

Before the Primus finished her report, Graves, the Investigator and I all walked down the ramps together, heading toward the exit. I liked the sound of the plan Graves had just come up with, and I thought it might just work.

-32-

The only good thing that came out of the cephalopod invasion was a new sense of cooperation between Legion Varus and the colonists. I didn't have to listen to any more muttering from the officers about taking them all out. They were humans and, even though they'd given us plenty of resistance at first, once they worked with us they'd been critical to our success. I dared to hope we were beginning to pull together as a species.

Tribune Drusus flew out the day after we took the ship to survey the scene of the battle personally. Graves invited me to be there when he met with the Tribune, but at first I declined.

"You should come, McGill," he said. "Your actions in this valley were as important as anyone's. We brought this campaign to a successful conclusion, and you might as well get some of the credit."

I shrugged, which was possible now because we weren't wearing battle-armor any longer. What a relief that was. My smart-cloth uniform felt absolutely cushy after spending days encased in steel and chafing polymers.

"That's it?" Graves asked, frowning at me. "You don't care?"

"Oh, I care, sir. That's why I fought so hard to end this. But I'm not into playing the game with the brass. They can read the reports and watch the suit vids if they want to find out what really happened. If I get into the middle of it, I'm liable to step on toes. It's not worth it."

Graves' eyes slid over to Primus Turov, who was doing everything short of putting on false eyelashes in anticipation of the Tribune's arrival. He looked amused for a moment, then looked back at me.

"Don't worry about her. To keep a high profile position, one has to worry about how one appears to their superiors. She's got to play that game—you don't. Not really."

I nodded. "Can I ask you how long you've served in Varus—and how long she has—sir?"

Graves didn't like the question. I could see it in his eyes. They became hard the way they looked before he executed a man for disobeying orders. But after that momentary flash of hostility, he relaxed again.

"Yeah, sure," he said. "I've been with Varus a long time. Most of the Primus-ranked officers are my juniors—I'll admit that. But that's because I play it my own way the same as you do, Specialist."

"So why do you want me to change my tune?" I asked, crossing my arms.

"Not for you," Graves said, lowering his voice. "For these people here—the locals. Their fate hasn't been decided yet."

"That is grade-A bullshit, sir!"

"Lower your voice, Specialist. And yes, I know it is. But you have to understand how things are. We're gambling with much more than our own piddley little lives. If we screw up, all of Earth will suffer. Hell, back home they are already blaming us for Cancri-9. I'm not sure how the Nairbs and the Galactics are going to take the violations that have occurred in this system. They might be in an understanding mood—or they might want to make a clean sweep of things."

I winced when he mentioned the Nairbs. They were the bureaucrats of the Empire. They were unpleasant beings that only cared about the letter of the law, not justice. I didn't have the best relationship with them. I'd had unhappy encounters with them on more than one occasion in the past, and I was pretty sure they weren't going to like anything about what had happened on this planet. Earth had colonized Dust World— even if we hadn't known until recently that we'd managed to do it. Worse, a Galactic ship had been destroyed. How would

313

the Nairbs mete out judgment and punishment in this instance? I didn't even want to think about it.

I frowned, took in a deep breath and uncrossed my arms. I knew Graves was right. The brass had to make some hard decisions about the colonists and the fate of the legion itself. You couldn't make choices like these with your heart—you had to use your head. The survival of our species wasn't always achieved in the cleanest manner. Legion Varus seemed to always be involved when things became particularly ugly. We were all about the gray-area of morality.

"All right," I said. "I'll tag along. You want me to keep quiet?"

Graves chuckled. "I'm not asking for miracles."

I followed him outside the alien ship and watched as a lifter floated down over the waters of the central lake. The ripples became furious as it dropped ever lower and landed on the shore. The ramp extended and squelched into the mud.

Rock-fish watched curiously as a delegation exited the lifter. At the center of a knot of officers was Tribune Drusus. He wasn't the tallest in the group—far from it. But somehow, the way his cloak of office trailed behind him and the purposeful manner in which he moved set him apart from the rest. You could just tell he was in charge.

Primus Turov marched past me and met the Tribune on open ground. I could tell she was trying to move with just as much aplomb as Drusus did. She damn-near pulled it off, too.

"Come on," Graves said.

I followed him, along with a half-dozen others. Most were centurions, the ones who'd died taking the alien ship. The only adjunct was Leeson, and I was the only enlisted man in sight. I felt like a fluffy cat in a dog kennel, but I tried not to show it.

Turov clasped hands with Tribune Drusus, enveloping his hand with both of hers. Drusus nodded vaguely and ran his eyes over the crowd. Those eyes paused on Graves and me. I thought there was a spark of recognition when he saw me—but that might just have been my imagination. Probably, he was just noting that the only enlisted guy was a head taller than the rest of the group.

Finally, he looked back at Turov. She was babbling something about her official report and the sacrifices we all needed to make for the good of the legion and the good of Earth.

"Well said, Primus," he said at last. "Have you got a secure location to talk?"

She paused for a moment. "I was planning to give you a tour of the alien ship. Don't you want to survey the prize, sir?"

His lips thinned, and I thought he was slightly annoyed.

"That can wait. Where's your nearest bunker?"

Turov's eyes drifted down the beach. I knew where she was looking, way back at our camp behind the ridge.

"That will be quite a walk, sir," she said. "I wasn't expecting—"

"Not expecting a counterattack? Or a second ship How about an attempt by the natives to remove this vessel from our possession?"

The Primus' mouth opened and shut again. To me, she looked like a curiously attractive rock-fish.

"Unacceptable," Drusus said. "Set up the perimeter now. I want a bunker at the base of each of these ramps that leads into the ship. No, let me correct that. I want two of the three ramps retracted. The last one, the one in the center, is to stay open for now. We'll set up bunkers with clear firing paths in all directions. Construct a few on the far side of the vessel. For all we know, it might be possible to open this ship on the other side as well."

"Yes, sir," the Primus said. She turned and relayed the orders to her staffers, who ran off like their butts were on fire.

Drusus walked toward the knot of officers I stood behind. "Graves? I might have known you were the one leading the charge into this behemoth ship. Congratulations."

Graves shook the tribune's hand. "I can't claim that honor, sir," he said. "Leeson was in command of the final push. I died right here on the doorstep."

"Pity," Drusus said, stepping up to Leeson. He had a frown on his face, as if he smelled something a little past its sell date. "Congratulations," he told Leeson, eyeing him.

"Thank you, Tribune."

"What are you doing here, McGill?" Drusus asked next.

Leeson opened his mouth to answer, but the Tribune stopped him with a raised index finger.

"Let the man talk, Adjunct. He's good at that, as I recall."

"Sir!" I said snapping to attention. "Centurion Graves asked that I come along."

"Why would he do that?"

My eyes slid toward Graves, but I could tell I wasn't going to get any help from him. He was watching us detachedly.

"I was one of the first into the ship—and probably the first man to set foot on the bridge at the end. That might be why, sir."

"Not just that," Drusus said. "You also organized local resistance to aid us. Without their help, we would have failed in our attempt to capture the ship. I'm sure you'll have valuable input before this gathering breaks up."

"That's true," I said. "The colonists really helped."

I wondered why he'd asked me if he already knew all that. But maybe he'd wanted to hear how I explained it. Sometimes, I found my officers tricky and tiresome to talk to.

Primus Turov had returned during our interchange and overheard us. She looked like she'd swallowed a bug.

"That's an overstatement of the colonists' contribution, sir," she said crisply.

"Not from what I've seen and heard," Drusus said, still looking at me. Finally, he turned toward the Primus. "Turov? Where were you during the assault?"

She looked startled. "At the final stages, I was marching through the ship to the upper decks," she said. "I led the relief forces that—"

"Yes," Drusus said in a voice that suddenly seemed bored. "Of course, I've read your report. Your cohort did very well under difficult circumstances. You're all to be commended. Now, do you have a secure location for us to discuss serious matters?"

"We don't have a bunker, sir. The big drones will take about an hour to complete the first of them, but we can go into a tent or the ship itself."

"Go into an alien ship with unknown properties? Are you serious?"

"We could go back to our camp, sir. It's behind that ridge."

Drusus followed her gesture and looked annoyed.

I don't know why—I really don't—but when I see a problem and I have the solution in my head, sometimes I just can't keep it from coming out of my mouth.

"We could go down, sirs," I blurted, "into the tunnels. They're quite roomy and secure."

"What tunnels?" Turov asked acidly.

"The ones we used to get under the enemy dome," Graves answered. "That's an excellent idea. Before the attack, they served us as a bunker for several hours."

In the end, we all went to the circle of rocks where our invasion of the ship had begun. Drusus surveyed the battleground with interest.

"There are laser strikes everywhere. This was a hard battle long before you reached the ship. What were your total revivals by the end of the assault?"

Primus Turov looked concerned. "We had somewhere over a thousand, sir."

Drusus whistled. "Effectively, you wiped."

"Not at all," Turov snapped back. "At any given time, the cohort was never below half strength."

"That is a technical distinction but an important one. You're all to be commended for a hard-fought victory."

He'd already said this, but I felt that he really did mean it this time. He looked troubled. He faced us all and spoke to the group.

"Look," he said. "Whatever happens, you did your jobs. Not everyone sees it that way, but I do. Other cohort commanders have second-guessed every decision made here, but that's only to be expected."

Frowning, I followed the group after the Tribune's strange little speech into the cool gloom of the tunnels. What the hell was the Tribune talking about? Why had the other cohort commanders seen fit to complain about our actions? I wasn't in love with Primus Turov, but we'd won in the end under her command. I didn't like the idea of other officers trying to

317

nitpick our difficult battle when they weren't even here to participate or support us.

The tunnels were dry and sandy. They smelled better than I remembered. Drusus circled up the officers, but I hung back in the shadows near the exit. I felt out of place.

"Turov," said the Tribune. "Have a security team explore each of these tunnels a hundred meters back. I don't want anyone listening in. Use buzzers as well, and do an electronic sweep. Oh, and everyone should put their tappers into conference mode."

These orders took several minutes to follow. Drusus waited until all of the security people were back out of the tunnels before he got around to the point.

He faced the circle of officers with a very serious expression on his face. "The Nairb ship has arrived," he said.

This caused a visible reaction. We'd all known he had to have a reason to bring us down here. The arrival of any Galactic ship was good news, in my opinion. Why all the secrecy?

These thoughts rang out in my head, but I said nothing. I could tell the other officers weren't clear on what the big deal was, either.

"Excellent news, sir," said the Primus experimentally. "We're as good as rescued."

"Not at all," Drusus said. "Tell me, Primus, how will the Nairbs judge our actions here in this system?"

"Uh...I'm not certain, sir."

"Exactly," Drusus said, nodding. "What if they find our efforts lacking? What if they decide the system is to be expunged?"

"It's just the Nairbs, sir," she answered. "Surely, the Galactics themselves will come to make their own decisions."

Drusus shook his head. "No. That's not how it will happen. The Nairbs will perform their investigation. They will make their decision, and then they will call for the Battle Fleet. At that point, action is almost assured."

"Why's that, sir?" Graves asked.

"Please understand that due to my office, I'm privileged with information that the general population is not aware of.

318

Hegemony follows cases like this very closely to make sure we know how to behave ourselves."

I frowned, as did Graves. "Are you saying Hegemony has access to information outside our home system? To information that isn't publicly presented by the Galactics for general consumption?"

"I would never suggest such a thing," Drusus said sternly. "That would be a violation of Galactic Law. And none of you had better breathe a word of it, either."

"Of course, sir," Graves muttered.

In my own case, I felt like a light had gone on in my head. *Of course* we were spying on the Galactics as much as we could. It would be madness not to. But it was dangerous to do it, too. I had to wonder who these spies were and how they operated. To me, that was a ballsy job that made mine look easy. I was pretty sure there wasn't a revival unit waiting around to make a fresh copy of our failed spies.

"Don't concern yourselves with how we gather intel. What we've learned from the process is alarming enough. When the Battle Fleet is called for a second time to any system, they sterilize every rock in orbit around the local star. *Every. Single. Rock.*"

"But why, sir?" Graves asked.

Drusus shrugged.

"Could they simply be lazy?" Turov asked. "Or irritated at having to leave port and fly out to do their jobs?"

"Actually," Drusus said, "we suspect it's a matter of efficiency. The Empire's resources are always stretched thinly here at the rim of the galaxy. They can't afford to come all the way out to a system and do nothing. They know there's a strong possibility they'll be called back years later to the same system if they take no action. So they don't fool around. When the Nairbs make a call, that's good enough for the Galactics. They wipe everything."

"I understand," said Turov in a haunted tone. "Why bother to take a second look around and decide justly? Who cares if it's a questionable case? Safer to err on the side of caution and be done with it. An extinct species can't appeal a verdict and can't cause further damage."

"Exactly."

I felt a sinking sensation in my gut as I listened to the officers discuss the matter. I knew Drusus was right in my heart. The local Battle Fleet had only made one trip to Earth, long before I was born. During that visit, the Galactics had given us their ultimatum. If they ever returned to Earth's skies with their countless silver hulls shining above the clouds— well, that would be the end of everything. As a kid back in school, I'd longed to see those ships, just once. Now, I hoped I never would.

"If the Nairb ship is in the system, how long do we have?" asked Turov at last.

"Less than a day."

I turned my wandering attention back to the conversation. The officers were leaning forward, almost huddling. They looked like a pack of conspirators plotting something.

"That puts a new light on the matter," Graves said carefully. "If we want to make any 'edits' to the situation, we have to act fast."

"*Corvus* was lost, so we can't run out of the system," Turov said.

"Obviously not," Drusus said.

"What if we all self-execute?" asked Graves. "Right now."

This question stunned me. I stared at each man in turn, wondering if it was a joke. From the look on their faces I figured it wasn't.

Drusus shook his head. "Not good enough. There would be bodies everywhere. The evidence would be indisputable. The Nairbs won't care about that level of sacrifice. The crimes they'll discover are too large. They can't be erased by a few deaths. The colonists who live here aren't authorized to be outside of our system. That's a serious violation."

Primus Turov leaned forward. Her eyes were shining and decisive. "To save Legion Varus, we're going to have to erase the evidence before the Nairbs get here."

"I agree," Drusus said. "The action is regrettable but necessary.

I couldn't' believe what I was hearing. I'd worked so hard, and the colonists had come so far. They were our allies now, our own flesh and blood. Our long lost kin.

"How could we do it fast enough?" Turov asked.

"The answer is the alien ship," Drusus said. "We'll never figure out how to fly it in time—but we just might figure out how to blow it up."

The group broke up into harsh whispering. By the time they'd formulated their plan, I was already backing down one of the tunnels.

I overheard the details of their plans to kill all the colonists as I began trotting quietly away. They were going to overload the alien ship's engines and turn this valley into a smoking crater.

As I got farther away, I moved faster. Dust fell over me, and I tried not to choke on it.

I thought I heard someone calling my name—but my tapper was off, and I was pretty far down the tunnels by then, taking random turns to lose any pursuers.

-33-

At moments like this, I wonder if I'm crazy. I think I probably am.

What was I going to tell my fellow legionnaires if I ever went back to Legion Varus? *"Sorry sirs, I had to run off to take a piss...and then I got lost, see..."*

I wasn't really angry with the legion's brass. After all, they'd been given a tough decision. The way they saw it, either we were all going to get permed; or the colonists had to die. For most people, situations like that turned into relatively easy decisions. They would simply opt to live and let someone else die instead.

But it was different for me than it was for the rest of the officers. I knew these colonists personally. Sure, they were weird and some of them were assholes, but couldn't the same be said of any group of humans?

Most of all, I couldn't swallow the idea of turning my hands against a local population. It was just plain wrong, and I wasn't going to do it.

When you're on the run in a series of dark tunnels, it's hard not to feel fear grip your belly. I didn't have anything other than a sidearm, and I barely knew where I was going. Fortunately, I was able to find a few peepholes and used them to look into the valley and get my bearings. They steered me toward my destination, which was the wreck of *Hydra*, located behind the northeast wall of the valley.

Cool dirt shifted under my feet as I made rapid progress. I wasn't running—not quite. I was trotting in the gloom, keeping my suit lights dialed down to their dimmest illumination levels. I wished I'd had armor and at least a rifle—but there was no way I was going back to camp for equipment now.

I knew that if Legion Varus ever caught me, I'd probably be executed as a deserter. I had to admit they had good cause for that. Probably, any Nairb in the Empire would have recommended it to them.

The situation was much bigger than my own personal life, however. I didn't want Legion Varus to get permed on this rock, but I didn't want us to survive by killing off everyone who'd been born on this world and lived a harsh life here. It was just plain wrong.

First, Earth had sent the colonists out here and forgotten about them. Then, we'd come along unannounced and started bombing their pathetic clusters of rocks. Now, after saving them from alien slavers, we'd changed our minds and decided to kill them after all.

"No," I said aloud to the echoing walls.

My plan was simple. I was going to warn them. I knew where the Investigator's lab was. I would convince him to take his people out of the valley, then deeper into the local tunnels or out into the badlands around the polar surface of the planet. My fellow legionnaires would never find them in time.

They only had to evade death long enough for the Nairbs to get here. After that, everything would be recorded. Killing the colonists wouldn't solve anything at that point and might even worsen the situation.

Would I get justice out of the Nairbs in the end? Maybe not, but it was worth trying. I'd talked them into letting me survive all their legal mumbo-jumbo before, and I was willing to give it another shot.

I followed the dark tunnels for what seemed like hours but was probably only about twenty minutes. I found the first of a series of apertures that looked out over the valley. I took a second to gaze down at the alien ship and the legion camp.

Feeling a pang of remorse, I wondered if I turned around right now and wandered back to camp, would they take me back? Maybe they would after a demotion or a good old-fashioned beat-down by Harris?

Shaking my head, I steeled myself. I had to warn the colonists. Then I could go back and give contrition a try. I doubted it would work. Turov hated me under the best of circumstances. Graves and Tribune Drusus were no dummies, either. They might like me, but outright mutiny wasn't going to sit well with either of them.

I forced myself to move faster. When I was moving along at a fast trot, turning up my light levels so I wouldn't trip, I heard something.

It was a soft, buzzing sound, not unlike that of a housefly coming near. But it wasn't a housefly. I'd heard buzzers too often before to be fooled.

I threw myself down in the dirt and rolled over onto my back. I couldn't evade it that way because buzzers had infrared and olfactory sensors. There was no way they'd miss a sweaty man down here in this tunnel. But my plan wasn't evasion.

Drawing my sidearm, I cranked the aperture open as widely as I could. Then I waited as the buzzing got louder.

Even with a diffuse spread, it wasn't easy to hit the buzzer. Fortunately, it slowed down as it sensed me and tried to figure out why I was lying there on the ground.

I fired my weapon. It took two tries before I nailed the buzzer. I'd always been good at swatting flies, and I smiled as the tiny singed drone did a spiraling nosedive into the dirt and died.

Jumping up, I stomped on the metal bug until it stopped protesting, then began running again. The buzzers couldn't be operator-driven directly when they worked in tunnels because the signals wouldn't penetrate thick stone walls. Whoever had sent this one would wait for it to return, eventually being forced to give up.

But that wouldn't be the end of it. If one had been disabled, more would follow.

The techs were after me. I could feel it. They wouldn't stop until they'd found me. There wasn't much time now. I forgot about dim lights and quiet steps. I was running all out scrambling over dirt and stone. I left bits of skin and blood on the sharpest protrusions from the tunnel walls.

A crossbow bolt snapped out of the darkness ahead and nearly took me full in the face. I tripped and went sprawling.

"Hold on!" I shouted. "It's me, McGill. I'm here to see the Investigator."

A pair of cautious colonists crept forward, aiming their black-tipped bolts at me. It took a bit of convincing, but they finally led me to *Hydra*. I felt anxious every step and kept looking behind me, ears straining to catch the whine of another buzzer.

The Investigator was back inside his labs. He wasn't in a good mood. As I approached, I heard him throw out an assistant. He poked his head out, glowering, but then he saw me. His expression changed to a look of curiosity.

"The schemer," he said. "The runner, the fornicator. What do you want here? You're like a ghost that haunts my world."

"Sorry about that, sir," I said. "I had to come. I had to warn you. Uh—did you say *fornicator?*"

"Yes. My daughter brags of little else. She's determined to have your child, you know."

"Uh…" I was honestly at a loss for words. He had to be talking about Della. Why hadn't someone—*anyone*—told me she was his daughter?

The Investigator walked out of his lab and cocked his head, staring into my face. It was a disconcerting behavior pattern, and I realized now that I'd seen it before. Della had done that more than once. I'd thought it was a cultural oddity unique to the colonists. Now, I suspected it was a family trait.

"Warn me about what, runner?"

"Sir…" I began, and I told him the whole thing. I tried to put a good face on it. I tried to explain that the universe was a harsh, cold place and my people weren't any more heartless than the next band of interstellar mercenaries—but I wasn't even buying it myself.

The Investigator seemed to be taking it all in with a remarkable lack of concern. But then I got to the part about how Legion Varus planned to kill the colonists.

"Did you say they want to *blow up* my ship?" the Investigator boomed suddenly.

"Yes, sir. The whole valley. It won't be long now. You have to pull your people out of this cave. You need to run somewhere—up to the surface, maybe. You have escape tunnels that lead up to the polar deserts, don't you?"

The Investigator stared at me with distant eyes. To me he looked at least half-mad, but I'm not the best judge of other people's state of mind.

His hand lashed out and grabbed up my shirt. The smart-cloth squirmed and writhed in protest, trying to smooth itself out again.

"*No one* is blowing up my ship!" he boomed.

Then he pushed past me and ran off, shouting. An alarm went off soon thereafter that sounded like a ship's klaxon. People on the lower decks began moving quickly after that.

I stumbled after the Investigator, not knowing what to think. The people I saw weren't grabbing up kids and belongings and making a run for it—quite the opposite. They were gathering weapons, painting their faces black and applying fresh nanites to their bolts and swords.

Finding the Investigator, I walked up to him and got his attention.

"Sir," I said. "What's going on? You have to get out of here."

"No, traitor. No, thing that crawls in the dark. No mercenary Earthmen are going to blow up *my* ship. We're going to take possession of her, as I should have from the very beginning."

"But sir, the legionnaires—"

He grabbed onto my arm with surprising strength. I saw that light in his eyes again, and I was pretty sure now that it was the cold, clear light of madness.

"We're *not* running," he told me with absolute certainty. "We're attacking. Flee if you want to, but don't interfere."

He left me standing there and rushed off with a growing mass of men and women behind him. I remembered then that these people who'd been left here in the darkness were the rats who liked to fight. All the others had long since been enslaved.

Only the hardest hearts among the children of Earth's lost exiles still survived.

Even though I sympathized, I was left wondering as I trotted after the swelling army about just what these people thought they were going to do with an alien ship…

Following the colonists, I had to admit I felt more than a little sick inside. I'd come here to save them after all, to warn them. Instead, I'd apparently kick-started the war I'd previously hoped to postpone in the end. The truce was over between my people and theirs, that much was clear.

As we marched, we came upon two teams of legionnaires. I felt sorry for both groups. The first was a trio of heavy troops in armor who'd no doubt been sent here to hunt me down. They went down hard in a storm of fire with nanites eating away their eyes and throats. I made sure I touched my tapper to theirs so the death would be recorded. They could be revived once I told the camp about it.

The next group was even more shocked. They were techs, and they'd already dropped their equipment and begun running. No doubt their buzzers had seen the colonist army on the march.

The techs didn't make it very far. I'd thought I'd become pretty good at navigating the tunnels, but watching the colonists I realized I was a clumsy surface-dweller. They seemed to know every stalactite and spur of limestone. They vaulted over obstacles with ease and ran full-tilt until they brought down the fleeing techs in a brief, furious action.

Following, I touched my tapper to each one in turn, shaking my head. At least I could make sure they wouldn't be permed.

A shadow watched me work as the rest of the colonist throng pressed ahead. A voice spoke, and I was surprised to realize I knew its owner.

"What kind of death rite is that?" Della asked softly.

I looked up, startled. She was standing over me, her long legs exposed and dusty.

"Exactly that," I said, "a gesture of respect for our dead. I'm wishing them well in their next lives."

She turned her head the other way and didn't say anything for a moment as I touched the last of the dead techs with my tapper.

"I chose poorly," she said. "I thought you were a great warrior—but now you've embarrassed me. If your seed quickens within me, I shall cut it out."

This statement got my attention. I straightened. "I was only trying to help," I said. "If you're pregnant, don't blame the kid for the sins of his father."

"His? Are you so sure I'll bear a son?"

I chuckled. "I don't know anything about that. But I came here to warn your people."

"You're a traitor to your own kind, an embarrassment."

I stepped closer to her, and a small blade appeared in her hand. I ignored it.

"Look, we're all the same people. That's why I'm here. Our real enemies aren't human—and believe me they outnumber us a billion to one. We don't need to fight amongst ourselves. We can't afford to. The way we bicker and kill one another—that's the embarrassment."

I pushed past her and didn't look back. I heard soft footsteps after a few minutes, but she didn't say anything.

I had to hand it to the colonists. They had serious balls. These people didn't know they couldn't win this fight.

Wondering about them, I figured they'd been changed somewhat by their circumstances. They'd come out here as a sophisticated group: Educated, trained and intelligent. But years of travel and a harsh life on Dust World had changed them. They'd become almost tribal—one might even say savage.

When darkness fell, they boiled out of the same hole we'd originally used to get close to the ship. They managed to creep on their bellies to within a few meters of the bunkers before they were spotted.

Glaring lights flared brightly, and bolts began to snap and sizzle. The front line of colonists fell, but the rest charged in closer. The colonists were too numerous, too close. They shot down the troops in Turov's makeshift bunkers and slid into the firing slits. A brief struggle inside ended with the colonists victorious.

"Damn, damn, damn," I said, staring and grimacing. "This is all wrong!"

I turned toward the distant camp. There had to be a patrol out here, something. Someone I could talk to. Things were spiraling out of control.

She was fast and almost silent. I hardly knew she was there until she slipped her nanite-blade into my back and shoved it deeply into my organs.

Gasping, I fell on my face, rolled over and clawed for my sidearm—but she already had it in her hand.

"Della," I gasped.

She bent and kissed me in the dark. I felt searing agony and cool lips at the same time.

"You can switch sides again," she said. "You've chosen to go back, so I've helped you on your way."

And then that evil little witch shot me in the face with my own damned pistol.

"Catch him! Don't let him roll off the frigging gurney, Charley. He's a big one."

Groaning and curling up into a wet, slimy ball, I howled in remorse and anger. I couldn't recall having felt so betrayed by one of my murderers before.

"What a bitch," I breathed, trying to get air. I felt like I was drowning in thick fluids. I coughed and retched.

"Come on, McGill," the bio said, slapping me twice with a hard hand. "Get up and off my table. This isn't your first time."

I got unsteadily to my feet. "Anne?"

"What is it, Specialist?" she demanded, checking my eyes with a blinding light.

Why the hell did they always do that?

"Charley," she barked over her shoulder. "Recharge the calcium. I'm getting a one-point low read on bone-density."

"On it, Specialist," said a haggard-looking orderly. He rolled a dolly around to the far side of the revival machine, and I heard the glugging sound of liquids loading into the back of it.

"The smell of this place…" I said as the world became more steady and distinct. "How can you stand it, Anne? So sour…like piss and vinegar mixed with bacon grease."

"It beats being on the line," she said, then her voice softened for a second. "It's not always this bad—it only gets like this during a pitched battle. Most of the time, we bio-types have nothing to do. How'd you die, James?"

"My new girlfriend knifed me in the back."

This brought chuckles from everyone present. I dragged on some sticky clothing. Then I remembered to check my tapper, and I did a U-turn.

"Anne," I said. "There are a lot of recorded deaths in my tapper from the tunnels."

"So? Report them to central. They'll be put in the queue with the rest."

I hesitated. "I'm disconnected from central. Can't I just give you their IDs directly?"

She came to me, frowning. The machine behind her was churning out a fresh body, and I tried not to look at it.

When Anne came close, she touched her tapper to mine; and the information was passed.

"You're in trouble, aren't you?" she said.

"Just see that these people get revived, okay?"

"Will do."

I hesitated. Anne Grant had helped me to live again on more than one occasion when I shouldn't have. She'd presided over my birth many times more than my own mother.

"Anne? Do you know anything about the attack on the ship?" I asked her.

"Yes, well…just what's on the feed. Those crazy colonists broke in and holed up inside. They closed all the ramps up tight. Turov is royally pissed. She'd massing up troops to retake the hatches."

"Damn. Can't anyone get along on this planet?"

Anne stepped close and looked up at me. "I saw something about you on the feed too, James," she whispered. "They're looking for you."

"Yeah," I said. "I'm a legion favorite. Can you forget to report my revival for a few minutes? Maybe mark me down as a recycle?"

"All right. You've got thirty minutes. Make them count." She squeezed my hand, gave me a worried, searching look and then disappeared back into the revival chamber.

After gearing up in armor and finding a new heavy weapon, I walked all the way out of the camp and back toward the alien ship. This wasn't anything unusual, fortunately. Plenty of people had been killed tonight, and the processing was expected to go on for hours. Walking in twos and threes, we were to report back to the ship as soon as we could to help with the new assault.

I caught up with a man I recognized as I came close to the ship, which loomed in the darkness like an artificial mountain, a hulking mass of metal from the stars.

"Carlos?" I asked.

He wheeled around in surprise. "McGill? You frigger, I hate you *so much*. Can't you just die and stay dead?"

"That's not in the cards, my man," I said, and I clasped arms with him.

Carlos suddenly turned serious and lowered his voice. "Might not be so easy to waltz home this time. The Primus really has her cute, tight little butt in a knot."

"I know, I know," I said. "It's all a big misunderstanding. It's my fault, really. I was led off by a colonist…but this time, she killed me."

Carlos stared at me for a second. Then he grinned. "You're *so* full of shit! Your eyes should be as brown as mine. You know that, don't you?"

"Yeah…can you help me out?"

"I'll try to play along. But I'm not getting permed for you. I'm not getting permed for anyone."

That was Carlos in a nutshell. He'd die for you—but not permanently. His loyalty had its limits.

It was almost dawn when we reached the ship. The day was clear, and it became oppressively hot as soon as the sunlight slanted down hitting the high walls of the valley a kilometer or two above our heads.

I quietly rejoined my unit, which had gathered around Graves. I stood at the back. None of the officers seemed to notice immediately. With a set of steel armor on, one man in 3rd Unit looked a lot like the next.

I'd yet to dare turning on my tapper because everyone would know where I was the moment I did.

"Okay, troops," Graves said. "This is going to be rough. We've got less than an hour to take this ship. Gear up lightly.

Just marching all the way up to the bridge will take half that time."

Carlos' hand went up. I could have shot him. He was standing right next to me, and the first thing he had to go and do was call attention to himself.

"What is it, Ortiz?" Graves said.

"Sir, we can't possibly sweep the whole ship in that amount of time. This thing is huge, sir!"

"Yeah, I know. But we've got a time constraint, and we're going to meet it. Hopefully, the rebels will meet us in battle, lose and have the sense to surrender. I don't have to—" he broke off then and stared right at me. "Good God! Is that you, McGill?"

"Sir, yes sir. Reporting back from revival, ready and geared as—"

"Get up here, you crazy bastard!"

The jig was up. I was in full bullshit-mode, but I had a feeling it wasn't going to work unless Graves wanted it to. He was a very hard man to bamboozle.

I trotted around the gathering, while troops stared and buzzed. I ignored them all and put a serious expression on my face as I approached my superior officer.

To my chagrin, Harris appeared, trotting alongside me. He had a grin on his face that was predatory.

"I told you I was gonna get you, McGill," he said. "I told you."

"Good to see you too, Vet."

When we reached Centurion Graves, Harris had his sidearm out. He flipped off the safety and kept grinning. "With your permission, sir!" he shouted.

Graves frowned at him. "This isn't Christmas, Harris. Have some decorum."

"My apologies, sir!" he shouted, grinning all the while.

Graves sucked in a huge breath and let it out again. "McGill, walk with me."

Harris looked disappointed as I went for a little stroll to the base of the ramp with Graves. I didn't say anything. I knew I really didn't have to.

"What's your line, McGill? Do you even have one?"

"Line sir?" I asked as innocently as I could.

I can lie, just ask anyone from my school days. I'm not a master like Carlos, but I can pull off the look and sound of an innocent man. I worked that angle now, as hard as I could.

Graves shook his head. "That's not going to fly. There's no way you're not getting permed without an airtight alibi. I know you don't have that, but you'd better at least try."

"Sir? I'm not exactly sure what you're talking about. I'd like to make a report on recent events, however."

"You do that."

"Well sir, it was like this: when our meeting in the tunnel was getting to the interesting part—well, I felt the urgent call of nature."

Graves put up his hand to stop me. "Are you shitting me?"

"Uh…"

"Seriously, McGill? You ran off into the tunnels and fomented a deadly attack on your own people because you had to take a crap? That's your story?"

"Not exactly, sir. While I was relieving myself, I was approached by a certain colonist who knew me."

Graves stared at me. "That crazy mother? The Investigator?"

"No sir, the colonist in question is his daughter."

Graves was frowning now. I knew that was a good sign. When you bullshit somebody and they start to believe, they always frown because they're beginning to doubt themselves.

"His daughter?"

"Yes. Della, the scout-woman, the person I first contacted. Anyway, we discussed matters, and I was taken hostage. The enemy was angry about our taking of the ship, and they were preparing to storm it."

More frowning from Graves. I dared to feel hope.

"You're trying to tell me you followed some chick off into the dark and screwed her, is that it? And then what—you got lost after that?"

I hesitated. Graves made a hissing sound through with his teeth.

"You're such a pain in the ass, McGill. Do you know that we had a lot of troops out looking for you? Also, a team with

334

techs and buzzers were searching those tunnels? They go on forever. And you were playing footsies with the locals. Our search party never came back, and we can't revive them without the confirmation of their deaths."

I held up my tapper until I got his attention again. "I've found a solution for that, sir. I met up with the search team as I was dragged along with the colonists. They killed three heavies and several techs. I recorded their IDs and reported them to the bio people. They'll be out and back on the line in an hour."

Graves narrowed his eyes, looking at my tapper. "How come your tapper hasn't identified you to the network?"

I shook my head and eyed my forearm. "It's the damnedest thing, sir. The organic circuitry must not be working—not even on this copied version. I'll have to have the techs look at it."

"All right," Graves said. "Your story is bullshit, but at least it's attractive bullshit. Maybe we can get past the Primus eventually, but you'll have to be demoted in rank. You're a regular again. You can still carry your heavy kit for the rest of this mission, as you're trained for it, but you're not a Specialist any longer, McGill."

This pronouncement gave me a pang of regret. I nodded.

"I understand, sir," I said. And I really did. Graves hadn't believed me. Not for a second. But he was willing to play along in order to not lose a good man on a lonely planet.

"Off the record," Graves said quietly, "I didn't think it would be right to kill all these colonists just to save our own hides, either. But I wasn't calling the shots when the decision was made, and it might be too late now. They've screwed up by taking the ship rather than running off into the desert. Now everyone in the legion wants them dead."

I nodded, looking up into the pinkish-blue sky overhead. Graves frowned at me.

"I'm letting you off easy McGill," he said. "The least you can do is pay attention."

"Remember what you said about running out of time, sir?" I asked, pointing upward.

As he looked up, his face sagged. There was a shadow coming over the valley. It soon darkened the skies and then the entire valley.

The Nairb ship had arrived.

-35-

The Nairb ship wasn't a battlewagon. Bureaucrats usually didn't carry a payload of Hell-burners with them ready to fall on our heads.

We feared them all the same. The power of the Empire was behind every word any Nairb spoke to a lowly species like ours. They didn't have to wield force directly; they ruled through the threat of a vast power that might be unleashed should we fail to please them.

Being an unimportant species on the fringe of the galaxy was both good and bad. As long as no one noticed us, we were effectively invisible to the great races of beings in the Core Systems thousands of lightyears away. Staying invisible had become our best trick. It was the goal of any world like ours.

Today, however, the cold light of Nairb logic was to shine down upon us. Once the ship had darkened the skies of Dust World, all attempts to hide the truth ended abruptly. We stopped fighting with the colonists and ignored them in their stolen ship.

Instead, we focused on organizing ourselves. Lifters rolled in from other valleys all day long, as the Legion gathered its full strength. We didn't know if the Nairbs would want to perform a headcount; but if they did, we were ready.

Within ten hours after the Nairb arrival, every legionnaire had been revived and given a full kit. We'd polished our gear, and the lifters had come from every valley on the planet to unload full cohorts on the open polar deserts. There we stood in ranks waiting for inspection.

I was near the end of a line of troops that had to be a kilometer long. Fifty ranks stood ahead of me and twenty or so more behind. We stood in the blazing sun with dust whipping into our closed visors. I had to admit, we were a pretty impressive sight standing at attention in our thousands.

The first four cohorts were light troops—those sorry bastards: Soft gear, cheap smart-cloth and substandard air conditioners. They cradled their snap-rifles with what had to be aching arms. My armor was much heavier, but I had better temperature controls and an exoskeleton to hold up the weight.

Each cohort was broken into ten units of a hundred troops, led by a centurion. Every unit had a flag, just as the Romans had so many centuries before us. The flags were red with gold print that identified our units. These days, of course, we didn't need flags to show us who to follow on the battlefield. We had tappers, heads-up-displays inside our helmets and a dozen other pieces of high tech gear to serve that purpose. But on special occasions like this, when we wanted to dress up and show off, we still broke out the old gear and unfurled the banners.

As the most senior non-com in the unit, Veteran Harris had the honor of holding up our unit's flag. It was emblazoned with the wolf's head emblem of Legion Varus and our cohort and unit numbers. Seeing the banner flapping there in the strong, hot winds gave me a moment of pride.

After a solid hour of standing around in the sun, however, my pride was fading. I waved at a tech running down the ranks offering power to any trooper who was running low. To my surprise, it was none other than Natasha.

"Hey, pretty lady," I called.

"Need some power, McGill?"

"Sure, give me a boost."

I let my plasma tube down to touch the dust that now covered my boots entirely and offered her an arm. She had a drone following her that was loaded with power-packs. She plugged into my external port and I watched my gauges turn green as the juice flowed.

"Talk to me, Natty," I said. "What the heck is going on inside the Nairb ship? Is the brass going to keep us standing out here until we're buried under a sand dune?"

She cast a nervous look over her shoulder toward the ship. It had landed on the planet's surface up above the valley floor. Naturally, we'd been obliged to come up here and stand in parade in front of it. We were arranged in a massive square between the hulking ship and our swarm of nine lifters.

"Let's just hope they let us live, James," she said quietly, not looking at me.

I reached out and grabbed her hand as she disconnected me. I made sure I didn't squeeze too hard. Powered gauntlets could crush a person's bones.

"You know something, don't you?" I asked. "Tell me about it."

She glanced at me worriedly and shook her head. "It's best I didn't."

"Come on," I told her. "Things could hardly get worse. Either we're screwed or we're not."

"I've only caught bits and pieces from officers as I've juiced them up. I think things are going badly. The Nairbs want to know *everything*. They aren't buying any of our cover stories. They want to investigate the colonists who are still holed up in that alien ship. They want to talk to any surviving aliens, the colonists—everyone."

I frowned. That didn't sound so good.

"They might burn us all down, James," Natasha said, sounding scared. "They might want to burn us all."

"The whole legion?"

"For starters. Earth could be in danger, too. We're not supposed to be colonizing new planets. We're not really supposed to even be out here."

"Yeah, I know. Hey, since this might be our last hour under the sun, how about you and I have a little good-bye kiss?"

Natasha snorted in disbelief. "As if I would—can you guess what Kivi told me?"

I sighed. "I have a pretty good idea."

Natasha walked off, annoyed. I watched her go wistfully. It wasn't long after that when a peculiar call came in to my

339

helmet. I answered and became concerned when I saw the caller's ID: It was Primus Turov herself.

"McGill? Get your ass up here, right now."

"Sir? Where's 'here', sir?"

"The Nairb ship, you moron! Get to the entrance. The Nairbs will direct you."

I lurched into motion. My legs were stiff from standing so long, but I ran anyway. Graves came to intercept me and got into my face.

"Leave your weapon—and your sidearm."

I knew what that meant. The officers didn't want a scene in case I was to be executed.

The look on Graves' face was as hard as his steel-gray eyes. I gave up my guns and trotted off at a steady, ground-eating pace toward the ship. I ran first down the ranks, then up between the units. I passed Natasha along the way, and she stared at me.

"Should have given me that kiss while you could!" I shouted.

Hustling up to the hulking Nairb ship, I had to wonder exactly what they might want with little old me. I didn't think Legion Varus could place all their sins on my head and get off with a warning after perming a single soldier. And the Nairbs had no reason to want me dead in particular. They didn't think in terms of individuals when meting out punishment, anyway.

With nothing to go on, I dropped my worries. I figured I'd learn how to play their game as I went along. Until then, I'd keep my mouth shut and act the part of the eager legionnaire.

Despite what Turov had said, there weren't any Nairbs to greet me at the hatchway. All I found was a series of flashing green lights on the floor. That was typical of Nairbs, they didn't make things personal.

As I hustled along, following the lights, I noticed that they vanished behind me. I passed what seemed like endless bulkheads and cavernous empty holds. I had to wonder why they'd brought such a big ship out here. Could they really be planning to rescue us and give us a ride home? That would be nice—if uncharacteristic of the Nairbs.

At the end of a particularly long passage, I finally found Primus Turov. Her eyes were so wide I could see the whites all the way around. I wasn't sure if she was scared or pissed off—I thought it might be a little of both.

"Good of you to take your sweet time getting here," she said.

"It was so nice outside I hated to come in."

She stared at me for a second, then shook her head bemusedly. She looked over my armor and dusted it off. While we spoke, she worked to clean my armor, which I thought was sort of weird. I'd never been spruced up before by someone who flat-out hated me.

"Don't even open your damned mouth in there unless called upon, McGill."

"Wouldn't think of it, sir."

"And don't accidently kill anyone, either."

"I'll try to remember that."

At last, the final hatchway opened. I walked inside, taking two steps forward, and then stood at attention.

I looked around, knowing that they probably couldn't see my eyes moving through my visor at this distance. The chamber was unlike any I'd seen yet aboard this ship. There were fat, fluffy chairs everywhere. On most of them were Nairbs, draped over their furniture like seals on rocks.

The Nairbs were an odd race. They were green-skinned and green-blooded. They reminded me of living beanbags. They'd reportedly started off as an aquatic race, but had evolved into a tool-using species with curling flippers that could manipulate objects with great dexterity. These days, they were the local accountants for the Empire.

Unfortunately, in an organization as large as the Empire, accountants and bureaucrats had grown in power. Every race we'd ever met lived in fear of the Nairbs and their heartless regulatory powers.

When I stepped into the room, a few Nairbs turned to look at me. They soon turned their attention back to the Tribune, who was the only other human in the chamber.

Tribune Drusus didn't look happy. In all the times I'd seen him, he'd always come off as a paragon of calm judgment and wisdom. Today, he looked like a perp in handcuffs—a guilty man who knew he'd finally been caught.

"This is the man," Drusus said to the Nairb Prefect. "He's the only one that might get an answer out of them."

I glanced at Drusus, hoping for a clue concerning what I was supposed to be doing here, but he gave me nothing.

"Immediate self-execution would be far less time-wasting," said the Prefect.

This gave my heart a squeeze. It began pounding in my chest.

"I'm within my rights," Drusus replied.

The Nairbs translating device made a rattling sound. I think it was trying to translate a grunt of disgust.

"Very well, tell it to speak."

Drusus turned to me. "James McGill. We need you to contact the humans inside the alien ship. Who was their leader?"

"You mean the Investigator, sir?"

"Yes, that's him. Get him on a com line."

"Uh…" I said, at a loss. "I don't think he's going to answer my—"

"Please try, McGill."

A com-link with an outside hook-up was brought to me. I removed my helmet and set it aside. Putting on the com-link, I tried to open a channel. We'd left our com equipment inside the ship before the colonists had retaken it—but, really, I thought it was a longshot that they were listening at all.

To my surprise, the channel did open. But no one answered my call.

"Hello?" I asked. "Can I talk to someone, please?"

Drusus looked impatient. "We've tried that. The communication is getting to the ship, but it isn't being answered by anyone."

"They might not even be listening—" I began to point out.

Drusus made a rapid hand gesture, as if he were erasing my words out of the air. "McGill, they *are* listening. The trouble is that we haven't said anything yet that they wish to respond to. Do you understand?"

I was beginning to. Drusus had made some kind of commitment to the Nairbs with regard to the colonists. Maybe they'd demanded to talk to them, and so far no one had been listening to our demands.

For a second, I considered the problem. Sure, there might not be anyone around to pick up the phone, but I had to try. I could tell from the Tribune's attitude that it was of the utmost importance that I succeed.

"I understand, sir," I said.

After a moment of thought, I opened the channel again. As before, it opened, but no one said anything.

"This is Specialist James McGill," I said, then paused. "Correction, I'm Legionnaire James McGill of Legion Varus."

Drusus made a rapid hand gesture that indicated I should get on with the show. I tried not to look at him.

"I need to talk to the Investigator," I said. I wracked my brain, trying to come up with something that might get the man on the phone. I didn't have much on him. "This is of great importance. It is in regard to Della, your daughter, sir. Please speak with me."

I waited for several seconds, but there was no response.

"Maybe you'd like to use code," I said, grasping at straws. "If you're having trouble with your com equipment, try keying the transmit button to inform us of that fact."

Drusus looked alarmed. The Nairb Prefect perked up.

"They have failed to comply for an extended period," said the Nairb. "Criminals frequently seek to evade justice through hiding in ridiculously obvious places. This case is no different."

"Please, Prefect," Drusus said. "Allow us a bit more time."

"Irritating. You have reached the end of your useful—"

"Please, sir. I beg of thee."

"Beg? You plead for Imperial Mercy?"

"Yes."

The Nairbs barked at one another for several seconds.

"Very well," said the Prefect at last. "It is within our charter to extend mercy in these circumstances, but I must point out that you are only inconveniencing my staff further with these pointless delays."

343

"I'm so sorry, sir," Drusus said. Even as he spoke, he made circular motions toward me, indicating I should proceed.

I was sweating now. Whatever the Nairbs had in mind for us, it couldn't be good.

"Investigator," I said into the com link. "If you don't want to talk about Della, maybe you'll be willing to discuss your own survival and the survival of your ship. The Empire will destroy it if you don't comply immediately."

The Nairbs squawked and shuffled on their flippers. "That statement was unauthorized," complained the Prefect.

"I'm so sorry," Drusus repeated. "This man is merely an enlisted interpreter. He's not fully versed in the—"

"Investigator? We're coming in there. Surely, you can see the Nairb ship. You told me you knew about the Empire. The squids knew about it, too. You can't be completely ignorant concerning the vast power you face. I would advise you—"

"No one is going to take or damage my ship!" said a voice suddenly.

I paused, blinking stupidly. Drusus looked as shocked as I was.

"Is this the Investigator speaking?" I demanded officiously. I decided to channel the Nairbs with their bad attitude. It seemed to be getting a reaction.

"We've been listening to your prattling demands for better than an hour now. I'm switching this box off."

"Investigator! Don't do it, please! I'm the star man, the fellow who came to your caverns and met with you personally. I forged a truce between our peoples that—"

"A truce? That arrangement was nothing but a ruse. The new ship is ours, and as soon as we figure out how to fly it you'll all regret your actions."

"Threats?" the Nairb Prefect said excitedly. "The humans have threatened us. That casts an entirely new light on the matter. Take note, scribes. New charges must be drawn up."

Drusus had his eyes shut in horror.

"Investigator," I said. "You have to be very careful what you say now. All our lives are in jeopardy. I'm not threatening you or your ship. I'm trying to help you; to help both of us out of a bad spot."

The Investigator was quiet for several seconds, and the Nairbs moved restively on their pillows. I began to wonder if he really had shut off the com box.

"Twice now, McGill, you used the possessive form when referring to the cephalopod ship. Do I take it that Earth accepts our ownership of this vessel?"

I had no authority to do anything, so I eyed Drusus. He looked at me, and nodded.

"Yes," I said. "We're willing to make that concession. But you have to help us out. If the Nairbs don't agree, the opinions of Earth mean nothing. You understand that you and I and every being in this galaxy is a citizen of the Empire at best. If not, you're nothing more than an animal: An insect that might be crushed at any moment."

"Hyperbole," complained the Investigator. "Idle threats invented to intimidate us and force us into giving up a superior position."

I almost laughed. "You've got a few hundred fighters locked up in a ship you don't have any idea how to operate," I said. "That is hardly a superior position. But let's not get into all that. Let's horse-trade."

"What?"

"Let's make a mutually beneficial deal, sir. Talking can hardly do any harm, and it might do some good."

"I find your premise flawed, but I'm willing to listen."

Turning to Drusus, I offered him the com-link.

"You're doing fine," he said. "Just keep him talking. He has to come out and allow the Nairbs to inspect that ship."

I winced. That was a tall order.

"Investigator?" I called. "Will you allow a Nairb delegation to board your ship and take a look around?"

"I thought we had a truce aligning ourselves against alien invaders, McGill."

"You broke that truce when you attacked us," I pointed out. "But we're willing to reinstate it—and you will maintain control of the ship."

"I understand something now," said the Investigator. "You were chosen to infiltrate my people because you're the most manipulative of your kind. I see it all now. You pretend to be

345

of low rank and of little consequence. Your own people even performed an elaborate pantomime operation going through the motions of chasing you through our tunnels—"

"Sir—" I tried to break in, but the Investigator just kept on going.

"You wormed your way into my sanctuary, attempted to impregnate my daughter—oh yes, I'm fully aware of that—and now you attempt to edge me out of my ship—"

"*Please* sir," I shouted. "Listen to me! We're all the same! We're all humans, and we need to work together. There are so few of us out here among the stars. We're a tiny population circling two tiny star systems."

"Ah, and now you provide me with a fresh emotional appeal! Yes, we're colonists from Earth. But we've been gone too long from our ancestral home world to count ourselves as one with you and your legions. Unlike you, interstellar mercenaries that—"

The Investigator continued his rant, but everyone had stopped listening. The Nairbs were barking like a pack of furless seals.

"A *colony!*" shouted the Nairb Prefect. He was quite agitated. "There are few undertakings possible by a subjugated species that can rival such an act! Further, you've attempted to hide this High Crime, accruing an additional charge. The transcriptions of this inquiry must be carefully gone over anew. Each count of perjury, obfuscation, conspiracy and contempt will be individually cited. I must say, Tribune, we must thank you for insisting we listen to this insane individual in the cephalopod ship. Together with your spokesman, he's brought many new dark deeds to light. You have greatly aided our prosecution, and the reckoning is becoming sweeter by the moment."

Tribune Drusus walked over to me and switched off the com-box. The Investigator was still complaining until the signal died.

The Nairbs wouldn't listen to anything else we had to say after that.

346

"We have no need of further evidence," their leader told us. "The accused ringleaders must stand here and await the final verdict."

They recused themselves in an adjoining chamber to discuss our fate privately. I watched them file out with a sick feeling in my guts. The hatchway clanged shut with a booming sound that reminded me of a tomb slamming closed. I turned to the Tribune.

"I don't think that went very well," I said.

Drusus didn't even look at me. The hatch swung open into the adjoining passage and revealed the rest of the officers. They'd been listening to the proceedings. They buzzed among themselves dispiritedly.

Primus Turov, however, walked up to me and put a hand on my shoulder. She had to reach way up, as she wasn't all that tall, and I was more than two meters in height in my armor.

"You're a real piece of work, McGill," she said, marveling.

"Why thank you, sir."

"Did you really screw that colonist's daughter?"

"Uh…it wasn't quite like that. She was no innocent flower. She's more like a feral cat than a farmer's daughter. In fact she killed me herself—twice."

Turov laughed bitterly. "I bet she had damned good reasons to do it."

-36-

The delegation filed back in about half an hour later. There were fifteen Nairbs all told. I guessed they were the same ones as before; they all looked alike to me.

But this time there was a single Galactic as well. I was slightly disappointed as I recognized his type. He was spidery, with a central body mass that looked like a black widow. He had six legs—or were they arms? It was hard to tell, as they all ended with a grasping appendage. These "hands" were used intermittently as feet or to manipulate objects.

Behind me, the hatch opened and ten human officers walked in. Every one of them was a primus, a leader of an entire cohort. Along with Drusus himself, this was every piece of brass Legion Varus had. They'd all been brought in to hear the verdict.

The head Nairb spoke up first. His title was Prefect, and he never gave us a name. I knew his type—all pompous, officious attitude. Nairbs were all pretty much the same both in personality and physique. They were fussy aliens who loved details. Born pencil-pushers and desk-jockeys, my father always said—even though no one used pencils anymore. To me, the Prefect was just another green sack of gelatinous flesh.

The Prefect started barking. Before he got through the first minute of his speech I was annoyed and bored at the same time.

After a flowery address concerning loyalty and commitment to the Empire, extolling the virtues of well-served

348

patronage within our local chapter of the enforcement bureau, the Nairb announced his verdict. We were all to self-execute, legionnaires and colonists alike.

I could not recall a less happy moment in my lifetime. I'd been killed plenty of times before, but I'd never heard a verdict handed down that required *everyone* I knew to die.

We were all going to be permed. That's what this order meant. There wasn't going to be anyone else around to revive us. No ships from Earth would come out and rescue us. Even if they did find our bones someday, they'd have to be crazy to revive us after they heard about what happened here on this dusty rock in space.

"Relay the order to all your sub-commanders immediately," the Prefect told Drusus in conclusion. "Chief Inspector Xlur is here to serve as a witness for Galactic Justice."

I nodded to myself. Chief Inspector Xlur... I'd personally killed this alien twice. He had revival equipment of his own, naturally, being a privileged Galactic. He didn't seem to recognize me, fortunately. If he had, he'd probably want to add an additional count to humanity's long list of crimes.

My commanders looked from one to another sheepishly. I guessed no one wanted to go first.

Taking in a deep breath, I reached over and plucked Primus Turov's sidearm from her holster. She looked shocked, but then watched me in fascination as I placed the muzzle of the weapon under my chin.

Everyone fell silent, except for the Nairbs, who were grunting in anticipation.

"Just a second," I said. "What about Earth? If we all kill ourselves now, is this matter at an end?"

"That is no concern of yours," Inspector Xlur said. "Obedience is required. That's all you need to know. Proceed, we are recording this incident."

I pulled the weapon away from my throat. Primus Turov reached down to my gauntlet and tried to take her gun back. As I was wearing heavy armor and she was in her dress uniform, I barely felt the tug of her hands. Squeezing slightly, I applied enough pressure to the grip of the gun to prevent her from taking it back.

"McGill," she growled in a low voice, "don't you dare do anything crazy. Earth could hang in the balance."

Ignoring her, I frowned at the aliens. Sure, I knew what she was talking about. If we shot a few of them, maybe they'd rule that all Earth was too vicious and humanity had to be put down like rabid dogs. But if these guys were going to kill us all anyway, why should I obey them? Maybe we could warn Earth. Even if Battle Fleet 921 had already been given the order, it might be a decade or more before they got around to disciplining us. If the game was over for humanity, I wouldn't mind living a little longer before I cashed in my chips.

"I want to appeal the verdict," I said.

There was a general hissing that went up from the Nairbs. I didn't care about them, it was all up to the Galactic now.

"Denied," Xlur snapped.

"Denied?" asked Drusus, stepping forward. "On what grounds? Imperial law stipulates that—"

"Due process has been suspended. This locality is currently understaffed. No appeals can be submitted."

Drusus shook his head. "Well then, suspend the sentence. We'll comply when the judicial system is operating again."

"Just as I expected," said the Galactic. "There's not a single law-abiding citizen amongst the lot of you. I've seen this sort of behavior far too often along the galactic fringe: No acceptance of centralized authority, dangerously individualized thought processes, and no concept of hive-mentality."

"What are you saying, Inspector?" Drusus asked.

"That you humans have no respect for your betters. Worse, you're all cowards. You're driven entirely by self-interest and individual life-preservation. Disgusting."

I couldn't take it any longer. I figured he'd already ordered us to die—how much worse could it get?

Stepping forward, I addressed the alien. "We're not cowards, sir!" I said.

"McGill," hissed Turov, but I ignored her.

Everyone looked at me. I have to admit, most of them looked sick. I wasn't totally sure if that was because they'd just been told this was the end of the line or if it was because I was talking for them.

"High Justice," I said, addressing the Galactic directly. "We're not cowards. We're quite the opposite. I would put a thousand Earthmen up against a like number of anything in this neck of the Galaxy. We'd win. I know this from personal experience."

The creature made an odd, huffing sound. The translator turned this into staccato laughter.

"You know *nothing*. Great events transpire all around you. In the Core Systems there are…disturbances. Millions of ships move like raindrops. And yet here you creatures are, oblivious and helpless. You embarrass yourself in your ignorance."

"That might all be true, sir," I said. "But Earth will not self-execute any more than Legion Varus will. It's just not in our nature. Now, if you don't like us, and you have the power to remove two of our worlds from existence, then we'll become extinct. But we'll fight you to the end, both legally and physically. This ship you have—I think we can take her from you right now."

The Galactic turned itself to face me more fully. "You threaten us? After your death has been sanctioned? I can hardly—"

"Just a moment," asked the Nairb Prefect suddenly. It looked at me. "Being, did you say *two* worlds?"

"That's right. This is a colony world, and it stands with us in addition to our homeworld."

"A confirmed confession!" shouted the Nairb in triumph. "You have committed so many violations as a race, I can scarcely credit it. There will be an accounting, and I will review the vid many, many times in—"

"We didn't violate *anything*," Turov said suddenly. She seemed to be suffering from my disease—she was no longer able to keep her mouth shut now that all was lost.

"You implicated yourselves," the Nairb said. "Colonization is strictly forbidden under the articles signed by your species—"

"The colony ship left Earth *before* we signed the treaty," she said. "This system was colonized before we even knew the Empire existed!"

The aliens began buzzing amongst themselves. Finally the Prefect spoke again. "You can prove this?"

"Yes, if it matters," she replied.

"Why was this information withheld?"

"We were ordered not to speak, and no one asked us about it."

The Galactic turned off the translation box. Together with the Nairbs, he began discussing the situation. I looked around into the confused faces of my fellow humans. We didn't know what to make of it.

Finally, the aliens turned the translation system on again so we could understand them. Instead of the Nairbs, the Galactic himself spoke with us.

"This situation is highly unusual and disorderly. The Nairbs tell me they suspect you are correct in your statements. They were at a loss to understand how colonists could have come from your planet to this world undetected now that the Empire had annexed the region. If they had arrived prior to annexation—that would explain the discrepancy."

"Good," Drusus said quickly. "Then we're not guilty."

"Not of that particular crime, no," admitted Xlur. "But you are far from innocent. Normally, I would have already scheduled your demolition."

We stiffened in horror. 'Demolition' was a term the Galactics didn't use lightly. They meant that our species would be erased from the universe utterly. In their view, *they* owned Earth, not us. We were like animals living on fallow acreage. If we didn't serve them well, we would be erased; and the world would be 'replanted'. The Galactics thought of themselves as something akin to farmers. They managed their worlds with careful, callous hands. Humans were viewed as noisy chattel. Just as a farmer might decide to slaughter his livestock and plant something new on his pasture next season, they had no qualms about slaughtering us.

"Is there any way we can make ourselves useful to the Empire?" asked Drusus.

I had to admire the tribune's calm calculation. I was in the mood to kill the lot of them and hope no one found out about it

352

for a while. With luck, we could still blame it on the cephalopods and let them be erased instead.

"Certainly not," said Xlur. "Why would a zero-level population be awarded further responsibility?"

There was a strange sound. It took me a moment to realize it had come from the Nairb Prefect.

"Inspector," the Nairb said, "I'm forced to correct you in this instance. The species in question is not zero-level. They are, in fact, a level-two civilization—technically speaking."

"What?"

"They passed from zero to one due to a series of achievements."

"Achievements? Absurd."

I heard the sound again. I thought now that it was the Nairb's equivalent of clearing his throat.

"I know it sounds surprising, sir, and much of it is based upon regulatory technicalities but nonetheless—"

"Present your case."

"Yes, Inspector. There are three criteria for statutory promotion to level-one. Seniority in the region, a proven trade good and a successful defense of said trade good."

"Seniority? They've only just joined."

"Ah, but a careful inspection of local star systems places them high in the ranking. High enough, anyway."

"These novel circumstances could only occur so quickly out here on the fringe of the fringe."

"Correct, Inspector."

"Level-two...I see..." Xlur said thoughtfully. Two of his six hands touched his bulbous body. He seemed to perform this gesture when he was thinking. "Once they achieved level one, level two is a given now that we've determined that they occupied two worlds before becoming a member state."

"Exactly."

Drusus waved for attention and bowed when they looked at him. "As the local representative of a level-two civilization," he said smoothly, "how can I better serve my Empire?"

"One more thing," the Inspector said. "Two worlds require two trade goods. What is your second commodity, human?"

Drusus sucked in a breath and held it for a few seconds. Everyone winced. We knew he had nothing.

"As we've only just been awarded this status officially, we'll require the normal allotment of time and budget to rectify this discrepancy."

"Time yes, budget no," Xlur snapped.

"Done," Drusus said, not wanting to push his luck.

"Unfortunately, there's another matter we must discuss," Xlur said. "I hate to do this, but my diligent secretaries are about to remind me I have no choice. I've been charged with finding a local species that would qualify for a difficult role in local governance. Although it will no doubt haunt my internal processes, due to regulations and your new status, I'm forced to consider your civilization for the job."

"We'll take the position, sir," said Drusus quickly.

The Inspector seemed amused. "Such eagerness to please. Why haven't you exhibited this pleasant trait before? Could this be related to the threatened demolition?"

The tribune stood tall. "We've simply been misunderstood."

"Very well. Are you willing to accept the burden of local Enforcement Services? Battle Fleet 921 has been called away for…extended duty in the Core Systems."

Drusus only blinked once. I had to hand it to the guy, he knew when it was time to be agreeable.

"We absolutely and immediately accept," he said. "It sounds like a wonderful opportunity." Then, without missing a beat, he continued with: "Ah…what exactly does our new burden of 'Enforcement Services' entail?"

-37-

"You've *got* to be shitting me!" Carlos said to me a few short hours later.

"I shit you not," I replied, chewing my first square meal of the day. "We're 'enforcers' now."

We were sitting together in the mess tent in the valley we'd help liberate so recently. Overhead, the skies were clear. The Nairb ship had vanished back into space from where it had come. I, for one, hoped it would be a long time before I saw another of their hulking vessels.

"Enforcers…what the heck does that *mean?*" Carlos demanded.

"I don't think anyone fully understands it all yet. But I know that we're the only local species with two populated worlds in this slice of the frontier, which makes us somebody special. This far out along the galactic rim, most species are discovered before they get to the point of colonization. After you join up with the Empire, it's illegal to colonize a second world, and therefore illegal to qualify as a level-two civilization."

"Yeah, yeah, but what are we enforcing? Who do we get to lord it over?"

I frowned at him. Leave it to Carlos to start right in with an immediate plan to abuse our new position.

"Basically," I said, "we're not mercenaries anymore. We're regional sheriffs. We're supposed to help other races when they get in trouble—and that doesn't just mean beating on them."

"This is so weird. We've been doing this mercenary thing for like, a century. How can that all have changed overnight?"

"It's still the same day, actually."

"Funny," he said, "very funny. Spoken like a true Nairb at heart."

"Hardly," I laughed.

Later, I spoke with Natasha. She was in a far more convivial mood now that the Nairbs had left Dust World.

"You know, James, I was certain you were going to be executed when you were summoned into that ship."

"It'll never happen," I assured her.

"It already *did* back on Steel World!"

I shrugged and smiled at her. She was sitting beside me, and the stars were out. We were on a boulder near the lakeshore. The rock-fish blew bubbles and stared at us from the inky black water.

"What I want to know is how we're going to get back to Earth," I said.

Natasha laughed. "We're not going in that ship," she said, indicating the cephalopod vessel that sat like a pool of shadow near the shore.

"Why not? Does it smell too much like rotting squid?"

"All the techs have new orders. We're to help the colonists figure out how to fly it. We don't own the ship anymore. Drusus gave it to them. That's why they opened the hatches again and came out."

I eyed the ship thoughtfully. Natasha watched me.

"Are you getting ideas about that Della character?" she asked.

I was startled, but I covered smoothly. This girl was telepathic.

"Don't worry," I laughed. "If I get near her again, I'm keeping my armor on. She killed me twice, you know."

"Good."

* * *

When I finally did approach the cephalopod ship, I didn't run into Della right away. Instead, I met up with Centurion Graves. He was there, watching the colonist fighters walk back and forth to their caves. They seemed to be carrying a lot of equipment out of the hollowed out *Hydra* to this new ship.

"Was I supposed to report here for duty, sir?" I asked him.

"No, McGill. I purposefully didn't call you."

It was dark again, and the bizarre insects of Dust World were creaking and blatting in the brush at our feet.

"I understand, sir. I have a history with these people."

"That's right. We didn't want them to get upset again. The truce is working for now. I heard some crazy things about your little conference with the Nairbs, by the way."

"All encouraging words, I'm sure."

Graves laughed. "Yeah, right. Everyone said they could taste their own balls, they were so scared. When you started mouthing off, they all thought they were dead. But somehow our whole planet got promoted by the end?"

"Yes sir," I said. "Diplomacy is an underappreciated art."

"Okay, all bullshit aside McGill, do you know anything about the pull-back? I've heard that the Empire is falling apart."

I shook my head. "I really don't know. The Galactic said Battle Fleet 921 was ordered out of our area and sent to the Core Systems. That does seem kind of strange. Do you think *all* the Battle Fleets have been pulled back home?"

"Yes, I think that's exactly what's happened. We're on the fringe. If you're calling in reinforcements from the very edge of your territory, you're calling in everything."

"Yeah...you don't think it's serious, do you? The Inspector said something about millions of ships like raindrops."

"That sounds pretty serious to me. Worse, they put us in charge locally. That's got to mean something. Why put an irritating species like ours in charge of local law and order?"

"Because you don't have anyone better who can do the job?" I suggested.

"Exactly. What else did the Inspector say?"

"Nothing much. Are we talking about a civil war in the Core Systems, sir?"

"I hope not, for the galaxy's sake. It probably hasn't gone that far yet. I'm hoping they're just getting nervous. Maybe some of the ancient races are having a little squabble over who gets what."

"You know what I think?" I asked him. "I think the Empire *is* going to fall apart. How can it survive forever when it's so damned big? In Earth's history, huge empires always fell apart eventually."

"Yeah, well, let's hope it doesn't happen in our lifetimes."

"Why not? I'm sick of Nairbs and snooty Inspectors."

"You'd rather have rolling fleets annihilating populations? Destruction on a planetary scale? Black holes nudged toward inhabited systems for the purpose of swallowing entire stars?"

I stared at him but didn't answer.

"Yeah," he said. "I didn't think you wanted to see that. No one does. We all hate the Empire. It sucks. But it *does* provide order. Don't ever believe chaos is better, McGill. We aren't all from the same species. There won't be anything holding us back once we start going for our neighbor's throat. You see how the cephalopods treated the local humans?"

"We're just animals to them," I admitted, "dogs to be domesticated and enslaved."

"Right."

"Speaking of which, what are we supposed to do about the cephalopods?"

"They've attacked an Imperial ship. They aren't part of the Empire. They must be put down. What did you think the burden of the Enforcer meant? It means no mercy, no quarter."

I looked up into the sky. I could see the warm-water planet that shared the Goldilocks Zone with Dust World. Reportedly, it was far more temperate and friendly than this planet. Unfortunately, it was inhabited by a particularly mean species.

"How can we even reach them?" I asked. "We only have a single legion, and nothing but lifters."

"You'll see," he said.

Troubled, I left him there manning the ramps. A shadow approached me soon after I left the ship.

"I thought you were coming to see me," Della said.

"I ought to burn you down where you stand."

"Would you revive me, if you did?"

I didn't answer because I wasn't sure what I'd do. I knew I was angry with her.

"Don't try to stab me again," I said. "I'm wearing my full kit now."

She walked alongside me in the dark as I headed back toward camp. She didn't speak.

"Della, I don't know what you want, but I'm tired and I'm going to bed."

"I accept your offer."

"Ha! No way."

"You're angry?" she asked in surprise.

"Hell yeah, I'm angry! You *killed* me, girl. I trusted you, and you stabbed me in the back—literally."

"Did it hurt?"

"Of course it hurt. Are you crazy?"

"You remember the pain?"

"Yes."

She walked in the dark beside me for a time. Finally, she sighed softly. "I'm sorry," she said. "I knew you would come back. I didn't think you would remember the final moments."

I heaved a sigh as well. "It's nice that you apologized and everything, but I don't think I can get over being murdered so easily."

"You were turning away from us. It was my duty."

She stopped and stood in the dark. I stopped a few paces farther on and looked back at her.

"Good bye, Della," I said.

"Good bye, James."

And that was it. I marched back to camp, flopped onto my bunk and tried to go to sleep. Even though I was bone tired, my mind wouldn't shut down for a long time.

When my dreams finally did come, they were troubled.

* * *

About a week later, we left Dust World. On the second day of the journey, Graves called me up to the top deck of the lifter without telling me why.

I knew that we were scheduled to fly to a rendezvous point where we would be picked up by a transport flown by the Skrull. It wasn't going to be a nice, custom-built ship like *Corvus*—God how I missed that ship. It was just going to be a no-frills cargo vessel. But it was reportedly big enough to carry all of us back to Earth.

"Come over here," Graves said, leading me to a porthole.

I gazed out into the dark beauty that we called space. Timeless, silent and infinite—I was immediately captivated.

"The ship is going to roll over," Graves said. "Look down."

I did, and the disk of a blue world hove into view. It was covered in oceans and streaked with white clouds.

"Is that the cephalopod planet?"

"No," he said quietly. "Not anymore it isn't."

I saw them then. Hell-burners. They fell from the aft end of each of our nine surviving lifters. They weren't very big—but I guess they didn't have to be.

Hell-burners were something I'd read about, and I knew that few humans from Earth had ever seen them fall on a world. They weren't fusion bombs—they were much more terrifying than that.

Back in school I'd read of neutron warheads, weapons that killed by burning an area with intense particulate radiation. Neutron weapons left buildings upright, but killed everything that lived and breathed on the surface. The hell-burners were like that, but they worked on a global scale. Most forms of plant life, microbes and buried insects would survive. But anything sophisticated, anything with a brain, was wiped out.

The atmosphere glowed redly until I couldn't see the oceans below us anymore. The destruction of life so complete and yet silent. Stunned, I watched as a species was erased forever.

I swallowed, stared and swallowed again.

Graves clapped me on the shoulder. "Remember hating the squids?" he asked.

"Yes, sir."

"Well, you don't have to worry about them anymore. That Nairb ship wasn't entirely empty. They brought just enough bombs to do the job."

"What I just witnessed—it was so *wrong*, sir," I said.

He frowned at me. "It was them or us, soldier. The Empire lost a ship in this system. Somebody had to pay. Just be glad it wasn't either of our two planets."

I didn't answer. I nodded and went below. There, I stared at a rusty bulkhead while the rest of the regulars around me slept and played games on their tappers, oblivious to the dead world in our wake.

Did I feel sorry for the squids? No, not exactly. They'd been vicious bastards who would have done the same thing to us in a heartbeat. But to wipe out an entire living world…

I had to admit to myself, I now hated the Empire even more than I hated the squids.

* * *

Earth changed after we reached home. Mostly, it was a good change.

There was energy in the air, and ships came down from space almost every day to deliver exotic goods. Wealth was flowing again, wealth like we'd never seen before.

I learned that part of becoming the local Enforcement world involved an Imperial stipend. I'm sure the credit amounts would have been sneered at in the Core Systems, but out here in our little ghetto of stars, it was an unimaginable fortune.

People had jobs again and hope. We were building things everywhere: Spaceports on the ground and shipyards in space.

Friends and relatives had done a one-eighty in their opinion of the legions. We were no longer failures; we'd brought home the bacon and then some. They understood that troops in steel ships had dragged this bounty back to Earth, but I don't think any of them appreciated how hard-won our new wealth was, or how difficult it might be to keep the money flowing in the future.

For me and my comrades, none of this had come easily. For us, this new era wasn't about spending credits and building new buildings. We'd paid a price in blood to bring back good economic times—the best Earth had yet to see in all her storied history. But would it all be worthwhile in the end? What would the Galactics make us do to keep our status? To my knowledge, no one had even thought to ask the Chief Inspector what had happened to the last Enforcers who we'd been chosen to replace. Maybe nobody wanted to know.

I didn't have any answers, only questions. I found solace in beer and companionship during my second shore leave. I guess in the end that's all any of us ever really have.

I looked up Natasha and she made a special trip to Atlanta to see me. That was never a bad sign, when a girl spent money to come visit you.

Natasha and I went out after I introduced her to my folks, who were busy looking at houses out in the suburbs. They both had jobs again, and I knew that made them happy. They had dreams of buying some land with trees and a half-dozen songbirds—real ones—if they could scrape together enough credits.

After taking Natasha to a few places we ended up at a bar full of military types. I don't know why—I guess I felt most at home in that kind of place now.

"How are you holding up, James?" she asked me when we were alone and settling into our second round of drinks.

"Pretty well. At the end of the first month, I got a happy surprise. My pay-mail arrived, dinging on my tapper. When I checked the amount I discovered it hadn't been reduced. Graves had told me he was demoting me from Specialist to grunt again—but apparently, he never did fill out the official screens."

Natasha smiled and squeezed my hand. "I guess that was his little way of saying thanks for negotiating the legion out of mass perma-death."

We laughed and had another round. We'd saved two planets while utterly destroying a third. All in a day's work for Legion Varus. Seen from that perspective, I guess I did deserve to keep my rank and full pay.

362

"I've been wondering about one thing," I said to her about an hour later.

"The answer is 'yes'," she said, eyes shining.

I laughed. "Great—but that wasn't what I was going to suggest—not yet, anyway. I was wondering what kind of trade good the Dust World colonists could possibly come up with. If they can't figure that out, we'll be busted back down to a single-system species again."

"Haven't you heard?" she asked. "They have an excellent trade good. The Nairbs have already approved it, and they're making shipments by now."

"What did they come up with?"

"Nanites," she said, "what else?"

I thought about that, and it made perfect sense. They had managed to steal some advanced nanotech from the squids and fine-tune it. Now, they were selling their wares to the Empire at large. I was glad to hear humanity's position as a two-system civilization was secure for now. It did seem ironic that the squids could have done the same thing, but had chosen to end their existence rather than knuckle-under to the Empire. I guess some species were too proud for their own good.

Natasha and I got a hotel room and spent several intense nights together. By the time she had to leave, I was feeling better about life.

Before our next deployment orders came a month or so later on, I'd had time to reflect on how much Earth's role in the Empire had changed since I'd joined Legion Varus. I now suspected that this wasn't all due to chance. Looking back on recent events, I'd begun to see a pattern.

Why had the Saurian peoples of Steel World tried to take our single trade good from us? Such things did happen from time to time, but the brazen behavior of the Saurians and Legion Varus itself during the conflict went beyond the norm. The Nairbs had let both sides get away with it, too. Could this lax attitude on the part of the Empire be due to internal weaknesses far, far away in the Core Systems?

I daydreamed of vast armadas floating in the cold void between the close-knit stars at the center of the galaxy. I imagined millions of vessels struggling, striving for dominance. Seen from the fringe of the Empire, the distant upheavals all seemed remote and yet ominous at the same time. It was like watching a thunderstorm on the horizon and imagining how it must be furiously lashing the ground with lightning.

The part humanity played in this galaxy was an infinitesimally small one. Frontier 921 was a tiny, far-flung province that meant almost nothing to the commanders of those vast fleets at the Core. If they thought of Earth at all, it was in terms of a category of planets and beings. We were ants to them, and they were a herd of elephants having themselves a stampede.

If I'd learned anything during my brief adulthood, it was that being the ant in such situations could be dangerous.

The End

More Books by B. V. Larson:

STAR FORCE SERIES
Swarm
Extinction
Rebellion
Conquest
Battle Station
Empire
Annihilation
Storm Assault
The Dead Sun
Outcast

IMPERIUM SERIES
Mech Zero: The Dominant
Mech 1: The Parent
Mech 2: The Savant
Mech 3: The Empress
Five By Five (Mech Novella)

OTHER SF BOOKS
Technomancer
The Bone Triangle
Z-World
Velocity

Visit BVLarson.com for more information.

Printed in Poland
by Amazon Fulfillment
Poland Sp. z o.o., Wrocław